MORNINGSTAR

STAR TRIBES, BOOK FIVE

BLAZE WARD

MorningStar
Star Tribes, Book Five
Blaze Ward
Copyright © 2020 Blaze Ward
All rights reserved
Published by Knotted Road Press
www.KnottedRoadPress.com

ISBN: 978-1-64470-145-4

Cover art:

ID 14224711 © Philcold | Dreamstime.com

Cover and interior design copyright © 2020 Knotted Road Press

Reviews
It's true. Reviews help me sell more books. If you've enjoyed this story, please consider leaving a review of it on your favorite site.

Never miss a release!
If you'd like to be notified of new releases, sign up for my newsletter.

I will never spam you, or use your email for nefarious purposes. You can also unsubscribe at any time.

http://www.blazeward.com/newsletter/

ALSO BY BLAZE WARD

Star Tribes

WinterStar

SeekerStar

SeptStar

SwiftStar

MorningStar

The Handsome Rob Gigs

Can't Shoot Straight Gang

Can't Shoot Straight Gang Returns

Hunting Handsome Rob

The Jessica Keller Chronicles

Auberon

Queen of the Pirates

Last of the Immortals

Goddess of War

Flight of the Blackbird

The Red Admiral

St. Legier

Winterhome

Petron

CS-405

Queen Anne's Revenge

Packmule

Persephone

Additional Alexandria Station Stories

Siren

Two Bottles of Wine with a War God

The Story Road

The Science Officer Series

The Science Officer

The Mind Field

The Gilded Cage

The Pleasure Dome

The Doomsday Vault

The Last Flagship

The Hammerfield Gambit

The Hammerfield Payoff

Shadow of the Dominion

Longshot Hypothesis

Hard Bargain

Outermost

Dominion-427

Phoenix

Princess Rualoh

Earth Force Sky Patrol

Birth of the Star Dragon

Flight of the Star Dragon

Call of the Star Dragon

Shadow of the Star Dragon

Trial of the Star Dragon

PART I

OVANII

1

———

Ndidi paused as she stood up and looked around her office, noting the shelf with knickknacks, the two chairs for people to sit on the other side of her desk, even the art painted directly onto the wall that had been there for however long it had been since the ship was built or rebuilt.

Her office.

Hers.

Ndidi Zikora, Speaker for the Anndaing Battlemaster *MorningStar*.

How much had changed. It had been nearly a year since the Sept had captured Tavle Jocia. Time spent for Crence Miray to catch up with them in Upynth space. Then back to Ogrorspoxu and the Merchants Bank. Negotiations for a new warship and crew. Training. Preparation. Even the time to sail across the darkness of K'bari space to get here today.

An object on a shelf caught Ndidi's eye. A small pink cube small enough to fit in her palm.

Tavle Jocia. She'd found it on that TradeStation a lifetime ago it seemed.

Nobody had been able to identify what it was then.

Later, they had at least figured out that it was made of some sort of heavy polymer that acted like a metal alloy.

She stepped close and lifted the heavy coolness into her hand. Weighed it against the tonnage of her soul.

The faces were all featureless, save for a button on one side that she pressed.

The cube leapt out of her hands and hovered in the air rather than falling to the deck. Like always, it glowed faintly. The lights in her office were dim enough that the device could calculate refraction and displayed three thousand five hundred stars in relative proximity and motion to one another in a sphere about two meters across, not counting where she stood.

Someone's homeworld sat at the exact center of it, and the tool provided the galactic navigation parameters for someone traveling within that area. Not all that far across as a region of space.

Not even Daniel's ghosts had been able to identify things from the night sky that would be visible at the center.

Ndidi had considered handing it off to an astronomer somewhere on Ogrorspoxu to investigate. None of the charts she had checked covered the space, but presumably an expert would be able to guess where the tool had come from originally.

She did know that it was about a thousand human years old, give or take, but nobody had been able to even guess how something like that might have ended up at Tavle Jocia, short of the sorts of random, interstellar tides that carried everything forward.

Ndidi captured it in her hand and powered it down.

For a moment, she almost put it back on the shelf, but slipped it into a thigh pouch instead. Ndidi couldn't even tell herself why, but it seemed like today was the day she should ask her Pilot to run the data inside the cube against *MorningStar*'s astrogation computer.

If nothing else it would give her Pilot something to do on the long sail pending.

Her Pilot. Ndidi's.

Speaker for the Ovanii Battlemaster *MorningStar*, currently in Mbaysey service and leased from the Anndaing Merchants Bank.

Ndidi pulled at her jacket to smooth things. She wore the pants of the Comitatus, a flame orange Daniel had called tangerine, tucked into tall brown boots. Black T-shirt. Turquoise jacket that buttoned on the front like something the Sept Empire might have cut.

The ship was even kept colder than a Mbaysey vessel would be, just because the officers should appear in uniforms that connoted seriousness of purpose.

Ndidi glanced at a small mirror she kept on another shelf, just enough to show her face and the seriousness of purpose there, as well.

She still woke from the dead of night occasionally panicked that she was in over her head and about to get everyone killed, but Ife and Kathra had both told her they felt the same way from time to time.

If those two women could overcome such feelings, Ndidi could, too.

Because they believed in her.

Many people believed in her. She had a responsibility to bring them home safe. At least as many as she could.

It might not be all of them, she considered as she opened the door to her office and strode out onto the bridge deck of *MorningStar*.

She had a war to fight.

2

———

Daniel was in his accustomed space on the bridge of the big war machine, over on the left out of everyone's way. He had thought that *SwiftStar* was a large vessel, until he got aboard *MorningStar* and came to understand what huge really was.

It was not the size of a Septagon, those Sept Empire battleships that waddled around space with a deadly lance and three hundred thousand human crew members. Instead, it was more compact, if still enormous. A full crew might only be five thousand, if they had loaded everyone they could.

This bridge reflected hugeness, though. *SwiftStar* had only a single Sword controlling the various gun turrets on that Ovanii Dueler. Here, she was in charge of a team of eight, each with responsibility for an arc of coverage and a class of weapons.

Ovanii Battlemaster. Anchor point for an entire battle fleet. Worse, Daniel had studied an ancient battle where eight of them had formed a line and attacked a K'bari formation made up of smaller ships, more of the class of the Ovanii Assailant.

And annihilated them.

He looked around the bridge again, still feeling like an outsider. There was no equivalent role in the Ovanii or Anndaing charts for what he did. Or human ones, either.

Acqueir Chanthraphone, the Anic sensors officer from *SwiftStar* had transferred over as part of the acquisition of this vessel. Daniel supposed that his job was closest to hers. She listened for other ships while he listened for other minds.

There was only one that mattered. Two, he supposed. Hadi Rostami had been transformed by the Ishtan into something like Daniel, only weaker. Amirin Pasdar was the man who had been the naupati of the Septagon *Vorgash*, the first time Daniel ever encountered such a thing.

He had also killed Daniel's ship, the Star Turtle, nearly killing Daniel in the process.

And he had led the invasion of Tavle Jocia that captured it for the Sept Empire.

Daniel had listened closely for both men, but neither were still in the vicinity, or even still in the Free Worlds. If Daniel's geometry was correct, both of those men were either on Earth, or at the Imperial Capital on Rhages. From here, the parallax wasn't all that great, and he could only sense a direction, but not a distance.

Acqueir seemed to sense his look, because she turned and smiled briefly at him.

An Anic pair-bond was not activated by sexual relations with a human. Or she had decided that he was different enough from her kind. She still came by his cabin occasionally, on some odd watch schedule that ensured he was alone.

Daniel supposed that the several women he occasionally entertained had worked out something amongst themselves, but had never asked. He still didn't fully grasp why it was that he was attractive to those women.

He was short for a human male. Slender, like an average male shrunk down to a 90% copy. His curly brown hair was coming in fully gray on the sides now, but he didn't bother doing anything about it.

At least he was in better shape at age forty-three than he had ever been in his life, but Daniel had no idea if that was the extra working out he had done or if the gem he wore on his sternum was burning off all the excess weight and fat he'd had when he first met the Mbaysey.

All he had going for him was that he was a chef from Genarde who had once been awarded a Golden Diamond by Gastropode magazine, headquartered in the shadow of the ancient and rebuilt Eiffel Tower, in Paris itself.

Not bad for a *Rabic* cook of Algerian descent, born several sectors away.

His gaze turned to the ship's Sword and he felt his breath catch a little.

A'Alhakoth ver'Shingi. Spectre Twenty-Three in the old days when Commander Omezi kept a comitatus of women, pilots and warriors sworn into her service. Daniel had been admitted later, the only male ever awarded such a place. Ndidi and Ife had come after that. These days, Kathra's command circle was much larger, given the vessels in her squadrons, but Daniel was still part of that innermost group. Along with A'Alhakoth and a few others.

She was studying her boards at the moment. No more Kathra's Ambassador to the Kaniea, the Anndaing, or the Upynth. Now she was Ndidi's Sword. The woman in control of all the guns on this monstrous war machine.

He turned his head some more and caught sight of Hirly, the only Anndaing officer on the bridge. Not the only one on the ship, but this woman had been good enough to be made

Ndidi's Shield, her second in command, when the Anndaing leased the vessel to the Mbaysey.

Daniel had originally been expecting a female Anndaing warrior to be a large specimen, something like Crence Miray or Jine Riffin, but Hirly was petite. Smaller than Daniel even, when most adult Anndaing women were taller.

In that, Daniel almost felt like a giant here at times, in spite of being a short *Rabic* man. Ndidi was only his height. A'Alhakoth and Hirly were smaller.

Even Tanuss Barleyne, the Engineer who had previously served aboard *SwiftStar* before coming over to *MorningStar*, was a shade shorter than he was.

This after living several years in the shadow of Kathra's comitatus, where all but two of those women had been taller, all the way up to Kathra's enormous height. Some days, it had been like standing in the middle of a valley, to be surrounded by woman like Kathra, Erin, Areen, or Joane.

Hirly turned her hammer just enough to point her left eye in his direction and wink. She was safe ground for him, with a husband and several pups back home.

The main door opened and Daniel felt the air in the room change as Ndidi entered. Everything became crisper, sharper.

Electric.

She caught his eye and he could see the bottom of her soul. If death could somehow look like chocolate brownies fresh out of the stove, that would be it. But they had already shared everything, going back to when Kathra instructed the young woman to learn the inside of his mind and to be his friend.

She needed friends, but forgot occasionally that she had so many. All of the comitatus were her sisters. The entire Mbaysey looked up to her. Random strangers on the streets on Ogrorspoxu might know the name Ndidi Zikora, as the first person other than an Anndaing to ever command one of the great Battlemasters, going back to the Ovanii themselves.

Daniel smiled at her and watched her relax a shade.

Not much, but maybe no longer feeling like she had the weight of the universe on her shoulders.

All the other women perked up. Daniel always found it amusing that he was the only male officer on this ship. And the ratio on the crew was close to the eighty-five percent female that the Mbaysey maintained across the entire tribe.

The Anndaing were more binary, but there had been sufficient women to fill the slots, when Kathra laid down her recruiting rules. A few Kaniea had answered the call, but weren't officers, beyond A'Alhakoth. A few more Anic and Wisp, like Acqueir and Tanuss.

And one human male. Chef and bloodhound.

Secret weapon, he supposed, but the Sept knew who he was. At least one of them even knew what he was.

Ndidi took her spot at the center of the bridge, with most of the other women in front of her but generally facing inward towards her. She took a deep breath and did her own quick inventory of the room, but everyone was poised.

"Open a line to *SwiftStar* and the squadron," Ndidi said simply. Quietly. Forcefully.

"All vessels on the line, Speaker," Acqueir replied a moment later, like she had already set things up and was just waiting.

Always staying ahead of the woman in command. Professional.

But the women on this bridge were also angry. It was an underlying flavor, like adding a dash of salt to something sweet, and letting the mouth pick it up last as that lingering surprise on your tongue.

Most of them had never been to Tazo, the homeworld the Mbaysey had abandoned when they became a Star Tribe.

Ndidi had not even been born there, but enough of the older women of the Mbaysey remembered.

They had gathered the officers and crew of *MorningStar* together a week before sailing, human and alien alike. Had told them of the history of the tribe that they were now associated with. Some might even choose to join later.

Grandma Ezinne had been there, a spry, ninety-year-old woman unbowed by the weight of her life. She had spoken about the tattoo on her left cheek, the one she had chosen to keep, sixty years on. The barcode put there by a Sept aristocrat of the *Vuzurgan* rank. The Grand Nobles of the Sept Empire.

She had spoken slowly and carefully, pausing to answer questions with a mind still sharp.

Grandma Ezinne had told these women what it meant to be a slave. To be *property*. Her granddaughter, Erin Uduik, Spectre Two, Kathra's Second-In-Command wore an identical mark. This was was so that Erin's daughter, Kwento, would grow up in a world where nobody ever had that happen to them again.

It had been a forceful speech, however quiet and prim the woman with the sparkling, laughing eyes had been while giving it.

The entire Mbaysey combat squadron had heard her speak.

Watching her, he could see Ndidi draw on that now, eyes slightly unfocused. Or perhaps seeing something measured in light-centuries, going back to Tazo. To Rhages. To Earth.

"We know why we are here," Ndidi said simply. "You have trained. Studied. Practiced. We who have been there before have taught you everything we know. Shared with you our dreams, our fears, and our blood. Commander Omezi has her comitatus. Once, they numbered twenty-three, but that was the past. Those were the ones she trusted to protect the rest of the tribe. Today, she relies on all of us. We protect not just the Mbaysey, not just the Anndaing, but everyone, everywhere, from an evil that must be denied, must be repulsed. Must be destroyed. We protect the future. That is why Kathra chose us. Why she put us here. Why we must face these costs."

Daniel forgot to breathe as he listened. His lungs reminded him, and he was not alone from the sounds around him. He wondered how many other people had hung too sharply on the young woman's words. He had twelve thousand years of ghosts to draw on in his memory, and had encountered few speeches with similar power, especially delivered by such a woman.

"Mbaysey Tribal Squadron, come to readiness," Ndidi ordered. "All vessels jump."

3

———————

A'ALHAKOTH HAD BEEN RAISED on various forms of martial glory. Kaniea history until four generations ago had been decidedly Iron Age, stable and productive, but still wrapped up in pre-electricity tales of beautiful princesses and questing knights.

Both of her parents had been Jarls, the lowest of the aristocratic ranks. She herself had been the youngest child and second daughter, so Father had been able to spoil her somewhat rotten. At the same time, he had trained her up like a fifth son, expert in all manner of combat skills and fluent in Anndaing to the point that she spoke like one of them.

And then the old witch had sent her off…

Out from Kanus on a Se'uh'pal ship, clear across the vast darkness and around behind what maps still called K'bari space, in spite of them being gone for a millennia. Into the human sphere, where she met Erin.

And Daniel.

A'Alhakoth ver'Shingi wasn't sure where her life had gone

so far off track from her childhood dreams, but here she was, poised on the edge of the Tavle Jocia system where her adventures had really begun, for all the craziness she had faced just getting this far from home.

At least her childhood had given her the right mindset to be in this chair today. She had wondered if Ngozi should have been promoted from the bridge of *SwiftStar*, but that woman was happier staying with Ife. Ife had been adamant that Ndidi take *MorningStar* and leave her the smaller escort.

That left a Kaniea warrior princess, or whatever she might qualify as at this point. Spectre Twenty-Three, when Kathra had still numbered her women warriors.

Today, she had eight gun commanders serving her. That term was as close as the Ovanii title translated over into the Anndaing that was the working language of the ship. Heavy guns and light. Dorsal and Ventral. Forward batteries and aft, sliced along a vague line she had picked almost at random, with the assumption that at least two thirds of the turrets were likely to be firing forward at any given instant, if not all of them.

A'Alhakoth's job, unlike Ngozi, was not to lay the guns themselves, to use the ancient term, but to tell her people who to go after and in what order.

Regardless, she would still be the person responsible for most of the deaths today. At least as many as Daniel, who had gotten them here. Or Ndidi, who was in command.

Or Kathra, who had decided to accept this alien girl into her inner circle and make her someone.

"All Arc-cannons, conform to this line," A'Alhakoth drew a vector on her screen and watched it appear on the eight stations around the outer edge of the bridge. "Ram Cannons set to engage defensive targets."

Ram cannons as a defensive weapon. Frightening, really.

They weren't the exact same thing, but were a close enough approximation for tactical considerations.

The Ovanii had used them defensively. That thought always took her breath away because most warships used the Ram Cannon as offensive weapons. The Arc-cannons were an order of magnitude bigger. That was how the Ovanii had fought their wars.

"Countdown to emergence," Acqueir called across the quiet bridge. "Zwölf seconds."

Anndaing had five fingers and a thumb on each hand, so they counted in twelves. The other bipeds with smaller hands had adopted it anyway.

A'Alhakoth glanced back at Daniel.

"Any change?" she asked, more for something to fill those last few seconds than any expectation.

Septagon *Singara* held Tavle Jocia, along with a half fin of Patrols. Six, using the boring way to count. She grinned at her own joke.

"*Non*," Daniel said. "As before."

She could tell how nervous the man was just from how clipped his tones got. But he had been shot three times with the only weapon in the upcoming system that was a true threat to *MorningStar*.

The Axial Megacannon. The star lance capable of destroying a city on the surface of a planet from orbit, if the people down there didn't surrender.

Or had just pissed off their Sept overlords enough.

An Ovanii Battlemaster could not easily resist such a beam. But the Septagon only had one. And it was fixed to the bow of the ship, so the aspbad or naupati would have to pivot the entire vessel on all three axes in order to fire. And recharge every time they missed.

MorningStar wasn't here to slug it out with such a beast.

He was a questing knight on a charging horse, riding by and swinging his terrible sword at a dragon.

Just like in all the stories.

A'Alhakoth's boards came alive.

SwiftStar had already come out of jump, faster than *MorningStar* even over such a short jump from the darkness at the edge of the system. *BrightStar* and *NovaStar* had joined them.

A'Alhakoth took a moment to confirm the three other pirate vessels were where she expected, a triangle arranged in front of *MorningStar*, two above on her corners and one below on her beam.

Already, they had opened fire on nearby Patrol vessels supposedly protecting this system from marauders.

Like ancient Ovanii raised from the dead for another, terrible war on the galaxy?

"Target locked and confirmed," Acqueir called out sharply.

On her board, A'Alhakoth caught the first scans with Septagon *Singara* centered. Her eight commanders would have the same, along with two Patrols nearby, and the massive harvest of civilian shipping that a pirate like her might have otherwise considered.

But that wasn't her mission today.

"All guns engage," A'Alhakoth said in a conversational voice.

There wasn't anything she could say right now that would top Ndidi's earlier words. A'Alhakoth might not hear something even close in the remaining two centuries she would live.

Assuming she was still alive tomorrow.

The Sept Empire did not field a military, for all the terrible force they built. These were internal security forces. Secret police. And not so secret.

A Septagon was an unstoppable fortress in space, a dragon with fiery breath to kill any fool of a knight challenging her. A Patrol was a team of ten armed escorts, police officers.

Thugs with truncheons, but not warriors.

An Ovanii Dueler like *SwiftStar* was a match for a single Patrol. Two might be a threat. Three would chase Ife off, or possibly damage the ship too much to recover from.

Three Duelers were more than a match for two Patrols in close range. The other four Patrols might manage to get themselves organized into some useful formation eventually. Assuming Ndidi didn't send her forces hunting like hounds after a fox. Daniel had shared that image with her, from some ancient book. It was silly, but it worked.

MorningStar could annihilate all the Sept Patrols present. But she had a Septagon to defeat instead first.

Nobody had ever defeated a Septagon, depending on how you wanted to quantify that. A'Alhakoth had once managed to force *Vorgash* to flee for its life.

Even that might have been the first time in the history of the Sept Empire.

Today, she wanted to see if she could actually kill such a leviathan with her harpoons.

"Down, starboard, and roll high," Ndidi ordered in the background. "Hold current speed."

That was why the Sword and all her gun commanders were here, so they could hear the instructions in real time and make their own adjustments.

MorningStar had caught *Singara* on a flank. Ndidi was maneuvering to rush past and under the massive castle before they could turn and breathe fire.

Nwanyiudo Gruffudd, Spectre Twenty-Two in the old days, and Pilot today, acknowledged the command.

"Aft teams, maximum deflection," A'Alhakoth said to her folks.

They would joust.

Singara had seven Ram Cannon turrets on each of those seven facings. Zwölf-two Heavy Particle Cannons that might be useful against the armor on a Dueler, but would not get through the tough hide of *MorningStar* with anything but luck.

No Axial Megacannon could range right now.

MorningStar lit up with all fourteen Arc-cannons centered on the Septagon. The massive array of Ram Cannons were either held against Patrol vessels getting too close, or were already engaging them, assisting the escorts by shattering the smaller vessels.

Singara awoke finally. Somewhere, a gun commander on a flanking Ram Cannon probably took his career into his own hands and ordered his team to do something, as only that one weapon was responding right now.

The Arc-cannon was a terrible thing to behold. Even the heavily armored hide of a Septagon could not resist the wrath A'Alhakoth's people were pouring into that dragon.

"Sensors, Daniel, what's the environment?" Hirly called.

A Shield was supposed to track all the other things, so the Speaker and her officers could fight.

"Eight Patrols identified," Acqueir called back. "Vectors identified. Two of them are way out on the edge of things and will not be able to engage. Local defensive forces also starting to awaken."

"Slow panic, Shield," Daniel completed the thought. "Possibly a headless chicken."

Ndidi would understand the term. A'Alhakoth had had to learn what a chicken was first, but she had spent enough time around the two amazing chefs to understand the reference.

"Gun commanders, go for their engines," A'Alhakoth suddenly decided. Previously, she had been aiming them at various sensor and weapon stations, on the assumption that blinding the beast would be useful.

Laming it right now might be enough to score her kill.

MorningStar came around that flanking corner hard and tight, exposing the four big thruster vents where a Septagon pushed all that mass forward. The valence drives were above and in front of them, safe from hostile fire unless an Arc-cannon got lucky and penetrated several bulkheads that should have held against it.

But the engines themselves had to be exposed to space.

Fourteen guns fired off in a single salvo so intense that the lights on the bridge flickered under the power draw. Fourteen harpoons entered metal flesh like a bomb going off.

On her screen, A'Alhakoth saw one of the engines actually go dark, from the normal white-light flame visible in the other three.

Sept Ram Cannons replied, but weren't going to be sufficient.

"All batteries, rapid fire," A'Alhakoth called. "Ram Cannons engage as well."

It would burn out barrels and charging mechanisms, but she could smell fear over there. And desperation, as the vessel staggered and began to slowly move.

They weren't even trying to pivot right now, where they might bring that terrible lance to bear, but seemingly trying to scamper for safety.

Her gun commanders seemed to understand. A'Alhakoth began to get heat warnings on her board. Pressure warnings. Generator overload complaints. Flashing notices that she needed to override from her station, in her hands just in case one of the commanders got carried away with themselves.

Here, it was all of them, but A'Alhakoth had trained them. Trained with them. Understood them.

And Ndidi had brought them here, after all these women listened to Grandma Ezinne, an alien to most of these women, but one with a compelling story about good and evil.

Right and wrong.

Knights and dragons.

Another mass salvo erupted, impacting *Singara* like birdshot entering the surface of a pond.

Unconsciously, she tracked the Sept Patrol vessels around *MorningStar*. They were doomed, but unwilling to flee, so the three Duelers were wreaking a terrible carnage there as well.

The Sept weren't likely to ever be caught this asleep again, so Kathra had ordered them to make this first battle memorable. The Sept sailors who were going to die on the various ships around her were just the first to pay the price for the centuries that they had enslaved her sisters, back on Tazo.

Singara disappeared. Gone in the blink of an eye, and only caught as an afterimage on sensors as the ship entered a jump portal to safety. Moments later, sensors showed the other Patrols, the ones that hadn't just been annihilated at Mbaysey hands, also flee.

Only the local defensive forces remained in-system, two minutes later.

Surrenders began appearing on boards immediately.

"All guns, stand down," Ndidi ordered, unnecessarily, but only because A'Alhakoth was half a second slow with the same command.

There was nothing left to shoot at.

MorningStar held the system, with *SwiftStar*, *BrightStar*, and *NovaStar* hanging in orbit.

A'Alhakoth had one gun sensor pointed in the direction of the mighty orbital factory ahead of them in orbit. The place where *SeptStar* and *SeekerStar*, Kathra's flagship, had been born. Right here at Tavle Jocia, where so many stories had begun.

Nothing had changed about the factory.

But everyone had just begun a new chapter.

4

———

Ndidi let the tenseness flow out of her body as the results became obvious.

Singara wounded badly. Twenty of the thirty Patrol vessels in close proximity when the battle began were now shattered. Not just hurt, but destroyed. Broken into pieces.

Foxes loose in the henhouse.

MorningStar looped into orbit near the main TradeStation. The one where a Free Worlds governor had lived the last time she had been through this system.

She was close enough that beams on the station itself could hit *MorningStar*, if someone was feeling utterly suicidal. Anyone firing on her now would be indicating Sept loyalties.

Collaborators.

She would be merciful at first. At least until someone gave her a reason not to be.

"Shield, what is our status?" Ndidi asked, glancing around the bridge.

The battle had lasted less than sixteen minutes from the moment *MorningStar* had emerged. Not enough time for much, but this ship was a tool. A thing to be used up if necessary. A sword to be blunted in the cause of forcing the Sept all the way back to Rhages.

Or Earth.

"All systems within tolerance, Speaker," Hirly answered a moment later. "Escorts report the same."

Now was when things got strange. When you had to plan a comitatus lunch in such a way that leftovers got fed into dinner and possibly breakfast without the women realizing it.

There had been any number of plans and scenarios laid out around how this would work, but none of them mattered until the squadron was actually sitting here in orbit of Tavle Jocia, holding the field.

If that was possible.

Ndidi decided on her campaign. "Order *SwiftStar* and *NovaStar* into pursuit."

It helped that she had been able to merge with Kathra, Erin, Ife, and the two other Speakers. All of them understood the overall plan better than mere paperwork might manage.

That would help them understand squadron Speaker Ndidi Zikora as well.

"Scout team in motion," Acqueir called a few moments later.

The plan had been solid. Two of the Duelers to chase after the Sept forces until everyone was sure that they were actually leaving. And then harry them for a time. Ndidi had even left their closest supply base intact, just so they had enough food that they could retreat.

There would be nothing worse in the galaxy than a wounded Septagon that might be desperate enough to return to Tavle Jocia.

Plus, Crence Miray and a frenzy of other Anndaing were out there, hiding in Scout-6 and Gun-6 or Gun-12 ships. Again, they were not to attack *Singara* nor the base.

At least not until *Singara* had begun the long march back to Sept Space and the sort of shipyard facilities that could repair the carnage *MorningStar* had just inflicted.

At that point the base was fair game. Assuming that it wasn't just wisely abandoned as indefensible.

"Hail the TradeStation and declare martial law across the entire system in the name of Kathra Omezi and the Mbaysey Tribal Squadron," Ndidi continued, working down a checklist in her mind.

Well, it was more of a recipe than anything. A set of ingredients and actions that would hopefully yield a palatable result for lunch.

Assuming it wasn't a recipe for disaster.

At least taking the place in Kathra's name, instead of the Anndaing Merchants Bank, would keep the sharks from being technically responsible. After all, Kathra owned *SwiftStar* in fee simple. *MorningStar* was a long-term lease. *BrightStar* and *NovaStar* were private service vessels Kathra had hired.

Piracy, pure and simple.

You'll believe that, won't you?

Ndidi unbuckled herself from the seat and stood up. She had spent most of her life standing and walking in a kitchen, so sitting was alien to her. She might have even considered how to redo hers and Daniel's stations so they could stand, just so they felt more at home.

But she needed to think like a Speaker now, and not a chef.

"A'Alhakoth, turn your teams loose to fix half of the guns only, with the understanding that we might need them online on short notice," Ndidi said. "*Singara* has fled, but we won't know if they are truly gone for a few days. Daniel, I need to chat with you in my office. Hirly, you're in charge."

She nodded to everyone and headed aft, back to her real

office, and not just the one attached to the bridge where Hirly or someone might do paperwork.

Daniel rose and followed. The other women picked up their chatter, but this was the aftermath of their first major battle as an Mbaysey Battlemaster.

One that had chased a Septagon off after wounding it severely.

Now came the hard part.

5

———

Daniel trailed Ndidi down the corridors and into her office like a remora. The image suited him, since she was as much a shark as Crence or Wyll. Maybe more so, at the end of the day. He barely recognized the young woman who had been brought up from *SeekerStar*'s crew kitchen to cook for the comitatus when it became clear that Daniel had other pressing concerns.

But then, growing up was a bitch. He'd fought it until he was nearly forty. Until Kathra and Erin had required it of him.

He sat in her office now and watched her. Saw the tired lines that had carved themselves into her cheeks. Realized how much weight she had lost from stress.

"I need to make cinnamon rolls," he said out of the blue, enjoying the way her eyes surged and then unfocused as she considered freshly-baked pastries coming out of the oven.

That told him all he needed to know about her mental state right now.

She realized it as well, but they had merged enough times

over the last few years that sometimes he had to remember that they really were two people

Ndidi nodded.

"Yes," she said with a sigh. "Immediately after this."

"Okay, so what terrible thing do we need to do to the locals first?" he asked with a grin somewhat askance.

"The Sept held this system for more than a year," Ndidi replied, hands flat on her desk like she was trying to push it through the deck beneath her. "There are going to be some bad apples. At the same time, there will be some good ones we might miss, because they had to work with *force majeure* around here."

"*Oui*," Daniel nodded. "Kathra envisioned that."

"I want you to go a little farther than the Commander expected," Ndidi said, eyes growing dark and terrible. "I intend to order you to do evil in my name, and in Kathra's."

Daniel flinched. He didn't even bother trying to conceal it from her, or deflect it somehow with his words. She knew what he considered evil. Every bit as well as he did.

And she was going to go there.

At least she understood that there were lines *he* would never willingly cross.

It would be too easy to wake up one morning and see Hadi Rostami's face in the mirror as he shaved.

Daniel drew a cold breath down into his lungs and hoped it wouldn't turn him to ice.

"I serve," he whispered once he got his equilibrium back, eyes coming up to meet hers finally.

"Yes," she nodded. "And we all love you as a sister, probably more than you're even willing to accept, Daniel."

"Whose lives should I look to destroy?" he asked.

Might as well get it out of the way up front.

"Nobody," she smiled, leaning back now and seemingly relaxed.

Like she had expected him to argue.

Him. Argue with her. When she spoke with Kathra's voice.

He might also have Kathra's trust, but Daniel understood what these many women meant when they talked about *agency*.

His place among the Mbaysey was to shut up and listen.

"Oh?" he managed.

"We're going to meet with people, Daniel," Ndidi said. "We've chased off *Singara* and hopefully have time before they can send something else in its place. The locals will be the problem."

"*Oui*," Daniel agreed as a placeholder.

"I want you to go beyond just identifying the good and bad people," she continued, eyes growing dark and malevolent again. "I want you to start shaping them. Not much, but I want them to develop an antipathy to the Sept. To even working with the Sept. To ever talking to them again. Many will have a hatred already, I want that to come to the fore. If they like the Sept, I want them to question that. Rethink why they did it in the first place and maybe come to a different conclusion today."

"You want the K'bari," he said in as flat a voice as he could, when he really wanted to snarl angrily at the woman.

"Here, yes," Ndidi confirmed his worst nightmare. "At Tavle Jocia. But only here. They took this system because this was a good place to hold, a base from which to build new vessels that could trade with Sept systems, as well as scout K'bari space. To break the Free Worlds in two, so they could either take all of human space under their cloak, or reach out and threaten Kanus and Ogrorspoxu."

"Urid-Varg modified the K'bari," Daniel reminded her. "Twisted them at a cultural level by adjusting every person he met."

"Yes, and it is one of the most evil things someone with your power could do," Ndidi's voice softened. "But I'm not ordering them to worship you or Kathra. Only to hate the same people we hate. And only for now. In time, it will wear off. I've seen that in your memories. Urid-Varg didn't understand that, so he let too many worlds wake up from his power and decide to resist."

"And when the locals develop a hatred of all outsiders meddling in their affairs?" Daniel sneered.

"Then the Anndaing Merchants Bank won't be able to slip in and take over, either, Daniel," she replied with a hard smile. "Nobody will ever conquer Tavle Jocia again."

Daniel felt like she had just punched him in the stomach. All the air whooshed out of his lungs and his head suddenly rang.

But he could hear Kathra's voice coming out of this younger woman's mouth.

He must have missed several conversations, but that was normal. He was just a chef. And a bloodhound.

Ndidi was Kathra's Squadron Speaker. Her naupati, except they didn't use Sept titles and the Anndaing didn't have an equivalent. Some of his ghosts had suggested things similar to the ancient human rank of admiral, but Daniel didn't care enough to suggest it.

Ndidi was in charge. Kathra's left hand clenched into a fist, even as Erin remained her right.

"Oh," he managed weakly.

"Yes," she acknowledged. "Evil in the service of all sentient life forms, Daniel. Not just humans, nor Anndaing nor anyone else. Something to cause the Free Worlds to wake up and decide to become a thing, rather than just a collection of systems that didn't want to be Sept."

"How big are you two dreaming?" he asked, feeling tiny and vulnerable around such terrible titans.

"Empires require mass, Daniel," she replied in a hot, hard voice. "Kathra would prefer human space to fragment down into lots of little independent groups that can't afford to field fleets of Septagons. The Merchants Bank maintains the backbone of the Armada, this ship for example, but they prefer to trade as much as they can, rather than conquer."

"So we're helping the Anndaing, but over a much longer term than even they realize?" he probed.

"Longer than anyone imagines," she said. "Far enough down the future that Hadi Rostami is destroyed and you can be free to cast your gem into the heart of a handy star and finally escape that *branleur* who tried to take you."

Daniel was cold, but he knew that it was him and not that the temperature in this office really had suddenly gone down several degrees. Sudden spikes of mad adrenaline rushed into his stomach and out into his limbs.

He was being asked to do the most evil thing he could imagine.

And he would do it.

Because he trusted these women.

6

―――――

Earth.

Hadi Rostami had never actually visited the homeworld of humanity before this, having been born on Maragheh once upon a time. Now, he was here, in a palace owned by Amirin Pasdar's clan, enjoying a quiet, afternoon view of green fields with interesting fences made of long white posts. Two of them, set knee and shoulder height. Hadi didn't understand why was that sufficient to keep in the horses he could see in the distance, but it did. Rolling green and the brown of horses.

In the ancient times, it had been a religious commandment to visit a spot in western Arabia from which the ancient religion had originated. Like many things, the allure had faded over time, but the Sept themselves had originated in the highlands northeast of there. Here on the Persian Plateau.

Like the even-more-ancient Muslims themselves, later the Seven Clans had swept out at the head of a conquering army. But they had taken all the planet in hand quickly enough, rather than being halted in southern France, or one of the great rivers in the East.

From there, the Sept had proclaimed their Empire. Seven for the continents on the homeworld as well as the count of clans involved.

And then outward, a pulse of conquest and absorption that had seen more than half of all human-colonized worlds taken, along with a fair number of alien worlds and alien peoples.

Power might reside on Rhages today, but the humans of the Sept still cast their yearning eyes Earthward.

For Hadi, that was enough in and of itself. But he also had a secondary mission. Amirin Pasdar, of the famed Pasdar Clan of the Sept themselves, had decided to start here with his campaign to conquer the galaxy.

It was no longer enough in Amirin's mind to just hold all of humanity in his hands.

No, Amirin Pasdar wanted all sentient creatures. Even the weird ones that could not possibly be mistaken for human in any light.

Vidu. Attar. Allah help us all, even the Bhaorajj. All united under one crown.

Hadi wondered sometimes if he had crossed over from sanity in this quest and completely lost his soul. Whether or not he was still even human, or perhaps if the power of the Ishtan, the price they had demanded of him, had been more than he could actually bear.

Whether being bound to them mentally at the moment when their corporeal beings died, had cast them permanently into his mind and soul and erased some level of his humanity.

Or all of it.

Many humans lived on Earth. No aliens were allowed. Ever. That was on rule that the Sept would not bend on. It had been necessary to move even the Imperial Court lest alien feet land on holy ground.

Should he even be allowed here?

But Hadi saw all beings as one, and knew that it was the Ishtan taint one his soul. All Ishtan males had shared a mental bond born of hunting and the need for silent communications. The females, when they had existed, had been only egg-layers, barely intelligent enough to speak.

Urid-Varg had ended most of the Ishtan when he killed the Ishtan Eldest and took his mindgem. The only six survivors had spent eleven thousand years in deathless pursuit.

Outliving even Urid-Varg, only to die at the hands of Kathra Omezi's *Comitatus*.

One human remained who had been Ishtan. Another human remained who had been Urid-Varg.

Hadi Rostami would see the entire galaxy fall before him, if that was what it took to destroy that human. Amirin Pasdar was merely the instrument of his vengeance. The Anndaing would protect the Mbaysey, so it would be necessary to destroy them. The Sept would need to be rejuvenated from their corruption and lethargy in order to wage a war large enough to break the hammerheads and all their allies.

And anyone else that stood in his way.

Kathra Omezi would die in battle, or she would flee into the interior, taking her precious chef with her.

Hadi Rostami would not rest until Daniel Lémieux was dead and cast permanently into the fires of a star for purification. Until the final mind gem was gone and no other being could grasp it and use such evil.

A footfall brought Hadi back from his musings with almost a jolt. How had someone managed to get so close to him without him realizing it?

He blinked and ranged his power all directions to be sure he was still safe from assassins.

Those would become a greater threat with each day, without any other humans knowing the truth about it.

If that information ever came out, no planet would be safe for him.

Amirin Pasdar stood at a careful distance. The two of them were on a balcony overlooking a valley. Behind him, the palace complex and city stretched, but the palace grounds with their horses had been permanently preserved by the Pasdar for its view.

Hadi caught the hesitation about his commander, his future emperor, and nodded.

"Your face forbade all visitors," Amirin said with a wry grin as he took the other chair, turning to watch the view across a small table.

Hadi relaxed the horrible rictus that had been his mien a moment ago, feeling how sore the muscles had gotten.

He needed to not fall so far into his Ishtan self that he forgot to occasionally be human. Fortunately, the horses would not see him from there.

"What news?" Hadi asked quietly as he recovered, as though he had just woken from a slumber measured in centuries.

"Tavle Jocia has fallen," Amirin glanced both ways before allowing some level of triumph to appear on his face.

Servants in the distance also realized that they had not seen to Hadi's needs in too long, held unconsciously at bay by his mental powers while he sat and thought. They began to circle now, drawing closer.

Hadi would say he meditated, but it was really an intense rage.

He had come so far, so close, and then died at the last moment.

Except he hadn't died. The Ishtan had. But all four of those remaining ghosts still tainted him. Probably would until his death.

Hopefully that would end it.

Hadi Rostami could not be sure until darkness claimed him for good, assuming Daniel Lémieux did not step up and capture him, like he had so many others.

No, Urid-Varg did that. The Chef lacked the strength.

Everyone hoped.

Hadi breathed slowly and tried to be human for a while yet.

"How have our people taken the news?" he asked.

"The Court has responded almost exactly as badly as one would imagine," Amirin said with a grin that vanished as a male servant stepped onto the balcony with a pitcher of lemonade over ice.

After their first visit to Rhages, Amirin Pasdar had removed all female servants from his immediate household. They had both watched young, nubile, frequently-alien women at the Imperial Palace, and what demands the so-called Grand Nobles placed upon such innocents with no thought whatsoever besides fornication with whatever creature one might rape.

Not slaughtering the entire Imperial Household had been one of Hadi's great emotional victories that day.

Only men served Pasdar now. Important visitors would have to settle for sexually assaulting their own servants when they got home.

If they made it without some terrible accident. Hadi Rostami had a shorter fuse than he used to and a sharper knife, if he wanted to twist a victim enough that they destroyed themselves.

A few had tasted his rage. Only a few, but enough.

Amirin Pasdar was developing a reputation for great

moral rectitude that played well with a general populace that had perhaps grown weary with debaucheries.

Hadi thought back to the force left to protect Tavle Jocia when he and Amirin had returned to Earth in triumph.

"*Singara*?" he asked simply, wondering what could capture a planet already held by a Septagon.

"Badly damaged," Amirin's voice got subtle, hiding the notes of triumph. "Apparently fled one step ahead of annihilation at the hands of some massive, alien warship."

"Truly?" Hadi allowed his surprise to the surface.

What existed that could threaten a Septagon? They had killed the turtle.

Was there another one? What other allies did the Anndaing have that Omezi could call upon?

"Truly," Amirin confirmed. "Afterwards, Kathra Omezi declared martial law and last news from our spies was that she was cleaning out the collaborators and building Tavle Jocia up as a new center of resistance against the Sept."

"And how has our dread emperor taken the news?" Hadi felt his brain engage as the next steps in Amirin Pasdar's complex plan began to move. "What punishment has he ordered for the naupati and governor that replaced you?"

"That's the best part," Amirin laughed. "The fools were down on the planet in a whorehouse, along with the aspbad. All were taken alive."

7

NDIDI HAD no choice but to allow the Sept scum onto her deck. It would not likely be safe for her to land on a Free Worlds TradeStation for decades.

If ever.

Kathra might never be safe from potential assassins, but she would probably never step off a Mbaysey deck for more than a few hours again in her life.

At least *MorningStar* had a contingent of combat troops aboard, as did the Dueler squadron.

Pirates, for whatever needs the Squadron Speaker might identify.

Right now, tall brown women and wide blue men were escorting a dozen Sept officials, slightly worse for the wear and all wearing iron manacles that an Anndaing artist had hand-welded and *distressed* with rust to Ndidi's exactly requirements.

Nothing was too good for her guests.

Ndidi sat behind a long conference table that had been lowered a handspan from Ovanii height to make it comfortable for her. Not everyone was Ovanii height. Only Kathra, generally.

Daniel sat on her right. A'Alhakoth on her left. Nwanyiudo, Acqueir and a few others were here mostly to make the Sept *salauds* nervous.

Hirly was with the guards accompanying Kamharida and her officers.

But Ndidi would do the talking.

The growls emanating from the women sounded bloodthirsty as they shoved or dragged the prisoners into the chamber. But then, many of them remembered Tazo.

And now everyone knew Grandma Ezinne.

Ndidi studied the two men thrust to the front. The Sept Governor of Tavle Jocia was only interesting because he was apparently a Sidiqi, one of the Grand Nobles of the Sept. The Seven Clans themselves. A Vuzurgan, formerly an Anusiya, one of the so-called Companions of the Emperor who were a poor knock-off of the comitatus.

"Interesting," Daniel murmured, leaning closer to her ear, rather than talking to her in the privacy of his own mind.

Ndidi turned to the man, ignoring her prisoners.

Let them sweat.

"The Shah has been altered," Daniel whispered just loud enough for her to hear. "I can see Rostami's fingerprints on the man's psyche, where adjustments were made with what Urid-Varg would classify as an amateur's touch."

"Amateur?" Ndidi asked.

"The welds are visible," Daniel flashed a grin for just a moment. "Not that anyone else I am aware of could detect them."

"What did that *violeur* do?" Ndidi asked.

Right there, she could see the evil Daniel was so afraid of committing. Just *fixing* someone rather than convincing them to change their ways.

"Nothing much," Daniel shrugged. His eyes faded for a long moment before they found hers again.

"No, I lied," he continued. "This one met Pasdar and Rostami at Rhages. Tried to stop the naupati from seeing the Emperor, but could not count on not being in control of his own mind at that point. They offered him this planet after it was taken, although I'm not sure why, except to perhaps gain an ally and move a potential foe out of their way."

"Is he more ally or more foe right now?" Ndidi asked, intrigued with the possibilities at hand.

"He blames the fool next to him," Daniel murmured. "The naupati who replaced Pasdar, after he conquered the planet just as he said he would. Pasdar and Rostami even suggested to someone else that this particular Sidiqi be sent to rule here. *Singara* failed to stop Kathra Omezi from taking it back, so his anger is focused on military ineptitude."

Ndidi took a deep breath and turned to the two men, Shah and Naupati. Glowered at them with a face she had borrowed from Iruoma, terrible and vindictive.

Both men quailed for a moment before they remembered that they were supposed to represent the Sept, and that women existed only to serve them.

Even the ones that had these *salauds* shackled in rusty, rattling chains.

"I will require more evil of you," Ndidi whispered, turning back to Daniel.

"*Bon*," he said with enough of a sigh that he had probably already seen where her mind was going to go.

They really were closer than even twins at this point.

"I will make it all up to you later, Daniel," she assured him, although both of them knew that to be at least a partial lie.

Ndidi had no idea how she might do that, short of

letting him return to his kitchen forever. Or a library filled with books to translate.

But the Sept had to be broken first. Doing so might use him up like a carving knife that has been sharpened too many times.

And they both knew it.

Ndidi took his hand and Daniel nodded as he quickly brought her into his mind.

His eyes got wide and blinked too rapidly a moment later.

"*Merde*," he murmured forcefully. Then a wry smile came over his face. "That's not even all that evil, all things considered. I like it."

Ndidi chuckled.

Twist the Sidiqi a touch, until he believed that Pasdar had put him here as a sacrificial goat, which he probably had, without telling the man. And had him removed from Court as a threat to be killed off-stage, with white gloves, while no stain would accrue to Pasdar's name.

She smiled at the Shah with all her terrible, accumulated rage.

"Commander Omezi offers you mercy, Sidiqi," she said simply. "*Singara* has already fled for the interior, its tail tucked between hobbled legs. We are not here to conquer Tavle Jocia, unlike the Sept, merely to free it from your tyranny. You will be sent home."

"Just like that?" the man managed to snarl just enough to make his point, without Kamharida or one of the others bashing his skull.

"There are two other alternatives," she offered with a smile like a twisting knife. "One would be to turn you over to the locals and let them deal with you as they see fit."

The Shah flinched.

They *all* flinched.

"And the other?" he asked, much more polite now as somebody had jerked hard once on his chains when he moved too much.

"We don't take slaves," Ndidi sneered. "Not like the Sept. Not like you. Many of us have been slaves in the distant past. You and your men could volunteer to serve aboard one of the ClanStars as farmers and do penance for the rest of your kind. Many of those old women still have Sept tattoos to remember you by."

That got a flinch so hard it might be a shiver passing through the man's entire being.

He blinked rapidly, like a man having a religious conversion. Or a vision suddenly appearing unbidden in his mind.

What was it Daniel had called the place? Damascus on Old Earth? Yes, that.

A vision on the road to Damascus.

Except that it wasn't their god speaking to the man. Only a mad alien named Urid-Varg, speaking through a false prophet named Daniel.

Ndidi waited a moment for his eyes to clear, wondering at all the things Daniel had done. He would show her later, but she had given him her needs now.

"So, *Companion to your Emperor*, what will be your fate?" she asked now.

He growled under his breath.

"I have been betrayed," the man accused the galaxy in a dark tone almost reminiscent of hers. "Pasdar sent me here to die."

"That is between foolish Sept slavers," Ndidi pronounced. "Kamharida, find them a Sept ship heading to safety and allow it to break the blockade with them aboard. I don't care what the locals think. They are not in command of this system until I decide to allow it. Communicate to such locals that all they can do is anger me right now, if they choose to complain."

The woman holding the Sidiqi's chains nodded fiercely and turned the man with a jerk and a growl. The others got hustled out as well, probably thankful for their very lives.

They would be grateful to the Sidiqi when he told them the story Daniel had planted, the lies and misdirections suddenly brought to light in an unfavorable way.

Somewhere, the one known as Rostami would be able to undo it, but by the time he discovered what she had done, the damage would have already spread well beyond this one man. It would infect the entire Sept if she was lucky.

Ndidi watched them depart with a smile.

Kathra had ordered her to destroy the Sept Empire.

Ndidi would grasp whatever tools she had, even if she had to use them up.

8

Daniel had slipped out of the conference room with his head down and made rapid progress back towards his cabin. Like *SeekerStar* and *WinterStar* before it, he liked to be separate from the rest of the officers, living down near the kitchen.

He didn't cook for many people these days, as he had an entire staff that were well trained and understood that their Speaker was at least as good as he was, so they never slacked in the kitchen. That was the fastest way to simply be fired and sent home around here.

All of his volunteers had known that going in, so the food was exceptional even on their bad days.

Still, he needed some comfort food right now. Something to wash the bitter taste out of his mind.

Daniel understood that his continued existence required his submission to these many women. And he knew what the cost would be, in terms of his eventual sanity.

Hopefully, Kathra would just shoot him one of these days when he wasn't looking and couldn't prevent it. Or let him strip this stupid lime green bodysuit off and cast it and the gem into the heart of a sun.

But he had promised her, and Ndidi and the rest, that he would hold fast. Hold that line.

Not go crazy or turn fully into the sort of mad god that Urid-Varg had eventually.

Well, that *salaud* had always been an insane narcissist. A megalomaniac. It was only later he got the godhead part down.

Daniel had started with all the power. It was the madness he was trying to avoid.

Fixing people bore a heavy price. Ndidi knew that. Kathra knew that. Erin knew as well.

He walked quickly.

It wasn't full-on jogging, but Daniel was done with people today. He would need some time to be away from Ndidi and her demands, however effective they would be against the greater evil of the Sept Empire.

A lesser evil like him was still evil.

"But necessary," a voice floated over his shoulder.

Daniel cried out in surprise and pivoted, hands up defensively and mind suddenly running away with itself like a generator with no weight on the transmission.

Was he already going crazy?

Tanuss stood there.

Had she been stalking him? Keeping up while remaining so perfectly silent he hadn't noticed her?

No, he'd been squirreling in on himself that badly.

"Correct," she agreed with a soft smile.

And he'd apparently been muttering to himself again. In a loud kitchen, nobody probably noticed. If they did, people probably marked it down as part of his genius. Or some equivalent stupidity.

Daniel pulled himself together as well as he could and stood up to his full height. He took a breath, even as his heart continued pounding so loudly she might be able to hear it from over there.

He studied the alien woman.

Bipedal. Mammalian. Gray skin with iridescent patterns in pink and purple like a hexagonal tartan. That tentacle horn thing emerging from her forehead and glowing ever so slightly, a human-shaped anglerfish, right down to the sharp teeth.

She was tall for her kind, just barely taller than Ndidi and shorter than most of the comitatus. Standing, they were close to the same height.

The vestigial gill slits on the sides of her throat were working hard today, so maybe she'd been chasing him after all, and hadn't just magically appeared in this hallway.

"I'm done with evil for now," Daniel said aloud, hoping that the words would invoke some sort of magical incantation that would make it actually work out that way. "Done with people."

"I understand," she said quietly, stepping close enough to place her hand on his chest. "I don't want to be people."

It took him a moment to parse that. Maybe.

"What do you want?" he asked, confused now.

Not that such utter confusion was all that rare. He found himself surrounded constantly these days by competent, intelligent women. Complicated women.

Before the Mbaysey, he'd spent decades around groupies and bimbos like Angel and others. It had been a poor training ground.

"Knowing you, you are about to go to your cabin and take a long, hot shower to try to get all that evil off your skin," Tanuss said, stepping a little closer. "Then you'll be down in the kitchen. That will result in either cinnamon rolls or ratatouille, depending on your mood when you arrive."

He considered it. She was not wrong.

"*Oui*," he shrugged. "And?"

"And you looked like you needed a lifeguard to keep you from drowning in the shower," she offered with a tentative smile, as though willing yet to be driven off by his…

Despair? Anger? Guilt?

Daniel didn't know which set of terms might best describe the dark places prevalent in his mind right now. None of them were pleasant.

And yet, she knew that. Kathra had initiated this woman into the deeper mysteries of the comitatus, so she had been inside his mind.

Tanuss had seen all the bad things he had done. Both as himself as well as Urid-Varg.

Still, she had a calming hand on his chest, as though offering touch.

He wouldn't say human touch, because she wasn't, but it was close enough.

A friend. More than a friend. An occasional lover who understood the insides of his skull better than he did, quite possibly.

Something loosened in his chest, an iron band like those vicious manacles the Sept had worn, gone, just like that.

He drew a heavy breath into his narrow chest, like a sigh in reverse. Let it go and some of the darkness seemed to flow out with it.

He studied the woman again. Closer. Saw the emotions in her eyes that he knew better than any other being in the galaxy, because he had also been inside her mind more than once.

It still took some getting used to, understanding that he had friends who cared about it. For too many years, he had been the chef with the golden touch, and later, the Golden Diamond. A rock star to be feared and fawned over.

Daniel took her hand in both of his and kissed her fingertip.

Maybe, just maybe it would be worth surviving this war, after all.

9

KATHRA SMILED at the shark's discomfort, but he really didn't have anybody but himself to blame. Even on the bridge of his own ship.

"I still can't believe I let you talk me into this," Crence Miray said.

On his lap, little Adaku Omezi bounced and gurgled, a happy one-year-old.

Kathra sat in what was normally Dane's seat, but that Anndaing was standing nearby and chuckling.

"It's your own damned fault," Kathra retorted without any heat. "You were the one that suggested I sneak out here with you and your little Scout-6. Ife and Ndidi would throw a complete fit if they found out."

"I didn't think you'd take me up on it, Kathra," Crence turned a serious eye her direction. "Weren't you the one that promised the old crones that you would outlive them all?"

"Oh, I fully intend to, Crence," Kathra said. "But I don't like having to remain back at Ogrorspoxu or Kanus while all this is happening. The lag is months, and you aren't sending information home except when a transport brings supplies. I'd go nuts with frustration and boredom."

"Admit it, you just wanted to watch us blow things up," Jine said from his station on Crence's other side.

"That's a boy thing," Erin spoke up now from behind them all. Kathra glanced back and they shared a smile. "Girls are builders, not juvenile delinquents like you three."

She had Kwento's pouch slung around her neck, but that infant was asleep right now. The little one would wake up hungry shortly.

Crence rotated his hammer back enough to look, but Kathra already knew that Erin would be getting an eyeroll as only an Anndaing could do it, at either end of that wide hammer.

"It was her idea," Crence added, a thumb coming up to point back at Kathra.

Kathra just smiled.

"My idea, Crence, was for all your little Anndaing vessels to help Ndidi and Ife go after this network of bases that the Sept have built out here," Kathra reminded him. "Without those, the threat against the Merchants Guild vanishes for now and the Free Worlds are much safer."

She paused to fix the three men with a brief glare that melted into a grin.

"Blowing shit up along the way is just an occupational hazard," she continued. "That's why I suggested it to Wyll and Obaj."

The others laughed.

"But why wait until after *Singara*, though?" Dane asked.

Kathra wished occasionally that she had the ability to look both directions at once, like their hammers allowed, but she instead rotated in the chair enough to see the shark.

"Nobody has ever defeated a Septagon, Dane," Kathra said with a much more serious tone. "Ever. That Axial

Megacannon is irresistible. Even *MorningStar* cannot survive it and continue to fight effectively. That was why Daniel had to place the ship so precisely for Nwanyiudo and Ndidi. Otherwise, there was a chance the Sept could actually win."

"Right, I get that," Dane said, his hammer scrunching forward and down a little in confusion. "But you're letting them get away. Why not pounce on them again and again? If we were blowing up these outposts, they'd starve."

"No, they would get desperate, which is even worse," Kathra corrected the man. "Here, they have a highway that will get them safely back to Sept Space, where they can be carefully and lovingly rebuilt so that they can come back out in a year or three and threaten people again."

"Exactly!" Dane exclaimed. "Why allow that?"

"Because she already defeated *SeptStar*, Dane," Crence spoke up now.

Kathra smiled wryly at the trademaster and nodded for him to continue. Obviously, he hadn't gone all that deep into the details with his command crew, which surprised her some, but Kathra supposed that Crence had any number of secrets contained in that hammer that shouldn't be shared.

It would probably be difficult to remember which ones needed to go to the grave with him.

Dane turned to Crence at the same time everyone else did. Adaku turned and held her arms out, so Kathra grabbed her off the shark's lap and cuddled the little warrior close.

"*SeptStar* got home safe," Crence continued in a heavy voice. "So the bosses of the Sept had to decide if they wanted to build any more of them. They haven't to date. The design is fragile, if extremely cheap and fast to manufacture."

"Right, we've had that discussion over boullo wine," Dane agreed. "Mbaysey did it for political as well as technical reasons."

"So now *Singara*'s going to get home safe as well," Crence

nodded, his hammer actually flexed backwards enough that Kathra wondered how tense the man was right now.

He paused for Dane to nod, but the man didn't have any comments.

"What happens to the myth of Sept invincibility when a mauled Septagon limps into port and has to spend a year in drydock, Dane?" Crence asked. "How many people suddenly wonder if maybe they don't have to pay Sept taxes, if there's somebody out there capable of telling a Septagon *no* hard enough to spank one?"

"They have hundreds of Septagons, Dane," Erin filled in that key detail. "Killing *Singara* won't affect the balance of power all that much."

Dane closed his mouth right back again.

"People will see weakness, where there was once only strength," Kathra added. "As Crence said, the invulnerability and invincibility is gone. That's going to get into minds like a needle, Dane. Is the Sept really as inevitable as they would like the whole galaxy to think? What happens if all the aliens have other options? What if the Free Worlds don't have to eventually become Sept worlds? That was the value derived from letting *Singara* get home safely. They'll tell everyone, just sailing by, that a Septagon might not be enough."

"And the Armada?" Dane asked, breathless.

"We're all just pirates, Dane," Crence spoke up. "Merchants Bank is paying the Mbaysey a tribute not to raid their worlds. It happens to just about break even with the cost of leasing *MorningStar*, the other two duelers, and all these Scout-6 and Gun-6 ships floating around out here."

"Because you've never used plausible deniability as an excuse," Jine laughed.

Kathra had no idea what the nightflier was referring to, but the three Anndaing all laughed hard, so it must have been good.

Dane's hammer remained scrunched up. His eyes were all squinty at the ends of his hammers. His lips pursed.

"Will it work?" he finally asked, turning his whole hammer to face her.

"On humans?" Kathra asked. "Absolutely. I'm betting the Mbaysey on it."

10

———

CRENCE HAD SEEN the two women and the two little future warriors off his bridge and to safety back in their own quarters aft. Dane and Jine were strapped in and focused down on their tasks like diamond cutters.

They had taken to calling this particular Scout-6 *GhostStar*, at least as long as Kathra and her people were aboard. She outranked him anyway, and was a visiting head of state to boot. Or something like that. And Wyll had put him in charge of this particular frenzy of ships, which was good enough.

"Nightflier, what is your status?" Crence turned to look at Jine.

The shark's fin was flopped completely over sideways like he was asleep, but that just told Crence how tightly wound Jine was in his head.

"All systems nominal," Jine replied laconically.

Yup, tighter than an atomic clock.

"Status from *SwiftStar* and *NovaStar*?" he continued.

"Ife scares me some days, Crence," Dane said quietly. "This is one of them."

Crence nodded. He felt the same way about that woman.

"Is the rest of the frenzy ready to engage?" Crence turned the other way.

"They all signal red, Trademaster," Dane nodded.

Sounded like blood.

That had been the weirdest part of dealing with the humans. Red was something bad to them, possibly a survival instinct honed from being arboreal creatures at some distant point in the past.

Anndaing had evolved up from sharks that were remarkably similar to the earth creature, except that they had been more apex predators like the whites, rather than quiet hunters like a Terran hammerhead.

Red was a happy thing. Especially to a frenzy of armed warship with their fins in the air.

"Fins upright and make your jumps," Crence ordered.

Jine was under penalty of dismemberment by Wyll if anything happened to Kathra, so they would be lurking at the edge of even the Scout-6 vessels. Let the Gun-6 and Gun-12 hooligans charge in blasting.

GhostStar's job was to track down any Patrol vessels that fled. He could take one of those, especially if it was running and possibly wounded.

Blood in the water, as it were.

There.

Sept snowflake station, lurking out in the middle of space like a jellyfish. Guns were already firing in all directions, so this was one of those stinging *salauds* you had to approach from above to avoid the tentacles. Except that here, you came at him on the plane, where only a few of his guns could engage you.

Stupid design, but there were three Patrol craft docked right now, so Crence was willing to bet that they were too badly damaged from Tavle Jocia to stay with the rest of the squadron.

After all, *Singara* only had a head start. Not a free ticket home.

Every station was getting rolled up after this, all the way back to Sept Space.

And maybe a little further, but that would be after Kathra and Erin were safely home.

Or at least safely someplace other than *GhostStar*.

Gun-6 and Gun-12 ships were mean little bastards. Crence watched them charge right at the station, pouring fire into the metal. Stupid things still weren't armored, which had struck Crence as a dumb design.

But then, a Patrol of ten was supposed to be enough to take down any pirate they encountered. And nobody was crazy enough to start a war with the Sept.

Except Kathra Omezi.

"Status?" Crence asked, just to keep Dane from forgetting to talk.

"Frenzy, Trademaster," Dane said with a bit of awe in his voice.

Certainly looked like it, with chunks already spalling off that snowflake as the team kept shooting.

Without this station, no Septagon could threaten Tavle Jocia from this direction. And Crence had no doubts that various Free Worlds had scouts out in every direction as well, resurveying all their worlds for infestations of Sept stations.

This thumb that had stuck out from Sept Spacewas about to be bitten off, one station at a time, with the Septagon needing to keep fleeing ahead of the frenzy chasing it.

Sure, the Septagon could stop and offer battle, but every day he did that was one day closer to starvation. Three hundred thousand sailors, plus all the support vessels, ate an enormous amount of food on a daily basis.

From here, the frenzy was going after all those Sept transports hauling food and supplies to forward operating bases.

Nobody said piracy couldn't be profitable, after all.

11

———————

NDIDI WATCHED the system map from her office like a hawk. She had to admit that her command crew was even better than *SwiftStar* had had, but that was partly everyone slowly growing into their jobs over there.

Ndidi and Acqueir had already known what they were doing when they got to *MorningStar*, and A'Alhakoth had been trained to the blade long before she took the job title *Sword*.

Even Hirly, the odd shark out, had meshed well, but Erin had met the woman by chance at some event with Wyll Koobitz. Erin had an instinct for that sort of thing. Look at A'Alhakoth.

Tavle Jocia had only hiccupped a little when they changed overlords from the Free Worlds to the Sept a year ago. But then, according to Daniel's scans of various minds, Naupati Pasdar, once their foe on Septagon *Vorgash*, had understood the sticks and carrots to use around here.

Money.

Feeding a Septagon force required a tremendous amount

of food. Locals had quickly gotten over themselves enough to start selling food to the Sept without poisoning it first.

Ndidi wouldn't hold that against them. Two weeks ago, a Septagon had still been invincible. Many people were rethinking balance sheets these days.

Equipment had largely still been carried on Sept hulls by Sept merchants, mostly because those folks hadn't wanted to create an even greater manufacturing base out here.

Still, men like Factor Isaev had made an astonishing amount of money, just building hulls for new Patrols for the Sept. Supplying metal and forms.

Trade.

The Anndaing Merchants Guild would be showing up soon enough and offering a different kind of trade for the newly-liberated folks. A whole raft of new calculations to be made.

A chime interrupted her about the same time as a new signal appeared on the edge of the sensor map Ndidi had been studying.

She opened the line to the bridge.

"Go ahead."

"New signal, Speaker," Acqueir said carefully. "Sensors flagged it as a Cargo-6, but they're wrong."

"Wrong?" Ndidi asked.

"Scout-6," Acqueir said with some pride. "Still have the vessel in my records. That's Crence, but the ship calls itself *GhostStar*. They've hailed us and are wanting to come alongside to send a SkyCamel."

GhostStar?

Her comm chimed a second time, which was exceptionally odd. Most people would knock.

"Go ahead and clear them for now," Ndidi decided. "Standard protocol but don't shoot without a good reason. Crence must have some secret he doesn't want to share."

"Yes, Speaker."

Ndidi switched to the second line and checked the ID.

Daniel?

"What's up, Daniel?" she asked, trying to sound casual.

He would certainly have walked here, but his cabin was aft of her day office off the bridge by a ways, so it must be important.

"Are you alone?" Daniel asked carefully.

"I am," Ndidi replied, tensing. "Why?"

"Kathra is on that vessel."

What?

12

———

Daniel had finally settled into a good rhythm of being able to cook at least one meal per day, but the galaxy kept intruding and he had sometimes been lucky to cook for the comitatus once in a week back on *WinterStar* and then *SeekerStar*.

Ndidi had taken the slack, but she was Speaker now.

Daniel had at least gotten smart this time and was training half a dozen new cooks to go with all the other staff he had. All of them had the potential to open their own bistro or taco truck one of these days. He had been a cruel farmer culling for winter when he had started recruiting.

"I will probably not be back until dinner is served," Daniel announced to the crew, catching eyes, fins, and tentacles waved or glowing in his direction. "Make sure you are prepared for an exceptional meal tonight, for reasons I will not share immediately, but will be obvious in an hour or two."

He slipped out of his domain without waiting for questions. Most of his folks knew better than to ask, anyway.

The landing deck on a Battlemaster was aft, between the

main engines on the centerline. He had always wondered about that, but he supposed that it made things easiest for a shuttle to line itself up and hit a hole, rather than trying to account for drift as well.

The Ovanii had been wanderers far longer than they had been marauders, but like the Mbaysey, they had never bothered to settle on a planet once they left. All his ghosts agreed on that topic, however little was known otherwise.

He still wanted to go visit the one world where the Anndaing had planted the survivors of the final battle, just to see what their legends had turned into, after falling from the Galactic Age to the Iron in a generation. Several thousand years had passed.

Who were the Ovanii today?

Tomorrow's question. Kathra was going to land on *MorningStar* shortly. Kathra, who should have been safely back on Kanus or Ogrorspoxu, instead of clear up here.

He knew that Ndidi would be tearing a strip of flesh off Crence at some point, to have concealed all this, but again, Daniel was just a chef. He left political matters to the women who understood such things.

When he was most of the way to the landing bay, Ndidi caught up with him. Daniel made sure not to be run over as she stomped angrily down the corridor, Hirly and A'Alhakoth trailing. Acqueir must be in charge up on the bridge.

Not like there were any weak links in Ndidi's chain of command. Even after you got to the wardroom kitchen staff.

He grinned and caught up with Ndidi, pacing her in spite of the woman's longer legs.

"She's not really here, you know," Daniel observed in the same way that folks talked about last night's ForceBall score.

It worked. Ndidi was derailed enough to turn his way in confusion. She even slowed down.

"What?" she demanded.

"Kathra," Daniel said carefully. "All this secrecy is a reminder that she's not anywhere close and you're in charge of heaven and hell in Tavle Jocia until you decide otherwise."

"And if she decides to take over?" Ndidi snapped.

"Will you allow it?" Daniel smiled cruelly.

That got through. Ndidi bit back something that was probably pretty salty, from the way her eyes flared.

"No," she said, softening. "But I do get to see my nieces."

Daniel grinned and started walking at a normal pace. She caught up this time and paced him.

"For a man who claims to be weak and ignorant, you do seem to know how to puncture pomposity at times," Ndidi observed wryly.

He glanced back to note the grins on Hirly and A'Alhakoth's faces before he spoke.

"I used to be an expert at being a pompous ass, Ndidi," he replied with a smile. "Angel and a few others cured me of that. My job these days is to see to the well-being of my crew, both physical as well as emotional. Kathra would have to have a good reason to be here, and I'm willing to take that at face value. You can always order her back to Kanus aboard Crence's ship. Pretty sure you and Ife can do that to the trademaster."

They paced the rest of the way in silence.

Ovanii shuttlecraft, in their day, had been larger than SkyCamels, which were just rectangular boxes the size of ground trucks for the most part. The landing bay could fit exactly one Anndaing transport, and the pilot had very little margin for error in the process.

They watched from a long picture window made of clear aluminum as the vessel touched down on a pin. The outer bay doors closed quickly and atmosphere flooded the room.

Crence and Kathra emerged, with Adaku on her hip. Nobody else.

Daniel wondered if she had flown the transport. Crence wasn't that good as a pilot.

They walked to an airlock and cycled through quickly.

Daniel could practically smell the rage emanating off Ndidi again. He could only imagine what it would have been like without him intervening earlier.

Kathra, for all the good it did her, had a sheepish look on her face when she emerged.

Crence seemed content to hide behind the woman's skirts.

"I would ask for permission to come aboard," Kathra said. "But you might say no, so I'll just surprise you and announce that I'm here and need to talk to you about the next stage of the campaign. I'm sorry for all the secrecy, but you, of all people, will understand."

Daniel wondered if someone could actually grind their teeth hard enough to throw sparks, like those magical weirdos in the movies who started fires. Today, he might find out.

Ndidi was utterly pissed.

But it was her ship. Her squadron. Her command.

"At least Erin wasn't such a fool," Ndidi snarled quietly.

Crence flinched and Daniel understood.

"She's on the Scout-6," Kathra admitted. "*GhostStar* is what Crence calls it."

"Wyll knows," Crence offered weakly. "He did approve."

"Why are you not at home, Kathra?" Ndidi managed to sound at least a little human.

Friendly was yet out there a ways.

"I want to make some drastic changes in the way your campaign is going to work, Ndidi," Kathra said. "You will execute them after I leave with Crence and his crew, but what we originally planned won't be sufficient."

"Alright," Ndidi nodded. At least she was going strategic again, rather than remaining angrily focused on Kathra. "Let's take this to the main conference room."

Daniel smiled at Kathra and caught her nod as Ndidi turned and started stomping forward. Crence looked chagrined, but like Daniel, he was in over his head with these women.

Thankfully, Daniel didn't have to do much around here except track Rostami on a daily basis and cook for the women he loved.

Because he suspected that things were about to get even more interesting.

13

Kathra knew she deserved all the anger and hurt Ndidi was channeling, but this was one of the times that the young woman needed to pause and take a step back.

It was still Ndidi's command. Would be her campaign from here. Kathra was going to make one change, and then depart.

This time, she would be returning all the way to Kanus, because her only other option would be to stay here and crowd the very woman she had selected for this task.

Plus, the old women she'd left behind were probably getting *fussy* by now.

Kathra looked around the table at the people she had placed here. Ndidi. Hirly. A'Alhakoth. Nwanyiudo. Acqueir. Tanuss. Daniel.

Adaku sat on Nwanyiudo's lap and squirmed a little, wanting to climb up on the table itself and crawl around. She was already starting to walk. It would only get more interesting from here.

Thus was the Mbaysey's future assured to some extent.

"This is yours, Ndidi," Kathra said, gesturing up and out with one hand to encompass *MorningStar*, but also the entirety of Tavle Jocia. "All of it."

The fewer people who knew where Kathra was, the better. She had no doubt that Sept assassins lurked around any corner that they could.

Ndidi surprised her by turning to Crence.

"Wyll put you in charge out there," she reminded him flatly.

"Ife's a much better top shark in a frenzy than me," the male replied carefully. "*SwiftStar* and *NovaStar* are ranging out on the next mission with about half my team, while the other half is at the jump point, robbing every transport dumb enough to come under their guns because nobody warned them about the change of plans."

Kathra watched the Speaker absorb this information silently. Process things like a chef cooking for a hungry comitatus that couldn't make up its mind. Breakfasts on *SeekerStar* had frequently been like that.

Finally, she came to some conclusion.

"So rolling the Sept waypoints up is no longer primary?" Ndidi asked, turning her eyes back to Kathra.

"It is," Kathra nodded, then tilted her head a little. "But our success—your success here—was greater than I had imagined possible, because we only planned for what we thought we could manage. That will still happen."

Kathra looked at the others and noted the fierce pride in all of them. Only a few were Mbaysey born, but all of them had absorbed that tribal ethic along the way. Several probably planned to join the Star Tribe at some future point.

"You don't need *MorningStar* for that, unless you plan to provoke *Singara* at some point, which seems stupid," Hirly spoke up now. "Since that's not it, what is the mission, Commander?"

"Vorgash," Kathra said simply, watching faces.

Surprise. Shock. Anger. Canniness on Ndidi's part as her eyes got narrow.

"Good for the goose, Kathra?" her favorite Speaker asked. Kathra nodded.

"What's going on?" Daniel asked. "I thought we didn't want to take on another Septagon unless we had to."

"She's not talking about Septagon *Vorgash*," Ndidi turned towards him. "She means the planet itself."

"Seriously?" he goggled. "Why?"

"Ogrorspoxu," Kathra said. "You were aboard *Windrunner* when Hadi Rostami came out of jump on top of you and would have destroyed you, except that Ife was able to intercept him. The lucky shot that killed the Ishtan was the reason you are still alive today, Daniel."

"*Oui*," he agreed, still a little lost.

But then, he was a chef, not a former Spectre pilot like many of her women had been.

"*MorningStar* will range ahead of Septagon *Singara*," Ndidi said. "We know the rough path they used to build their network of bases originally to attack Tavle Jocia, because they originated at Vorgash. According to reports, *Singara* was brought in to protect the system when Septagon *Vorgash* headed out."

"Good for the gander," he saw it finally. "Will we need all three Duelers with us?"

All eyes turned to Crence and his hammer flexed down and forward.

"I need to send Kathra home with one of my gunships," he said. "If I could have one Dueler as a sledgehammer, the rest of my frenzy could easily continue raiding closer and closer to Sept Space. Eventually, they're going to hear the news over there and send out a large enough force to protect those stations. Gun-6 and Gun-12 ships are mean bastards, but an Ovanii Dueler is enough to chew up a whole Sept Patrol without even breaking a sweat.”

Kathra focused on Ndidi now. Took a deep breath and smiled at the woman.

“You are in charge, Ndidi,” she said. “I would like you to raid Vorgash directly from here and rattle Sept sensibilities. But this is your force. Your decision. I have delivered the message I needed you to hear, so I need to step back and let you decide how to plan your campaign.”

Everyone went silent, even little Adaku, but she looked hungry, so Kathra reached over and lifted her up. Sure enough, the bottomless pit needed feeding, so Kathra took care of her while she awaited Ndidi.

Interestingly, Ndidi turned to Daniel.

“Do we assume a Septagon at Vorgash?” she asked. “Perhaps our old friend *Vorgash* has returned home?”

He started to say something but stopped when he realized that he was truly the only expert on the Sept in the room. Kathra had been born on Tazo, and both Ndidi and Nwanyiudo were Star Tribe children, born aboard a ClanStar and not a planet. The rest were aliens that had rallied to Kathra’s cause, either out of nobility of purpose or because the dread of the Sept was so great.

Only Daniel had been a Sept citizen in good standing at one point. That he was a wanted criminal today would not change that.

Daniel paused and his eyes got that distant look when he was falling in on himself.

Kathra had no idea what he might ask his ghosts, since none of them knew the Sept except through him, but perhaps he needed their support.

Daniel Lémieux was still the only male officer on this ship, and one of a few males at all.

Mbaysey.
Kathra watched her favorite chef and waited.

14

———

Daniel took the long dive down into the great cathedral where all his ghosts waited. In the early days, only a few had been willing to interact with him, but that had changed when he went there to ask about the Ovanii, on that momentous trip to the planet Tnesu. The one where he first laid eyes on the remains of the ancient Ovanii fleet and the ship that would eventually be named *SwiftStar*.

A'Alhakoth had met them all once, as had Kathra and Erin, but they generally tended to be circumspect when dealing with outsiders.

They waited like a field of wheat today, blowing in some unfelt breeze that created tides and eddies. All of them.

All of them.

Like they knew.

"I am not a warrior," he announced simply. "We are surrounded by such women, and they have a question that only you might help me answer. What should we find at Vorgash?"

He had never been there, personally. From Genarde he had ranged out further and further. Getting to the edge of known space in his mind, but now he realized that he had been constrained by old thinking. There was a whole galaxy out there that had been blank space on a map.

Here there be dragons.

It would have been nice to have a few Ovanii in his Greek Chorus, but Urid-Varg had never met the ancient roamers.

The Roahrt he had spoken with previously emerged from the crowd now, to stand next to Daniel's favorite K'bari, Arsène.

Pheryoutl. All the ghosts were Daniel's size, regardless of what they had been like in life, but this one conveyed great size and strength in spite of it.

He had a look of pain on his face, but it cleared a moment later.

"The Destroyer would walk in there and either claim the place for himself, or wreak a terrible havoc in passing," Pheryoutl began slowly. "You have not the muscle, nor the inclination, but Ndidi Zikora has the will and the power in her own way."

"She does," Daniel nodded. "And in me, us, she has the potential to do just that. To devastate the place known mostly because of the name it gave the Septagon who was my greatest enemy, before those two men left that ship and returned in *Singara*. Do we wish that?"

"Evil must often be fought with iron and blood, Daniel," the Roahrt nodded. "The costs will be high. The repercussions generational in nature. But the Mbaysey will not pay them, because the Commander will never return to Sept Space, even as a conqueror in her own right."

"She won't?" Daniel asked, surprised.

But then, he was facing twelve thousand years of accumulated experience and possibly wisdom. That was why he asked these ghosts.

"The Star Tribe will head ever outward," Pheryoutl noted. "You and A'Alhakoth will perhaps guide them into the other darkness, or Commander Omezi will seek beyond the Anndaing. Again, these tides move generationally. You have no strong feelings, either way."

"*Non*," Daniel agreed. "I will cook for amazing women, and perhaps make love to a few of them, but I will likely never return to human space, either. Too many will suspect the truth, and only the Mbaysey will be willing to shelter me, until such time as we all must die."

"That frees you, Daniel Lémieux," Pheryoutl acknowledged. "You can choose to do terrible things to the people of Vorgash, because it is in her name. Her requirements. Not a thing you would do on your own. Not a thing we would object to. And it will strike a heavy blow against the Sept Empire itself. That edifice may begin to crumble under the assault."

"Could we bring down the Sept?" Daniel asked, astonished at these beings and their willingness.

But then, each of them had once been a man with his own life, until the fateful day when each had happened to cross paths with a megalomaniac who refused to die.

It had finally taken a puny, human chef with a fire extinguisher. And a rage as terrible as had first launched Urid-Varg into space, twelve thousand years ago.

And many of the men around him knew that.

"We cannot," Arsène spoke now. "Urid-Varg could have, but he would have claimed them instead. You lack the power amplification that the Star Turtle provided. And you are not him."

Daniel nodded, thankful that these ghosts would also protect him from turning into another Conqueror, just as the women would.

He was not Urid-Varg. So many people watched. But the women could only use their will on him.

These ghosts held Daniel's soul.

"But at Vorgash, you can teach them fear, Daniel," Pheryoutl said. "The Sept believe that they are destined to conquer all of the galaxy and bring all species under their yoke. To date, only Kathra Omezi and Ndidi Zikora have been able to dispute that. The Anndaing Armada is merely a collection of warships that could argue with a Sept invasion of their worlds. Perhaps they prevail. Perhaps they fail. That is the material world."

"We must fight on the spiritual plane," Daniel agreed. "But we will echo the terrible Urid-Varg when we do so."

Pheryoutl smiled. Arsène as well. Looking around, all of his ghosts had their equivalent on their faces.

"A wolf is calling to them from nearby in the darkness," Pheryoutl said. "But not a wolf. A man playing a terrible practical joke on other men, that they no longer can sleep comfortably in beds, and perhaps are no longer safe from the predation of wolves."

"And Septagon *Vorgash*, if it is there?" Daniel asked.

"*Uwalu* remembers your hunting call," Arsène said. "*Vorgash*, both the Septagon and the planet, should also be infected with such a fear. Let them offer sacrifices to whatever gods they may venerate. It will not be enough."

Daniel nodded. He took a breath and was suddenly back aboard *MorningStar*, surrounded by Kathra and all her women.

His smile grew terrible.

15

Ndidi knew that look when Daniel went to consult the ancient ones. Watched him return an eye blink later.

The smile on his face turned cold and cruel. Something about it blunted the hot rage that had consumed her since Kathra had appeared at a place that woman had no business being.

Daniel had been asked about Vorgash, both the planet and the Septagon.

"There will be a Septagon there when we arrive," he said simply. "The ghosts agree on that tactical and strategic maneuver from the *salauds*."

"But?" Ndidi asked, hearing the catch in Daniel's voice. That burr that suggested he was holding something back.

"But it will not matter," he turned to her and she saw the abyss itself opening up in her twin's eyes.

That thing, that bottomless darkness that had convinced Kathra to admit this man into the comitatus, when no other male had ever impressed her even remotely.

Daniel had looked Death in the face again. Just now. Talking to his ghosts.

Perhaps *become* Death itself.

"Even a second Septagon will not matter, except as that means twice as many victims," he continued.

Ndidi heard the gasps around the table. Hers might have joined it.

Victims.

Not sailors. Not enemies. Not even people.

Victims.

"Are you okay, Daniel?" she asked.

As Speaker, he was her responsibility as one of her officers. But Kathra had also once commanded her to be possibly his only friend in the galaxy, when he found himself completely alone. She had never rescinded that order. A'Alhakoth, Tanuss, and even Acqueir had done things about the loneliness, but this was still her twin brother.

"*Non,*" he replied. "But *they* are united in the need to do something terrible at Vorgash when we arrive. It will not be as powerful as it once was, but the memory of it will stain the Sept until the very end of time."

Heads came up. Some in confusion. Some in indignation.

Kathra started to speak until Ndidi silenced her with a look.

This was *MorningStar*. Ndidi Zikora *Spoke* for the ship.

Kathra Omezi was only the Commander of the Mbaysey.

Ndidi waited as Daniel found the words.

"You were there," he said, staring directly at her.

And Ndidi knew the truth. Understood the terrible thing that Daniel had planned.

His ghosts would help, because he no longer had the Turtle.

Yes, that would be terrible indeed.

Ndidi began planning her campaign around such a thing.

"What?" Crence finally asked.

But then, he had only seen the truth in Daniel's mind. He had never actually merged with the man in such a way as to learn Daniel's secrets.

No male would be allowed that depth of knowledge, because they would then understand how to take it away from the chef.

How to become gods themselves. The Mbaysey would never allow that.

"The place doesn't even have a name," Ndidi said. "Only a string of digits on a Sept navigational chart to identify it. It was the place where the Sept first discovered the existence of the Star Turtle, when an Mbaysey traitor gave them the coordinates."

Crence shook his head, still missing something.

Ndidi nodded to Daniel.

She had been there, carried along on his hip through space with nothing but a shirt and capri pants to protect her. And Daniel's powers.

Diving down into that gas giant, until *Leviathan* emerged from the depths of a permanent storm, hiding in the darkness.

Boarding the ship by being eaten.

And then flying up into the sky to confront a Septagon.

"We're going to do to them, what we did to Septagon *Uwalu*," Daniel said.

Ndidi shuddered in spite of herself, but the nightmares of that scream had largely passed.

And she had only heard the echo of it.

Septagon *Uwalu* had taken the full brunt so hard that the vessel itself rebooted all mechanical and electronic systems while she and Daniel made their escape.

Yes, the Sept would never erase that memory.

Ndidi's smile echoes Daniel's.

16

———

Hadi was coming to like Earth.

All planets had been modified along the way, either by aliens or by humans expanding and seeking to establish colonies, but he could see them all now as faint shadows of the homeworld.

Everything felt right here, because this was where humanity had been born. The right gravity. The right air. Even the right sky over his head, though Hadi was much more accustomed to being inside starships.

As always, he trailed close down hallways and past important men and messengers, walking behind Amirin Pasdar, great conqueror of the modern ages who had driven the Mbaysey clear off a human map of the galaxy and taken one of the jewels of the Free Worlds in a surprise attack that left the place almost undamaged.

That other fools had subsequently lost control of the planet just played to the legend of greatness that circled around Amirin's name. Aided, of course, by subtle touches along the way as Hadi encountered people whose esteem of Pasdar was important.

They had been summoned to the court of the Shah of Earth. Because Rhages was so distant, the man who held this title was not in the direct line of inheritance to the current Keyaksar, Emperor Dana Bahram Tabatabaei, supposedly called The Wise in history books, but Hadi generally referred to him privately as The Drunkard.

An afternoon at the man's Court on Rhages had cured Hadi of all thoughts of the Divine Right of Kings. Not even Allah would support such a fool.

Here, the Shah of Earth was a Sardari. All seven of the Clans were nominally allies, but as a ruling caste of a star-spanning empire, there were always tides. Swirls in the darkness that might sink an unwary ship like rocks.

And the man was a power unto himself. He ruled the ancient homeland in the name of the Keyaksar. Amirin would need his support when the next several steps played out.

It helped that this Sardari was a model of moral rectitude. In that, Hadi already liked the man.

The Court they were attending today was located in the mountains north of the ancient capital of Tehran. The building was largely open to the elements today, but the weather was perfect and promised nothing but cool, clear skies and just the right amount of breeze.

Hadi studied the men around him as Amirin chatted and glad-handed.

Everyone wore simple robes that their ancient ancestors would have recognized, even going so far as to wear cotton and linen, rather than expensive silks or artificial fibers developed by technology or aliens.

Sober. Metaphorically as well as literally.

Hadi even allowed himself a brief smile, but that was him wondering again if perhaps Rhages should simply be bombed out of existence. If the Capital was moved back to Earth again, perhaps this sort of sober thinking would infect the next generation with the need to set a better example to the population of the Empire. Rhages's moon held most of the important bureaus and agencies of Empire anyway, so nothing great would be lost if all those scum on the planet below were annihilated.

How far we have fallen from the dreams of our ancestors...

The man Amirin was speaking with now was from Mirzadeh Clan. A lesser noble, only in the sense that he was not a first son, so he would never bear the title *Vuzurgan*.

At least not unless something happened to his brothers and possibly nephews.

Not all politics was handled across a negotiating table, after all.

Hadi reached quietly into the man's mind and studied him using skills honed by alien bloodhounds seeking to track down the most dangerous predator in history and developed at the hands of a human with political needs.

Yes, the Mirzadeh had the elements of a quiet, irrational rage from being born a third son. The man could be important, but only in the way that dynastic marriages would improve the wealth and power of the family. He would never lack for money or opportunity, but true power would be denied him based on nothing but birth order.

Hadi understood why Amirin was taking the time to chat with the fellow. He was not just an ally for what was coming, but a man with reason to support overturning the ancient ways. If every son could perhaps aspire to power, then anything was possible.

Hadi already had far too great of an understanding as to why primogeniture was such a poor idea. Eventually, you gave birth to a moron, and then handed him absolute executive authority.

Like they had done at Rhages.

The Sept had only survived as long as it had because it had a bureaucracy already in place that could keep things running when drunkards sat on the throne.

That, and Septagons.

No force in the galaxy had been encountered yet that could resist an Axial Megacannon.

Hadi suppressed a shudder at the Ishtan nightmares of a universe where Urid-Varg had encountered any other human vessel besides Kathra Omezi's. Where the creature had learned about the Sept and decided to found a new empire on the backs of a Septagon fleet rather than debauching himself onto the bodies of human women.

All would have fallen before him, and humans would have venerated the creature as a god, because he would have been human, at least in his outward guise.

As would the victims he continued to take for however long humans thrilled him, or until some other alien emerged from the depths of darkness to challenge his power.

Hadi had memories of the Ishtan aiding the K'bari rebels when they finally decided that they didn't want a living god anymore. Anndaing warships sold into K'bari service as mercenaries.

He mourned the K'bari, but only a little. Many of them had chosen to keep worshiping a god that had been forced to flee when too many K'bari resisted.

The civil war had eventually been xenocidal in scope.

Hadi shook his head and tried to pretend to be human again, hoping nobody had noticed his lapse. He expanded his senses enough to sniff the mental breeze, but detected nothing untoward, so he reached out to the Mirzadeh speaking with Amirin and planted a few seeds.

Nurtured, them, really, as they were already present, just stunted. Hadi poured a little water and some fertilizer on them. Directed that resentment to grow against rigid aristocracy and towards a more meritocratic system, where Shahs and Emperors were chosen on ability, rather than birth order, even if they were still only drawn from children of the Seven Clans.

It would still help break down the old model, and hopefully let Amirin build something better in its place.

The Ishtan had known it was coming, and told him that Amirin Pasdar would be able to overthrow the Sept.

Could they replace it with something that would outlive them?

17

—————

KATHRA USUALLY APPRECIATED how spoiled she had gotten by Daniel and Ndidi when Crence's chef served dinner. It wasn't that Mase Jacksanch was a bad cook, but the kitchenmaster was a fussy old fish, tasked with keeping things simple and running for the thirty crew members of *Koni Swift*'s crew that now served on *GhostStar*.

He had learned a few things from his competitions with Daniel on that first flight to Ogrorspoxu, but most them hadn't stuck. Mase had his rotation of dishes that he liked to work through, and you could almost predict them a month out.

Today was rice in a green sauce with some sort of baked fish. Nothing that would poison a human. Daniel and Joane had seen to that. But it was an exceptionally pedestrian meal.

Adaku and Kwento were asleep aft, watched over by Areen, so Kathra and Erin could have a private dinner with Crence and Dane. Jine just wanted to fly, so he avoided all political discussions like they might infect him with *boringness* or something.

Mase had retreated to his kitchen, no doubt already

planning whatever bland meal would be served for breakfast. Kathra found that she really could wait.

"Maybe we should ask your recruiter to find me another chef?" Crence asked sidelong, staring at a piece of fish with almost as much enthusiasm as Kathra had right now.

"Human for an Anndaing crew?" Erin asked.

Kathra noted that her best friend must be feeling extra feisty today. She still had the mohawk going, but had shaved the sides clean, rather than just keeping them buzzed short. Still, motherhood agreed with her. With both of them.

Dane managed the most excellent eyeroll.

"Mase," he offered with a chuckle. "Low bar to clear."

They all laughed. The meal was perfectly adequate. And not much more.

Something Ugonna might have served, when she had been in charge of the comitatus kitchen. Fortunately, Mase had been cleared of any treasonous thoughts by Daniel.

"Would humans integrate well into Anndaing space?" Kathra asked. "I appreciate that the Merchants Guild is open to everyone willing to sit for the exams and having the requisite time as a crewman to qualify, but most of those folks are Anndaing or one of the species you uplifted to technology."

"The Se'uh'pal have their own equivalent rating system, to which we offer reciprocity," Crence shrugged. "The Bhaorajj hate everyone equally. The Upynth aren't really explorers. Going the other direction, there are a few species further out that we occasionally trade with, but there are some strange gaps in civilized worlds that direction. One of them represent the z'lud according to Daniel's records. They appear to be completely extinct, rather than just fallen to barbarism, like the K'bari or Ovanii. Others are just quirks of the galactic arms. So yeah, humans are really the next group likely to be a big presence to the Guild."

"And?" Erin prompted when Crence fell silent.

"Small groups would be easy enough to handle," Dane stepped into the conversation, but he was studying to be a trademaster eventually. After he got rich working for Crence. "It gets hinky when a group of proposed colonists want to move out and set themselves up on one of our worlds in a big block. It works for the Kaniea, like you said, because they're one of ours. Things would be harder to judge with humans."

"The Mbaysey make a poor baseline against which to judge our kind," Kathra smiled.

"Well, yeah," Dane said. He paused to glance at Crence and got a nod before he continued. "On our own trips to Tavle Jocia, we had a few walk-ups who wanted to see the galaxy, but Crence figured most of them were probably Sept spies or saboteurs, ya know?"

"Oh, indeed," Erin barked a laugh. "We never trusted singles or large groups wanting to join a ClanStar. A couple of friends were far more believable, and we could vet their backstories easily enough, even before Daniel."

"You'll be working closely with the Free Worlds in the future," Kathra acknowledged. "Assumedly, at least. What about the Anndaing? Will you or one of your cousins want to colonize former K'bari worlds? Or even consider uplifting the K'bari again?"

"Not while there's a war going on," Crence shrugged. "Those worlds make a nice firebreak. At the same time, I could see the need for us to start seeding some colonies, just because they could produce grains and meat pretty easily and sell them to forward Anndaing bases that no doubt will be cropping up. If just to keep the Sept from doing the same."

"So let's talk about doing just that," Kathra looked right at Crence. "Colonies can be expensive things to set up, because they don't have much of an industrial base, but can produce foodstuffs pretty easily. Especially if this is a K'bari world where they died out after the war ended."

She liked the way both sharks perked up.

"What do you have in mind, Kathra?" Crence asked.

"Drop a small station over a world on a good travel corridor," she smiled. "Put farmers on the ground and tell them to just grow stuff. The Mbaysey can go back to what we've always done, mining metals and water from the systems themselves, and getting exotic gases and chemicals from the giants. We trade that at the station for grain and meat, like always. The Merchants Guild will send traders like you out to keep the place supplied with advanced things, plus I'm sure you'll want to make certain the TradeStation is maybe more of a military base. Or add one, so Scout-6 and Gun-6 ships can range over the sector without having to return to Acran constantly for resupply."

"You're serious," Crence's voice got nervous.

Dane's eyes followed suit.

"I have a much greater interest in keeping the Sept out of K'bari space than even the Anndaing do, Crence," Kathra said. "Plus, the old women are probably getting fat and lazy now, with civilized worlds wanting to trade for exotic goods. It will do them good to have to return to their roots, at least for a while. And eventually I need to build up a great deal of financial reserves against future need."

"Why is that?" Dane asked.

"*SwiftStar* is an expensive vessel to maintain, Dane," Kathra turned to him. "Right now, the Merchants Bank is paying me a bribe that's enough to keep everything in motion, and for me to supposedly hire all the ships accompanying it. Not just *MorningStar*, but the other two and all the gunships. Eventually, the war is either won or lost, and the Anndaing will stop paying bribes. You'll get all those ships back, but I'm keeping *SwiftStar* if I can afford it. It will possibly replace *SeekerStar* as my flagship, if the war ends and we're all still around."

"Have you talked to Wyll or Obaj about this?" Crence asked.

"No," Kathra said. "Only Erin. We must measure things now in the lifetimes of our daughters. It might be enough for the Sept to start minding their manners. What Ndidi is going to do with Daniel's help might force the Sept back within their own borders for a time. Better the Anndaing or the Free Worlds claim K'bari space than Sept infiltrators start breeding like ticks."

Dane turned to Erin with a stage voice now.

"Does she always think like this?" he asked, almost humorously.

Erin grinned.

"I talked her out of colonizing all of K'bari space directly and creating an entire Mbaysey homeland on those worlds when you folks weren't looking," she laughed.

Dane and Crence both turned a little white around the gills.

It hadn't been *that* serious a conversation. Kathra was never going to be beholden to a planet that could be bombarded from orbit. That was exactly why the Sept and their Septagons were so irresistible.

Those things could destroy a world, but when they had to chase you across deep space, the ClanStars could always flee farther and faster.

Maybe Adaku's daughter would want to build such a homeland. Kathra didn't think that putting it between the Anndaing and the humans would be all that wise. Sure, you could get rich on trade, but both sides would eventually want to incorporate you into their political and mercantile systems.

That would mean warfare.

No, better to be off on the edges, like that place Daniel had described where his Roahrt ghost had come from. A dark pocket of worlds, one with no immediate neighbors.

Such a thing had served the Upynth well enough, at least until the humans came calling.

She would need to go even deeper into the galaxy.

Crence had been studying her face. He nodded.

"I'll talk to Wyll, but I'm pretty sure they've already considered something like this, and either not told me, or not worked out the part where they could entice someone like the Mbaysey to help," Crence said.

Kathra nodded in turn.

It would be risky, but she had already known that. The risk would be offset by the potential reward.

And she wasn't about to trust anyone else to dig a moat deep enough to keep the Sept at bay.

18

Daniel sat in the darkness of the bridge, late in the evening shift, and listened to the galactic winds play about the hull. Space, for all it was a vacuum, was a noisy one, if you had the right ears to listen.

Planets crashed with lightning as solar wind impacted magnetic fields and got twisted. Stars hissed and roared with fusion wind like an angry dragon. *MorningStar*, *BrightStar*, and *NovaStar* hummed contentedly with the hungry wrath of focused humans and Anndaing going off to do something about those wolves preying on the flock. His ghosts were generally asleep, or whatever they did when they weren't prodding him.

Daniel was in his usual corner of the bridge tonight. The ship was in real space for a time, coordinating with the other two as everyone did maintenance. This would be a tremendous voyage, and much could go wrong, but everything was still within the bounds of predictable, at least according to Ndidi, and she was the one he trusted on the topic.

The bridge itself was quiet.

Acqueir had come on duty off-shift when he appeared, but she frequently did that on those middle of the nights where he was restless enough to come forward to the bridge. If something happened, she wanted to know about it immediately, and was senior enough to take charge, at least until she needed to rouse one of the others.

Her station was across the way from his. *SwiftStar* had a compact bridge, at least by Ovanii standards. Humans found it comfortable, but *MorningStar* had him sitting far enough away from her that he had to raise his voice. Daniel didn't want to think about the symbolism there. She occasionally knocked on his hatch, but far less frequently than any of the others who did.

Hopefully, he still showered often enough and hadn't acquired the wrong soap somewhere along the way.

He knew where Earth was from here. Could turn his face as though to the sun and feel it in the vast distance off their right hand front. Starboard bow, he thought they called it, but he was a chef, not a sailor.

It happened to have him staring almost at the back of Acqueir's skull, with her pinkish-purple mohawk too long right now and flopped over onto her left ear. Lighter than eggplant. Maybe fuchsia? There weren't many plants or spices to compare it to.

Rostami was on Earth. Daniel could sense him now when he focused on the task after the tremendous battles that they had fought in mental space. No doubt, the aspbad could sense him as well.

At least they would be able to find one another when that terrible final battle came due. That, or the one would be able to chase the other to the ends of the universe.

Daniel had nightmares that involved the two of them flying in Spectres somehow, riding the valence drives forever from star to star, always chasing, but never catching one another.

Daniel wanted to kill his power one of these days, but he could not while Hadi Rostami still held the remaining power of the Ishtan within him. Nobody else would be able to stop the man.

How strange it was that the two of them, complete strangers to the Ishtan and Mnapyre, from a species that only came to understand metals much later, would inherit that endless war, eleven thousand years later.

But they would see it through to completion.

At least, he hoped so. Daniel lived in terror that something would manage to kill him and Kathra would then be forced to rely on some other male to complete the chore.

How many other men could be made into gods and not turn into Zeus immediately?

No, just kill Rostami and then he could live out the rest of his life cooking and translating old books. That would be the best possible outcome anywhere.

Like Kathra, he would never set foot on a Sept world again. Even Ogrorspoxu might be too much, and he would need to just fly forever.

Take a Spectre and never look back?

They were closer to the edges of Sept Space now. Two-thirds of the way, if his math was right. Close enough that they needed to take a week fixing everything, but far enough away still that nobody should stumble over them out here.

Not that anybody but a Septagon could argue with *MorningStar,* but surprise would treble the force of the impending blow.

Movement brought him back to himself from his daydreams.

"What do you see?" Acqueir asked, gesturing at the walls around them to encompass the universe.

"Earth," Daniel pointed, and then moved his hand as each name came up. "Rhages. Vorgash. Even Singara."

"Can you actually see those worlds in your mind?" she asked, half focused still on her boards.

"I can smell concentrations of what my mind interprets as Septness," Daniel tried to explain. "They think different than the Free Worlds, even the close ones, so I can tell when there is a cultural boundary, such as this one. It is clearer with humans, because I understand them better, but I can also detect Kanus when we get close enough, or Ogrorspoxu."

He noted the way her eyes narrowed at the mention of the Kaniea homeworld, but there was nothing he could do about her feelings. If she had them, they were not as strong as two Anic pair-bonding. At least nothing he had seen suggested it.

A'Alhakoth had claimed more of his off-duty time than anyone else, but he didn't want to think about the implications of him falling in love with a woman who would be only getting into her middle age when he was an old man on his last legs, even with modern medicine.

Kaniea could live for two centuries, at least in both of A'Alhakoth's families. Daniel figured one hundred would be an impossible feat for him to achieve.

But he was human, and none of these women were. Well, Areen was, but she had been assigned by Kathra as a bodyguard on *SeekerStar* and *GhostStar*. Plus, she had only ever occasionally dabbled in bisexuality.

Daniel was just a male handy and non-threatening when she had needs.

Maybe all of them saw him that way, except for the occasional predatory gleam he saw in their eyes.

Merde, was he doomed to fulfill even Urid-Varg's lust-filled nightmares?

Daniel fell into himself and studied the inside of his skull as well as he could with all the blind spots a middle-aged man erects to protect his sanity.

Nothing, but he was half-blind on the topic.

Had that *salaud* infected him with a need for a harem? Had Daniel unconsciously altered these women around him to fill that role?

He'd known groupies when he was a rock star chef. Those were a dime a dozen. In the Mbaysey, he was just a cook. And a scholar, which would have made his mother howl with laughter were she to hear it.

Daniel surfaced in a complete panic and studied Acqueir's face.

"I need your help," he whispered hoarsely.

She clicked something on her board and it beeped a moment later. She rose from her station and crossed to him like he was having a heart attack.

He wasn't, was he?

No, heart rate normal. Pain only psychic.

But she was there. Friendly, and more.

He needed the more part.

Daniel held out a hand. She understood the gesture and took it.

They fell into his mind.

19

ACQUEIR HAD MERGED with Daniel on several occasions. The Commander required it of all the women that she had admitted to her expanded comitatus. That included an Anic who still wasn't sure about all these humans.

She had even lain with Daniel on occasion, human and Anic being compatible enough to find the process mutually pleasurable.

They were in the salon that he kept for visitors. It was a human place, soft with cotton and embroidery in ways alien and even harsh to her Anic sensibilities. But their sense of touch was less advanced than hers. And they saw further into the red and less into the ultraviolet than her kind did.

"Someone else is watching all the sensors," she told him. "Are you okay?"

"Scared," Daniel admitted, not understanding that the willingness to be vulnerable was one of the reasons so many women found him attractive.

Doubly so when it didn't define the man. He was still a cold, hard killer underneath, but few people saw that. They only saw the Golden Diamond that was the result of his drive for excellence.

The two of them leapt outward into his memories. Tanuss and Ndidi had described it as pulling various books from endless shelves and reading them at a glance.

She was standing on the deck of *WinterStar*, the Commander's first warship, before it was destroyed by *Vorgash*.

Somehow she was one of the women Urid-Varg had lined up for inspection and eventually rape, rather than being Daniel, as she normally was when they did this, but she felt him close.

"I have a blind spot here I only just stumbled into," his voice whispered in her ear. "All of you are tasked with keeping me from turning into a mad god, but I fear that I might have been able to hide it from everyone, in spite of the mergings."

She was Erin now, instead of Kathra, disrobing without emotion as the conqueror commanded it. Except that it was Daniel standing there, rather than the creature that had been Urid-Varg's mount on that fateful day.

Ah, so this was his nightmare.

Acqueir reached out a hand and pulled more books down from the shelf. Yes, the man indeed had a blind spot around those sorts of things. He was surrounded constantly by women he found to be amazingly sexy based on attitude and confidence, rather than shape or texture.

And he also had the power to reshape minds.

Had he touched all of them and drawn them into his bed, like a spider enticing flies?

In her vision, Acqueir walked up to the Conqueror in green and grabbed him by the lapels. He did not resist, except to squawk briefly in surprise. She dove into his mind like he did others, and she understood why he had chosen to place her in Erin's body.

Erin was the killer. The deadly Right Hand of the Commander. Comitatus Second, even though Ndidi really was better.

Erin would not hesitate to kill him if she thought it necessary, and he loved her all the more for it.

Love.

What an interesting concept. Erin loathed even the thought of a male's touch, and Daniel knew it. Respected it. Still loved her, perhaps more than anyone else, because she would kill him when it came to be time.

And he would let her. She would shoot him again, and this time he would not stop it.

Would even welcome it with joy at the release.

Around her, Acqueir heard the chorus of all Daniel's voices as well. Most of them also welcomed the eventual release of death.

But only after Hadi Rostami preceded them into hell.

Daniel was unable to look behind that pillar in the middle of his vision. The one obscuring his sexual needs, even from himself.

He needed her to approach and peek.

Acqueir was still Erin in her waking dream, so she did, pistol in hand just as the real woman would have done.

Daniel was afraid that his unconscious mind had reached out and touched A'Alhakoth, Tanuss, her, and several other women. Had drawn them all into the harem that had been Urid-Varg's original reason for emerging from hiding after so long.

Had raped them, because to a woman unable to make her own choice, that act was rape, regardless of the pleasure she might derive.

Standing there, hidden from even Daniel's view, she understood why he had hidden such things.

Secrets that he was afraid to even admit to himself, let alone allow others to discover.

She saw Kathra Omezi, stretched out nude on her bed like the most magnificent panther, black as coal and deadly as a sword.

Daniel was seated on a chair within easy reach, but fully clothed.

He reached out a hand to take hers as Acqueir watched and sent Kathra into the greatest series of orgasms the human body was capable of surviving, approaching his task like a diamond cutter splitting shards off a perfect stone.

She lay there for several minutes, mindless and unseeing, before she turned to him with a smile.

"Thank you," Kathra Omezi said. "I was right."

"*Oui*," Daniel agreed. "Now I need a cold shower."

"I'm sorry," Kathra replied.

"*Non*, it is good," Daniel nodded, rising and departing. "I needed to know that I could do such a thing, in spite of the women involved."

That was a secret unknown to any, as far as she could tell. Not even Erin knew, although Acqueir thought she might suspect.

Erin had never tried something similar.

Just the guilt of doing such a thing when the Commander asked him had blinded Daniel to other things.

But she understood better the relationship between Commander and Cook now. For all his amazing power, he lived a life now where he chose to exist without agency. To not exercise the enormous influence he had been given, lest he accidentally wander down those dark pathways he always feared.

Instead, all the women around him were granted that

power. That control. He served, however they required. Whatever they demanded.

Daniel would not ever knock on her door when he had physical or emotional needs.

She had misunderstood that about the man. Had thought he was aloof, when really it was that Daniel Lémieux was very, very frightened.

Not of her, but for her. Of himself.

She studied this place, but saw no evidence that he had done anything to any of the women to make them knock on his door. All were adults, making adult decisions. Women drawn to him because of his amazing strength and willingness to subsume it to them.

Daniel saw himself as a tool, rather than a man, much of the time.

That was the only thing that had kept him sane.

That, and friends. Ndidi and Erin, as well as the lovers that came and went.

She broached the surface of his mind and they were back on *MorningStar*'s bridge.

Perhaps three seconds had elapsed.

"You are fine, Daniel," she told him, watching the man's shoulders come down from around his ears.

She took his hand and pulled him to his feet.

"What?" he asked, somewhat confused.

"Someone else has the duty," Acqueir said.

"Then where are we going?" Daniel stammered.

"What you did for her?" Acqueir turned and smiled at him until he reciprocated. "You are going to do that to me."

20

MorningStar was a two-handed claymore of ancient legend in Ndidi's hands, even though A'Alhakoth was the woman who held the rank of Sword on this bridge.

Standing at the center of her bridge, Ndidi spoke for the entire Mbaysey today. For the Anndaing Merchants Guild. Even Merchants Bank, that entity that was the corporatist government of the Anndaing sectors.

She thought back to that speech she had given at Tavle Jocia, when she started her grand campaign of liberation. Not conquest.

Never conquest.

Liberation for a galaxy that feared the reach of the Sept. Feared those acquisitive eyes turning their way and conquering them. Fear of a Sept collar around their necks someday.

Freedom from fear was what she offered.

Ndidi did not need to give a speech to her crew and her squadron. Grandma Ezinne had said everything that needed saying on that last afternoon before they left Ogrorspoxu.

Still Ndidi spoke for Kathra. Even today, she found that

a heavy weight on her shoulders. To speak in the Commander's Name. To make decisions that the Commander was not here to make, because this was Ndidi's deck.

She Spoke.

Ndidi was seated at her station in the center of *MorningStar*'s bridge. Hirly was close on her left as Shield. Daniel beyond that, out of the way, but still central to all things, especially today.

A'Alhakoth was on the right, supervising the eight women in command of the many guns around them as Sword. Nwanyiudo sat between Sword and Shield on the fourth point of a diamond with the Speaker, from which she would Pilot this great ship of devastation. Acqueir was opposite Daniel, listening with sensors limited to the merely physical. It made a nice symmetry.

On her screens, echoed onto Ndidi's, she could see icons for *NovaStar* and *BrightStar*, escorts keeping close duty in their own ways.

The bridge was poised on the edge of violence. This many women, this closely aligned mentally and emotionally, had even fallen into similar patterns of mere biology, but today was simply a day when all of them had ascended to terrible heights.

Ndidi felt like one of the ancient barbarians sitting at the top of a hill, looking down upon a village below.

Except that this wasn't a harmless village. This was a castle some *salaud* had erected on her land, threatening to evict her and her tribe if something wasn't done about them.

Ndidi was here to Speak the words of doom to them.

Like before, she rose.

Kitchens were not places where you ever sat, so she felt more natural standing. It was like facing a hot stovetop with a pan, a spoon, and a stack of ingredients, about to do battle with the culinary gods.

Only Daniel truly understood what that meant.

"Acqueir, bring *NovaStar* and *BrightStar* online," she ordered, taking a deep breath and contemplating British infantry pushing south across the veldt to lay waste to anyone challenging their queen.

She must have picked the image up from Daniel at some point, because the cultural context was not Mbaysey. Her ancestors had been metaphorical neighbors to the Zulu on that fateful day.

The Sensors officer turned to her with a calm smile.

"Both ships standing by at full readiness," Acqueir replied.

Ndidi took a breath and saw the words she needed to *Speak*.

"Today is not the day for pretty words to be recorded for all time," Ndidi said in a clear voice. "Let some future Shakespeare put those words into my mouth when they celebrate their own version of St. Crispin's Day. We are not here for sisterhood or righteous glory."

Ndidi turned slowly from right to left, catching the faces smiling back. She faced Daniel.

"Who lurks at Vorgash?" she asked, feeling like a terrible witch instead.

"One Septagon," Daniel said. "I think it is *Vorgash*, but I am not sure, Speaker. Other forces that are normal for a border world."

"Customs inspectors and enforcers?" Ndidi asked, sneering the word in case anyone had any doubt as to her opinion of the Sept Empire.

"Pimps and thugs," he growled back.

But then, he had been forced to listen to the immense symphony of their combined voices to make sure of this day.

Two Septagons would have challenged her thinking, but Daniel was sure he could do something terrible here. That his ghosts would be able to achieve that thing they had shown her when she doubted them.

But she remembered *Uwalu*.

Ndidi took a breath and scowled. It felt like the sort of thing Iruoma would have unleashed on an unsuspecting world. The faces looking back at her all quailed a bit, so she was close.

It was good to have Iruoma as a favorite aunt.

"All tribal members, this is the Speaker," she said slowly, deliberately. "We liberated Tavle Jocia from Septagon *Singara*. The next target is Vorgash itself, home system of our ancient foe. This is not about liberation today. We are here to carve our icon into the very souls of this system, because the Sept have forgotten the meaning of fear. I intend to remind them what it tastes like. All vessels will align on the Septagon when we emerge, and pound it mercilessly. Patrols can flee us until it is their turn, but we are here to add a note of terrible horror into any history the Sept ever choose to write, starting tomorrow."

Ndidi turned to Nwanyiudo and smiled.

"Pilot, take us in."

21

Daniel had listened to the system as they sat here, aligning everything just so. He had placed the Septagon for Nwanyiudo and A'Alhakoth and everyone else.

His nerves were a little shot at this point, but much of that was dread. The rest was just the slimy feeling of listening to Sept minds in a mass measured in something close to one billion souls, if he remembered correctly.

No Sept worlds were as densely populated with humans as Earth. And might never be. But there were still so many minds down there that he could actually sense the flavor of the population as though it was a single entity.

Urid-Varg had never developed such an ability, but he had never needed to. With his powers, his other gem, even the Star Turtle, he had been able to control tens or hundreds of thousands of people at a time. Enough that any government would support him.

Humans were bad enough followers that perhaps a third of any large group would have eventually come to worship the creature. Such had it also been with the K'bari.

The z'lud had been closer to fifty percent, which was why there were no more z'lud these days.

One Septagon awaited on the other side of a jump. The Sept imposed a west-to-east orbital path, when seen from above the north pole. The ship had maintained its current orbit for half a day, so chances were good that it remained so.

MorningStar and her companions would pounce on it like panthers chasing an eland. Or something. Daniel wasn't entirely sure which big cats chased what prey.

It would be fast, messy, and ugly.

Arrival.

Daniel always found it weird that he was just as blind inside a jump tunnel as the ship's systems. An Anndaing scientist had explained the purely physical by saying that everyone was in a different universe for a short period. A smaller place, where everything was closer together, but still vibrating on a distinct pitch, which was why you didn't see anybody else.

Hadi Rostami, were he paying attention, would have probably noted a parallax as Daniel approached the edge of Sept Space. At least, if he was remembering the term correctly.

He was thinking too fast for his own good right now. Daniel was aware of that.

But he had to make sure nobody else here had the sorts of power that he and the aspbad had stolen from others.

Daniel leapt out of his physical body, even as *MorningStar* was still vibrating slightly out of pitch with the Vorgash system.

Everything would center shortly.

Vorgash. Both the planet below and the Septagon in front of him, so bright that Daniel was nearly blinded.

They had dropped out of jump at something sharply close to perfect range for those monstrous beams A'Alhakoth called Arc-cannons. Far enough away that the Ram Cannons were going to tickle when they awoke, but the Septagon was going to be suffering punches in return.

Daniel grasped the mind of this thing called Septagon *Vorgash* with both hands and studied it.

Naupati Pasdar was not here, but had left his fingerprints on the entire crew in his time. Aspbad Rostami had selected a great many of the men in command, because this new commander and naupati had not had time to replace the key individuals with their own men.

In fact, the two newcomers were not the strict disciplinarians of before. Nor were they warrior monks dedicated to a singular task.

No, both of these men tasted like the two fools Daniel had met at Tavle Jocia when Ndidi had captured the Shah and the commanders and sent them home to start their own counter-revolution to Pasdar's.

It felt odd, smelling the alcohol on the mind of a man who was outwardly dedicated to a religion that forbade such things. But Allah also forbade many of the things these two practiced with great regularity, including maintaining their own collection of sex-slaves just for themselves, in addition to the ones forced to service the crew.

Yes, the Mbaysey had only been one such exotic culture for the Persian nobles to exploit. There were many others.

Daniel turned and tasted the despair from the lower decks. All of it was female.

Tazo, times a hundred. Perhaps a thousand.

But none of these women had ever had the luck to know a woman like Yagazie Omezi, or her daughter Kathra.

Not even a heartbeat had passed. Daniel turned outward and studied the night sky around him.

The Septagon was at rest. The two Patrols permanently assigned to the vessel were doing various chores, but no single ship was anywhere in a position to threaten the squadron.

Further out, TradeStations, NavalStations, orbital bases, and various manufacturing foundries dotted the night sky of Vorgash, but again, none were in a position to hurt Ndidi's command.

But all would bear witness today.

Deep in his soul, a thousand voices growled. It felt more like an earthquake awakening than a sound one heard. This was down in the keel of his sternum, a ripping and tearing note building to apocalypse.

Daniel returned to his body and found A'Alhakoth across the bridge, dark blue eyes studying him with worry, but possessed of a fierceness as great as anybody but Ndidi.

"No change," he said simply, letting everyone know that no sudden surprises would cause the entire plan to be thrown into disarray.

"All gunners, execute as you bear," A'Alhakoth replied with a hungry smile.

Two seconds had passed.

22

———

A'Alhakoth had the most complicated screen to study, echoing each of her eight gun commanders, plus sensors from Acqueir and a half dozen other things that might be relevant.

She did not fire a single weapon, but A'Alhakoth ver'Shingi was responsible for all the damage *MorningStar* would do today. At least the physical.

She still quailed a little at what Daniel thought he might be able to accomplish. She had been him enough times to remember *Uwalu*, but much of that had been the turtle, not the man.

Right?

Arc-cannons opened up. Twelve of them could bear forward right now from exactly dead aft of *Vorgash*, but there was nothing in range for the four aft, else she would have prioritized them.

Soon.

Vorgash was orbiting faster than stations that kept pace with the ground below, so the two of them would fly overhead and A'Alhakoth's women could wreak their terrible rage and vengeance there as well.

The Sept would never forget her name, even if she had never been to a Sept world.

A'Alhakoth was still the *Sword* of *MorningStar*.

The Arc-cannons erupted like a volcano, spewing molten death into the aft facing square of a Septagon.

One enormous blast that ranged almost like a single bolt, before various guns fell into their own rhythm based on generators and aiming mechanisms.

Unlike Tavle Jocia, A'Alhakoth had instructed her women not to use up their guns today. They had a great distance to sail to get home if something broke. But *Vorgash* was just as surprised as *Singara* had been, and the mission today was destruction, not liberation.

If she could sharpen a razor enough to split the two.

Idly, one portion of her mind wondered if it might be possible to synchronize twelve or more Arc-cannons, so that they fired like a Axial Megacannon. Such a weapon might be just as irresistible.

Vorgash staggered under a zwölf blows.

Each gunner had taken those two seconds before the firing order came to line up on the same thruster vent, a hole large enough to fly an Anndaing transport in and not touch the sides.

You could armor the throat of such a thruster to a certain extent, but it still had to be exposed to open space for the gases to push the enormous mass of the vessel around.

Until *MorningStar*, the Sept had never met a vessel big enough, tough enough, *dangerous enough*, to fight a Septagon directly.

Twelve Arc-cannons slammed into a small targeting ring on the ass end of the vessel.

A'Alhakoth might have compared them to Terran hornets swarming, but the impact was much greater.

The rear of the vessel was suddenly hidden behind a fog bank, except that instead of cold water vapor in the air, this was metal converted to plasma so quickly that it hadn't had a chance to turn red yet.

Or even white.

"Secondary targets now," A'Alhakoth called to her deadly Valkyrie, another image she had drawn from Daniel, but Kaniea culture had something bizarrely similar, except that the human version of the women lacked wings, so they had to ride flying horses.

But Kaniea legends were so much more fun and colorful anyway.

Each of the eight women dialed in new places to wound the beast. Around them, the hull actually hummed and groaned as enormous turrets began to adjust firing mechanisms to bear on the next place that A'Alhakoth wanted destroyed.

Vorgash had three more engine vents available to destroy, depending on which way the ship moved...

A strobe of light caught A'Alhakoth's eye.

It took her a long moment to realize that someone had opened fire on *MorningStar* already, just in the few seconds since they had landed and fired themselves.

That it was just a heavy particle cannon turret making the attempt did not lessen the impressiveness of the feat. But at this range, a hit might scour as much as a millimeter off a slab of bioarmor several meters thick. The kind that would regrow given time, current, and raw materials treated with the correct chemicals.

Apparently, though, that level of professional competence from a Sept gun commander pissed someone off.

One of the Arc-cannons answered a few moments later,

blasting a crater in the side of the ship where the offending heavy particle cannon turret had been trying to make a difference.

Around her, the big guns attacked the Septagon like lumberjacks, while all her smaller turrets, what the humans would classify as Ram Cannons, went at it like angry woodpeckers.

There had been a bet going, informally.

Could Daniel place the Septagon in Nwanyiudo's mind perfectly enough that the Pilot could drop *MorningStar* exactly aligned on the flat, aft facing of the ship? Was *MorningStar* agile enough to make such a jump, even over such a short distance?

Would Septagon *Vorgash* be able to begin a pivoting turn on its axis in some vain attempt to bring the Axial Megacannon to bear?

MorningStar was much smaller. And a purpose-built warship designed by people for whom war was a vocation as well as a joy.

The Ovanii had lived lives just as large and emotional as any human or Kaniea ever had. Perhaps more than her kind, because the Kaniea had reached a level of cultural stability that had given the Anndaing a reason to contact them and uplift them from late Iron Age to the Interstellar.

MorningStar was a warrior. A dancer. A Chooser of the Slain flying with her own wings, rather than relying on a silly horse.

A'Alhakoth was her Sword.

She slashed again and again at the terrible dragon, but he had not awakened enough to try to turn.

To face them.

To bring that terrible maw around where he might breathe fire on them.

Around her, death raced downrange.

23

———

Ndidi *Spoke* for *MorningStar*. *Spoke* for Kathra.

Spoke for all the women like Grandma Ezinne who had been taken by the Sept and returned broken.

Or never returned at all.

She had looked around her soul on this long flight, alone in her office. The raucous arguments with Kathra when they were alone had not changed anything about Ndidi's outlook either.

Ndidi Zikora was possessed of a terrible, implacable rage.

Perhaps that was why Kathra had noticed her in the first place.

In those days, the short, half-blind child had been *driven*. *The Haunt* was denied her, so she could never belong to the comitatus, but she had found a place where she could get close.

Daniel had even demonstrated to her that a mere chef could become so much more, and given Ndidi a path. A map.

Competence and controlled rage had brought her here.

The Mbaysey would remind the Sept about Tazo today.

Ndidi would remind them personally about women like Grandma Ezinne.

"He's still not turning," Acqueir announced in a breathless sort of surprised voice.

Ndidi didn't bother explaining Sept arrogance to the woman.

Sept conceit. The belief that they were greater than all other species in the galaxy. That all were beneath them. That they were in fact ordained to rule all other sentient creatures by some god-given right.

Ndidi had met a god. Had even been one, standing at barely a half remove from Daniel in their combined memory.

It had reinforced a grand atheism in her.

No god was so loving that she would allow her children to be subject to such treatment as the Mbaysey had survived. No just god would allow her followers to do such things to others.

That left evil.

Ndidi Zikora, Speaker for *MorningStar* and the Mbaysey, understood evil.

She had *been* evil, at least in Daniel's memories of such things.

He would never reach those levels of depravity. All the women in his life watched him like hawks for such shadows. Even today, the things he did were because his Speaker *demanded* them of him.

Ordered the man to step closer to the ledge than he would have ever gone of his own volition.

To do evil.

Ndidi looked around her bridge at the other women. Even Daniel was an honorary sister here, welcome and one of them.

But only she *Spoke*.

"We are coming up on the first NavalStation,"

A'Alhakoth said loud enough that all these women would hear and understand. "Prepare to target with the rear weapons."

"Negative on that order," Ndidi called out sharply, snapping several heads around to look at her. "I want all attention focused on the Septagon until he flees. Those stations aren't going anywhere. They cannot escape my wrath later."

A'Alhakoth blinked, hard, once. Her pupils slit down horizontally like a porthole closing, and then snapped back open again.

She nodded, tight and compact.

"All gun commanders, maintain your targeting locks on any station as you bear, by priority sequence already set, but hold the rear cannons for defensive purposes for now," the *Sword* of *MorningStar* countered her own order. "Continue pounding *Vorgash*."

Ndidi smiled grimly and unmuted a channel back to engineering.

"Tanuss, this is Ndidi," she began, much calmer. "How are your systems holding?"

"All is well, Speaker," the Wisp woman answered. "We can maintain this pace for another hour before heat and wear probably becomes a risk to operations."

"It will be over long before then, Tanuss," Ndidi said, muting the line again.

On her screen, Ndidi watched sledgehammers of energy and matter pound the Septagon mercilessly.

Because she was without mercy.

Turrets on the rear face of the monster were starting to awaken now. Local officers no doubt taking it upon themselves to *do something*, even as the aspbad and naupati in charge were not issuing orders.

It would require a pilot to decide to bring the vessel

around to the point where the Axial Megacannon was a threat. Or even to bring a new facing to engage *MorningStar*, one not already savaged.

Of course, without the engines to harass, her gunners would have to concentrate on destroying Ram Cannon turrets instead.

Vorgash was a city in space. A castle some *salaud* had erected on her people's land with a thought to claiming it and driving her off.

That was not allowed.

Sept invincibility had forged a legend so great that none dared challenge them.

At least until today.

But they had never faced someone with her rage. Or the ability to study the designs of a Septagon and identify the exact weaknesses that such a design contained.

They had nothing heavier than a Ram Cannon, because anybody thinking to disrespect a Septagon could be destroyed by an Axial Megacannon.

Even an Ovanii Battlemaster was at risk of such a beam.

If Ndidi ever decided to fight fair.

What utter foolishness.

Vorgash finally seemed to be awakening from its contented slumber. Seven minutes had passed since *MorningStar's* arrival sounded the trumpet signaling a new age.

Or perhaps the Armageddon that so many human cultures contained somewhere.

The Septagon began to turn finally. Two engines glowed white hot now, rather than the four she could see.

The hull began to shift, like a moon orbiting as someone tried to bring the ship about, turning, exactly as Ndidi had known they would, to the right.

They were a right-handed folk. Most humans were.

Ndidi was not. In that, she and Daniel had an unfair advantage, perhaps.

She turned to her twin brother now and smiled her terrible, merciless smile on him.

Daniel licked his lips with nervous anticipation at he stared at her. Perhaps a note of fear was there as well, but he was a chef first and only a killer second.

Ndidi had only taken up cooking later as a way to focus her lethalness into constructive pursuits.

"Now, Daniel," she said implacably.

24

———

Daniel had been Ndidi enough times. She considered them twins of the soul, if not the flesh.

The blade cut both ways.

He knew her mind at least as well as she did. Had seen the things no other human would ever know, not even lovers if she ever found one enough to her liking to become a permanent thing.

He would do this thing, because all of his guilt could be placed at her feet, when he finally met whatever treacherous *salaud* of a Creator had brought all this to pass.

Daniel closed his eyes and found both Arsène and Pheryoutl standing in his salon, awaiting him, like twin nightmares of their own, here to haunt his dreams.

And then he saw the rest of them.

All of them.

Every single ghost contained within the gem was here.

He had never seen them together like this. Nor here. Only when he went down to the place where they slept restless.

Even the Mnapyre were going to stand with him today.

Daniel swallowed past the frog that had taken up residence in his throat.

"What we do is foul and wrong," Pheryoutl announced to the collective.

Many heads bowed, as if in prayer.

Daniel held his breath.

"Why we do such a malevolent thing is what makes it *righteous*," Arsène took up the chant now.

Daniel wondered if he was going to have a heart attack, as rapidly as his pulse was pounding in his ears right now.

A thousand hands reached out now, clasping other hands or resting on shoulders, until Daniel was physically connected with every single ghost Urid-Varg had ever stolen from his life and ridden to death like a cheap horse.

The surge of energy that flowed into his soul make Daniel wonder if he was suddenly zwölf feet tall.

"The Sept are evil," a thousand voices intoned like a bell's tolling to call the faithful in from the fields.

Daniel took a deep breath.

He had carried the living on several occasions. Kathra and several of her women had ridden his shoulders that first time when it became necessary to judge Ugonna and execute the traitor.

Now Daniel was riding on the shoulders of the dead. Uplifted by their hands.

The instrument of *their* rage.

He stepped into the darkness between worlds and called *Vorgash's* name to eternity.

He was there.

Standing on the thing they called a Command Node, like a tongue sticking out, or a stage overlooking the orchestra pit.

Two thrones stood before him, one greater and one lesser.

Naupati and Aspbad.

He sensed the two men furiously running this way from whatever drunken debaucheries had been underway when an avenging angel decided to call.

Looking around, twenty men were being displaced by twenty more, *MorningStar* like her name having arrived at the very end of night aboard this vessel.

The fighting crew was desperately trying to do something to save their Septagon.

Daniel would not allow it.

Three hundred thousand minds ranged around him. Only now were they finally beginning to suspect something.

To taste fear, perhaps.

To discover that the god to whom they prayed had turned her face away from them now, if she had ever really cared in the first place.

Daniel was also a god.

Unwilling, but unable to return such a gift to the true gods that had decided to play such a malicious prank on a mere chef.

One thousand ghosts began to chant.

He could not understand the words, but it didn't matter. They were composed of nearly a thousand cultures as well, scattered across twelve thousand years of history, and each was invoking whatever vengeful spirits that had brought them solace in life.

Daniel was nothing but a tool for retribution, but that was not an unfamiliar feeling. He was a tool Kathra Omezi used.

Erin Uduik.

Ndidi Zikora.

Comitatus.

Mbaysey.

Anndaing.

And every child yet to be born in the future history of the galaxy.

He watched the Aspbad and Naupati arrive.

Heard the cries of surprise. The shouted orders.

Smelled the ammonia fear begin to pervade the room as the truth became known.

Now, indeed.

Daniel Lémieux took a deep breath and screamed.

25

Acqueir watched the Septagon on every frequency available. Every scanner she could point at the beast. Anything anyone knew about how Ovanii technology had worked, or how it had been filtered forward to the modern Anndaing.

Or an inquisitive Anic like her.

Daniel's aloofness had been fear. Not of her, but for her.

For all women he touched, that he might accidentally break them, however tough and implacable they thought they might be.

Until she had merged into an entity with Commander Omezi and Speaker Zikora, Acqueir had always thought she was the toughest person she knew.

And both of those hard women paled by comparison to a chef from Genarde.

She heard his scream of fury. No sensor could notice it, or even measure it directly.

She didn't have to listen on those frequencies.

Septagon *Vorgash* went dark.

Every sensor beam they had been projecting ceased.

Every gun, regardless of size, stopped firing at the exact same instant. Even running lights on the hull failed.

The two remaining functional engine vents flickered and went out.

Septagon *Vorgash* went dark.

He had warned her. Had warned everyone.

Acqueir Chanthraphone had not *believed*.

She turned back to Ndidi, her head moving almost of its own volition. The Speaker looked like how Acqueir had always expected Death should be painted, had the artist ever met a human with eyes that weren't supposed to glow.

Not like an Anic's.

Not like Ndidi's seemed to be doing now, even half-hidden behind those strange lenses that were her symbol.

The Speaker smiled at her.

"*Uwalu*," the woman said simply, as if that explained everything.

It might. Acqueir had seen her memories as well as Daniel's.

"Against *Uwalu*, Daniel had a simple rage-fear," Ndidi told the bridge crew in a conversational voice that made it all the more frightening. "The outpouring of all the terror he and I had felt as we raced to save the Turtle and see if we could escape a Septagon, then the most frighteningly-powerful thing in the universe. To get there, we flew through deep space protected by nothing but his power and his conviction that he could do this thing."

She paused and Acqueir found herself unconsciously leaning forward to hear more, trapped like a fly in a spider's web.

"Daniel has consulted all his ghosts," she continued, still sounding like a teacher with a classful of precocious children at story time. "They had learned a few things the Urid-Varg never did. But then, that one was merely a conqueror. A *violeur* intent on raping whoever he met that tickled his fancy. Mental, physical, or emotional, it did not matter. Nothing could stand before Urid-Varg and his Star Turtle."

She took a breath and Acqueir felt the other shoe drop.

"But Urid-Varg was never a chef," Ndidi concluded. "He was not tough enough to stand in any competent kitchen against a man like Daniel. Gunners, I want all four of his engines destroyed."

Acqueir shook her head like a woman awakening from a dream. A'Alhakoth did the same, as did her killers.

As did the entire bridge.

Maybe all of *MorningStar*.

The guns had never ceased their own rage, even as the minds had drifted back to hear the Speaker's words.

A sound caused Acqueir's head to snap around.

Daniel had collapsed onto the deck and lay there insensate.

"Hirly, get him to medical," Ndidi's voice cut through everything.

Acqueir didn't have time to contemplate what had just happened.

Over on *Vorgash*, lights were starting to return.

26

A'Alhakoth felt her heart stop as Daniel lay crumpled on the deck, too far away to even touch.

For a moment stretching to eternity, she wanted to rise. Run to him. Confirm that his heart was still beating.

"Sword," Ndidi snapped. "Do your duty. Hirly will take care of him."

Ndidi knew the truth. Had probably specifically searched for it in their minds. She was the Speaker, but she was also Daniel's closest friend.

The rest of them were merely lovers, however close.

A'Alhakoth ground her teeth in a rage so intense that a small portion of her mind feared that she might spall off enamel splinters before she was done.

But the Speaker needed her. Right here. Right now.

The *Sword* of *MorningStar*.

Dealing death.

A'Alhakoth focused herself back into the present tense as much as she could, wondering if she was feeling dreams die.

Her dreams, down there on the deck, even as the Shield was in motion.

"Pilot, he's got a drift going," A'Alhakoth called. "I need you to snap us around where he cannot turn tail. Keep us on that stern as much as possible while we punish him. Gun commanders, I want everything into the engines. Ignore all other targets until ordered otherwise. Arc-cannons and Ram Cannons alike."

Two of the four had apparently been damaged sufficiently to flicker out. Or whatever a Septagon's engines did when things exploded inside the hull.

Nwanyiudo showed her amazing abilities now. A'Alhakoth knew the woman could fly. She had been a wingsister to Spectre Twenty-Two, back when they had numbers in addition to names.

MorningStar danced like a Spectre gunship this morning. Nwanyiudo had them rolling, twisting, and sliding like a primitive aircraft riding on atmospheric winds. The dorsal Arc-cannons lost their firing arc as *MorningStar* turned away, presenting the flat hull rather than the armored edge. All the ventral guns continued to harass the beast, even as Nwanyiudo fought the edges back down to bring the other half of A'Alhakoth's firepower to bear.

Ram Cannons were slower to awaken than heavy particle cannons, so the damage *MorningStar* was suffering wasn't nearly as severe as it might have been otherwise.

A'Alhakoth ignored that. Hirly or more likely Ndidi was responsible. The Sword existed to kill things.

On *Vorgash*, something failed.

A bulkhead. A reactor. A feed line.

Vibrations, or shrapnel, or even just beam energy got to someplace deep inside where they never should have.

One of the two remaining engines exploded.

The others had simply fallen dark, snuffed out like candles.

This one erupted like Daniel's torch making crème brûlée for dessert.

A'Alhakoth wondered what might have happened had *MorningStar* been closer. The guns were point-blank, but the distance was still measured in tens of kilometers, so the explosion, as impressive as it was, did not threaten an Ovanii Battlemaster.

But Septagon *Vorgash* was crippled.

"Acqueir, confirm these readings," A'Alhakoth snapped over the moans of surprise or delight flowing around her.

"Speculation," the Anic woman glanced back and made eye contact. "But strong evidentiary support."

Meaning: *I'm willing to put a lot of money on it, but not my life.*

Good enough.

A'Alhakoth had learned to share the woman with Daniel from an emotional standpoint. His innocence and blind spots, coupled with that intellectual capacity and hunger, made him amazingly attractive, even if the Mbaysey women generally considered it little better than bestiality.

Human women were only a tiny fraction of *MorningStar*'s crew.

But she and Acqueir had come to an understanding. It helped when they could both see the inside of Daniel's head to know his truth and the other woman's.

Right now, sensors were showing the rear quarter of Septagon *Vorgash*, off-center and mostly on the left, dead.

That explosion had ruptured something. There were almost no energy signatures or power flows detectable.

Had they actually crippled a Septagon?

"Gunners, last engine," A'Alhakoth reminded them. "I want another explosion like that."

Vorgash was still drifting, but suddenly it felt like a tumble. Acqueir's boards reflected it thus. Accelerating even, the result of that explosion pushing so hard against one corner of the ship like an oversized engine.

You can't escape me that easily.

The Septagon was tumbling on all three axes now, if the sensors were correct. Grav Field Inducers were failing as well, with engines and generators off-line or destroyed.

Guns attempting to stop her were fewer with every moment.

Septagon *Vorgash* was on the verge of going dark again.

Part of her mind registered Hirly literally picking Daniel up with the help of someone, slinging the smaller man over a shoulder, and hustling out, presumably aft to where a med bay would hopefully be able to fix him.

To save him.

To keep her dreams from dying.

If that was possible.

"Sensors," Ndidi called over the noise and voices that A'Alhakoth had blocked out. "How are *BrightStar* and *NovaStar* doing?"

"Engaging successfully," the Anic woman replied. "Local space remains clear of hostiles."

A'Alhakoth had gotten so focused that she had forgotten they had brought two Duelers as escorts today. That the Sept kept Patrols vessels in groups of ten as units of force.

Two Duelers could shatter three Patrols easily enough. A'Alhakoth checked her boards and noted that they had been busy doing just that from the wreckage and tumbling ships sharing this orbit with them.

Nineteen minutes had passed.

MorningStar continued to pound the hapless Septagon.

"Kill shot!" Acqueir's voice had a note of triumph, but A'Alhakoth wasn't willing to gainsay her on it.

Septagon *Vorgash* had gone dark again, just like it had when Daniel raged at them. Lights weren't off, but scattered when they worked. Guns still chittered at her, but again, random, as though power had failed at the macro level, leaving only backup generators and battery arrays to power local things.

Vorgash had pitch, roll, and yaw, all at once, an enormous child's toy poised at the top of a ramp and just starting down the slope.

A'Alhakoth blinked hard and realized where that slope ended.

The planetary surface of Vorgash itself.

"Speaker?" A'Alhakoth asked, making eye contact with *Death*.

Ndidi nodded.

Smiled.

A'Alhakoth felt all the blood drain out of her entire body to puddle somewhere, leaving her skin puckered with chills.

The Speaker meant to deorbit a broken Septagon.

Thirty-two hundred meters each on seven facings. Seventy decks tall. Seven kilometers from bowsprit to engine cluster.

Three hundred thousand men of the Sept navy, plus however many women had been enslaved aboard the ship as sex objects.

Plus however many millions would likely die when this monster impacted. It would not matter if the hull retained integrity or failed and came apart under atmospheric turbulence, except for how localized the damage would be.

Whether the planet of Vorgash suffered a merely catastrophic incident, or an extinction.

A'Alhakoth ver'Shingi was a warrior. The daughter of a pair of Jarls. Inheritor of a warlike culture that still clung to some of those ancient traditions.

She had killed, both in Kathra's service as well as her own name.

This went above and beyond anything she had ever even had nightmares about.

A'Alhakoth wondered if the Anndaing had understood what they had done when they handed Ndidi Zikora the most dangerous warship known.

Probably.

A Septagon was an implacable foe, armed with a lance capable of killing anything if they could not maneuver away from such death.

Or had a man who could place the exact location and facing of such a ship, so that *MorningStar* could land close behind it and unleash an apocalypse so great that it would echo for millennia.

Wyll Koobitz had made the point that the war could be fought above Anndaing worlds, or in Free Worlds space. Today, it was coming to roost on the Sept overlords intent on conquering and enslaving the universe.

"All guns, identify and target the connection angles of the Septagon itself," A'Alhakoth ordered in a voice she hoped sounded calm and commanding. "I want to see if we can break the vessel apart before it enters the atmosphere."

The Sept would never forget today.

They would likely never forgive it either, but a wounded planet was a better thing for her conscience than a dead one.

A'Alhakoth caught wild glances back from the women manning her guns and grimaced harshly at them.

They gulped as well and returned to their duty.

Kathra Omezi and Ndidi Zikora wanted *Vorgash* to be turned into an example, both the Septagon and the planet.

Goddess help them all.

27

Ndidi surveyed the damage displayed on her boards.

It was about where she had expected to be by this point in the battle.

BrightStar had been pounded pretty aggressively by a Patrol that eventually died. *NovaStar* was running through weapon filters and power systems at an alarming rate. *MorningStar* had the least amount of damage, but pitifully few people had been able to shoot back effectively, given her amazing escorts.

Ndidi still knew she was pushing her luck.

Had been for more than zwölf minutes now.

It had been theoretically possible to actually break a Septagon with guns, but would probably requires days of perfect alignment, and she didn't have that. Forward in orbit, a swarm of Patrol vessels were finally organizing themselves to strike.

They were only Patrol vessels, but *WinterStar* had been almost destroyed by the time Ndidi's Sword had decided to ram that one Septagon and drove it off. *MorningStar* would do no better if some Patrol Marzban or Savaran decided to sacrifice himself and his ship.

"All guns, stand down," Ndidi ordered the room. "Acqueir, order *NovaStar* and *BrightStar* to come about and jump as soon as they can. Pilot, we're done here. Jump as soon as you have a clear escape vector and then calculate us a path to squadron Concursion from there."

Voices acknowledged her with something of relief about them. All of these women were sworn to serve, and it wasn't that much different from joining the original comitatus.

Dying in the line of duty was always a high probability, when knifes or pistols came out. All of them had that in the back of their heads, even as they had given her everything they had today.

It hadn't been enough to actually break the Septagon into pieces, but they had been faced with a monumental task to begin with.

Septagon *Vorgash* was utterly mauled. Septagon *Singara* would be a year in a repair dock when they finally got home. *Vorgash* might be cheaper to simply scrap, if someone could bring themselves to admit to that level of defeat.

That brought a smile to Ndidi's face. This one even felt like joy, rather than hostile rage.

A'Alhakoth had understood, eventually, that actually damaging a Septagon enough to crash one into an inhabited planet had been within Ndidi's ethics.

Grandma Ezinne had spoken to these women.

This wasn't a war to make the Sept respect certain boundaries on a map. Nor to perhaps change their behavior enough that their greater angels came to the fore.

Ndidi wanted them destroyed.

Broken.

Shattered down into something that made the Free Worlds look organized and regimented by comparison.

She was willing to kill an astonishing number of humans to get there. Enough that even Kathra had been nervous.

But the Commander had backed down eventually. *MorningStar* was Ndidi's ship. She would handle this raid her way.

Ndidi and her crew had failed only in that heroic measures would successfully keep *Vorgash* the ship from meeting Vorgash the planet.

It would still require heroic measures.

Ndidi Zikora had killed a Septagon. Never forget that part.

MorningStar leapt into bluespace.

These engines weren't valence drives, but functioned close enough to compare. You opened a portal and fell through it, emerging at some physical distance measured in light-years or light-decades.

MorningStar would need repairs. And time to repair itself. None of that required the Speaker to remain here.

Normally, she would hand things over to Hirly as Shield, but that woman was aft with Daniel. The Sword would be next, but Ndidi couldn't imagine being cruel enough to leave A'Alhakoth behind. Nor Acqueir, when it came down to it.

Tanuss would be in charge of repairs, so she would be unable to join them.

"Nwanyiudo, you have the bridge," Ndidi said as she unbuckled and rose. "A'Alhakoth and Acqueir, would you care to join me?"

The looks of surprise on their faces was telling, but she knew how they felt. And how Daniel felt.

Hopefully, her favorite chef wasn't dead or dying. Stranger things had happened, like when Erin and the others had been forced to escape the dying turtle on a shuttle nobody but Daniel could fly, even if it had been the only thing capable of crossing between stars.

Out they went, Ndidi flying with two wingsisters back a step and flanking her.

Hirly looked up as they entered the medbay, studied the three of them, and nodded.

"Trade you," Hirly said with a quick smile.

"Nwanyiudo has it handled for now," Ndidi countered. "You stay with us for a while, and maybe Tanuss will need you supervising something later."

Hirly nodded, all business now.

The Anndaing Physician had been listening to Daniel's heart with a device so primitive that Ndidi always wanted to giggle when she saw it, but Tuuf Klaskat swore by her stethoscope, claiming that it let her hear things that no machine could ever grasp properly, regardless of how fine the digital signal could be parsed.

She was taller and thinner than most of her kind, with a wider hammer that looked like it would overbalance her at any moment. Tuuf always claimed that the extra parallax made her a better doctor, but Ndidi had never been a patient, so she couldn't be sure.

"How is he?" Ndidi asked.

Tuuf fixed her with a scowl that reminded Ndidi of Iruoma on a cross day.

"Heart rate elevated, but nothing out of the ordinary," the physician said in almost a growl. "All vital signs showing stress, but I get more adrenaline out of a scary movie. He will not, however, awaken or respond."

"How so?"

"It's almost like there's nobody home," Tuuf shook her hammer back and forth with a grimace on her lips. "Anybody but Daniel, I would be greatly concerned, but this is not even the first time his medical records show something like this."

Ndidi nodded. Daniel had retreated from the galaxy after they killed the Star Turtle. He had done lesser things in other moments of great stress, because Daniel was not a confrontational man.

On the contrary, he was amazingly stubborn, but had his limits, and if you pushed him hard enough, far enough, he would eventually just let go and allow you to push him backwards off the table.

And you would never again get him to engage you once you had done so.

Ndidi was reminded of Angel, a woman she had never actually met in the flesh.

But she also knew Daniel's secret.

Knew all of them. Even the ones he didn't tell himself out of personal fear.

Ndidi moved around to stand next to his head, glancing up to note the various vital signs being displayed on the overhead board. Yes, everything about where a chef might be at the tail end of a dinner rush.

But not gladiatorial combat.

Ndidi leaned her weight against the edge of the bed and slipped a hand under the top of his shirt, reaching down to the gem at the base of his throat, covered over with several layers.

She rested her hand on the gem, a stone small enough to fit in her palm, still cool in spite of resting against his skin.

She remembered being Urid-Varg and killing the Eldest of the Ishtan to acquire this gem. Remembered the other thing Urid-Varg had built, where he had rested his soul once his original body got too old and frail.

Kathra had killed that piece with a bolter pistol. Ndidi had been there that night, watching from one side and ready to throw herself into battle if necessary.

That had been her initiation into the world of the comitatus.

The gem was gendered. She could never wear it as anything but a pretty bauble, if she ever chose such a thing.

But she had been Daniel, as well as Urid-Varg. She could not tap it, could not control it, but she could damned well make it listen to her.

Ndidi focused herself onto the gem and probed.

Nothing happened.

She growled. Snarled an obscenity, but she wasn't sure if the word ever made it to her lips.

She pushed.

Fell.

Darkness.

Cold.

Light.

Two strange men stood before her in Daniel's salon, that place with the wood furniture and the picture window overlooking a tiny front yard, somewhere on the surface of a planet Daniel didn't even recognize. She recognized both of them.

Arsène stood next to that window, the gray, foggy sun making his sand-colored fur almost glow. Pheryoutl sat on the couch.

The Roahrt's skin was also covered, but with a lighter fur, much like Terran horses were reputed to, rather than the cats that the Mbaysey had brought into space with them against vermin. He had strong hands, like they kept expecting to grasp a hammer and walk up to a forge at any moment.

As a woman constantly missing her kitchen, Ndidi understood. Even her uniform had a special pocket sewn into it for her sakimaru knife, so she could always cut fish or chop vegetables at the drop of a hat.

Daniel was nowhere to be seen.

Ndidi rose from the corner chair so she could pace. She had never been in this room without Daniel being here first.

Was he dead?

"No," Arsène answered her unspoken question, but was anything really unspoken inside another's mind.

Pheryoutl grinned at her in answer.

"What happened?" Ndidi asked the two, her head pivoting between them.

His death would be her guilt, as much of it as she would accept. This was war and they were all tools that Kathra Omezi could use up as she needed to.

Comitatus.

"Something the Conqueror never envisioned possible," Arsène answered her, so she turned that way and began to pace the long axis of the room.

"Explain," she commanded the being.

"Urid-Varg had his own power source," Arsène replied. "Plus the turtle. Plus the gem that contains all of us right now. But he always thought only of himself. His influence, his needs, his desires. He never once considered doing something for someone else. Certainly not at a personal cost. That is why he is not Daniel, and Daniel will never be him."

Ndidi nodded. No doubt someone could more succinctly parse the two men, but they would be hard pressed to do so as accurately.

"He did not have the Turtle, as he did when you were with him," Pheryoutl continued the conversation. "Instead he had us. We chose to band all our power together and focus it outward through Daniel. He had never done something like that before, because only a fraction of our power is normally available. The gem is almost a sentient thing itself, separate from all the ghosts. But we called upon it and it answered us."

Ndidi considered his words.

"Did you burn out Daniel's mind?" she asked.

That might explain them being here and him not.

"No," Arsène spoke up. "But we came extremely close accidentally."

Ndidi turned to the K'bari scholar and considered the implications. Daniel Lémieux was a pillar of strength capable of holding the entire Mbaysey on his shoulders if necessary.

"Yes," Pheryoutl agreed. "And we gave him everything we had. It was almost too much. But we understand our own limits now."

"And Daniel?" she asked.

"He sleeps," Pheryoutl nodded. "You must protect his body. We will watch over his soul, until it is ready to rejoin you."

"When will that be?" Ndidi stopped her pacing and stared at the two men.

The shrug they offered in harmonious answer was possibly the most frightening thing Ndidi had ever encountered.

What if he never awoke?

PART II

SEPT

28

Earth was still Hadi Rostami's idea of paradise, even after nearly a year on the planet. The breeze on his skin. The color of the sky. Even the gravity as he stood in the great hall of the Shah of Earth and watched Amirin mingle with the rich and powerful men who made up this Court.

It was only those nights when Hadi awoke from some terrible nightmares that he missed fur. Or had to throw off all the covers because the heat was overwhelming.

At least until he remembered that he was human.

Or perhaps a wolf in human clothing.

The Court of the Shah had stepped immediately past the stage of ugly rumor-mongering and character assassination when news of Tavle Jocia arrived, but Hadi had been there to squelch the misfits and redirect most of the high emotion into asking why the vuzurgans were the only ones granted power.

What was it, after all, that made a first-born son everything and classified the rest as bricks with which to build treaties?

So they had instead gone beyond *Why not?* and started asking instead *What if?*

What could the Sept Empire be like if second sons could be Shahs of planets or Anusiya, Companions of the Emperor himself?

Hadi and Amirin had always been exceedingly careful to never suggest anything but the Seven Clans be allowed to rule. There were Secret Police agents everywhere, and Hadi would never find them all in time to prevent rumors of treason from being reported outside his reach.

But within the Clan structure, men were freer to ask harsh questions.

It helped that most of the Secret Police who came into contact with Hadi Rostami achieved enlightenment. Not all of them, nor immediately. That would raise red flags and cause other people to ask questions.

But they fell in line with the men of the Shah's Court asking similar questions.

Tavle Jocia had been lost, *after* Amirin Pasdar had been removed from power and returned home to Earth covered in glory.

On the one hand, men were upset at the loss itself, and blamed it on incompetent naval commanders more interested in politics than power. Amirin did not deny nor encourage such commentary, so the talking heads chattered.

On the other hand, the fool who lost Tavle Jocia was beginning to make noises that he had been set up for failure. Amirin Pasdar's name came up, but only tangentially, as the scar running backwards on Pasdar's bald skull from just over his left eye served as a reminder that the man had seen ground combat from close enough to bleed.

Almost none of the men they encountered these days could say that. Nearly all of them had served in the navy at some point, a few even rising to command. But for most, it was enough to say they had once served.

None of them had taken personal risk.

Even that fool of a Sidiqi wouldn't provoke a physical confrontation with a killer like Amirin Pasdar.

If he did, Hadi had this Court in the palm of his hand.

A messenger arrived.

The man moved anonymously through the crowd, but contained a tightly-constrained energy that was as good as a spotlight illuminating the night sky, from where Hadi watched.

Hadi moved close enough to Amirin to murmur something in his ear, but merely nudged the man to study the same movement Hadi was watching.

Courier. That was it. They had a walk to them. A petite arrogance because they were allowed to hand documents directly into the hands of important men and relay verbal messages.

What news was so interesting that it could not wait?

Hadi could not get close enough to the Shah without a damned good reason, so he instead made his way to a nearby bench, sitting next to a woman who was there for serving some man's needs.

He reached outward and engulfed both of them in a sphere that would keep any other man at bay, much like he did with servants he didn't want overhearing things.

It wasn't much, but the woman would perhaps gain an hour or two with no man making demands. That was all he could offer her.

He reached out and listened to the room and the man on the throne with Ishtan senses as the courier bowed low and handed a letter into the hands of the Shah of Earth.

Excitement damped down immediately to rage followed by fear. Again, a lighthouse marking danger.

Hadi rose and moved back into Amirin's orbit. Great, terrible things were about to occur. He could sense Pasdar's name on the Shah's mind, but could not read deeper from such distance.

Hadi felt the Shah's eyes turn this direction in the way relief flooded the man's mind.

How bad had it gotten? Was the Emperor dead and a civil war erupting?

A Court official was summoned by the Shah and gestured this way as Hadi watched. Andarzbad, another commoner like him that had risen on the strength of mind and will, rather than birth order.

Another Andarzbad stepped to the fore of the raised platform where an old man rested, and took a deep breath.

"This Court is closed," he announced without any explanation, causing any number of rumors to immediately be birthed.

Hadi found a bright spot in his soul that the men would immediately depart and the woman behind him might remain unmolested for the rest of the day.

In Hadi's mind, Erin Uduik scowled heavily, but even she relented after a moment and nodded at him.

Around them, men began to form into smaller circles and cliques, while others started towards the exits, intent on other pastimes, with the excitement of Court thwarted.

The first Andarzbad approached with a careful note of diffidence about his mind.

"Naupati Pasdar, a moment?" he spoke just loud enough for Hadi to hear, and the men around Amirin, but no others.

Amirin was not surprised, but he had been warned. The others registered shock, but also noted that the Shah seemed to have sent for the man, and politely.

Also, quietly.

Good rumors would be born of it. Just in case, Hadi

planted such notions in their minds against future need. Eventually, the Court of Earth would be the basis Amirin used to overthrow the Court of Rhages.

The Andarzbad looked askance at Hadi, but Amirin intervened.

"I will need my aide if this conversation is business," he said flatly.

The man didn't know otherwise, so he withdrew any objections and led them to a side door.

The same one the Shah of Earth had just left from a moment ago.

Something terrible had happened, but Hadi could not identify what.

29

───────

Amirin watched with experience born of decades of court intrigue. None of the men escorting him and Rostami knew what had happened, and Hadi had known only that something was about to unfold.

Thus he was treated with great deference. Care born of fear.

The room he was taken to was a much smaller chamber. The sort of drinking salon that contained so many side deals and conspiracies on Rhages. Here, the oversized array of whiskey, whisky, bourbon, and every other intoxicant known to mankind had been replaced by jars of tea on one wall and sealed containers of coffee on the other.

The room had an earthy smell that brought a smile to Amirin's face.

He blinked in surprise when he saw that several men sat around a table, when Court rules dictated that only the Shah sat. Amirin nearly swallowed his tongue when he recognized the Shah himself at the head of the table.

The Shah of Earth scowled past Amirin when he noted the arrival of Hadi.

"Your Excellence, this man's genius is a significant portion of my success over the last decade," Amirin nodded and spoke placatingly, aware that Hadi was no doubt adjusting things as he needed them to be. "I have no secrets from him, so with your approval, he should know everything."

A reputation for ferocious military genius, combined with spending the last several years as a Court ponce played well here.

Amirin Pasdar could serve any needs you might have, My Shah.

A moment later the man nodded and gestured them to sit. Amirin found himself at the low end of the table, facing the man with Hadi on his immediate right. As metaphors went, perhaps not the greatest, but the symbolism would play well with the half dozen other men around them.

"Tavle Jocia was lost," the Shah said, immediately raising a hand to forestall any commentary. "That was after you had conquered it for the Sept. The Sidiqi who had been given the planet makes accusations that are nothing more than a whisper campaign."

The Shah paused and fixed every face with a harder glare than the man usually achieved. Amirin took the moment to study this man.

Old without being elderly or frail. Skinny in the ways of an ascetic, when so many of the men around him enjoyed too many decadences. Brown eyes that seemed to glow with fire right now. Hands that were liver-scarred but did not shake.

Eighty years old, give or take, and still in the top half of the men in the room when it came to being physically dangerous.

Amirin was so happy that the man had turned out to be so upright and respectable.

"There is news," the Shah's voice dropped now, perhaps unconsciously, perhaps drawing all these men deeper into his wake.

There were no outsiders present, save him and Hadi, and Amirin had the feeling that he would not be considered an outsider by these men tomorrow.

If he came out of this room alive. Nobody had weapons except a few guards nearly invisible around the walls.

He had Hadi, who was no doubt touching every mind in the room. He did that.

Adjusted them, without them ever noticing.

Amirin wondered if the Ishtan had changed him thus at some point. He could remember the old Amirin, the man who had decided that his reputation was too warlike and needed to soften. That had been before the aliens, but how much of what had come since then represented their influence?

Even Hadi was a different man.

Hopefully, they were both human enough still.

"This news is from Vorgash," the Shah finally continued, once he had satisfied himself. "The planet, as well as the Septagon that was your command for so long, Pasdar."

Amirin found himself leaning forward with the rest, such was the Shah's charisma, even today.

"The report is sketchy at present, and I expect a more detailed package to arrive with particulars, but you need to be prepared when it does," the old man intoned, showing where his loyalties and expectations lie. An ally, but he might have been without Hadi. "I do know that another one of the ships that attacked Tavle Jocia and damaged Septagon *Singara* raided Vorgash."

The gasps and angry growls weren't just from his mouth, or from Hadi.

"How bad?" Amirin asked when it became clear the man was waiting.

"They did not destroy the Septagon," the Shah explained. "It came close to crashing out of orbit and was perhaps damaged beyond economical repair. Casualties were worse than a decimation. Several Patrols were destroyed as well."

"And the raider?" Amirin tried to make his voice sound normal, in spite of the sudden dryness.

"Escaped with only minimal damage," the old man nodded. "The report in my hands does not have much more than that, and serves mostly as a warning to all worlds that Sept Space is no longer inviolate. That aliens might attack anywhere."

"These are not aliens, Your Excellence," Amirin offered carefully. "Or rather, the vessels are alien, but the commanders are human. The ones I was chasing."

"Mbaysey," the Shah nodded.

Amirin was surprised that the man had done that level of homework, but he supposed that with a war hero politely exiled to Earth, the man might have wanted to know who and what he was dealing with.

Amirin nodded.

"Kathra Omezi has alien allies," Amirin said, turning to Hadi now as the encyclopediac genius.

"The Anndaing are a species best described as erect bipeds that might have evolved from a hammerhead shark, Your Excellence," Hadi began. "Gray-skinned and predatory. They had had starflight for several thousand years longer than humans, but largely kept to themselves, coreward and spinward a great distance beyond Tavle Jocia and the Free Worlds."

"The planet your ship raided," the Shah said without heat.

"Correct," Hadi acknowledged, blushing a bit.

"And it would have been like attempting to raid Earth, for defensive forces, yes?" the old man pressed, again showing friendliness that Amirin didn't think Hadi was encouraging.

At least not much.

"Exactly so, Your Excellence," Hadi nodded. "The Mbaysey have made treaties with the Anndaing, and gained access to their worlds and a great number of other alien species. We do not know where these new warships originate, because Anndaing vessels look completely different, even their combat vessels."

"Unknown aliens?" the Shah asked.

"That is our working theory, sir," Hadi shrugged just perfectly. "A most warlike species we have not yet been able to identify, but one friendly enough to the Anndaing, or the Mbaysey, to place a number of warships at their command."

"Two Septagons badly damaged, gentlemen," the Shah turned a withering gaze across the entire room, largely skipping Amirin and Hadi. "And our greatest commander rusts on Earth, far from the fleet. Far from Rhages. Do you suppose they fear him?"

Amirin worked exceptionally hard to have no emotional reaction right now. The Shah himself was verging over into treason, but Amirin didn't think it was Hadi's doing.

They were too early in his plans for that.

Except that Omezi had apparently gone on the offensive and attacked Vorgash. Amirin doubted that the choice of targets was accidental. There were other worlds closer to Tavle Jocia that could have been hit. Vorgash had a major shipyard, and was where *Singara* was headed for repairs.

Could she have known that?

Something must have shown on his face.

"Pasdar?" the Shah asked.

"Were the repair facilities damaged, Your Excellence?" he asked.

Blankness. The Shah turned to the man on his right for an explanation. That worthy was flipping through a small document and reading furiously for details skipped before.

Finally, the man looked up and shook his head.

Amirin sighed with relief.

It was just personal, then. He could plan around that.

Trying to fight off a full-fledged invasion by Omezi and her allies while simultaneously undermining that drunkard on Rhages might have caused him to lose his grip somewhere.

Fools fighting in a burning house.

If she had struck *Vorgash* and withdrawn, then perhaps they were only repaying him for sending *SeptStar* to Ogrorspoxu in the first place.

The Shah of Earth was not a man to be derailed, however.

"Orders from fleet command are to raise the level of alert across all systems," the old man said. "To send out Patrols and scouts to prevent the aliens from surprising any more Sept worlds. They had done the unthinkable twice, gentlemen. For the first time since the Founding Wars, Septagons have been attacked and damaged by enemy forces."

There was a fire there now. Rage at the insults offered by a bunch of women who had only wished to be left alone to pursue their own destiny.

But they were black women. Native ethnotype from the western, central coast of the African continent, originally. They could not be allowed to challenge the nature of things. Amirin would see them destroyed, since driving them into the darkness had merely shown them other allies they could recruit against the Sept.

The Shah studied him, largely ignoring Hadi except as an extension of their will.

"Septagon *Terra* has a naupati," the old man said. "One I approve of, and am not willing to displace."

Amirin felt himself grow cold at the implications of those words.

Had the revolution already started?

"Amirin Pasdar of the Pasdar Clan will thus take up a position comparable to Anusiya, here on Earth, until the fools in charge of the fleet get their collective heads out of their asses," the man continued, voice growing harsh now. "You will be my representative to the fleet, and I charge you with overseeing the defenses of Earth, Pasdar. Whoever else might think they can argue with you will answer to me, so I expect you and your aide to bring that brilliance to the defense of the homeworld for now."

"For now?" The words escaped Amirin's mouth before he could stop them.

The old man smiled cruelly.

"Eventually, they will realize that you should be in charge of protecting the entire Sept Empire."

30

Kathra hadn't thought much of the system marked Hanai Gozra on the ancient K'bari charts, but she did have to hand it to Wyll and Obaj. When those two sharks said *Swim!* they got results.

Hammers down and tail fins thrashing.

The planetary system on her office vidscreen had been chosen for a central location that was still a little ways off the trade route civilian vessels had been blazing to Thrabo in the Free Worlds. That was important, since the first thing that the Merchants Bank had done was deploy a heavily armed station into orbit of the third planet.

Planet Number Two was actually the more habitable one, an oceanic world that was a little too close to the orange star and reminded Kathra of a jungle horror movie, where everything had grown big and nasty. Good place to fish and hunt the local equivalent of cetaceans, but you had to get by the local alligators first.

The Anndaing farmers had decided to settle on Three instead. It was cooler and drier here. Not as many things grew, but there were bands down near the equator where the plains went on seemingly forever, so dryland crops would grow well enough. And it wasn't like they needed to support an entire planetary population here.

Just themselves and those crazy *salauds* over on Two who produced meat and hides for trade.

Interestingly, there had also ended up being a major Kaniea population on both worlds in addition to the regular mix. Kathra put that down to folks wanting to impress her personally, as well as all the Kaniea in her direct trade network these days because of A'Alhakoth's father and eldest brother.

The Mbaysey wouldn't get as rich here, but they also didn't have to compete across as many vectors, nor worry about Sept or even Free Worlds warships threatening.

Not with a passel of Gun-6 and Scout-6 ships stationed at Three that liked to range outward with hungry eyes.

She shut off the monitor and leaned over to check the little one, fast asleep in her crib next to the desk with a cute, cheerful smile on her face. Adaku was walking whenever someone turned their back on the scamp. Talking nonstop and playing silly games with her half-sister when the two of them were together.

Would she really be three shortly?

Kathra shook her head with a chuckle and listened to the footsteps approaching her open door. She smiled as Areen peeked carefully in and looked around before actually entering. All the aunties had learned to move like big predators when the little ones were sleeping, lest they incur Kathra's wrath. Or worse, Erin's.

The Commander gestured her to sit. The visitor had a troubled look on her face.

Kathra waited for her to find the words.

Areen eventually shrugged.

"The usual bitching from the Clan elders," she began.

"Who got fat and lazy at Kanus," Kathra remarked. "Now I'm making them work their asses off again in a dark system: mining, smelting, and processing."

"More or less," Areen replied. "Some wanted to stay at Kanus. Others wanted to go inward beyond the writ of the Merchants Guild. A few have the fire to return to the Free Worlds and have their say."

"Mark that last group as troublemakers who should be encouraged to join an Anndaing warship," Kathra smiled grimly. "This is as close as I ever intend to get to the human sectors again."

"A few still want to set down roots here," Areen broached the topic carefully.

"Those are welcome to resign from the Mbaysey first," Kathra growled.

Quietly, though, because the little one would wake and be cranky until she got food in her.

"Noted," Areen said. "Mostly these are just rumors and women bitching. Nothing will come of it. The hotheads will sober up tomorrow and realize how good they have it."

"But?" Kathra noted the hitch in Areen's voice.

She had wondered a few times if the woman would have taken a berth aboard either *SwiftStar* or later on *MorningStar*. Of the humans in the comitatus, she was the only one who have ever been physically intimate with Daniel. A few others had considered it but never moved fast enough.

Of course, with Ndidi gone and Erin gone maternal, Areen was something of a second-in-command these days. The woman everyone else would have to get through to reach Kathra.

"Do we trust the Anndaing?" Areen finally asked bluntly.

Kathra considered the woman. Not the oldest or longest serving in the comitatus, but certainly part of that inner cadre who had her greatest trust. She had earned her answer.

"No," Kathra said simply. Bluntly. "We are allied with them at present, but things will change eventually."

Areen goggled a little in surprise, but kept silent.

"Not the answer you were expecting?" Kathra smiled.

"No, not really."

"Allies of convenience," Kathra continued. "They need us to help blunt the Sept. To use our knowledge and hatred of those folks to help the Free Worlds resist. I have no doubt deals are being done in quiet rooms for more Gun-6 and Gun-12 boats to be leased to Free Worlds governments. Or hired out to private corporations willing to focus their piracy on the Sept, like we do."

"Then what?" Areen asked, leaning forward now.

"At some point, full on war between the Merchants Bank and the Sept Empire," Kathra said. "With the Free Worlds possibly being split right down the middle as to who they help. Or get conquered by."

"And the Mbaysey?" Areen looked uncomfortable, but the woman was a pilot, not a diplomat.

Warrior, not planner. That was why Ife and Ndidi held those commands, rather than former Spectre pilots who had good reflexes, but not the ability to handle a broad campaign like a chef might.

"The Mbaysey are a tool that the Anndaing see as useful for now," Kathra shrugged innocently. "They would use us up if we allowed it. If we got in over our heads with the situation and let the Merchants Bank force us into that opening."

"But you refuse?" Areen asked, some light dawning in her eyes now.

"The human crews of *SwiftStar* and *MorningStar* only amount to about one hundred and fifty people combined," Kathra said. "Against an original tribal roll of seventy-five hundred. Granted, many of the best, but nothing that would destroy the tribe if they were lost."

"And that's why you refused when they offered you the other two ships?" Areen guessed.

"Yes," Kathra nodded. "Too easy to thin ourselves more than was smart, just because we might be able to hurt the Sept. We cannot stop the Sept Empire from conquering the galaxy."

"No?"

"We don't have to," Kathra reminded her. "We can damage them. Frighten them, especially with what Ndidi is going to do at Vorgash. But it would require the entire Anndaing Armada and all their allies to truly stop that many Septagons from sailing where they wanted to."

"So the raids?" Areen asked. "The mission to chase *Singara* all the way home?"

"Each of those bases was a place the Sept could threaten K'bari space, once we destroyed the one that let them reach Ogrorspoxu the first time," Kathra replied. "Now, they have to build new ones to replace them. And they will. But each base has to be protected against Anndaing patrols and Ovanii warships. That ties up resources. The Sept cannot build Septagons that fast."

"And if they have to protect their own worlds from Ndidi…"

"Then they build even slower so they cannot threaten the Anndaing," Kathra nodded. "We gain time."

"What are we doing with it?" Areen asked.

"Building up our reserves here," Kathra said. "Someplace safe enough, surrounded by Anndaing warships, but making a statement by still putting ourselves between the sharks and the humans."

"Except that we can sail away if we have to," Areen blinked.

"We can sail away if we have to, yes," Kathra smiled. "A Septagon cannot be resisted by anybody but a Battlemaster, and even that requires surprise and skill. Patrols are a threat, but not to the sorts of forces around us here. Nobody will catch us that much by surprise at Hanai Gozra, because the sharks want to keep this system for themselves."

"Why?"

"You're seeing the first baby steps by the Anndaing towards colonizing those worlds that used to be K'bari, as recently as a thousand years ago," Kathra said. "Eventually, that brings them into closer contact with the Free Worlds. More trade, certainly, but a greater threat by the Sept, assuming that nothing can be done about those *salauds*."

"And Rostami?"

"He can pursue Daniel anywhere in the galaxy," Kathra said simply. "Daniel is one of us for the rest of his life, so that means that the Sept can chase us for all eternity if they want. Rostami will probably try. Pasdar will help."

"Then why did they return to Rhages and Earth?" Areen asked.

Kathra grimaced.

This was the question that kept her awake at night.

Why had those two allowed themselves to be removed from the field of maneuver? Nobody could remove Rostami if he chose not to allow it. In that, his powers were the sorts of things that Daniel could do, were he a lesser man.

A junior varsity version of Urid-Varg, if you will.

Two Septagons sailing together would be disastrous. Three or perhaps a full squadron of six, like the ancient days, would be cataclysmic.

"I have a theory," Kathra said, trusting Areen to keep her silence from most of the women. She waited for Spectre Three to nod. "With Pasdar's connections, and Rostami's power, the Naupati is going to make a play for imperial power."

"Pasdar?" Areen asked, rocked back onto her heels. "Could he?"

"Not according to their laws, no," Kathra explained. "He is a second son, or fourth. It doesn't matter. Not the Vuzurgan that one of his brothers is. And the crown is supposedly hereditary, passing father to eldest son. The current one, from all reports, is not a particularly impressive specimen, either mentally or physically. What is to stop Rostami twisting enough minds to open a path for someone like Naupati Pasdar to rise to the top?"

"Nothing," Areen replied a little breathless.

"No, there is one thing," Kathra said.

"What?"

"Daniel."

31

———

Earth orbit. Home system naval command facility. A quiet office near the diplomatic section of the station, rather than the military wing of the base.

Amirin Pasdar was no longer a naupati in his current role, even though that was his rank. He was a special Companion to the Shah of Earth, that man being perhaps the fourth or eighth most powerful human in the galaxy, depending on how you wanted to cut it.

Rostami moved in Amirin's shadow, as always. The perfect bureaucrat, capable of actually adjusting enough of the human systems of governance to make the Sept Empire work.

Or tear it all down.

Hopefully, they could build a new system fast enough that the other worlds did not fall into anarchy and chaos.

Somewhere, Amirin was certain there was a fuse burning. That smell was there when he awoke sometimes, but he knew as his mind returned that it was only in his dreams.

Or rather, the Mbaysey flagship wasn't a fuse.

It was a black swan. An event so utterly unpredictable

that no mitigations could be created, other than to establish an overwhelming superiority of force.

But there weren't enough Septagons.

Amirin looked around the office he had been given by a nervous command staff. The Shah of Earth was not in their military chain of command, but one word from the man would be sufficient to break any number of careers if they crossed him.

They knew that.

They also knew Amirin's reputation for brutal efficiency and willingness to get bloody when necessary.

He was a bull in a china shop, surrounded by fearful little pots.

The funniest part was how much he needed all these men to remain intact, even after he reached above them all and broke the government itself. The navy would be the only thing between the Sept and the aliens.

The Mbaysey had chosen sides. They would not even be granted the courtesy of humanity under Sept law, when the time came.

A knock at the door and Hadi entered a moment later with a sharp nod and a stack of binders containing printouts the man could reference as needed.

Amirin was always surprised when other officers resorted to the pocket computer every one of them carried. It was lovely, when you needed to look up exactly one detail.

The moment you needed two details, or more, you were forever flipping back and forth between screens trying to keep things straight. Amirin preferred printing on paper where he could add notes, shuffle things around, and find new conclusions that would otherwise elude you as screens slid back and forth.

Hadi closed the door and settled the stack on his side of the desk. Amirin had left it purposefully empty today, going so far as to move his coffee mug to the filing unit behind him.

"What do we know about *MorningStar?*" Amirin asked the most intelligent, details-driven officer he had ever met.

"One vessel, provenance unknown," the man said. "Same cultural notes as the smaller vessels, identified as *SwiftStar*, *NovaStar*, and *BrightStar.*"

"The same species built all four?" Amirin confirmed.

"The smaller three are functionally identical, within manufacturing limits," Hadi nodded. "*MorningStar* was built by the same people, but we are reasonably certain that such a species were not known to the Anndaing."

"What have our spies learned?" Amirin asked, confirming what he had already read in the voluminous folders supplied when the navy decided that the Shah was serious.

"Precious little," Hadi muttered with a snarl. "I expect that we will need to burn some agencies to the ground and build replacements rather than trying to separate the wheat from the chaff."

"Yes," Amirin agreed. "They spent too much time chasing after civilians at Thrabo and barely dedicated any effort to the vessel known as…"

He paused, thinking backwards through what he had read.

"*Koni Swift*," Hadi filled in the name, flipping open one of the binders and extracting an executive summary.

The Anndaing aspbad was shown. Except they called the rank Trademaster.

What did that say about the species and the culture?

Ugly. Gray. Almost frightening-looking, with that hammer that projected a pair of eyes out sideways. Gills, although apparently largely vestigial at this point their evolution.

Koni Swift. Cargo-6 design, which apparently referred to

a set of six shipping containers that the vessel could haul, in addition to voluminous interior cargo holds.

And guns. The thing had managed to escape that fateful ambush at Tavle Jocia, when pirates in Sept pay had attempted to take it.

Amirin Pasdar was certain Crence Miray was a spy for someone, but nobody understood the structure of the Anndaing Merchants Guild or Merchants Bank well enough.

How did you run a government like a business? It didn't seem remotely efficient, ancient Italian or Chinese examples to the contrary.

Amirin considered his co-conspirator.

"There is only *MorningStar* in our records?" he confirmed.

"And the three smaller ones, which have all been seen in the company of Anndaing warships comparable to Patrols for size, but with greater firepower," Hadi agreed. "They apparently use a different gravitational system than we do. Much more efficient and compact, so better than Patrol vessels, ton for ton."

Amirin considered.

One warship like *MorningStar* was a terrible thing, but it feared a Septagon like the turtle aliens had, so he presumed that the Axial Megacannon could hurt or possibly destroy such a vessel.

Solution: sail two Septagons in close order.

Except that there weren't enough Septagons to protect all the human worlds.

Amirin was happy to write off many systems for now. Enough had sufficient defensive arrays that they should be able to prevent Omezi's flagship from doing that much damage. And if she took to raiding shipping, eventually he would be able to track her down.

Or her bases, which were what he needed to kill.

Cut off her supplies, and she would have to sail to a friendly port. Those could also be blockades, until she faced starvation or surrender.

Septagons could not go for long without food shipments. Surely *MorningStar* had similar problems, as large as that vessel was.

Yes, two Septagons could destroy her. It might require an entire fleet of Patrols to locate her, but he could prepare by convincing the right people to move forces forward.

And someone might do to *MorningStar* what the Mbaysey had nearly done to Amirin, ramming when all other options were denied them.

"What about the Anndaing?" Amirin asked, leaping outward from a purely military solution to something political, confident that Hadi could keep up.

"They have ceased all attempts at diplomacy," the man said with a grunt. "Granted, such efforts were not that great originally, and were met with the sorts of specism one might expect from Sept bureaucrats convinced of their innate superiority."

"Have they left?" Amirin pressed.

"Vanished," Hadi confirmed. "Presumably, they were warned somehow, and got to safety ahead of the sorts of reprisals the Sept are infamous for."

"Fools fighting in a burning house," Amirin said succinctly. "What if we assume that the raid on Vorgash was payment for your attack on the chef at that Anndaing world? What happens if we ignore the Anndaing for a time, and bring pressure at home to stop trying to conquer the Free Worlds?"

"Would they accept such a status quo?" Hadi asked.

"Could they resist you?" Amirin countered. "I need time. We cannot break the hold of that fool at Rhages and supplant him while we also fight a major war on multiple fronts with aliens that might have a technological edge on us. If nothing else, we do not have vessels that can counter *MorningStar* and her peers. We have grown complacent."

"Such complacency was the reason you could attempt to make yourself emperor, Amirin," Hadi noted. "All of the Sept had grown a little rotten."

"Agreed," Amirin admitted with a grimace not pointed at this man. "But I have sixty good years in front of me if I remain healthy. Plus another twenty or forty where I should have retired and allowed some other second son to rise to power. This is no longer a chase against Kathra Omezi and her pack of deviant women. If we do this thing, if we move to conquer, then we must confront the threat that the Anndaing bring."

"Which is?" Hadi settled back on his chair, papers forgotten.

"They are another star empire possibly as powerful as the Sept," Amirin admitted, much as it pained him.

He remembered the time, not all that long ago, where Sept superiority was a thing to take for granted. Where conquest of the entire galaxy, and subjugation of all the native species he encountered was merely a matter of time and effort.

Before he knew *Doubt*.

Amirin Pasdar had inspected the insides of his mind as much as he could. Had ordered Hadi to do the same to both of them, somehow convinced that the Ishtan had altered him almost as much as they had his assistant.

Except he had known doubt before that.

The Star Turtle. It had started there.

Other aliens, other technologies. Things so vastly unlike human culture and civilization that they had no analog.

Today, Amirin understood Urid-Varg. Several times per day he had taken to thanking all the terrible gods of the galaxy that such a monster had stumbled across Kathra Omezi and decided to start his new empire with a scene to make the rape of the Sabine women look tame by comparison.

But for Daniel Lémieux, however eternally that man should be cursed, it was entirely possible that the Keyaksar at Rhages would have worn lime and white now. Would have proclaimed a new Sept Empire, centered around a deathless, psychopathic alien.

Hadi had shared as much of the past as the Ishtan had known, forever hiding in the shadows while seeking an opportunity to undermine the creature.

Eventually, they had attempted to destroy the chef, but failed. Hadi still spoke with respect and occasionally envy of women such as Erin Uduik and Iruoma Emeka.

He found himself staring at Hadi and wondering if he had gone entirely wrong.

No, only mostly wrong, which was even more frightening.

"We need peace with the Anndaing," Amirin decided. "Trade, however diluted and delayed as it will probably have to pass through the hands of Free Worlds smugglers and pirates rather than honest merchants."

"What do we gain?" Hadi asked. "Besides time. Where does your campaign take you?"

"They have better technology than we do," Amirin ground the words out of his soul like a smith pounding on a thing that would become a sword. "Better gravity systems. Better weapons. Quite possibly better everything, if the notes your spies did manage from Tavle Jocia and the trade voyages of *Koni Swift* are accurate. How long would it take for us to build a new class of vessel, if we could understand Anndaing equipment?"

"A generation," Hadi decided. "Human specists would

refuse to admit to such a thing, but the military could be brought around easily enough. They always demand better toys. But yes, it would take time to rebuild everything, and then to train everyone to use it effectively. Would the aliens remain complacent?"

"Probably not, but they would have to force their own technology forward ahead of ours, while we might be leap-frogging any number of intermediate steps to catch up," Amirin shrugged. "We would need to invest in better spy networks, at a very minimum. But we will need to break the current, ossified manner of thinking in the Sept and bring everyone to a new way of looking at the galaxy."

"Sounds revolutionary," Hadi smiled. "But we will have the problem of the chef. If the Ishtan were to be believed, then I have only a few years remaining before the power fades, and I am nothing but a mundane human, unable to twist minds for you."

"Have you seen any decline in your power?" Amirin asked.

So much of his plans hinged on Rostami being able to move things that nobody but the chef could detect, let alone thwart.

But yes, it introduced a mania to his planning.

Amirin Pasdar had been expecting to take twenty years to maneuver himself into a position where the Clans demanded that he take power and overthrow the old dynasty.

Depending on a group of dead aliens, he might only have three years.

He circled back to his most ancient education. Those most hated enemies from the west that had threatened his ancestors time and again. But they had also built two of the most enduring cultural empires in human history, echoing all the way down to the modern era with their vocabulary.

Amirin Pasdar was camped on the banks of the river in

ancient Italy known as the Rubicon. Crossing it would be to cast the dice to the fates, that he would either be crowned Emperor, or killed like a dog and left in the streets to rot.

"Assume we have at most three years from today," Amirin said. "By then, the crown must be stable on my head, and the throne warmed under my butt. We can start the effort of remilitarizing today by simply using this pulpit the Shah has given me to agitate for modernization. That will be my job."

"And me?" Hadi asked.

"You will twist your spy network hard," Amirin said. "Use up men if you have to. Destroy any that uncover your secret, as you did retreating with the broken *SeptStar*. Get me the crown while we can still do something to prevent those damnable aliens from deciding that the Free Worlds should be free from the Sept. If we wait too long, they might be able to box us into this tiny realm we hold now, and we will have to fight our way out into the broader galaxy."

"Should we build a better Septagon?" Hadi asked, broaching the most taboo subject of all.

But hadn't *MorningStar* now twice shown men that the dreaded Septagon was not the most powerful warship in space? What other surprises did they have for him?

And what better wedge to draw the military even more fully onto his side?

"Find out what technologies we could incorporate tomorrow into a new design," Amirin ordered. "Better, find one of those think-tank engineers who has designed a better Septagon, but been ignored or suppressed because contract and contractors would have to change, causing families to lose money. Get me his blueprints."

"It shall be done," Hadi replied. "Should I move on those orders immediately, or are there other things to cover today?"

"Nothing so important as a new Septagon and a new

bully pulpit from which to ask dangerous questions," Amirin decided. "Dismissed."

Hadi rose with a grim, hungry smile and departed, leaving him alone with the stacks of paper.

Time was suddenly his enemy again.

Once, Omezi had been in a position where she could simply flee into the interior of the galaxy beyond sectors known on any maps. That might have been sufficient, except she had found allies out there, time and again.

Once, he had lived in utter ignorance of the recent history of intelligent life in the galaxy around them all. Now, he knew just how common other species were. How much basic physics and energy efficiency favored an erect bipedal design that might be mistaken for a human in the distance or the dark.

A young Amirin Pasdar had expressed all the species, racial, and gender superiority stereotypes of his class and station.

An older one knew *Doubt.*

It would make him a better emperor, he knew, but it also made him wonder if the ancient Roman and Byzantine model might not be an improvement. Had not the original armies of the desert eventually absorbed any willing to convert with a good heart?

A human empire was doomed. It might last for a time, but it could not challenge the Anndaing, or some of the other, more distant aliens that had not yet appeared on a human border.

Would he need to take whatever power Hadi had and use it to infuse new blood into the Seven Clans? Just thinking such thoughts was a heresy bad enough to get him denounced by many on Rhages, but he no longer had a need for anyone on that planet.

Should they consider adopting enough aliens into the

Seven Clans that alien children could carry the Sept imprint and help him conquer the rest of the galaxy?

If a man was of a mind to destroy the very culture that birthed him, in the process of conquering it, with what should he replace that thing?

32

Coming out of jump, Ndidi was always a little frightened when she contemplated what *MorningStar* was really capable of. What the Ovanii had achieved in their time. Looking at a readout from her bridge computer as the ship cruised in towards the station just reinforced it.

The outer armor of this ancient horseshoe crap design was almost organic. Tack specially treated plates of metal over damage and apply the correct current. A week later, it had fused on like flesh, usually leaving some layer of discoloration behind.

Inside and outside, every Ovanii vessel had been painted with all manner of geometric designs across the entire rainbow of colors. Now she understood why. An enemy vessel could not tell where prior damage had been healed over, because the entire hull was colorful.

Not only were they warriors, but poets as well. She had read enough Ovanii literature, as translated by Daniel, to understand that, both before taking command of this warship as well as after.

Today, they were out of jump and as close to home as *MorningStar* would get for a while.

Or, as close to home as Ndidi was willing to go right now.

Tucked into a pocket, surrounded by darkness. Closer to Vorgash than to Narlpynth or Cylou in the Free Worlds, but located in a rough triangle formed by those three.

The system from which the Sept had once attacked Tavle Jocia was behind her on a right wing flank, when looking at Vorgash from here.

SwiftStar was already docked to the station that the Anndaing Merchants Bank had caused to be constructed here. *NovaStar* and *BrightStar* had taken more damage from the battle, so they would dock as well, where repair crews conversant in Ovanii technology could repair things.

No hits had actually penetrated the outer armor hard enough to get through the honeycomb layer behind it. The only casualty from the battle had been a sailor that had a box break loose and fly off a shelf to strike her in the back of the head, cracking her skull and adding the most amazingly complex bruise to her hammer.

She was healing almost as fast as *MorningStar*.

Ndidi looked around the bridge and counted noses. All her primary officers were present.

Save one.

Daniel still had not awoken. Nobody could say for sure when he would.

If he would.

What would happen to the Mbaysey without Daniel?

They could flee the Sept, never to be found again. Just sell *SwiftStar* back and sever technological ties with the Merchants Guild. Load up the various Stars and look beyond Anndaing space.

Except that Ndidi wasn't done with the Sept just yet.

"Message from the station," Acqueir spoke up into the bubble of silence that had engulfed them all and broke her reverie. "Crence sends his regards and inquires about news."

"Did he flag it *GhostStar?*" Ndidi asked, looking over that way.

"Negative," Acqueir nodded, acknowledging the question under the question.

Kathra was not with him. Had finally taken the hint, however verbally abusive it might have been when Ndidi delivered it, and returned to Anndaing space, well away from Sept assassins and Septagons that might threaten the future of the Mbaysey.

Ndidi, Ife, and all the rest of the women could be lost and not jeopardize the tribe. Adaku was not old enough to step into her mother's shoes.

Most people apparently hadn't believed that Kathra had what it took, back at seventeen, to take charge. They had been wrong. Ndidi could have told them then.

She liked to occasionally remind them today.

Ndidi opened a channel aft.

"Tanuss here."

"Any changes in docking?" Ndidi asked her engineer. "The others need it more than we do, and we might have company shortly."

"I'm good here," the Wisp woman almost sounded cheerful. "Low on everything, so tell whoever to bring a load with them on a transport, and then expect their chariot to leave as soon as its empty for the next one to come aboard."

"Noted," Ndidi chuckled.

Engineers were the same, regardless of the shell around their soul. Adanne might have given her the exact same speech from the deck of *SeekerStar*.

Rather than ask her sensors officer, Ndidi closed the channel and brought up a list of ships in scanner range, updated constantly by Acqueir. None of the Stars were here, save for her squadron of four.

SeekerStar had no business being anywhere in hailing range, but Ndidi needed to remind herself to keep a high level of paranoia. Too much weight on her shoulders most days, and nobody to share some of it with, if Daniel was no longer an option.

"Flag Crence and invite him aboard," Ndidi told Acqueir. "Pass along Tanuss's suggestion as well, so he doesn't expect to take up our landing bay."

Other chuckles. They all liked and respected the trademaster, but he was a male, and occasionally that type got a little full of themselves if they weren't Mbaysey.

"Anything else?" Ndidi asked, aware of all the paperwork she could be doing right now, instead of just being seen and smelled by her women.

Acqueir shook her head, so Ndidi turned to Hirly.

"You have it for now," she said. "Ask Crence how big an audience he wants and then let me know or set up a conference room."

Ndidi rose and made her way back to her office. Time to sit and prepare for news from home. Wherever home was. Whatever news might be relevant enough to be carried by the Merchant Bank's top spy.

Her eye fell onto that star map projector, so she rose and retrieved it from the shelf, turning the lights down in here as she did.

A thumb on the button and it floated, projecting someone else's home into the air around it. She understood better now why the device called to her.

She commanded an Ovanii warship. The Ovanii were gone, culturally, reduced to a low iron age civilization on the distant fringes of Anndaing maps. But their technology lived on.

Daniel had found K'bari books and translated them. That had actually been the breakthrough that caused his ghosts to consider the man in a better light and eventually help him.

But the K'bari were gone as well.

As were the Roahrt and so many others. Mostly, victims of Urid-Varg's unquenchable desire for male dominance. A few simply swallowed up by time or other species, since not everyone was as open-minded and welcoming as the Anndaing.

And then there were the humans. The other humans. The ones she would have to break of their male issues.

Ndidi wondered if some unknown alien might find a toy similar to the one floating above her desk and wonder about humans that had been forgotten after some apocalypse.

She captured the device in one hand and deactivated it as she opened a channel back to her favorite Wisp.

"Tanuss here," the woman sounded less cheerful now, but that was the consequence of someone intruding with need outside the regular channels.

Engineers were like that, too.

"Ndidi," she replied.

"Oh, what can I do for you, Speaker?" Tanuss asked in a friendlier voice.

Another sister-in-law that she liked, depending on how one wanted to calculate all the women who had decided that Daniel was as special a human as Ndidi already knew he was.

"You know that device I found?" Ndidi said. "The star map with no coordinates that would let us identify where it is right now?"

"I do," the engineer warmed to the subject. "Were you able to identify something?"

Always the problem solvers.

"No," Ndidi felt a little bad, crushing even that tiny bit

of hope, but maybe this would make up for it. "I would like you to make me another one, Tanuss. Centered on Earth, but I want you to include enough other stars, the major, distant ones, such that some future scholar could locate it on a map."

There was a long pause, but not unexpected.

Tanuss was an engineer, not an artist.

Not a chef.

"Why?" the Wisp woman finally asked.

"So some future woman doesn't have the same questions that we do," Ndidi answered honestly. "Either they will know those coordinates because humans exist, or they will be able to find them and visit the place from whence my kind originated."

"Oh."

"Thank you," Ndidi cut the line and moved to put the device back on the shelf.

She would meditate for a bit.

Maybe she needed to take Daniel's place and cook everyone dinner tonight.

The news about Daniel would be terrible enough.

33

———

THERE WERE days that Crence resented being the first Anndaing to encounter the humans in numbers. Specifically the Mbaysey, much as he had come to love these feisty women and all the things they had done to Anndaing culture.

But he could have been out there getting filthy, stinking rich.

Combat pay was nice and all. And he didn't have to pay upkeep on the ship he occasionally slipped and called *GhostStar*. Plus, storage for *Koni Swift* was covered as well.

But, damn, the places he could have gone in the Free Worlds. The cargo he could have carried to places that still hadn't met his kind.

The profits lost.

But all that melted like fog when he was ushered into Ndidi's office and saw what the young woman had turned herself into.

Crence slipped into a chair and kept his usual sarcasm on a shorter anchor chain than usual.

She looked like hell.

Not sad or anything like that.

Tired, maybe.

No, if Crence had to really apply some vocabulary to it, she looked like a creature who had faced some level of demonic possession. Except that she had killed the stupid demon and eaten it afterwards as a statement of toughness.

He really hadn't believed Kathra when she told him what the woman seated over there could turn into.

Not until this moment.

He skipped all the usual formalities and banter, mindful that she might fin him and toss his silly ass out an airlock, just from the look on her face.

"How can I help?" he asked instead.

She blinked.

That was good. Meant she was still an organic creature and *NOT* a demon.

Hopefully.

She even breathed, relieving him of some quiet, desperate fear that she had turned into an Ascended Being who had then come back to teach them all some manners.

Not that Crence had that guilty of a conscience.

Most nights anyway.

"Your news first," she finally relented, about the time he was beginning to wonder if Ndidi was going to turn him to stone.

Crence leaned back and sanded all the sharp edges off his words and tones as he explained.

"So Kathra and the rest of your folks have moved a little forward from Ogrorspoxu," he said tentatively. "They are currently based in the former K'bari system known as Hanai Gozra, where an Anndaing base is protecting her and two colonies on planetary surfaces. She's doing the usual things with ForgeStar, IronStar, and the rest. But she's remaining way the hell away from the Sept and the Free Worlds, like she promised you."

Ndidi had started to say something, but subsided. He'd only gotten Kathra's side of the story. Must have been good.

"While it is impossible to build a true firebreak in space when dealing with valence drives and related technology, we have scouts and such out constantly, monitoring for passage and traffic indicating that anyone has done anything. To date, several small-time piracy rings have been annihilated, and half a dozen religious cults, mostly human, have been discovered, but no Sept bases. How did Vorgash go?"

"The Septagon survived."

Ndidi smiled. It was the most terrible thing Crence thought he might ever see on a human face.

"Will it ever fly again?" Crence asked.

He'd had Jine and Dane scan *MorningStar* as it approached. Nothing about the ship suggested a naval apocalypse over a human world, so it must have been rather one-sided.

Ndidi shrugged nonchalantly.

Okay, that tops the smile for scary.

Crence pasted a friendly smile on his face and kept his hammers from flexing, as much as he might have a headache later from it.

"We surprised them," she said slowly, almost lovingly. "All four engines were broken, so I instructed A'Alhakoth to try to break his hull into pieces with the Arc-cannons. We were not successful before I decided that we'd been there long enough and needed to skip out ahead of the check."

How did you break the engines of a Septagon? Crence figured he'd be up all night with some boullo wine and maybe a muscle relaxer, just reading reports. He had a high enough security clearance, unlike most of the people in this system right now.

He just wasn't sure he wanted to know what a truly angry human woman was capable of achieving, given the right tools.

"And?" Crence ventured, wondering what monster megalodon was about to emerge from the depths and bite him in half. "I feel like you're leaving some interesting detail out. Something I might need to know."

Not quite as dumb as climbing a hill in a lightning storm with a long, steel rod in one hand, but really close, all things considered.

Ndidi lapsed into silence, as though herself trying to find the right words.

Damnit, this just keeps getting scarier. What can't she say to me, *of all people?*

Crence held his breath and his hammers.

"Something happened to Daniel."

Oh, tunashit.

"What?" Crence managed to croak like a broken frog.

"You've heard the stories of what he did to Septagon *Uwalu*," Ndidi offered.

Crence nodded, mutely, not trusting his own words right now.

"He didn't have the turtle as a focus or battery this time," she continued. "But that didn't stop him from unleashing a death scream so powerful that Septagon *Vorgash* actually shut down for about ten seconds."

Double tunashit.

"His ghosts used all the power they had," Ndidi continued. "They don't think they burned out his mind, but nobody knows for sure, and won't until he chooses to awaken."

Crence had never gotten as high as a *triple tunashit* before now.

"They don't think?" he asked, truly, honestly frightened at this moment. "Who don't think?"

"Two of his ghosts," Ndidi explained, as if talking to dead men was *THE MOST NATURAL THING IN THE UNIVERSE.* "I spoke with Arsène and Pheryoutl."

"I recognize the K'bari name," Crence said after a moment, deciding to just go ahead and treat necromancy like an everyday thing.

Tunashit, with humans it just might be.

Why the hell not?

"The other is a Roahrt," she smiled grimly.

Okay, fine. *Quadruple tunashit.*

Crence knew that Daniel contained a Roahrt. He spoke and read their language, after all.

One of them was acting *in loco parentis* right now? With a K'bari?

My mother always wanted me to study medicine instead of business. Should have listened.

Crence managed to swallow.

And breathe. Can't forget that part.

"And nobody knows if Daniel will ever wake up again?" Crence asked a woman who might just be the galaxy's scariest necromancer.

"Correct," Ndidi said.

Okay, that explains looking like hell. Pretty sure I'd be worse right now.

"I already asked once, but here goes nothing," Crence gritted his teeth. "What can I do to help?"

At least Ndidi leaned back now. Possibly even relaxed a little. Her shoulders no longer looked poised to rake him with talons, in any case.

"I've given it a lot of thought on the flight here from Vorgash," the Necromancer of Doom said. "I think we'll need Kathra and Erin to break him out of whatever trap he's crawled into to hide."

Crence Miray, Doctor of Cranial Medicine. Boring never sounded so appealing.

"Why?" he asked, dreading the answer.

Human necromancy, and all that.

"Daniel and I are functionally twins at this point," she explained. "I can't reach him. But he and Erin have a very different relationship, because she was the first Mbaysey he ever met. And Erin has told me more than once that Daniel was the first male to ever impress her."

"And Kathra?"

Crence tensed all his stomach muscles, like she was about to gut-punch him.

"I've since had a couple of really interesting brainstorming sessions with the women who know him best," Ndidi said. "A'Alhakoth, Tanuss, Acqueir and a few others. Acqueir took me aside and shared a story she didn't think anybody but her knew. Let us just say that I think Daniel will respond to Kathra's voice, even as he might ignore the rest of us."

Crence wanted to ask. It was right there on the tip of his tongue. But something in the serenely evil smile on her face stepped him backwards several paces in his mind.

The Mbaysey, as far as Crence was concerned, were nuts. Not bad. Just crazy.

Gender imbalance by choice, eighty-five percent female and just keeping men around for reproductive purposes, but making them earn their keep as teachers, nannies, or artists.

At least the Anndaing sectors remained much closer to even along those lines.

He decided that he could go to his grave not knowing what bizarre practice might have bound Daniel to Kathra such that she could call him back from the dead.

As long as it helped squish the Sept and let him eventually get back to trading for a living, Crence really didn't care what consensually weird things the humans did in the privacy of their ships.

"Are you coming back to Hanai Gozra with Daniel?" Crence asked.

"No," Ndidi said with deathlike finality. "My doctors know how to treat humans and yours don't. He'll stay with us on *MorningStar* until you get back with Kathra."

"I can go ask her to come," Crence offered. "I assume you'll send a letter with all the details she needs. But that roundtrip is about seventy days, even if I push really hard. Were you planning to stay put?"

"Oh, no," Ndidi said, smiling and pronouncing a Doom that was really just the cherry on top of today's pudding. "There are still places that need to feel my wrath."

34

Septagon *Terra*. Amirin was impressed, but for all the wrong reasons.

Along with the other flagship, Septagon *Rhages*, they were the pride of the Sept Empire. But that generally meant that the two vessels were pretty, rather than tough.

As Amirin walked forward from the landing bay to the elevators, he noted the paint and the carpeting in the hallway. As naupati aboard *Vorgash*, he had ordered the carpet removed everywhere. And the cream-white paint covered over to head height with an industrial gray that was almost abrasive enough to sand off flesh.

The number of tons of carpet on a single Septagon was sufficient to actually improve speeds on the valence drives when they were removed. That was important when every other vessel in the galaxy was fast enough to escape you.

And this paint would probably have to be touched up on a weekly basis, just from shoulders rubbing against it in everyday use.

Pretty. But it was an art installation. A knife could also be pretty, but there was no mistaking it for a killing tool if it was fashioned correctly.

He flashed back to Rhages and some of the men he had known there. Pretty. But not lethal in an alley. Any alley.

Not like Amirin.

Two troopers escorted him as they walked through corridors. A savaran escorted him. Just a medium level officer, so possibly someone that the naupati wanted Amirin to meet, as opposed to subtly insulting him.

Perhaps.

Four aides trailed, plus Hadi. The four came with his rank as adviser to the Shah of Earth, and were adequately intelligent creatures. They could handle the paperwork tasks and errands he or Rostami needed handled, but they were no conspirators by any stretch of the imagination.

It felt alien to still be wearing his desert robes on this vessel, loose and flowing, cotton and almost homespun, when the navy men were wearing traditional uniforms. Riding boots. Tight pants. Belted tunics. Short-brimmed caps. All of it dark and muted, like black holes emerging from the bright white of the walls or the homey sand color of the carpet cushioning feet.

At least the elevator was functional. Stripped down to just a thing that carried people and cargo up and down the many decks. That was the first thing Amirin had seen since he boarded that reminded him that he was on a warship, rather than a pleasure palace.

He made a note to change the fitting out process of all future Septagons, either as adviser or emperor. Every day, some new thing like this bubbled up into his conscious mind, showing him just how bad things had gotten in the Sept Empire.

Just how decadent. Just how flawed.

How far they had strayed from the early, ascetic days.

He would ask Hadi later if all empires decayed the same way. That man had carried an encyclopedia in his head even before he learned of so many other cultures no one within a light-millennia had ever heard of.

They emerged in one of the command towers forward, centered more or less on the beam and midway to the great bowsprit of the vessel where the Axial Megacannon would emerge.

More troopers. More flunkies. A few bureaucrats who were probably useful.

The aspbad had been standing at attention, rather than sitting. Or had risen early.

A good sign. Respectful of his rank as one of them, rather than a visiting fop to be fawned over.

"Ambassador," the man greeted him warmly.

Two naval officers of high rank, relatively unknown to one another, but brothers in uniform.

Amirin realized he had been spending too much time with career civilians. Men that did not engender respect for anything except the power they had accumulated as first born sons of first born sons.

Men without merit.

"Aspbad," Amirin approached and shook the man's hand. "Thank you for hosting me and putting on such a proper display."

After all, Amirin represented the Shah, in off-hand ways, so they needed to respect that power. At the same time, Amirin Pasdar was a known quantity. Or had been, when he had been a warrior.

And human.

At least he had Rostami to draw a much more complete spectrum, with humans at one end and Amirin only a little ways removed. Unlike his Ishtan assistant.

"This way, sir," the aspbad gestured, before turning and

leading the way through a door into one of those officer conference rooms that had largely defined Amirin's career.

This one was lush, as was to be expected with a flagship of this type. Other than Founding Day celebrations, the Axial Megacannon had probably never been fired.

Hopefully, he wasn't about to alter that streak.

The naupati was from Clan Tabatabaei, a man that Amirin had only tangentially encountered over their last twenty-some years. Older enough to have already been commissioned when Amirin was in school, learning to be a warrior. Powerful enough politically to be given this position. Competent enough to not embarrass himself from this deck.

They shook hands as equals.

As polite fictions went, it was sufficient for today.

They sat quickly. Enjoyed a round of tea and finger snacks produced by a cook so good that Amirin considered stealing the man at some future date. He had learned much from the memories of Daniel Lémieux.

Listening privately to Hadi's stories describing his nemesis had given Amirin a much greater appreciation of the art of cooking. And how it tempered its own kind of warriors.

Or, as Daniel was apparently fond of describing them: *tattooed psychopaths with knives.*

Amirin even stretched out the pleasantries today beyond the usual with sailors, until the men around him were beginning to grow restless.

See? I can outlast you at anything I choose.

But he didn't say that out loud. Didn't even think it too much, but Hadi would be listening in anyway. It was the four of them at a small table, plus four more around the edges of the room, two aides and two troopers for whatever need emerged.

Perfectly mundane in every way.

"You do me great honor by visiting us, Ambassador," the Tabatabaei finally said. "Your reputation, of course, precedes you. How may we be of service to you and the Shah?"

Amirin smiled friendly enough. This man was a just another aristocrat. Certainly not a threat to Amirin's plans.

"You have heard the reports from Vorgash," Amirin nodded, turning to catch the aspbad's reaction.

That man was a commoner raised to great heights, and more likely to be an ally going forward. Or at least someone Amirin could use.

Both nodded.

"I have studied the two battles now where the alien vessel known as *MorningStar* appeared," he continued.

Both men leaned forward. They were warriors at their cores, and that ship had done the impossible.

Twice.

Singara would recover. *Vorgash* might be rebuilt only for the political reasons that nobody could admit how close it had actually come to destruction.

Amirin Pasdar would never trust that vessel in combat again, but it would fly the flag of Empire just fine. Safely behind the lines.

"Their tactics show that a single Septagon is at risk from the alien," Amirin continued. "They know to avoid the bow, and have heavier cannon elsewhere."

"What can be done?" Naupati Tabatabaei asked.

"In the short term, my recommendation to the Shah and others will be to have two Septagons in place guarding important systems," Amirin replied. "The alien can maneuver with one to avoid the Axial Megacannon, but not two. If nothing else, the two can pivot inwards and provide complete coverage."

"And the long term, sir?" the aspbad asked, already moving beyond the tactical.

But then, aspbads on Septagons were frequently commoners of uncommon talent, commanded by aristocrats of common skill.

That had been sufficient when nobody had the might to challenge the Sept.

Those days were over.

Amirin studied the man, giving Hadi a long moment to do the same with other senses and indicate if Amirin's reading of the aspbad's records were wrong.

Nothing, so Amirin proceeded.

"I intend to work with some engineers I have identified," he said. "The Septagon design has not changed appreciably in more than a century, and while technology has not advanced much, I believe that the ships can be upgraded significantly. Prior to this, there was no need, as our only foe was the Free Worlds."

"Are the Anndaing that dangerous?" the aspbad asked, plainly willing to press, while his superior officer watched with a political eye.

As if Hadi would allow either man to harbor any hostility when they left.

"They can be," Amirin allowed. "*MorningStar* is not an Anndaing vessel, but plainly an ally of some sort, as it has operated with those creatures in harrying *Singara*. It and the three smaller ones are also a new alien we have not identified."

The man licked his lips for a moment. Glanced over at Tabatabaei and got a slight nod before he proceeded.

Amirin assumed that in that instant, Hadi had rifled the man's mind, but hopefully nothing bad had passed that would need radical action.

"Will the war come to Earth or Rhages?" the aspbad asked. "What should we need to do doing to prepare against such a thing?"

"That is part of the reason I am here," Amirin allowed himself a smile. "*SwiftStar* has already shown itself to be the equal of any single Patrol, having destroyed several. The others are expected to be comparable. We don't currently have a larger vessel, something in-between a Patrol vessel and a Septagon, so I am going to work with some designers to see what can be done. In the interim, my suggestion will be to move another Septagon here and place it under your command, acting as a small squadron. At Rhages and as many as twenty other worlds, a similar pattern might be sufficient."

"For now," Naupati Tabatabaei spoke up. "What is the long-term goal you work towards, Ambassador?"

Amirin studied this man as well, but he had already read extensive intelligence files that the Shah had accumulated defensively on the naupati. Still, the Tabatabaei was safe and competent, or he would have never been given this command.

Rubicon, though. Amirin still had to ford that river and do so publicly.

"Renewal," a prospective *Emperor of Man* offered. "The Empire has grown stale and a little inward-looking over the last century or two. It was enough when all we needed to do was slowly grind away the Free Worlds, but now we have a true foe. Humanity needs to return to the roots that once set out to conquer all of human space."

The man before him was a cousin at some remove. All of the Seven Clans were cross-linked by marriage and blood. The two aspbads were merely servants in that context, but Hadi could reshape the minds of every man in earshot as needed.

Amirin hoped that this naupati might come to see things his way without modification, as there was no guarantee that such things would last.

"Conquest?" Tabatabaei asked.

"It is either that, or eventually dilution to the point that humanity is absorbed into some larger, galactic entity of aliens and vanishes without leaving any appreciable trace," Amirin replied. "We can be servants of the aliens, or their masters. I plan to propose to the Shah that he use some of his immense power to shake things up here on the homeworld, in the hopes that such a revival spreads naturally to the outworlds, as well as upwards to Rhages. We cannot go on as we have in the past, because there is someone out there now willing and able to fight back for the first time in over a century."

Both men paused, a little white around the edges and shallow of breath as Amirin watched them.

Naupati Tabatabaei was just like Amirin in education and upbringing. He would see things in those words that mere commoners would miss.

He did now. That much was obvious in his otherwise guarded eyes.

"It is safe to speak," Amirin said into the complete silence. "Everyone in this room can be trusted to keep their mouths shut, under imperial penalties."

Technically, only the Emperor himself could make such a threat, but again, commoners might not parse the legalisms that finely.

Tabatabaei barely suppressed a gasp.

"How radical a change might you counsel?" Tabatabaei asked, glancing up at the four men along the wall.

At least one of them would be a spy. That was the nature of things.

Spies were only dangerous if they were allowed to speak. Or retain their original loyalties.

Amirin had no doubts that Hadi had been diligently fixing those men.

"The current system has failed us," Amirin said in a quiet, scholarly tone. "Not badly, but bad enough. Men of talent in the Seven Clans are denied true power merely for being third sons."

Third. Like Naupati Tabatabaei. Or a second, like Amirin Pasdar.

The aspbad gasped now. So did one of the assistants along the wall.

Clarity was a two-edged sword, when such knowledge might get you killed as an accomplice.

"What if any noble's son could aspire?" Amirin asked Tabatabaei before turning to the aspbad. "Or any banker's son?"

Yes, Amirin and Hadi had done their research before making this trip.

Both men concealed it well, but Amirin was already watching their eyes for the signs of avarice. Amirin hid his smile as he watched it take root.

"You are suggesting something revolutionary," Tabatabaei offered weakly, his voice catching.

"Yes," Amirin nodded with a firm smile. "Without it, we are all doomed."

35

HADI WAS A BUREAUCRAT. That much was a given. Exceptional at what he did. Brilliant and capable even before he had been *modified*. He was still occasionally amazed when a man like Amirin Pasdar turned on his charisma like a light switch and aimed that spotlight at strangers.

Walking back to the elevator and descending to the lower decks for departure, Hadi was still a little astonished.

He had been locked in tight on all the minds around him, just touching each one lightly to gauge their emotional response to the conversation as it progressed. Ready to grab hold of anyone suddenly prepared to denounce them as traitors.

Nobody had.

They had all listened to the worlds calmly. What Amirin proposed might be revolutionary to the elders of the Seven Clans, but for commoners like him not much would change. Perhaps things would be run better if competent men were promoted instead of first sons.

Men like Hadi Rostami might find an easier path into strategic marriages, if women were suddenly calculating that all their children might rise to power, so they would wish to mate with competent men, rather than whoever might make a good alliance.

Nothing Amirin had proposed would even bear fruit for a century, were they to change things today.

But Hadi was measuring empires with eyes fifteen thousand years old. A pebble pushed off a ledge now might be an avalanche when it got to the bottom.

Certainly, if the rumors got out and triggered a wider discussion, then either he and Amirin would need to be executed quickly, or they would infect the ruling caste of the Sept Empire.

Thus had the Ishtan seen. And warned him.

What was it that compelled them to overthrow the current incarnation of the Empire and replace it with something else?

But he knew that answer.

Rhages. A drunkard sitting on a throne. A Court of sexual deviants raping alien women for no better reason than they could. A strict, legal structure of caste and race and species delineating your rights. Or lack thereof, if you weren't of the Seven Clans.

This was not the thing Hadi had been raised to believe in. Nor Amirin, even though he had been so much closer to the center of things his whole life.

In that, it was obvious that someone would come along and try to make it better, but you could not, within the structure. The structure would have to be toppled, so that something else could be attempted.

It was a story as old as human history.

The elevator delivered them to the flight deck level and Hadi followed Amirin to the transport that would return them to the surface.

Behind him, the minds that Hadi had been prepared to twist to suit Amirin's needs were untouched.

The two men were already revolutionaries, but until today had never understood what needed to change. Until Amirin Pasdar suggested that they could personally make a difference.

Frightening, really.

Those two men would infect others, like rats carrying plague. Amirin was merely suggesting aloud what they and so many others were thinking, but afraid to voice.

Could he really help topple the dynasty and place Amirin atop it instead?

It had been a theoretical exercise ere now. A compulsion on Amirin's part and Hadi would serve, because that was what he did.

They crossed empty decks and made their way into the bay itself, treated at every step with all the regal courtesy of a representative of the Shah. Hadi moved silently in Amirin's wake, as always, surrounded by a bubble of force and order from a system the two of them were working hard to undermine.

Hadi would serve. That was what he did.

Why?

Because Amirin Pasdar had chosen him as a young officer and brought him along. Understood that thing that made him a good savaran and cultivated it. Placed him in harm's way, except that Hadi had thrown himself on that sword to save Amirin from whatever would have become of the man had Amirin been the one to accompany the Ishtan to that Anndaing world and contained them after they'd died.

Even Hadi was not silly enough to suggest that Amirin Pasdar would have survived the experience. He would have died. The Sept Empire would have continued on for centuries, slowly growing inward with entropy until it finally failed.

The Anndaing would have found them eventually, but the current Sept would have ignored the sharks until it was too late to stop them from extending their trade network over the human worlds.

Nobody would remember the existence of Hadi Rostami in future histories of Amirin's empire, save that he had been there from the beginning, a loyal soldier.

Was he?

They boarded the shuttle and prepared for flight. Everyone was used to the aide being a quiet, introvertive type. None would question him remaining silent on de-orbit. Amirin was filled with great enthusiasm for what he had accomplished, and would ignore his aide, riding that emotional high for a time.

Hadi reached inward and wondered why he felt so empty.

He leaned back and studied the cosmos around him, looking for that one signal that pointed him at the only other being he knew who might understand him.

Daniel was hard to locate. In the past, that meant that he was in a jump somewhere, invisible until he arrived, and then detectable. The signal he saw was wrong.

The man was almost not there, as if he had folded in on himself. Faint, like a distant star, when he had been a solid flame in the darkness before this.

Had something happened to the chef?

On the one hand, that would be exceptional news, because nobody else in the galaxy could stop Hadi from putting a new emperor on a throne.

At the same time, he would be completely alone for the rest of his life. Or at least until these powers faded, but Hadi suspected that only his death now would bring such an outcome.

Worse, given the Ishtan themselves, had he absorbed enough of their essence that he might live forever?

Could he turn himself into a lesser form of Urid-Varg?

Everyone saw the conqueror, but Hadi had seen something else in Daniel's memories that had been stolen and then transmitted.

He had seen the scholar. All those strange, little ships on the four flight fins. Each still largely flight-capable, which must have required regular and ongoing maintenance. And that done by the creature himself, since he lived the most solitary existence possible. So much easier to just dump them into cold space, since Urid-Varg didn't need a ship besides that Turtle.

Or the assembly of strange land vehicles from a variety of technology levels. That was the mark of a collector. Even the halls of skulls, each of them a man Urid-Varg had ridden in his life to their death. Preserved until the moment that Amirin Pasdar and the Ishtan had caused them to be destroyed.

What would Hadi Rostami do if he was cursed with literal immortality?

Until this moment, contemplating Daniel actually being gone, Hadi had not understood what loneliness might be like. But his world had changed again.

The transport backed out of the bay and began the transition back to the naval station where they lived at present, but Hadi was only present physically.

He knew that Amirin Pasdar was arrogant enough to decide that he had to destroy the Sept Empire in order to save it. That Amirin could build a better empire. Replace the Sept with something greater.

Hadi Rostami wasn't sure he still believed.

36

———

A'ALHAKOTH SUPPOSED that at the end of the day, she was either the perfect person for this job, or as perfectly wrong as one could get.

Other Mbaysey women would be joyous at a fast raid deep into Sept Space, attacking a world with almost no economic or cultural relevance whatsoever, but they had a burning hatred of all things Sept to begin with, so they might let their emotions get the better of them.

As an alien, A'Alhakoth saw this from a different place. Ndidi wanted to stretch her cloak of fear over all human worlds. Not because *MorningStar* could actually do that much damage by itself, even with *NovaStar* and *BrightStar* as escorts today.

Frankly, there wasn't that much here worth destroying.

That was part of Ndidi's logic. In that, A'Alhakoth agreed completely.

Vorgash was a sector capital. The kind of place important enough to have a Septagon named after it, and frequently assigned there as well. A couple of billion humans called the system home, and had probably watched the battle overhead, at least metaphorically.

Krusskyo was a mining colony in the middle of nowhere, along a complicated series of seams where four human political sectors more or less came together. On a map, the lines looked like drunk rivers, but that was partly the result of where each colony had emerged from and who claimed precedence.

It was the kind of system the Mbaysey would have loved. No inhabited worlds, because a gas giant had come along at some point and ejected some planets forcibly while breaking up others before they could properly coalesce. The result was a navigational mess.

Asteroid belts always brought fear to the hearts of sailors, but most of the rocks travel at the same speed in the same direction, so they can be evaded. Big ones are usually so far apart that you can't ever see more than one at any given time.

But they provided ambitious miners a vast wealth of possibilities.

Almost everything was either nickel, iron, or carbon, but there were always interesting things floating around.

Some corporation somewhere had even taken it upon themselves to build a smelter out here, rather like a big version of ForgeStar. Miners would run around in their little ships, staking various claims and prospecting for things until they found something worth actually collecting.

MorningStar was overkill for this. Even *SwiftStar* might have been, except that they didn't have Daniel to exactly place targets into the minds of the pilot and gunners before they arrived, so the single Patrol moving around might have been enough to take on a Dueler with some expectation of success.

Two Duelers and a Battlemaster had just emerged from jump.

A'Alhakoth had images of a farmer with a hatchet in one hand, studying a yard filled with chickens. That smelter station and the various inhabited hubs around here had about as much chance to win a battle as the chickens did.

"Sword, what is your status?" Ndidi asked in a hard voice.

"Main station acquired," A'Alhakoth replied. "Eleven smaller stations identified. Seven of them appear to be long-term housing. One is governmental. Three are industrial facilities of various sizes. One hundred and seventy plus individual ships within immediate scan range, including three that are standard bulk cruisers designed to haul cargo. Presumably ore or refined metals. One Sept Patrol appears to be moving to engage."

Chickens. Hatchets.

"Kill the cargo ships first," Ndidi ordered. "I want economic damage. Have the escorts engage the Patrol. Under no circumstances are any beams to be fired at the governmental station or housing. The rest are fair game."

A'Alhakoth glanced at the Speaker, almost in shock.

"I want someone alive afterwards to provide a most detailed report of what happened today to the authorities at Rhages," Ndidi smiled.

That woman had grown frightening, but A'Alhakoth recognized the warrior fighting the next three battles today.

Fear me.

Flee me and you might live. Fight me and I will annihilate you.

Word would get out. No place was safe if they were attacking insignificant targets like Krusskyo. People would demand better protection.

When that wasn't forthcoming, they would start questioning the Sept Empire itself.

Hard questions. Uncomfortable questions.

Mean ones, designed to weaken the Empire itself.

That or they might flee to the Free Worlds instead.

"Gunners, I have laid your priorities," A'Alhakoth said to the eight women with axes in hand. "Pilot, take us down this path to engage the biggest targets. Escorts to destroy the defenders first and then go after stations as designated."

That had been Ndidi's plan. Blow up the transports hauling the megacargos. Then the expensive stations that made the system economically viable. Kill the Patrol.

Leave all the rest of the little guppies alone.

On the one hand, that would save innumerable lives, if enough ships were available to pick up emergency escape pods as people fled her wrath. But those people would have to go somewhere else, because Krusskyo wasn't going to be worth mining until everything got rebuilt.

Those people would return to their original homes, or more central locations, with stories of what had happened here today. And questions.

The first Arc-cannon reached out and slammed into the ass end of a freighter like a hammer. These ships were built durable to haul heavy cargoes, but this was an Ovanii Battlemaster.

Chickens.

Hatchets.

37

CRENCE HAD JUST GONE AHEAD and started calling his ship *GhostStar* at this point. There was no way in hell he'd make that long run all the way back to Ogrorspoxu for updated orders, so he had prepared a message packet for Wyll and Obaj. Someone would haul it the rest of the way home.

Until then, he was on his own, trying to make the best decision possible when they were all likely to be wrong. Wyll could only fire him once. Crence was pretty sure that he needed Kathra up on the front lines again, if the war was to be anything but generational in nature.

He'd read histories about the K'bari conflicts. Centuries of low-grade raids and tunashit back and forth until everyone mostly settled into routines and left the stupidities to the pirates.

How long would it last with the humans?

"Status?" he asked, pulling himself back out of the water in his head to look around his bridge.

Jine was almost asleep from the look of things, so they weren't that close. Dane was studying a screen.

"We'll drop in about six minutes," Dane said. "After that, it depends on where *SeekerStar* is and how many people we have to yell at for them to tell us."

Dane was only kidding. The locals knew *GhostStar*. And Crence Miray. If they pissed him off right now, he'd add that to the report going to Ogrorspoxu.

Careers had been broken for less, but Crence wasn't in a particularly grand mood.

Egregious, maybe. Given to rampant stupidity instead of asking someone twice when they should have answered him the first time.

Crence took a deep breath and reminded himself to be cool here. Nobody but him knew how dire things had gotten with Ndidi and Daniel. They'd be as flippant and sarcastic as always, and he didn't dare say otherwise because somebody would talk.

Silly sharks over there with nothing better to do but gossip.

They dropped. It felt like zwölf seconds or maybe zwölf years. Hard to gauge, but he was a bad judge right now.

"Find me *SeekerStar*," Crence growled, but Dane was already doing that, and snapping at the man's fin wouldn't make him go any faster.

"Got her," he said. "Close enough over Three, with both WaterStars and IronStar. Guessing the rest are off mining."

"Plot me a course to rendezvous," Crence glanced his hammer to Jine now, watched that shark snap to. "Dane, tell Kathra politely that we'd like to come aboard soonest with news. Nothing more. Nothing less. Deflect everything else to your paranoid, pain in the fin boss, whoever asks."

"Got it," Dane said.

He left it at that.

Nothing good was going to come of this meeting, at least as far as Crence could tell.

Wyll could only fire him. Kathra was going to have to decide not to shoot the messenger for the tidings he brought.

38

———

Kathra had read the message and arranged a play date for the girls elsewhere. She had added several other mothers with similar age toddlers to *SeekerStar*'s crew, just so Adaku had a whole cast of friends growing up. If it was anything like her own childhood, she would see the beginnings of a new comitatus take shape over the next decade.

Hopefully, her daughter wouldn't ever need such a thing.

But it got her and Erin alone into a room for Crence, without the little ones being fussy or distracting. Something about the message from Dane had left her on edge.

Partly, that was the lack of snarkiness. Dane was relaxed enough around her people now to make rude jokes and non-serious propositions.

There had been none of that. Just a cold, emotionless request for a meeting.

Not a good sign. She wondered what had happened with Ndidi.

Erin looked over, studying her face.

"Relax, Kathra," she commanded lightly. "If nothing else,

there is always the far edge of Anndaing Space to flee through."

Kathra nodded.

Always they had an escape. Without *SwiftStar*, she wasn't tied to any planet. The only thing she would still need would be a fab capable of making advanced electronics, and not even all that advanced. From there, no planet, no culture could hold her.

"Maybe we need to raid a Free Worlds factory at some point?" she asked. "Pure piracy?"

"They'd never see it coming," Erin grinned.

"Food for thought," Kathra nodded.

The door opened and Crence Miray entered, with his escorts staying outside, by request.

Kathra didn't figure the shark was any kind of personal threat, but she and Erin were both in uniform. That included a knife and a pistol.

She was still in the top five of her old comitatus for accuracy with a beam.

Crence sat heavily. Breathed just this side of a sigh. Stared at her face.

"No easy way to say this, and I've spent the flight here asking myself," he began. "Ndidi sent me. Something happened with Daniel."

Kathra tensed involuntarily. Her breath caught.

Erin leaned forward like she might strangle the shark with her bare hands.

Crence waved a hand defensively.

"They raided Vorgash, like you ordered," he continued. "Daniel did that thing he did to Septagon *Uwalu*. Apparently, they used too much mental energy or something, and nearly cooked his brain. He's unconscious and has been from that moment until the time I left to come here."

"But still alive?" Erin asked in a voice just this side of a snarl.

"Still alive," Crence confirmed. "I have all the medical reports, if you want them. Ndidi said that she went into his mind, and talked to a pair of his ghosts to get confirmation, but Daniel won't respond to her. She thinks he will if you two ask."

"Both of us?" Kathra asked, mildly shocked.

"Her words," Crence agreed.

Kathra turned to Erin and noted just how big the other woman's eyes had gotten. Erin had as complicated a relationship with Daniel as Kathra did. Erin had been the first woman of the Mbaysey that Daniel met, way back when.

Kathra had just been his Commander.

"Where is *MorningStar*?" Kathra asked the shark trademaster.

"At the forward base we've been using to scout Sept communications when I left," Crence replied. "But she was going off to hit some meaningless world deep in Sept Space as a black swan, since it would take me so long to round trip this. Ndidi's supposed to be there by the time we get back."

"Both of us," Erin stated, rather than asked.

"I'm only the messenger," Crence actually cringed. "Please don't shoot me. Remember, dumb male here."

At least he understood how the Mbaysey worked and didn't think that his gender automatically gave his words merit. That was one of the many reasons she liked and respected the shark so much.

If the Mbaysey added Anndaing to the tribe, she'd been planning to make sure he made contributions to the sperm bank. His own alternate immortality, as it were.

Kathra turned to Erin and considered her options.

Again, she had promised the old women that she would

outlive them all, even before little Adaku gave her alternatives. Normally, she would leave Erin in charge, but if Ndidi wanted both of them, that meant that the two children would need to remain here in the custody of aunties. Iruoma and Areen, most likely.

Maybe she needed to end the comitatus and have them all get pregnant together so that Adaku had her own clique of troublemakers, if it became necessary later on. It wasn't like *SeekerStar* was a combat ship in the old sense anymore.

"Both of us," Erin grimaced.

"I was thinking Iruoma and Areen," Kathra replied.

"Feeling morbid?" Erin asked.

Kathra shrugged, willing to have this discussion in front of Crence because the implications of any decision would weigh heavily on the Anndaing. On his bosses. Best they got it from the shark's mouth directly.

"This feels bigger than just the surface," Kathra said.

"How so?"

Erin had always been her wingsister, even when they were eleven and being troublesome. She would play devil's advocate for no better reason than she knew how far to push and when to finally shut up.

"We have to leave Adaku and Kwento here," Kathra said. "And go forward. I would like to think that we're there for a day and do whatever Ndidi and Daniel need, but I fear that it won't be enough. We might have to remain that far forward. That far separated from the Stars."

"Leave them all here, including *SeekerStar?*" Erin asked.

"We have *GhostStar,*" Kathra looked to Crence, who nodded immediately. "Ndidi is absolutely the woman I want in charge, but things might have gone beyond her. Maybe the whole war is poised to reach beyond what a simple chef with a Battlemaster is equipped to handle."

"Two chefs," Erin corrected her. "The most dangerous creatures in the universe. After grandmas."

"After grandmas," Kathra agreed. She turned to Crence. "What's your turnaround time?"

"I pulled rank," he said simply, indicating just how serious the Anndaing trademaster took the situation. "They are loading me priority, because I needed to head back to Ndidi as soon as physically possible, whatever your decision was."

Kathra nodded. On the surface, it was a decision, but she could already feel the star tides pulling her sideways. Better to float atop them than try to resist.

"How many ships do you have at that forward base?" she asked bluntly. "Or could you pick up here and along the path?"

"How stupid do I need to get?" he countered. "How likely is Wyll to have me fired and prosecuted?"

"Fifty/fifty," Kathra guessed the odds. "If it works, you'll be covered in glory and groupies. If it fails, you might be dead and beyond his reach."

"You haven't seen Ndidi," Crence muttered before he slammed his mouth shut and flexed his hammers in embarrassment.

He blinked. Kathra waited.

"It was like dealing with a necromancer, Kathra," he finally said. "Scary. Daniel's not there, so she just went and raised his other ghosts to talk to instead. Like some ancient fairy tale. And did it more than once. Humans are just scary."

"This is Ndidi, Crence," Erin spoke up before Kathra could. "We already knew that. You should have learned."

Kathra appreciated the shudder that went all the way through the shark. The trademaster was a hard-ass, but

Kathra had understood the sorts of places Ndidi Zikora could go if she thought it was necessary.

That was why she Spoke for *MorningStar*, and nobody else. She spoke for Kathra and the entire Mbaysey as well.

And she needed help. Kathra was a little surprised and quite pleased that Ndidi was mature enough to understand something might be beyond her and to bring in the experts.

Kathra wondered if Ndidi should start her own clan one of these days soon. Maybe after the war was over, or at least receded some. Build out a new ClanStar and show the old women how it was done. There would be no shortage of volunteers, and they could always hit a few Free Worlds ports for more humans if they needed to, but what would an alien clan look like, if the sperm banks ran deep enough?

Kathra ran through all that in an instant.

"You get packed for flight," she ordered the shark. "Ask the locals if you can borrow a few gunships for a forward raid under my authority, rather than yours, in case Wyll or Obaj want to object later. We'll make arrangements here and join you as soon as we knock a few heads together."

Crence nodded.

"Do you think it will work?" he asked quietly.

"We are Mbaysey, Crence," she snapped. "So is Daniel. You'll get your chance to see what that means soon enough."

He shuddered again.

Kathra smiled.

39

───────

AMIRIN HAD BEEN EXPECTING a midnight knock at some point. Secret police come to arrest him for the things he had been speaking in quiet salons. Hadi would deflect as many as he could, but an unknown recording could be played back later, when nobody was there to twist the minds hearing treason.

It was late in the day for Persia. The Shah kept far different personal hours from the Court at Rhages. He rose before the sun each morning and prepared for first prayers with an austere focus. As a result, working breakfasts in the palace were common among the senior bureaucrats.

Such as Amirin had become over the last several months.

The Shah also retired at dark, known to spend time with his wife in domestic life before reading and going to sleep at a reasonable hour. Again, the Court had followed.

On Rhages, the debaucherous orgies usually only started after the sundown call to prayers had finished. Many of those men heard the morning call before getting around to sleeping.

As if hiding such things under the cloak of night made them somehow more forgivable.

Amirin had retired to his personal chambers at the same time the Shah had, having finished a meeting filled with technical details and naval proposals.

Sept bureaucracy moved with slow deliberation. That had kept the Empire from falling under fools, but it also prevented the sorts of radical innovations and revolutions like Amirin proposed today.

He had still been expecting a knock at some point.

Amirin, like the Shah, led what might appear to be a monastic existence to outsiders.

Sparse chambers reminiscent of a Septagon, where space was still compact, even for a commanding naupati. Two bookcases filled with actual tomes he had accumulated and kept, the rest being on a tablet reader. A narrow bed some might mistake for nails or stone, depending on their disposition. A trunk for clothes, with most of his old uniforms stored back at a family palace.

But for wood walls instead of raw stone around him, he might have emerged from the era before space flight.

Amirin rose to the sound, powering off his reader and placing it on a bookshelf for now. He checked his robes before approaching the door.

If one is to be arrested, at least one should look professional.

He opened the door to his suite and peered at the single messenger waiting. Unconsciously, or perhaps consciously, he had been expecting men with guns in their eyes.

"Yes?" Amirin looked at the man.

"The Shah inquires as to your availability for a brief, private meeting to discuss something while it was still fresh in his mind," the young man said in a singsong voice carefully replicating the message without any emotions behind it.

Inquires? The Shah was within his power to command any man on Earth right now. And they both knew it.

Private suggested that Hadi would also not be welcome.

Amirin knew a moment of fear so pure it was like ice stabbing his belly. Had he grown so reliant on his Ishtan-made-human?

Was this a polite way to separate them, that Amirin could be arrested without being able to call upon the creature able to defeat all others?

Was he doomed?

Of course he was, Amirin realized after a moment. The only question now was what form the doom took. Robes of silk or a coarse rope about his neck?

He would still die on his feet.

"Please, precede me," Amirin said after no appreciable gap.

Nothing in his chamber was incriminating. Everything existed in his head, or that of Hadi. And nothing would be needed otherwise, else the Shah would have done this at a more reasonable hour.

Such as, when he was supposed to be awake.

Amirin wondered what other things one might hide under the cloak of night, if a man maintained a sober reputation for keeping hours like a farmer, rather than a drunkard.

Had he underestimated the man?

Through the halls and corridors to a section of the palace Amirin did not visit all that often, until they arrived at a non-descript door with nothing marking it but a number.

The messenger knocked politely and waited.

Amirin heard the lock open and the door move perhaps a hand span inward.

"Please enter, sir," the messenger said, bowing and withdrawing silently.

Literally, the man turned and walked away without another word or even a glance.

Amirin wondered what trap lay beyond.

What doom awaited?

Death, but how soon? How embarrassing?

He put a hand on the door and pressed it inward, willing to walk to his own execution with his head up proudly.

The room was someone's private quarters. A small living space with chairs, a couch, and an entertainment unit on one wall. Amirin could see a compact kitchen and other doors beyond, but the man seated on the couch drew his eye.

And his breath.

"Close the door," the very Shah of Earth said with quiet command.

Amirin did as he was bade, standing in the entryway still cold and numb with surprise.

The most powerful man on Earth appeared to live in a space not much larger or more innate than Amirin did.

"Come," the man gestured to one of the stuffed chairs. "Sit with me. The tea will be ready shortly."

Amirin finally processed a coffee table with a pot and two mugs before the man.

The Shah smiled.

Death probably knew that smile, but had been defeated by the man more than once.

Amirin stumbled over on legs that felt like bloodied stumps, almost collapsing into the chair before he dared draw a breath.

The Shah smiled even wider.

It was a different smile. Colder, and yet warmer. Knowing. Dangerous.

"Yes," he said with a grin that looked like it concealed a blade. "You understand."

Amirin nodded weakly, still trying to find his center.

No battle he had ever fought had left him so off-kilter.

"I would like to discuss the future of the empire with you, Amirin Pasdar," the Shah said. "You will treat me tonight as if I was merely Umek Sardari, rather than Shah."

Amirin gulped. Nodded with more energy. Found that ball of fire that had caused him to reach for an imperial crown.

Umek Sardari, Shah of Earth, would not be treating him as an equal unless the man already presumed such a thing.

"Sir," Amirin finally managed. "What do you not already know that you would like to discover?"

Crown or grave. He had slipped up somewhere, but Amirin wasn't sure where. Probably a device nobody else knew about, in the hands of someone who was still themselves because nobody had thought to fix them.

Umek studied him closely. Amirin returned the favor.

The man was exceptionally old. Eighty and some number. Rail thin like the ancient desert mystics. Cold, sober, and rational.

"You are a threat to the very empire itself, Amirin Pasdar," Umek announced in a quiet voice.

He knows.

Amirin bowed his head to the man.

"Only to the thing it has become," Amirin countered. "That thing that has infected Rhages and turned it away from the dreams of our forebears."

"You have whispered uncomfortable treasons into welcoming ears," Umek continued.

Treasons. Not a word any politician used lightly, as many things might be open to *interpretation.*

Amirin held his peace. Umek Sardari was forty years

older than he was. In a physical contest, Amirin could kill the man quickly. And they both knew it.

Allah Himself knew how many secret police might lurk around them, but Amirin had the distinct impression that the only person within earshot right now was Umek's wife, presumably asleep or back in their sleeping chambers waiting.

That was the measure of a man like Umek Sardari.

This was what courage looked like. Amirin had seen it in others so infrequently that he sometimes forgotten its appearance.

"I have asked questions that should have been asked before me," Amirin offered.

It was not a defense against the charge of treason, but perhaps a deflection of an admission.

"You challenge the very basis of the Sept," Umek accused.

Amirin felt his chin come up before he could stop it.

Pride, but he was a proud man.

"The Seven Clans should remain," he rasped, trying not to shout. "But there are many competent men who did not have the luck and courtesy to be born first."

"Like yourself?" Umek asked.

Amirin could not tell if the man held deadly mirth or amused malice in his tones.

It would take a finely-sharpened blade to separate the two.

"Like most," Amirin said simply. "A man with seven sons has one heir, one spare, and five hungry mouths that might find solace in the conquest of alien worlds. Or the debaucheries of their wealthier brothers."

"And you would challenge that?" Umek asked bluntly.

"I would ask you, a man whom I greatly respect and admire, what he thinks of his cousin who warms a throne on

Rhages?" Amirin countered, letting a little of his emotion show now.

Controlled rage, with control being the key.

It was acceptable to be angry, as long as one could use that like a knife and not a bomb. Such things had seen Amirin Pasdar into this room, this night.

Discussing treason with this man.

Umek's eyes also held a rage, but a first son never faces that particular disappointment. He will gain power from merely being alive when his father dies.

Second sons must carve out their place.

Sharp knives become critically important tools.

Umek smiled a much warmer acceptance and leaned back into the couch so suddenly that Amirin almost fell over.

"He drinks," Umek said in a tone that somehow conveyed lightness and warmth to Amirin while referring to something one might find on the underside of your shoe. "He fornicates with as many alien creatures as he can summon to his palace. One suspects, but cannot prove, that not all of them are female, but those are only rumors, as such a truth might finally be the man's undoing."

"They are all like that," Amirin stated. "Anusiya, Andarzbad, or the rest. You have just described most of the male population of the capital world of humanity."

"And that offends you," Umek observed.

It wasn't a question.

"More than might be acceptable to admit," Amirin acknowledged, at least to this man. "They have grown dependent on their debaucheries to even get out of bed in the morning. As a result, the Sept Empire has drifted for several generations. Possibly centuries."

He rose to pace now, unable to remain seated. Amirin missed that long Causeway of a Command Node on one of his Septagons, as a place to meditate in motion.

This chamber was not a quarter as long.

Umek Sardari watched, silent but not impassive.

"We conquer Free Worlds systems because they cannot stop us," Amirin continued. "Not because they mean anything to us. It has become like the ancient Nihon art of Kabuki. But we do the pantomime without any emotion. The Free Worlds resist, because they have no other option."

Amirin paused at a wall and rotated to face the man.

"We have already fallen," he pronounced in an angry whisper. "But the corpse has not yet grown cold."

He stood there, waiting for the man to shoot him. Or something.

Umek chuckled instead.

Amirin didn't think he had ever heard a more disarming sound in his life. He deflated like a punctured balloon.

"Sit," Umek gestured him close. "Let me share a story with you."

Amirin found himself stumbling into that chair for a second time, unsure how this man had so defeated him.

Umek Sardari, Shah of Earth, began to pour tea. For both of them. Himself.

"Once upon a time, it was not thus," Umek began in a storyteller's voice as he worked. "Men rose on merit, rather than birth."

Amirin nodded. But that was centuries ago, when the Sept were young.

"In time, it changed, because we stopped losing so many sons to wars and revolutions," Umek continued. "As you said: an heir, and spare, and five hungry mouths. In the early days seven births might only yield two old men."

Such had Amirin remembered from early histories. Hadi had confirmed it with the encyclopedia in his head.

"And yes, we have grown stale, Amirin Pasdar," Umek nodded. "You have done a masterful job of concealing yourself from the many men whom you threaten, but at no point have we detected any threat to me."

Amirin quailed, ever so slightly, at the word *we*.

Both men understood that the secret polices had been watching. Not all of them had been twisted.

"I mean no threat to you, Umek," Amirin offered, deciding to resort to simple honesty with the man most likely to have him executed right now. "You are one of the few men in the entire Empire that I respect for what you have done with your life, rather than the power you inherited from your birth. You are the thing I wish more men emulated."

Umek nodded and grasped a mug, but Amirin had the impression that those words, heartfelt as they were, were accepted as a truth.

"But you offer revolution," Umek said. "Treasonous words whispered, but never confirmed by any man questioned. You have built yourself a following of amazing loyalty, but they are perhaps even more loyal to that ideal you espouse than the man who embodies it."

Amirin nodded, mouth dry. He reached for a mug and let the scalding heat burn his tongue. Anything, to keep himself focused.

"There was always a risk that I would fail," Amirin offered after a moment, when he realized that Umek was waiting. "But the Empire requires rejuvenation if it is to mean anything. Second sons of talent should have better options than strategic marriages and horse farms. Commoners should be seen as a resource to be brought into the Seven Clans by marriage, rather than limited as a result of their own birth."

"And if you were executed for your treason, Amirin Pasdar?"

"Then I have tried to make the Empire better," Amirin answered. "Given my entire life to the Sept Empire and tried to make it a healthier place. A more powerful realm. A success. If it also requires my death, then that was the price I acknowledged when I opened my mouth and asked."

Umek studied him for several long moments.

Perhaps he would call for the secret police now. Maybe it was all being recorded for his eventual execution on Rhages.

Or Umek Sardari was going to just shoot him right now.

But Amirin had tried.

Umek chuckled. Amirin flinched in spite of himself.

"Oh, it's much worse than you imagine, Amirin," the Shah of Earth pronounced, staring intently at him. "I'm going to help you."

40

———

Hadi liked to rise early. Resetting his personal clock to Court time on Earth had been easy enough, and it allowed him to get up well before most people and meditate on what it meant to be human.

What it had meant, when he had been one.

There was no doubt in his mind these days that he was Ishtan on two legs. When shaving in the morning, he was occasionally surprised not to find pink fur growing in.

The palace had a flavor. He couldn't describe it using any other sense, because the humans around him lacked the necessary apparatus to understand what he saw.

What he tasted.

It was something like cookies baking and just pulled from the stove, but in his mind, rather than his nose.

Rhages had frequently tasted of anger and despair, both human and alien. Earth, especially the area around him, brimmed with purpose.

But something had changed. The flavor had moved from where it had been two days ago.

Two days?

Yes, something had changed yesterday. The implications were still moving outward like the waves a rock generated in a still pond, but the damage had been done.

Hadi reached out to locate the guards outside his suite. He was not a prisoner, but a valued guest. That had not changed. Those men were still in awe of him, in a good way.

But that was mostly because they didn't know the truth. Either of them would have shot him in an instant had they learned.

And he did not have the power to turn a pistol's beam like Daniel could. Hadi lacked the suit that Urid-Varg had created to contain and channel his powers in useful ways. At best, he might stop a knife by stopping the mind controlling it, if he had enough warning.

Thus were the humans on this planet safe. They could always shoot him.

The Ishtan part of his soul raged at the thought of dying before Daniel did, afraid of whatever evils that being might unleash on a defenseless galaxy. But the remaining human element, that might be all there was left of the original Hadi Rostami, was tired.

He had pushed and twisted so many minds around him that even Hadi could only tell when he looked at someone and saw the marks already in place. The Court at Tehran was safe. The Shah appeared to be an ally.

Hadi turned his mind that way, looking for the unique signature of their dread overlord. His jaw dropped open when he did.

That was the change in flavor.

The man smelled of revolution.

He knows.

Hadi had no idea how the man had pierced all their obfuscations and shadows, but he had.

A thought was sent in the direction of Amirin, but his light remained unchanged.

No, he also glowed with a new fervor.

The two must have met last night and worked out treason. Hadi was not offended to be excluded. Many of the Seven Clans maintained such a superiority about them. A classism that kept the lower ranks of society at bay, regardless of ability.

That, itself, almost defined the Sept Empire.

But treason was in the air. Far more so than yesterday.

Hadi checked his clock and noted that he had perhaps an hour before morning prayers would be called. He rose from his meditation and headed to shower.

Refreshed, he wore the best robes he had acquired, expecting someone to summon him for some terrible rendezvous where such seditions were to be discussed openly. Coffee brought his mind to full wakefulness and a simple flatbread roll with butter and jam served to prepare him for the trials of the day.

The knock was almost perfectly predictable, two minutes after morning prayers had completed.

Hadi no longer even bothered with the forms. Allah might be All Merciful, but he had chosen a badly-flawed vessel to use. And infected it with alienness so great that Hadi was surprised that humans could not sense it when he found himself so distant.

He opened the door to a messenger, a young man from a good family hoping to impress the right authorities that he might find a better job than what was normally a sixth son's lot in life.

Hadi emptied the man's head and confirmed the shallow contents, before assembling them into a new pattern. Still the same man, but less satisfied to be given whatever crumbs might be allowed him.

He had done it to so many men by now that he could almost print instructions, were there anybody else capable of doing such a thing.

Well, Daniel could, but the chef would carve him with a long knife for what circumstances had demanded of Hadi Rostami.

"His Excellence summons you to a meeting," the messenger said, already less anxious than he had been when he knocked.

Thus, a small revolution gained another adherent.

Hadi nodded and stepped from his chambers, indicating to his two bodyguards that they should accompany him.

The destination was a meeting chamber where Amirin awaited, along with several others. Hadi recognized many of the faces, but these were not the men that were normally present in such meetings.

With the exception of the man who commanded Earth's defensive squadrons. That gentleman had already been a respectful adversary of Amirin's when the Shah decided to shower glory on a Pasdar warrior. Amirin's suggestions to improve the fleet had won him over as a friend. Doubly so when it became obvious that Amirin had no interest in displacing the man in local command.

The humans all had petty souls, but the Sept was what it was.

The others here, rather than being top assistants to senior officials were instead the officials themselves. Men Hadi had not been close enough to modify before now.

He withheld his power now, only because he wanted to see who else had decided to assist Amirin.

They waited with fresh, hot tea for a few minutes, making small talk at the high end of the table, while Hadi and several key aides nodded commiseratingly at the low end.

The Shah entered with a jaunty stride and everyone rose.

He fixed them all with a stern, patriarchal gaze as he made his way to the head of the table and sat.

"Join me," he ordered, and everyone returned to their chairs.

Hadi didn't have to do much more than glance at the Shah to know the truth. He would get the full story later, so he concentrated on everyone else, taking their temperature before the news came out and someone decided to inform the authorities on Rhages of whatever plot was about to unfold.

There was always one. Hadi had spent too much time in other men's minds to have any hope that everyone in here was what they appeared to be. Someone would present a loyal front, while calculating odds in the back of his mind.

No few of them had not been men Hadi considered worth keeping, so accidents had occurred. Suicides by drug, knife, or motor vehicle, where they were removed from the gaming table in hopes that someone less disgusting replaced them.

It was a measure of how rotten and corrupt the system had gotten that Hadi felt he was fighting a losing battle against that game where rodents kept popping out of different holes for you to hammer.

The Shah of Earth drew a heavy breath, pulling all eyes and minds to him, Hadi included. Such was the man's charisma and force of character.

"Interesting questions have been asked," he said simply, gazing around the room but not focusing on Amirin. "They rise from various quarters, but share one important detail in common. Namely, why is it that only Vuzurgan, the First Born Sons, can inherit the pinnacles of power and prestige? Why are second sons shunted off to the military or diplomatic service, or even business?"

Hadi watched the room split along expected lines. Most of the men in here were not first-born. Would not ever sit on any throne, unless they or the fates did something to alter inheritance lines.

Warriors and diplomats, like most of the second or fifth sons present.

Still, they stirred uncomfortably.

"Yes, I have heard the whispers," the Shah confirmed, eyes narrowing like a schoolmaster with misbehaving children. "You have as well. In many places, other places, such things might be considered tantamount to treason."

Hadi joined the many other gasps around the table, to hear such things not just spoken openly, but by this man.

The one who could simply order them all put to death.

But he was not setting this room up for execution. Far from it, the old man was asking an honest question.

Living a pure life, unlike so many of his cousins.

But this was why Amirin had asked Hadi to make sure they ended up on Earth, rather than Rhages. The air was cleaner here. As was the living.

"But what is treason, gentlemen?" the Shah of Earth himself asked rhetorically. He paused and shook his head, again, the adult surrounded by precocious children. "The Seven Clans control the Empire. Do not doubt that. We will not allow that authority to slip. But within that, it is not treason to ask why mere birth order entitles a lesser man to rise above his more capable brother. If the Empire itself is to be strong, are we not best served by placing each man where he can make the best contribution to society?"

Heads nodded now. Hadi watched minds like a raptor spying for movement in the grass below. The first stirrings of discomfort were obvious, but none had turned to betrayal.

Not yet, anyway.

"There is no law stating that the Vuzurgan, the First-

Born, must be preeminent," the Shah continued. "I have studied the books at length for just such a thing, once the rumors were known. It is not there."

The whole room might have just suffered an earthquake, but it was only in the minds Hadi was watching. Third and fourth sons suddenly reminded that culture, mere tradition, held them at bay, rather than laws.

"So these might be difficult questions to ask," the Prophet of Doom spoke from his altar at the high end of the table. "But the answers should trouble you, as they trouble all good men. Why are lesser, first-born men elevated in spite of whatever incompetence would disqualify a second son?"

It helped that the Shah of Earth was not a position normally passed by primogeniture. Technically, the Emperor on Rhages was the legal Shah of Earth, but in moving the Court off of the homeworld, that worthy—when he was worthy—was forced to rely on another man to fill the role. When the current inhabitant died, another would be selected to take his place.

Assuming that words of treason and revolution did not make it to Rhages quickly enough that the current Keyaksar moved to unseat this man.

A figure on the left promised to be the first to tattle. Hadi reached out with his mind and took the fool.

Accountant. A man who had dedicated his life to rules and numbers. Yes, it made sense that upsetting the old ways would unsettle such a creature. He was almost exactly the opposite of the naval officers around him in every way, but they lived with life and death decisions routinely. They sent men off to die.

Accountants merely made sure that the wheels of commerce and government continued to turn.

This one had already decided to betray the Shah.

Amazing, how quickly some men hide their souls in fear of change.

A mental hand reached in and made adjustments between breaths. Loyalty to the Emperor, the current emperor, dialed down significantly, without altering the man's feelings about the Empire itself.

Feelings of indignation, previously suppressed ruthlessly, were given greater sway, allowing the man to ask those hard questions and come to some other answer than the secret police. Hadi would still watch him, in case the core came to be too strong to hold back.

Then it might be time for the man to be caught in such an incriminating situation that the authorities just destroyed him. Two men found in bed together would be desperately out of character, but within Hadi's power.

After all, destroying an empire often required breaking any number of men and eggs along the way.

The accountant would merely be the first of this group to be sanctioned. Not the first Hadi had destroyed.

"Thus I say to you, gentlemen," the Shah looked around and smiled at everyone. "How can we make the Sept Empire a stronger place than we found it? How can we return it to that epoch of glory that seems to have faded from us in this generation? Speak with your peers and impress upon them the importance of thinking about our empire, rather than merely our own pleasures. Ambassador Pasdar, I will leave this meeting in your hands. Thank you for bringing these rumors to my attention, and understand that I will be giving them much thought going forward. But I leave it to all of you to find me answers that do not merely rely on the old ways of doing things."

The man rose on spry feet, nodded with a wide smile on his terrible face, and departed, taking half the bodyguards and aides around the walls with him as he did.

Hadi looked around, but the men besides the accountant were still in shock at this turn of events.

The Shah of Earth had just sanctioned treason and revolution in a way that might not even be considered such, except by a man on Rhages and his friends who stood to lose from any such changes as Amirin Pasdar might unleash.

Hadi saw a path to empire suddenly opening up before them.

What could he do to Daniel with the entirety of the Sept behind him?

41

Ndidi was up on the bridge of *MorningStar* when the big warship dropped out of jump at the station she had taken to calling home. For now. At least until it came time to build a base even farther forward, so she could go after other targets, deeper in Sept Space.

Like say, Earth. Or Rhages.

Both of those would be suicide right now, even for an Ovanii Battlemaster and three Duelers. She would have to gather up every Gun-6 and Gun-12 she could lay hands on to even consider it.

And that would be a mess, since eventually the Sept were going to decide that they needed two Septagons in close sailing formation to stop *MorningStar*. It would be like rats attacking a bear.

Maybe she would need the rest of the Battlemasters and Assailants from the Anndaing reserves. The entire Anndaing Armada.

It still might come to it.

"Signals, I have more ships in orbit than usual," Acqueir called in a voice tinged with concern.

MorningStar was still far enough away to escape, but if the Sept had gotten here, she would have to sail lean and careful to get to another base or world where she could take on supplies.

"All appear friendly," her Anic sensors officer reported a few moments later.

A'Alhakoth, sitting close by, had ordered all the guns unlocked anyway. A little light on Ndidi's board had gone green in the gap.

Ndidi was concerned, but only because this scenario suggested a significant change in strategic planning on the part of the Merchants Bank.

Like say, Earth. Or Rhages.

Did she really want to go down that path?

"Hail the station and ask for guidance, but only vaguely," Ndidi decided. "Make sure everyone over there minds their manners and we'll mind ours. This is still an Anndaing warship. We're just borrowing it. They might have decided they wanted it back. Pilot, time to rendezvous?"

"On current trajectory, we'll be close enough to talk in real time in under an hour, Speaker," Nwanyiudo answered instantly. "Should we push?"

"Wait until they respond," Ndidi turned to Spectre Twenty-Two and nodded. "If it looks good, go ahead and push, assuming we can refuel from their stores for what we burn now."

Normally, Ndidi would retreat to her office at this point to do paperwork. Hirly would have charge of things, or one of the other women. Ndidi had an exceptional team around her, enough so that she could trust any of them to make a good decision.

She wanted time to think, but didn't want to do it in her office. Too much like a kitchen in the middle of the night, when the stoves have been shut down and everyone and everything put to sleep.

A time when smart chefs were deeply asleep, preparing for the morning prep crew to come in and start everything over again.

As Executive Chef of *MorningStar*'s crew, Ndidi decided to sit here.

"Hirly, you can take off for an hour or two," she said to her Shield. "Acqueir, you're in command, but understand that I'm going to sit here and ignore everyone. A'Alhakoth, you and yours can cycle watch as well, but keep someone ready to unleash hell if something has gone wrong."

Heads nodded. Hirly rose and exited, probably to catch a quick nap, as they had arrived in the middle of the woman's normal sleep period. Others moved around and the bridge calmed down as Nwanyiudo took them closer.

Time passed and Ndidi watched her boards, thinking about the excess number of Anndaing warships in close proximity, and what that implied.

"I have a message from *GhostStar*, requesting clearance to send a transport over with messages," Acqueir said.

"*GhostStar*?"

"Affirmative," Acqueir looked back and nodded. "Just text. Just that much."

"But it tells us far more than it might tell anybody else listening," Ndidi agreed. "Nwanyiudo, park us farther out than normal when we get there, and instruct *GhostStar* to send their transport ahead to our coordinates. Then tell the station to prepare for resupply shortly. No doubt they are poised, but we'll move over to them if this is what I think it is."

Ndidi unbuckled and rose. That was what had kept her here.

Kathra had come. And brought help. Lots of help.

A frightening number of assistants, all with hammers and probably fins upright with righteous indignation, just waiting for *MorningStar* to return.

"Update Hirly when she wakes up, and tell the kitchen and quartermaster to prepare for guests," Ndidi scowled. "I'm going to go get coffee and a beignet and then down to the conference room where someone will deliver all the guests. Set up watch cycles so all the main players can be in the meeting, including Tanuss."

She noted the responses and headed aft.

Crence had come through. He wouldn't identify his ship as *GhostStar* unless Kathra was aboard otherwise. Erin as well.

That meant that she had a superior officer again. That it wasn't just Ndidi Zikora taking on the entire galaxy, even with a few of her friends.

She stopped by medical to check, but Daniel had not stirred. Not even moved except where they had plugged various machines and cords in to keep him hydrated, fed, and exercised regularly, lest his muscles turn to goo from so long in bed.

Ndidi leaned down and kissed her brother on the forehead, but nothing was getting through and she didn't feel like talking to the others right now.

Kathra would be here shortly. And Erin. Either they would be able to break Daniel out of wherever he had gone, or the Mbaysey needed to make significant reevaluations about their future.

Did they still need to destroy Hadi Rostami, if it might be enough to sail into the darkness and never look back?

But that was Kathra's decision.

Ndidi would happily keep killing Sept stations, Sept ships, and Sept worlds until they made her stop.

If they could.

42

Kathra was just a passenger here. Not even the Commander, as this was an Anndaing vessel and not Mbaysey. Crence's crew, men and women Kathra knew well, but answering to the trademaster.

She and Erin were just messengers. It was liberating, in a way, not to have any responsibilities.

Not that she believed any of it for an instant.

Much larger things rode on this voyage. Had Daniel been destroyed? Had he accidentally killed himself?

Kathra doubted that the man would commit suicide. Those two Sept warriors still threatened everything, and only Daniel could stop them.

If he could.

If he couldn't, then it would be up to Kathra to do it.

If anyone could.

Which was why Ndidi had needed her, reading between the lines of her message.

Could anyone?

The transport docked. Her, Erin, Crence, and Dane. Jine

was in charge on the bridge of *GhostStar*. Others didn't know enough to be included in a council of war like this.

Mbaysey, and her allies, against the Sept.

Kathra rose, checking her pistol and knife automatically, just as Erin did. The Anndaing were unarmed, but they were just visitors here. This was an Ovanii vessel, commanded by the only Ovanii warrior alive, at least far as Kathra was concerned.

Ndidi had transcended them all and become something only Daniel still understood.

And hopefully Kathra.

She led them out the hatch and onto the compact flight deck of *MorningStar*. Followed the escorts to the main conference room. Entered and noted the way these women had changed since she had sent them after Vorgash.

Ndidi rose from her seat on the side of the table, rather than the end. Kathra moved to sit next to her, rather than at the end, gesturing Erin there.

She wanted to be close to Ndidi.

The woman had aged, but not in a bad way. Finally overcome her youth and whatever immaturity she might have once had.

It was the difference between an ingot of steel and a sword that had been hammered out by a master, folded however many times and purified.

Kathra smiled at her and noted the way it took a moment for the woman to smile back, like it was an alien emotion.

Around them, A'Alhakoth, Hirly, Acqueir, Tanuss, and Nwanyiudo.

All women, with Crence and Dane the outsiders here solely to witness for Wyll and the Board of Directors. Daniel would be the only male welcome otherwise, but he wasn't here.

Hopefully, that wasn't her fault. She had ordered it. He had always submitted to her, whatever demands Kathra had made.

Had this one been the death of him?

Kathra settled and watched all the women relax.

"You brought friends," Ndidi began carefully.

Something seemed to lighten her voice, like the woman had been carrying the weight of *MorningStar* on her shoulders.

Kathra nodded.

"I suspected that things might have changed on the front lines," Kathra acknowledged.

"Vorgash will never forget us," Ndidi noted with a hint of a smile. "Nor will Krusskyo and a few others."

The other women around them smiled, but Kathra could tell how forced it was on their faces. Ndidi made them nervous.

Ascended Ovanii Warrior.

"As you were ordered to do," she said, watching that tidbit of information impact the women who might have thought that Ndidi was acting this way by herself.

No, Ndidi just embodied the tools and mindset that Kathra had needed, when she herself could not be forward with them.

Like Daniel, a tool that might have to be used up.

"Tell me about Daniel and *Vorgash*," Kathra said as everyone recovered their equilibrium.

Ndidi began, starting with even the little, normally-esoteric details of the attack and carrying through to the various times the woman had climbed into Daniel's mind to talk to the two aliens.

Kathra nodded and turned to A'Alhakoth next.

"And Krusskyo?" she asked. "Walk me through the attack."

Again, deep details, filled in by the other women as they went. Kathra almost felt like a confessor figure, but all of these women had been left alone, trying to guess what the best outcome might be, without necessarily any guidance from her.

She could blame the old women back home for that. It had been sufficient before.

The war had changed.

Perhaps the entire future.

Now was not the time to recklessly charge into some final confrontation with Hadi Rostami, even if Daniel recovered, but Krusskyo would rattle things even more than Vorgash had. Just in different places.

The first attack would make the news on every planet, a Septagon thrashed in clear sight of everyone. The mining colony would generate whispers on the other hand. Fear.

Panic.

That was what would undermine the Sept faster than losing all their precious warships.

Losing the people.

Kathra smiled at all of them, and let them bask in it.

"I'm proud of all of you, but Ndidi has gone far and above anything I could have hoped for when I sent you out," Kathra said with a smile broad and encompassing enough to take them all into her arms. "You have done things Crence's bosses only dreamed about, and made the Sept look incompetent in doing them."

"Will it be enough?" A'Alhakoth asked now.

"We have provided an opening," Kathra said.

"So you brought all those other vessels to attack a Sept world?" Ndidi asked.

Kathra nodded.

"Perhaps many," she smiled. Ndidi returned it. "Piracy might run rampant through those nearby sectors now, as everyone demands a Septagon and enough Patrols to keep the wicked and dangerous Ndidi and *MorningStar* from falling down upon them."

"To what end?" Tanuss asked.

But the Wisp was an engineer to her core. Always problem solving.

"I want Daniel to return to us," Kathra said. "That's why Erin and I are here. If he has recovered, we might be able to do terrible things to places where the Sept will really know fear."

"Earth or Rhages," Ndidi said simply. "No other place matters. Will they be dumb enough to leave us an opening?"

"What will they do if Crence and all his friends start hitting nearby worlds and plundering their transportation networks?" Erin spoke up.

"Chase us," Hirly answered. "If you can sufficiently bait them. Will they fall for it?"

"Most of them don't matter," Kathra observed. "The only two men who are a threat to us are Amirin Pasdar, who was the naupati on *Vorgash* and later *Singara*. He knows enough of the truth. The other is Hadi Rostami, the one the Ishtan infected when they died, according to Daniel. We will aim our war at those two men. Draw them to us. If we can defeat them, that might be enough to break the back of the Sept."

The whirl of emotional energy that ran through the room at her words was electric. Even the two Anndaing, silent until now, reacted with wild eyes at the thought of actually defeating the Sept Empire.

If anybody could do such a thing in less than a century of concerted effort. Kathra had read about the encounters with the K'bari, back in the days before Urid-Varg turned those people inward.

But she had a tool nobody else in the galaxy had. Something that only Urid-Varg had probably understood.

Certainement, that monster had contained vast mental powers that he used for evil. But he also had no home, save the turtle.

The creature could just sail into the darkness when he needed to escape.

Or sail out of it to attack someone.

MorningStar had just done to the Sept what Kathra had only been able to dream about for nearly fifteen years.

She looked around now and studied her women. And her men. Crence was her tool, and Dane, just as much as Ndidi, even if he only suspected that truth.

This was her war.

The Merchants Bank would have probably waited another century or more to truly engage the human sectors, had Crence happened to locate Thrabo or someplace similar on that fateful voyage.

The Sept would have gone right on carving off Free Worlds systems.

Kathra was done playing.

"I need to see Daniel," she said. "Talk to him, if Erin and I can. Too much of what comes next hinges entirely on how much he can contribute to the future."

Her women nodded.

They needed Daniel, but the Mbaysey would still go on without him.

If they had to.

43

Erin had worn the long pants today to cover over the mechanical portion of her leg. *MorningStar* sailed like a Sept ship, with the temperature down enough to make her normal shorts insufficient.

Even if she was tougher than everybody else.

She and Kathra were only sisters of the spirit, since they looked nothing alike. But her sister needed her here.

And it was Daniel.

She had never suffered the touch of any male, even one like him, which put her in a strange minority among some of the women crowding into the medical facility. The doctor had moved him into a larger room, apparently, expecting something of a circus.

Erin doubted the woman would be disappointed.

Kathra had led them all down here. Her, Ndidi, Hirly, A'Alhakoth, Acqueir, Tanuss, and Nwanyiudo. The two Anndaing had followed, but they understood that they were just observers. Participants, but not powerful.

Pawns on the front row.

Daniel looked like he was just asleep, but had apparently

been like this for nearly six months now. Since attacking Vorgash.

He was a little more pale than normal, but his *Rabic* skin didn't change colors like the *Anglos*.

What startled her was his hair. It had been going gray gradually for as long as she had known him. But the sides were coming in entirely white now, almost to the ridge of his skull on each side. The rest was still in place. Still curly but not like hers.

Close enough. And he was close enough to one of them in blood these days.

Erin walked all the way around his bed to the far side, carefully avoiding a few wires and tubes keeping the man alive. She was at his head, directly across from Ndidi, with the Anndaing doctor at the foot of the bed and everyone else scattered around them.

"The Speaker has done this a few times," Dr. Klaskat said. "I am not an expert on Daniel's physiology. Each time he has stirred a little, but returned to quiescence afterwards."

"I know what to expect," Erin turned to her grimly. "Daniel has submitted to all of us at one time or another. But I was first."

On that TradeStation at Renneth, where the little male first impressed her by shutting his mouth and taking orders. Offering advice when asked and not presuming to make decisions.

Traveling light and compact, physically as well as emotionally.

She glanced up at Kathra and caught the woman's nod.

The doctor had pulled Daniel's blanket down enough to reveal the gem. It wasn't embedded in his torso, but it gave that impression. As far as Erin knew, nobody but him could remove it while he was alive.

They had eventually cooked a maintenance robot getting

it off Urid-Varg's corpse. And hacked his body apart to get the rest.

Before Kathra finally managed to kill the *salaud.*

Erin studied the gem. It was almost as dark as she remembered from the first time they had handed it to Daniel and asked him to sell his soul to the devil. Only the tiniest fire seemed to burn within, when normally it glowed like a reading light.

Or turned into a supernova when he did something big.

Kathra reached out a hand to her and Erin took it.

Both hands went down onto the gem. It was colder than she remembered as well.

Sticky, somehow, like maybe it was trying to pull her in.

Was Daniel trapped and trying to reach out for help? Ndidi had said she had spoken to the K'bari and the Roahrt more than once, but each time had been forced to push her way into Daniel's mind. To force entry.

The gem felt like an open door.

Kathra did something and Erin felt a jolt, but they stayed in the medical room.

She thought about talking aloud, but Daniel wasn't there to hear, so she forced the thought down her arm and into the gem directly.

Daniel, it's Erin and Kathra.

And then she fell into darkness.

44

Erin recognized the room. Daniel always brought his visitors here. Nobody had ever figured out what childhood fantasy had created it, as he had lived in a tower block as a child, and none of his grandsires had had a yard.

But she was here. Kathra, as well.

Arsène and Pheryoutl, with the K'bari seated in the chair and the Roahrt by the window.

"Thank you," the Roahrt said.

He walked closer to offer her a hand and she realized that the man was Daniel's size. He gave the impression that he would look down on Kathra, were he in his original body.

Erin took the hand and felt the warmth of his skin.

"How do we get to Daniel?" Kathra asked the two ghosts.

"We do not know, Commander," Arsène answered now. "Ndidi has tried several times, but he is hidden from us. All of us. I had not thought it possible, but there appears to be a place in this gem where the rest of us cannot go."

Kathra turned to her with a questioning look.

Erin looked around, wondering why Ndidi and the

ghosts had insisted that she be here, when Kathra should be sufficient.

What was it about Erin Uduik? What could she know or do that none of the other women contained?

As soon as she asked, Erin knew the answer.

She turned away from the others and walked to the bookshelf that contained Daniel's life on it, if you understood how the books were arrayed.

Genarde. Tavle Jocia. Ogrorspoxu. Kanus. Carggi. Azgon. Dozens of others.

One was missing.

It was a tiny slot. A gap you would miss if you didn't look close enough.

Didn't understand Daniel well enough.

Most of the women knew him at a deep level. A few had even joined with him in a physical and emotional way, but the mere thought of it turned her stomach.

But there was a gap.

Erin nodded and turned to the others. None of them would understand why that gap existed. What it implied.

Or why Erin Uduik, Spectre Two, had to be here.

"You know," Kathra said flatly.

Erin nodded.

"Where has he gone?"

"Renneth," Erin answered.

"Why there?" Kathra seemed perplexed, as did the two male ghosts who almost reminded her of Crence and Dane from the way they stood nearby hovering.

"He had fled Genarde and Angel," Erin nodded, as much to herself as to the others. "But not yet encountered Urid-Varg. The Mbaysey were yet in his future, with all the terrible things he would know and do only prophetic nightmares at this point. When I first met him, he had abandoned almost all of his past, save for that one duffel, which was less than I would need. I remember thinking of the man as a sword that had been beaten dull, but knowing him now, I would compare him to his favorite sakimaru knife in need of the whetstone."

"Can you take me there?" Kathra asked.

Erin looked around the room, trying to visualize the way to make Daniel's mind work without him. He always did the thing, rather than her.

But Daniel was hiding from them.

She returned to Renneth in her mind. Walked through that first day, when she had arrived with several other women to deliver a load of cargo.

SkyCamel Six. That was the key.

Erin envisioned a SkyCamel airlock hatch as they had used in the old days, before gaining access to Anndaing transports. She still flew one occasionally, mostly for qualification, but had a decade's worth of memories.

The hatch was suddenly there in her mind. Erin realized with a start that this room had never had any other doors, and that one had never once opened from somewhere else.

She found the space between two bookshelves on this wall and pulled the memory of a hatch out.

It appeared on the wall in place of a bad watercolor and a plant with some useless green thing that never bore fruit.

Just like the inside of SkyCamel Six.

Erin reached out her right hand and triggered the lock open.

The door beeped and began to move.

45

Kathra followed Erin through a SkyCamel hatch and emerged onto a Sept TradeStation concourse.

Except there was nobody here. Emptiness as far as she could see in any direction.

There were almost always people in view on a concourse like this, even if only moving around in the distance. This felt like a movie set after all the actors and crew had left, shutting everything down until it was dim with half-lights. There was a smell of cooked meat lingering in the air.

Kathra recognized the place. They had been to Renneth more than once, back in the old days before the Sept declared war on her openly.

But it was abandoned now.

A sound caused her to spin around, hand dropping to her pistol automatically. Erin did the same.

Arsène jumped in fright, almost falling backwards until Pheryoutl caught him with a grin.

She hadn't expected the two ghosts to come here with her, but Kathra supposed that they had just as much interest as she did. She nodded and turned back to Erin.

"I don't remember the details," she said. "What happened on that day?"

"I was here with Marra and a couple of others," Erin said, head down as she visualized things. "Daniel wasn't in sight, so I pinged him, already a little pissed at that point because we were on time. Except I was like fifteen seconds early, and he was just emerging from that bar when his vox beeped, so he would have been here exactly on time."

Erin turned and pointed. Kathra did as well. The two males spread out on either side like junior wingsisters.

Daniel did not emerge from the place.

"Then what?" Kathra asked.

"Short, *Rabic* male," Erin recounted. "Dark clothing. One bag. Shorter than all the women, because I'd brought tall ones with me that day."

Kathra shared Erin's grin. Height would probably have daunted most males.

Nothing intimidated Daniel.

"We talked about food, and he offered two suggestions," Erin continued. "That place, which he rated yucky, and a burger bar where we did end up eating. It was pretty good, until that little *salaud* spoiled us all forever for station food."

Kathra laughed. Oh, how those women had howled at how bad station food had gotten these days, when it used to be the thing they most looked forward to, such that they had to draw straws to see who got to go, and who had to stay behind with Ugonna's cooking.

"Burger bar," Kathra said.

Erin nodded and began to move, taking point with a hand on her own pistol.

The place was unsettling.

The two males trailed, moving more quietly now, once they understood Kathra's need for silence.

Down the main corridor a bit, and then inward on a spoke. Lateral on ring corridor from there.

The station was the same, but empty.

Kathra stopped just long enough to make sure she was actually wearing clothes, flashing back to other dreams every woman had growing up, walking into some important meeting utterly naked and unprepared.

This was a different nightmare, at least.

Erin led them to a wider hatch, open and partially obscured by those same two big ferns in pots, busy cleaning the air.

The interior was dim. A young, Anglo woman, human even, stood behind a lectern excitedly, menus already in her hands.

"This way," the stranger said, automatically turning and expecting them to follow.

Erin led. Kathra followed. Pheryoutl brought up the rear, feeling like a warrior to her in spite of his maleness.

The girl brought them to a table in the middle and seated them. Every other table and booth had been set up for customers, but none had come.

Menus were distributed.

Between one blink and the next, glasses appeared on the table. Kathra knew from the color that hers contained cold sweet tea, a taste she and Daniel shared.

A sip confirmed that she was on the right track. Erin's eyes got big when she tasted hers.

The two men, on her right and Erin's left, had their own something, one green and one red.

And matching surprise.

They were expected.

"Yes," Erin said. "This was the place. Daniel was where you are, Kathra, minding his manners and answering any questions we'd had the wit to toss at him that day, few though they were."

The waitress returned now, bearing plates, even though they hadn't ordered.

Except that the menus were gone.

The woman placed a burger in front of Kathra with all the perfect fixings and a pile of Belgian fried potatoes seasoned with something red. Erin had a similar plate, as did the two men.

Erin's mouth was open, but she closed it.

Kathra nodded.

"It's his dream, but he already knows what we want," she told her best friend. And the two ghosts.

Kathra picked up the burger and took a bite, unsurprised that it was the best burger she had ever encountered.

It was Daniel's dream. He could make the food utterly perfect.

They ate in relative silence, with only quiet moans of delight at the taste breaking things up. She knew she would regret this memory when she awoke.

Dessert arrived without ordering either, a chocolate mousse for her, topped with a white cream somewhere between a flan and a cheesecake for taste.

Utterly decadent.

"He's here," Erin said as she finished her carrot cake. "Watching?"

"Waiting," Kathra said. "I think it is time we went to retrieve him."

"Will he come?" Erin asked.

Kathra noted the silence of the ghosts, but then, they were really just figments of Daniel's imagination.

Much as she was right now.

"I could order it, and he would obey," Kathra offered. "But this needs to be his choice now."

She rose, unsurprised that the young woman had vanished. That one had existed only to serve the customers and the food, and was even less real that Arsène.

Kathra took point now, letting her senses direct her through the dimness just this side of dark, like you got when the lights were on the lowest setting before pure darkness.

She found the doorway to the kitchen and smelled the exquisite taste of meat grilling in the smoke that still hung. Entering, Kathra found herself in a radically different kitchen from the ones she had known.

This was a larger space, as befit a restaurant serving hundreds of meals each day, rather than the twenty-five or so people for each of three meals on *WinterStar* or *SeekerStar*.

But it was just as empty as everyplace else. In her own memories of Daniel's life, this was the place from which he had launched into space.

Pain du Soir. Evening Bread, on Genarde.

She found the Golden Diamond on the wall, reminding the staff that every meal, every plate going out the door, had to be perfect.

Every time.

Never a chance to experiment with things, except to add the occasional Chef's Special and see what the customers thought of it.

Locked in and locked down by the enormous weight of that diamond. Daniel had called it the heaviest thing in the universe to hold, with only being awarded a second one being worse, to say nothing of those few places with a third.

Godhead, at least on a planet like Genarde. And a man like Daniel Lémieux.

Until the night he had had enough.

Kathra made her way deeper into the labyrinth of Daniel's kitchen, finding a door at the very back that she knew led to his office.

It was closed until her hand fell upon the knob and she pushed.

He was seated behind the desk, looking like a much younger version than the man she knew. The dark hair was still wavy but not curly, and in this image of himself it was just starting to gray in streaks. Eyes that almost seemed black with rage, and hands and arms scarred from the kitchen wars a man fights on a daily basis.

Daniel looked up with a smile as Kathra moved into the office and sat on the left.

Erin was always on the right in her office. Kathra saw no reason to change that here.

Erin joined her and she and Daniel stared at each other for a long moment.

"I hurt," he finally said.

"I know," Kathra nodded. "I was afraid I had asked too much of you this time."

"We came close," he agreed, nodding to the two ghosts in the doorway.

As she glanced back, both men seemed to fade and disappear.

She turned back to Daniel with a question in her eyes.

"They are all me, just as I am each and every one of them," Daniel shrugged. "Once you got here, they knew this place existed, and if another captures my soul later, then perhaps I will be able to cook for all of us for the rest of eternity. There are worse places I could end up. All of us."

"What do you want?" Erin asked, leaning forward and focusing on the chef. "We have always taken from you, but rarely have the scales been balanced, and I'm probably more guilty of that than any of the others. How do we make it right for Daniel the Chef?"

He lapsed into silence.

She could see him as he must have been on that last night

before he met Erin, staying in a cheap coffin room here on Renneth while he waited to find out what the fates had in store for him.

Who could have possibly imagined the things that would come?

"I want to be free," Daniel said, glancing right and left. "Both of you know how much weight I carry. What things I alone make possible, and what costs I have to bear for the rest of you. I'm tired."

"Then you should rest," Kathra said. "But you are also comitatus, Daniel Lémieux, and that brings other costs with it."

He nodded, like a victim placing his head on a block for the executioner's axe, but remained silent.

"I also serve," he said.

"You and I have one last mission together, Daniel," she said.

His head snapped up at that, those black eyes showing surprise now, instead of resignation.

His mouth asked *"One?"* but his breath could not animate it.

"The Ishtan are not all dead, just as Urid-Varg is not gone," Kathra said. "We must destroy Hadi Rostami, and nobody else in the galaxy that I am aware of can do that besides the two of us. After that, I will free you to do whatever it is that will finally bring you solace."

She could see the options multiply in those eyes, but she and Erin had been probably deeper into his soul than even Ndidi. That woman was merely his sister, after all.

She and Erin had become his gods.

He wanted to be free, but that might be a simple return to a kitchen. Or to a library somewhere to translate ancient texts so old the language names had been forgotten.

Or he might choose death. That was in his eyes as well.

With the last of the Ishtan finally gone, Kathra would allow him that option as well.

She had, like Erin said, taken far more from this man that anyone had ever given. Even A'Alhakoth or one of the others had never balanced the scales with Daniel.

He nodded, and she saw the tears begin to roll down his face.

She felt the same way.

Looking over, even the dangerous creature known as Spectre Two was crying now, but that was okay.

They had one, last battle, and then Daniel could go home.

46

NDIDI HAD NOT MOVED. Had barely even dared to blink.

She knew how little time passed in the real world, in spite of the appearance down in Daniel's mind. Days might pass in the blink of an eye.

Kathra and Erin held hands, fingers interlaced on the gem.

How much trouble had Urid-Varg caused by killing the Eldest of the Ishtan? How much pain and grief had that fool unleashed on an innocent galaxy because he was the most arrogant *salaud* ever born?

But they could not just toss it into the heart of a star. Not while another Ishtan survived.

At least Daniel had done something good with it.

Still, Ndidi felt like she watched over a dying man today. She glanced over at a sound and realized that Acqueir was quietly crying, with Tanuss comforting her with a hand.

Ndidi reached out and pulled both women close with one hand, and grabbed A'Alhakoth with the other. All of them were crying, and that was fine. She would watch over them just as she had watched over Daniel.

That was what sisters did.

Daniel stirred for the first time in months and everybody jumped.

Dr. Klaskat was there immediately, poking and prodding and staring at the various readouts overhead.

Kathra opened her eyes, as did Erin.

Both sighed.

Ndidi felt the women in her arms surge and recede with emotions, shaking with fear, for the most part.

She held them all upright. That was her job.

She *Spoke* for *MorningStar*, but that was so much more than just a length of killing blade made by the Ovanii.

Ndidi also represented this crew. These people. These various women who might all form a bizarre harem of sisters-in-law, even as they were also sisters of the comitatus.

Each brought Daniel joy in her own way.

His eyes opened, squinted, focused, found her.

A hand came up and she moved to take it, dragging the others along with her.

"You were there," he whispered in a voice rusty from disuse. "In the darkness, watching over me."

"I was," Ndidi answered, finding that she was crying now, too.

"Thank you," he said.

She felt his hand squeeze hers.

"Now you're back?" she asked.

He looked up at Kathra first and then Erin, before returning to her.

"I have one last mission," he said ominously.

"Oh?"

"I need to kill a man."

PART III
____

MBAYSEY

47

NDIDI *SPOKE* FOR *MORNINGSTAR*. That fact kept resonating with her. Only Kathra and Ife had truly understood the terrible weight such responsibility brought.

She and Kathra had merged one last time with Daniel's help, so that they were almost closer that any others on this bridge.

She found a memory that was Kathra's, one designating the Commander and Erin as Daniel's Gods, and her as merely his sister, but that had changed. Ndidi had been elevated as well, so that Daniel now had a trio of terrible women to worship and fear.

And love. She could not forget that. He did love each of them, as much as they would allow it. Served them willingly, when he had once held resentment at such a need.

But the fires of Vorgash had burned everything out, taking all the impurities.

She glanced over and noted the way his soul seemed to glow like a freshly sharpened deba knife today. The other women had it as well, even the ones that only knew Daniel as an officer, and not as a lover or mind-partner.

MorningStar had purpose. No, it had always had purpose, for it was an Ovanii Battlemaster, forged for war.

Today, it had a mission.

A dream.

"Signals, open a channel to *GhostStar* and the squadron," Ndidi called out. "Conference mode."

Acqueir nodded and pressed a button. The air changed resonance, so the Anic woman already had it prepared, and had just been waiting.

Yes, they had a mission, didn't they?

"You're live, Speaker," Acqueir said with a serious tone.

Ndidi took a deep breath. She called up the hologram of local space to see all the blue stars and arrowheads projected, plus three larger sharks swimming along her own flanks.

It wasn't the Armada of legend, but this was still the largest aggregation of Anndaing warships put together for anything but training in the last several centuries.

Nobody had challenged the Merchants Bank in lifetimes.

Until now.

"This is the Speaker," Ndidi said simply.

Other vessels also had Speakers. At least the three Duelers. Anndaing ships traditionally called their commander a Trademaster.

But there was only one Speaker for this squadron, just as there was only one Commander of the Mbaysey, out there within reach of her voice.

"We have been to Vorgash," Ndidi continued, letting her tones range low and ominous, in fitting with her mood. "They will never forget us there, because any number of fools could discount Tavle Jocia as a fluke. *Singara* was, after all, commanded by a fool. *Vorgash* as well. But all of the Sept cannot expect every naupati to be a fool."

She looked over her bridge, starting with Acqueir and ending with Daniel. Most were focused on their own screens, just listening, but he turned to her with a fierce, angry smile that seemed to match hers.

"We have also visited Krusskyo, lest the lesser worlds feel that they are safe by hiding behind their mother's skirt," Ndidi smiled at her women. "All of those things were useful. But they do not satisfy our need. We cannot defeat the Sept by ourselves, but we do not have to. We only need to draw out one man and kill him. Two if we are lucky, but that naupati is largely irrelevant by himself. He has an alien serving him, guised in human flesh but another one like Urid-Varg, and all that it implies."

She could only imagine the gasps of shock anywhere except on this bridge. And maybe *GhostStar*.

Not many men and women knew Daniel's secret, and those had been sworn to secrecy, perhaps reinforced by Daniel himself to protect him and the Mbaysey.

But Urid-Varg was the bogeyman that Anndaing mothers used to frighten recalcitrant pups.

Be good or Urid-Varg might take *you*.

"We are invading human space now," Ndidi confirmed for her expanded squadron, with nearly three-zwölf additional vessels, mostly Gun-6 killers, but a few Gun-12s and a finful of Scout-6s like *GhostStar*. And a group of Cargo-12s loaded up to act as a forward base for the raiders Ndidi led. "We need to draw our foe to us so we can kill him and return home. It is as simple as that, my friends. We need to kill that wolf in human form to save the galaxy."

She paused long enough to take a breath and let some of her rage bleed out, where it might infect all the others around her.

"All vessels transition to jump."

48

———

Daniel had had a hard time these last few weeks, no longer being dead. Or whatever it was. Even returning to his kitchen, his real kitchen and not the one in his mind, barely helped.

The pain was there still, like a toothache that no amount of medication could mask, but he could generally live with it.

He didn't have much longer that he needed to do this, and then he could be free.

Interestingly, while *MorningStar* was in jump, the pain got worse, even though most of the universe had vanished from his mental sight, leaving only the three thousand-odd souls of *MorningStar's* crew to hear.

Or was it the silence that grated on his nerves?

Daniel had never considered that being able to taste the mental winds of several trillion sentient beings, flowing around him like tide waters, might actually bring him solace.

Bon, perhaps he needed to finally settle on a planet again, where he never again had to travel on valence drives. Except he knew that was a lie as soon as he thought it.

Kathra would not be bound to a single system, and he was Mbaysey for the rest of his life.

However long that might be.

Daniel would travel with her. With Erin and Ndidi. With any of the others who decided to leave Anndaing space behind forever when *SeekerStar* lived up to his name and departed for the galactic interior.

He would just need to learn to live with the silence. Maybe.

The kitchen was dark. It was the middle of ship's night, the time when he liked to meditate, but he hadn't gone forward to the bridge to hide. They were several days in, with a few more before everyone arrived at whatever secret destination would become their pirate's den for a time.

His evening crew had cleaned everything spotless, like usual. Without him around, apparently Ndidi had taken it upon herself to inspect things regularly. That had been even worse than Daniel doing it.

The crew was fast asleep now, most likely exhausted. The morning shift would awaken in a few hours and arrive to start prepping.

He no longer cooked for twenty-five to thirty women, like he had once. Now he supervised the officer's mess, although he had proper chefs under him. Executive Chef again, but none of them would turn into Ndidi.

That was a benefit as well as a sadness, but perhaps training her was enough of a legacy for him. Certainly, if she returned to the kitchen afterwards, none would doubt her earning a Golden Diamond.

Or whatever cultural equivalent existed, wherever the Mbaysey passed.

Daniel sat on an overturned wash bucket. It had been dry enough that the water he had dumped on the floor would evaporate before anybody got yelled at.

Hopefully.

He had a glass of boullo wine in one hand, courtesy of Wyll Koobitz and friends, who probably wanted to remind him that he could retire to Ogrorspoxu and open a wine bar or bistro. He had considered it, if only because the University at Therly would offer him whatever he wanted, to come in and train a new generation of linguists.

Maybe he should just retire to academia? It wasn't as if he had anything left to prove in the kitchen at this point.

And it would be utterly rude to open a hot dog cart out on the sidewalk in front of the Treasury building. Profitable, no doubt, but still rude.

A door opened. He felt the pressure differential, even before the ambient light changed.

Someone entered, carrying a light, so they knew to expect darkness when they found him. Not that anybody should be surprised to find him thus.

Correction, she bore the light on her forehead, that glowing, semi-rigid tentacle dialed all the way down to almost nothing. It only went out when she slept, and even then nightmares or intense dreams lit her up.

Tanuss paused at the corner separating the front from the back, that one spot where the counter turned and servers didn't cross unless one of the cooks invited them back to do something on the hot, sharp side of the border.

He looked up and smiled at her.

Death had done something to Daniel, but he didn't have the vocabulary to adequately describe it to the living, like Tanuss.

Daniel had always wondered what caused alien women to be interested in a short, swarthy, severely-graying, *Rabic* chef. He supposed it had been his own special kind of arrogance, to believe he didn't deserve such attention.

Certainly, the Mbaysey had, for the most part, cured him

of looking at a beautiful woman and doing anything more than passively desiring her from a safe distance. Only a few of them had ever expressed any interest in a man.

But *SwiftStar* and *MorningStar* only had a few humans serving aboard them. Most of both crews were Anndaing, who didn't particularly find humans interesting, but Anndaing space was also populated with Anic, Kaniea, and Wisp like this woman, among others.

She studied him, like he was alien again.

Being dead would do that to some people.

How much had he changed?

A'Alhakoth and Acqueir had both confirmed in the last week, in their own ways, that he was hale and hearty. Hirly had even made a few jokes that Daniel took to mean she had considered it. Humans didn't have the right equipment for an Anndaing, but he only needed to hold Hirly's hand, and apparently someone had told her that while he was dead.

But Tanuss had kept her distance. Her reserve.

Daniel didn't know Wisp culture well enough to know if they had ghost stories like humans did, or how they interpreted them in the modern era.

So she paused on the other side of that invisible line, watching him.

He watched her.

The scale-looking pattern to her skin that was gray with iridescent patterns in pink and purple like a hexagonal tartan. The sharp, tearing teeth as she smiled carefully. The vestigial gills slits on her neck that she liked to have kissed.

That long, skinny body that was still only a little shorter than him, even though he kept expecting her to be as tall as Kathra, when spied from a distance.

"What do you see?" he asked her.

"You were dying on that table," she answered perhaps a shade more brutally than he had expected, but this was

Tanuss. The woman was an engineer, not a poet. "Most of you has come back, but not all. Your hair will be almost all gray, the next time you cut it, unless you add color."

"*Oui*," he nodded. "The beard is already there, which is why I shave every morning. I am not quite ready to face that in the mirror."

"More lines around the eyes and mouth, but I looked that up and all humans do that as they age, silly as it is," she continued, still not crossing that line. "Thinner than you were. Thinner than you've ever been, and I've seen pictures of the pudgy you that first joined *WinterStar*. You have gone too far into thinning everything down, but I expect that you'll rebuild bulk and muscle tone over the next few months."

Daniel had been a slightly rotund teenager, the result of too much rich food and not enough of the stresses that one derived inside a kitchen filled with professional killers. *Tattooed psychopaths with knives*, as it were. Kathra and Erin had indeed worked him harder than ever in his life, just to keep up with such vigorous women as they walked.

But he was not the man he'd been a year ago, let alone ten. Wouldn't ever be. Wasn't sure he even missed that person.

He shrugged.

Death will do that to you, he suspected.

But good enough. He reached out a hand and grabbed a bucket that had been filled with carrots when it arrived from ClanStar Okafor. He pulled it close and flipped it over for her to sit and smiled.

She took the invitation and entered the terrible dragon's lair of Daniel's kitchen, perching athletically on the pillar upholding her beauty.

"What can I do for you, Tanuss?" he asked as she got settled.

"I don't know," she fired back at him. "I wanted to see you and decide if you had changed too much. If dying made you someone else."

Again, engineer. Not one for circuitous evasions. Straight to the heart.

"It did," he said. "I had several years to sit inside that gem and contemplate who I was and what I wanted."

"Years?"

"Time moves very rapidly in that other place," he nodded. "The others do not notice it passing at all, except in my presence, but I was living in there. Several centuries occurred. And nothing at all."

"So what did Daniel Lémieux learn about himself?" she asked, at least smiling a little now.

"That I am surrounded by friends," he said. "That for the first time in my adult life, I have a family, where before I only had rivals who were peers, and family members who were largely current or former employees."

"Indeed?" she pressed.

"Several women, all of whom I love in different ways, and all of whom love me in their own style," he continued, smiling at her.

"So Kathra's threat of a harem?" Her eyes got devious now.

"Accidental as far as I'm concerned," he shrugged, attempting some level of innocent levity, even at this late of a date. "I was around Mbaysey, who consider it a significant perversion for the most part, so nobody warned me that I would run into so many amazing, sexy, alien women that I would have to seduce."

"Snickerdoodles are a terribly effective seduction," Tanuss observed drolly. "Possibly a crime in some jurisdictions."

"*Oui*," he grinned. "And I have come up with new things, hiding inside the kitchen in my head for so long, with nothing to do except meditate on my crimes. But new recipes kept popping up and disturbing my calmness."

"New recipes?" she asked, leaning forward a little now.

"I suspected that death would throw something of a kink in my relationships," Daniel said. "So it might be necessary to seduce all of you, all over again. That might be the only way I could wheedle my way back into your beds."

"Sounds intriguing," Tanuss offered, perhaps the littlest bit breathless. "You might have to seduce me, after all."

Her horn was also glowing a little more than it had before, which was a terrible giveaway.

There was a reason Wisp made such lousy poker players.

Daniel rose from his bucket and placed the mostly-empty wine glass on the counter.

He glanced slyly at her and nodded her to stand as well.

Tanuss did, moving close enough to press her hip against his as he reached up onto a shelf. Her arm went around his waist and he felt her warmth through his black shirt.

Daniel retrieved a square tin painted red and pulled the lid off.

A new smell filled the air around him.

Well, two smells, the scent of her arousal warring with the treats he had hidden away when he baked them earlier. Daniel pulled one of the triangular prizes out, thought about it for a moment, and grabbed a second for himself.

He handed it to her with a lascivious grin.

"Have a more proper seduction," he offered.

"What is it?" she asked, already nibbling on a corner.

"Start with a sweet scone, so a harder bread than most, and more rigid than a cookie," he took a bite and spoke around chewing. "Blueberry, because I wanted to. Instead of dropping it, these were squares that I filled with a pineapple cream reduction and then folded before baking. The frosting on top is the same as I drizzle on rolls, so milk, powdered sugar, and vanilla."

She took a bigger bite and got filling all over her chin with a surprised squawk. Daniel found a rag and handed it to her as he ate his own.

"And when were you going to share these with the rest of us?" she asked tartly, still close against his side, but turned into him now.

Daniel faced her and reached his free hand around her hip to hold her close.

"I wasn't sure who I needed to seduce first," he leaned over and kissed her.

She nodded sagely.

"This is an acceptable opening bid," Tanuss grinned. "But utterly insufficient."

"I had hoped that might be your conclusion." Daniel finished his scone and stashed the tin up where the morning crew wouldn't accidentally discover it. "Now I would like to attempt a more thorough seduction, Tanuss Barleyne."

Her arms came up around him and Daniel felt another weight vanish from his shoulders. She kissed him back and pressed herself against his chest.

"Give it all you've got," she purred.

Daniel nodded. Being dead, this had been the thing he missed the most.

49

AMIRIN UNDERSTOOD INTELLECTUALLY that he would never give orders from the Command Node of a Septagon again, but it rankled. There were a few other naupatis out there that he considered his equals in combat commands, but most of the men who could have done as good a job were commoners who would never rise above aspbad.

That was not a war he could win in his lifetime, so he had to settle for opening the Seven Clans up to new thinking, and hoping that with the time he had remaining that he could slowly infect the rest of humanity.

It would be a new Sept Empire. Either they would defeat him and he would be dead, with the lurching corpse of the old system slowly following him into the grave, or he and Hadi would win and start a new thing.

Or an old thing, depending on how you wanted to envision it.

Looking out the wide window from the station, Amirin watched two Septagons maneuver in near orbit as a team. That had not been necessary in more than a century, since the last revolt against the crown had been put down, annihilated by loyalists with a septuple of Septagons, the most irresistible force in the history of his species.

The Free Worlds could not even resist a single Septagon, except when they unleashed massive numbers of tiny ships and tried to nibble one to death.

MorningStar was already a novel enemy for him to consider, but nothing those women had done suggested that Septagon *Terra* and Septagon *Cyrus* would not be sufficient, were the women to come here. Likewise, Septagons *Darius* and *Xerxes* protected the Court at Rhages, along with increased numbers of Patrols.

Even the Mbaysey and their Anndaing allies would be hard pressed to risk such a collection of firepower.

A sound behind him caused Amirin to return his attention to this room and the man watching with him.

Umek smiled and toasted Amirin with a glass of orange juice. Tart and sweet and heavy on his tongue.

"Already, your genius is showing results, Pasdar," the Shah of Earth said quietly.

They were alone. Not even Hadi was welcome, but his assistant was just outside the chamber, waiting with others while the two leaders negotiated the future.

Amirin bowed his head and stepped close enough to accept a second glass from the man.

"I am merely the instigator asking questions, sir," Amirin said.

It was not a false modesty, at least he didn't think so. Amirin knew that in a different universe, one without Kathra Omezi and her women, he would have already begun to maneuver himself in such a way as to rip a crown from the bleeding corpse of the fool wearing it now.

Urid-Varg's death, and that of the Ishtan, had moved things up perhaps a decade, but Amirin didn't feel like he had that decade to work slowly.

If nothing else, every day that passed was one day closer to that eventual collapse Hadi had shown him from the dreams of the Ishtan. The actual death of the Sept Empire, even if those aliens had expected it to occur in a few centuries without Amirin Pasdar's ego intruding.

But he was not duplicitous enough to deny that his ego would not let him rest.

Amirin Pasdar would save the empire if he could, but he didn't know any other man he trusted to actually make it a better place.

The rest would have been content to simply lop off a head and replace the Emperor with themselves, or a more tractable fool. The system itself would not change.

The unseen bureaucrats of the civilian world or the navy would continue to fight a losing battle against entropic decay, spending their lives and sanity and still failing.

After time on Rhages, surrounded by men he wanted to strangle with their own entrails, Amirin needed something better.

Umek studied him as Amirin thought and sipped from the glass, wondering, as always, if it was poisoned.

Was Amirin Pasdar too dangerous to keep alive, once the revolution he had instigated started to gain momentum?

"What are your next steps, having protected the key worlds against another Vorgash raid?" Umek asked innocently.

As if anything that man did was innocent, appearances be damned.

Rubicon?

The Shah already had more than enough evidence to have Amirin executed. He didn't even need a reason, except as it might be necessary to mollify other men and Pasdar allies that might object otherwise.

But Umek Sardari had proven to be an ally. Or else he was the greatest triple agent in history.

Amirin turned back and took in the view of *Terra* and *Cyrus*, completing a twin, inward turn that would allow one or the other to kill *MorningStar*, whatever fancy maneuvering those women wished to engage in to evade an Axial Megacannon.

Umek moved to stand next to him, apparently also enjoying the image. Perhaps also considering ancient rivers on the Italian peninsula, and how their names had infected human culture down thousands of years.

"At one point, I might have believed that a new emperor at Rhages could be enough to save us," Amirin committed the cleanest, most understandable treason he could imagine. "But the many candidates to replace the *Padishah* Dana Bahram Tabatabaei are all just as bad."

He considered the juice in his hand. Freshly squeezed from oranges reputedly grown on Umek's own estate.

"At Rhages, I saw enough alcohol consumed on any given day to drown all of them, if I was of a mind," Amirin dug his grave deeper. "And these supposedly upright, moral men fornicated constantly with an astonishing array of women. And alien creatures we presume were women from external appearances. Slaves, like the Mbaysey resisted being and freed themselves from, before anyone else realized that they could."

"She still bothers you?" Umek asked. "Omezi?"

"Her and the others," Amirin nodded, sipping slowly and savoring the clean sweetness. "Erin Uduik. Ndidi Zikora, Ifedimma Ogu. A'Alhakoth ver'Shingi. Many more that my spies have identified. The raid at Vorgash was *MorningStar*, which puts Zikora presumably in command. And the alien pretending to be Daniel Lémieux was certainly there as well, since it did the same thing to Septagon *Uwalu* at the beginning. But yes, Kathra Omezi started all of this."

"Will you have her head before you take Rhages?" Umek asked simply. "Or as your first official act afterwards?"

Amirin's head snapped around, but the man was smiling wryly.

But then, Umek Sardari had known from the beginning.

Amirin wondered if the man had spent his entire life hoping someone would come along who could fire others with a dream of making the empire a better place.

50

Hadi leaned his head back against the wall behind him like he had a sore neck, but really he just wanted those extra centimeters of space. The power he wielded declined on an inverted cube, so twice as far away meant only an eighth as much strength.

He almost always had to be in the room with someone to affect them. Daniel had the mindgem of the Eldest to focus his power through, so he could disrupt an entire Septagon somehow.

Hadi listened to the minds of Amirin and Umek as they discussed treason. Out here in the antechamber, he kept a palm on the minds of the guards and bureaucrats. Most of these were weak-minded fools, so it was easy enough to just change them as Hadi demanded they be.

There was no treason here, because all of these men now believed they were acting as their Shah expected, which made it right. Out there, dozens of senior officials had felt his touch and come to a new understanding of morality, but even Hadi wasn't arrogant enough to assume that it would make any difference.

Not in the long run.

Rhages was an infection clear down in the soul of the empire, too deep to merely cut out and hope the patient survived. Extraordinary methods would be called for, just as had been necessary to save Septagon *Vorgash*.

The outer door opened and a low-level messenger appeared, looking around for a moment to find someone more senior. He bore an envelope, but Hadi could read the fear and excitement emanating off the man like waves of light.

He grabbed the messenger and read the man's memory.

No.

Damn them!

Hadi leaned his mind back and tapped Amirin on the shoulder, warning him that trouble had arrived, far sooner than they had expected.

The messenger delivered his note. The bureaucrat read it, turning white and gasping before he rose to knock on the door and intrude, fearful himself of the reception.

Before the bureaucrat could, Amirin opened the hatch and gestured the man inside. The Shah might notice the discrepancy, and Hadi would need to fuzz things later, but time was of the essence.

The man handed Amirin the note and stepped back, but was bade to enter.

Amirin found Hadi and nodded, so he rose and joined them in the office.

Umek Sardari, Shah of Earth, had gone white. Collapsed into a chair and gasped, before a sudden flush of what tasted like pure rage suffused the man's face nearly crimson.

"How could she know?" he demanded, looking up at first Amirin and then Hadi.

He held out the paper and Amirin took it.

Hadi listened to the man's breathing become hoarse and angry.

Amirin turned this way.

"They've hit Aeovan," he said unnecessarily, so Hadi reacted as if that was news, rather than having read other minds along the way.

Hadi decided to speak unbidden, confident that the situation called for a relaxation of social mores.

"Perhaps spies have alerted them to your location, Naupati Pasdar?" Hadi asked in a formal tone intended to stick in other men's minds.

Spy hunting made a good cover to destroy certain men that might be otherwise unimpeachable. Those who were also standing in the way in their belligerent stodginess.

"Perhaps," Amirin reflected. He turned to the Shah now, both men white hot. "I think it would be best if I went to Aeovan to see for myself. Who knows what the men there might think to hide, rather than reporting to us here."

"Is that wise, Amirin?" the Shah asked in a careful voice. "You have mentioned that these women are cannier than most men give them credit for. Could this be a trap to lure you to Aeovan where they might seek to destroy you?"

Hadi cursed, seeing the brilliance of the trap. Amirin was barely an eye blink behind him.

It would require two Septagons to be safe, but two were necessary to protect Earth. None were close enough to come for him as a taxi.

And Daniel would know where Hadi was.

Daniel.

Damn him!

Hadi had looked and listened for the man in vain for so long that he had unconsciously wondered if Daniel had died after Vorgash. He had been present in the galaxy, but his scent had been so faint that Hadi was unable to identify where the man was.

He dared not look now, as such meditation would be obvious. Hadi would need time alone in his chamber.

Daniel had done nothing mental to Aeovan, from the reports, just as he had avoided using his powers at Krusskyo. How much had it taken out of him to nearly destroy *Vorgash*?

"Truly, a cunning trap," Amirin conceded with a growl so intense that the bureaucrat cringed.

But not the Shah of Earth. Interesting.

Amirin turned to face Hadi.

"I will need your thoughts later," he said simply, evasively, but only to someone who might know the truth about the Ishtan standing here. "For now, we need to find a way to chase them down."

"Are we chasing them?" Hadi asked carefully. "Aeovan suggests that they might be chasing us?"

Amirin blinked, but then, the man had never been hunted.

Always the hunter, seeking people thinking to elude Sept justice.

Perhaps the tables were turning?

51

———

Daniel had actually considered moving to Aeovan
early in his career, before the twists of fate that eventually
took him to Genarde. *Certainement*, he would have found it
easier to earn that Golden Diamond there, living, as it were,
in the shadow of Earth itself and the office complex in Paris
from which such blessings emerged like the ten plagues of
ancient legend.

That had been decades ago, though, so he was almost as
much a stranger here as the women around him.

Aeovan was an old colony, into its second millennium
now and largely tamed. A movie lot copy of Earth itself, with
little of the original life human explorers had found. A bit
more land, a bit less water. Two small moons, like Mars in
the home system rather than Earth. Second planet from the
star, of only four, all close in, which had always suggested to
Daniel that it had been born in a busy neighborhood, where
someone had come along and stolen most of the material.

But a paradise in most senses.

Aeovan had enough population to be important, but not
enough to be central. Off the main trade routes outward, so

it had grown a little insular and strange, but only forty-some light-years from Earth itself.

On a stellar projection of any scale, the two stars usually touched.

What better way to get someone's attention?

Hadi Rostami was on Earth, not Rhages. *MorningStar* was close enough now that the two worlds were more than ninety degrees apart when he opened his mind to the *salaud*.

Salauds. Plural. Millions of plurals.

The Sept.

A busier system than Krusskyo, from the memories Ndidi and A'Alhakoth had shared with him, but barely any better protected.

There was almost nothing here worth taking. Or destroying.

Except peace of mind.

Fortunately, Ndidi and Kathra had brought that exact purpose.

One major TradeStation. Three manufacturing platforms big enough to qualify as addresses. Hundreds of little ones. Hundreds of ships in motion, coming and going, maybe thousands.

But only six Patrols of Sept enforcers.

Daniel opened his eyes and looked at the hungry women around him, all waiting for him to finish scouting this place.

"Unchanged," he said simply, nodding to Acqueir and then A'Alhakoth.

Ndidi's terrible scowl became an even more terrible smile, but neither Iruoma nor Kathra were here to appreciate it.

"Signal the other three to jump," Ndidi gave the order.

It might be a trap, so Ife was going to lead, *SwiftStar* with *NovaStar* and *BrightStar* as if that was the entirety of the raid.

Somebody might have hidden a Septagon out there

where Daniel had been unable to see it, but he had taken the time to look.

Hiding three hundred thousand minds was nearly impossible. Daniel wanted to make sure of that.

Ndidi didn't mind being the surprise that arrived later.

The three Duelers vanished from Daniel's mind and his screens. They would reappear a few moments later deep in the system, in orbital space above Aeovan, where a Patrol base was about to be hammered by all three.

It helped when Daniel could sit in deep space and listen, placing the exact coordinates on a screen without having to be close enough to refine them. Ovanii jump controllers were acceptably accurate over this distance.

"Daniel?" Ndidi asked.

He nodded and stepped back outside of his body.

52

———

GIVEN HER HEAD, Ndidi would have not even dropped *MorningStar* into the scanners at Aeovan, but she understood the need. Three Duelers were enough, unless some previously-unknown military genius just happened to be stationed here, but nobody believed that for an instant.

She needed to send a message. Kathra and Daniel wanted Pasdar and Rostami. Both were safe on Earth, so Ndidi would blow things up until they came out to stop her.

Even the Ovanii hadn't been this brutal, but they had been artists. Ndidi was just a plague.

But she still remembered Grandma Ezinne's words. That tattoo on her face, identical to and the source of Erin's.

Tales of Sept gentlemen with ruthless perversions.

Ndidi would see them all destroyed.

She looked around the bridge now, studied the women who were waiting with her.

Poised. Pissed, too, but all of them had absorbed the meaning of Mbaysey from the survivors of Tazo.

Didn't matter what her shape was. What color or pattern her skin displayed.

The Sept were rapists. Mind, body, soul.

Bullies who took because until today, nobody had been strong enough to stop them.

Having Daniel unleash another scream today would have been satisfying, but she needed him to rest. To prepare for when that Ishtan *salaud* finally emerged from the den where he had been hiding.

Armageddon, as the ancients had once called it.

"Time?" she asked, looking at the countdown on her screen.

"Close enough?" Acqueir glanced at her.

"Indeed," Ndidi agreed. "Pilot, take us in. Sword, prepare to kill fools."

MorningStar leapt.

53

A'Alhakoth had only learned the term *target-rich environment* by studying translated records from the ancient Ovanii that had built this mighty machine in the dimness of time. Neither Kaniea nor Anndaing faced warfare with as much gusto and energy as humans or Ovanii had, but she had learned.

The Duelers had come out close enough to the Patrol Base to bombard it almost before anyone noticed the arrival of danger. It was already out of the fight and the three ships were now hunting down singles and smaller groups of ships that were frantically scrambling to do something, anything.

And then *MorningStar* appeared from jump.

"All gunners, engage as you bear," A'Alhakoth announced in a stern voice.

Arc-cannons began to speak. There was no Septagon to focus on, so each gun commander had a zone around the ship they were responsible for, and generators on standby with orders to overload for short periods as necessary.

TradeStation. Manufacturing platforms.

Destruction. Devastation.

As with Krusskyo, they were avoiding habitat stations today. Not because of a squeamishness on her part, but because Ndidi and Kathra wanted the economy destroyed. That was easier to do when the factories exploded. People could not work but they would need to eat, so they would have to migrate, taking their horror stories with them to other systems.

MorningStar was infecting an entire generation of humans with fear, when they had known only racism and glory before this.

A young, blue woman from Kanus was the instrument, but the Mbaysey would get the credit.

A'Alhakoth found it to be sufficient.

"Sensors, find me that third station," A'Alhakoth spoke up now.

Acqueir was close enough to whisper to, but A'Alhakoth wanted all eight gunners paying attention. One of their targets was on the far side of the world right now. *MorningStar* would have to either chase it down or let it catch up.

Being separated from the main grouping was not going to save them today. All it would do was to give the inhabitants time to abandon ship in lifepods, to be picked up by other survivors later, or make their way down to the surface.

The station was forfeit.

A target vector appeared on her screens. Hmmm.

"Speaker?" she turned to Ndidi.

Ndidi nodded and studied the screens for a long moment.

"Stern chase," the other woman said a moment later.

A'Alhakoth agreed. Slowing down made more sense, but it also let other ships elude them.

Or a Septagon sneak up.

Better to think like a shark.

"Pilot, begin your acceleration," A'Alhakoth ordered. "Gunners, hammer everything hard now, but remember that we can come back in a later orbit. The stations won't be running."

Harsh laughter answered her from around the room. Arc-cannons continued to strike targets with lethal energy, but the Ram Cannons began chasing ships in orbit. Not to destroy them, unless somebody got lucky, but to damage them at a time when the repair yards were going to be annihilated.

Fright.

Expensive terror visited on people whose only crime to date was not demanding that the Sept Empire behave like civilized creatures.

A'Alhakoth watched things explode around them.

54

Amirin paced, hands clenched behind him so that he didn't just punch the wall and break his fist.

Damn them all!

Hadi was seated, out of the way and studiously not reacting to Amirin's current rage.

Amirin's quarters were large enough for a small salon. Eight paces and turn. Repeat.

Adequate.

"Are we trapped?" he finally asked, not bothering to look.

"Daniel was there," Hadi replied quietly enough that Amirin had to listen carefully. "He might still be there, but it is hard to say."

"How?" Amirin stopped pacing and studied his bloodhound. "I thought that you could always place him."

"I could, in the past," Hadi nodded. "After Vorgash, his signal grew so faint that I wondered if he had died. Now I can only see a direction, but not a range."

"What?"

"Something has changed about the man," Hadi

shrugged. "Without getting close enough to touch him, I cannot tell you what."

Amirin cursed under his breath.

His plan all along had been to use the ruse of these attacks to undermine the Emperor as an incompetent fool, more interested in sex and whiskey than ruling. But Aeovan was far worse than Vorgash.

Omezi had upped the stakes, blowing up stations like she had done at Krusskyo, but not Vorgash.

Was she getting desperate? Or just taunting him louder and louder because he had not responded?

When had the Sept ever allowed anyone to snub their noses at authority?

Even Kathra Omezi's tiny tribal force had warranted a Septagon, just because of that. Finding the alien allies that had taken Daniel Lémieux only made it worse.

Someone needed to respond, and those fools at Rhages were incompetent. Getting them to pair Septagons had required far more time and effort than it should have, just because tradition leaned against such a thing.

Worlds were safer, where such a pairing orbited, but any other system was at risk. Just look at what those dangerous cows had done at Aeovan.

"The horns of dilemma," Amirin finally admitted. "I can convince the Shah to give me sufficient forces to chase Omezi. But is that a good use of our time? Do we take the throne from an incompetent and then save the empire, or use that glorious victory to assure our rise?"

The encyclopedia that was Hadi Rostami lapsed into thought.

"My powers do not appear to be fading, even though they should," he said with a distracted tone. "Perhaps they will just turn off overnight, sometime soon. Perhaps they will be with me until I die. But momentum favors you right now, and the many minds I have tampered with will eventually revert. I can adjust things, but unless I completely alter someone, it is like tightening a bolt. Eventually, it will vibrate loose again."

"So Rhages, and then Omezi?" Amirin asked.

"My suggestion, yes," Hadi said. "She cannot expect us to do anything but be dragged around by the leash she has given us. Can we ignore her?"

"Ignore her?" Amirin gasped. "The woman shattered Aeovan. And Krusskyo. Two Septagons have felt her wrath so far."

"And she fears fighting two now," Hadi responded. "We could take a Septagon to Aeovan, but it might require two, and that would leave Earth open to the same sort of attack."

"Do we take the two to Rhages instead?" Amirin asked. "Someone is bound to whisper of my treason eventually. Should we simply march on the capital and demand the man stand aside?"

"Others will still dispute you, Amirin," Hadi noted.

"Let them," he said. "I will have you thwart such fools or destroy them, as necessary. But we need time to repair the Empire and start to rebuild it. I cannot do that while we are also fighting Omezi and her Anndaing allies."

"In our lifetimes, then," Hadi said. "As the Ishtan proclaimed. We would destroy the Empire, and then attempt to build something new in its place."

Amirin nodded.

All of his life had been secretly dedicated to exactly that end, even before he met Hadi Rostami, to say nothing of the Ishtan or the Mbaysey, who might have granted him the power to do it.

"*Singara*," he decided aloud.

"The Septagon?" Hadi was confused, which was good. If

he did not see it coming, nor would the others who sought to outguess him, Emperor or Rebel.

"The ship was broken at Tavle Jocia and returned home limping," Amirin nodded. "It is not a warship capable of engaging even another Septagon, let alone *MorningStar* and Omezi's allies. But it will be a powerful symbol. My symbol. You and I took that vessel and conquered Tavle Jocia with it. Another man foolishly lost everything afterwards. Many will see an emperor in that failure."

"And if they destroy us?" Hadi asked, but clinically, not emotionally.

"Then we are dead," Amirin declared. "And the eventual fall of the Empire becomes someone else's problem, except for the footnote that announces that I might have been able to save everything in my time, but for being executed."

Hadi studied him for a long moment.

"Will you care what becomes of the men that might wish to stop you from recruiting Septagon *Singara* to your cause?" he asked.

"They can join me, or they can die," Amirin said simply. "Those are now the stakes we are playing for."

55

Daniel noted the faces around the room. The expressions tight with anticipation, perhaps tinged with a little fear. Only Kathra and Ndidi seemed immune to emotion, but he knew both women well enough to understand what roiled beneath calm surfaces.

"I have been trying to track Rostami," he announced, turning left to right to take them all in.

Kathra and Erin. Crence and Dane. Ife and the other two Speakers. Ndidi and all her women. His women, he supposed, if you wanted to look at the whole thing sideways. Even Hirly had overcome her squeamishness.

"Trying," Kathra echoed, not asking but stating.

"When one of us goes into jump, we vanish from the universe for a time," Daniel stated, perhaps unnecessarily. "Hadi is on the move now."

Faces perked up. Heads elevated just the slightest bit.

Daniel imagined he could smell wrath in the air right now, if it actually had a scent. Not the sour rankness of adrenaline and sweat, nor the musk of arousal.

Perhaps it tasted like fire and brimstone?

Or was that just in his own soul?

"Where?" Kathra asked.

"I do not know yet," Daniel managed to shrug without feeling weak or helpless, even as he was. "I must now spend time every hour or so looking for him until I locate the man when he comes out of jump. From that, Acqueir will be able to judge a direction. Eventually, we will know his destination."

"Will he come to Aeovan?" Crence leaned forward and put his chin on his elbows.

"Possible, but unlikely," Ndidi spoke up now. "Unless we were to camp over the planet long enough for a message to transit and a fleet to return. We made our point and left."

Daniel noted the calm certainty on the faces of the women he shared a bridge with: Ndidi, Hirly, A'Alhakoth, Acqueir. He was merely a chef by training, not a warrior, so he could only rely on experts who had killed people with their own hands, something he had never done.

"But he is moving?" Dane asked, perhaps the least comfortable here, but Crence considered the man his own second-in-command.

And Crence probably needed another male in the room with him during these war councils.

Daniel didn't count.

"He has vanished from Earth," Daniel nodded.

More than that he could not say.

"If he doesn't come to Aeovan, where would he go?" Hirly asked.

"Rhages, perhaps," Kathra offered.

"Or some fleet base where Pasdar could take command of a Septagon assigned to chase you again," Ndidi smiled grimly. "Us."

"Like the Mbaysey have somehow forgotten how to stroll casually away from a waddling Septagon," Erin laughed.

The rest joined her harsh mirth.

The Sept had planets to defend. The Mbaysey did not. Kathra would never allow it in her lifetime, and would raise Adaku the same way.

In a generation, Daniel wondered if the Sept might build something like a Dueler or Assailant. More capable than a Patrol vessel, but far faster than a Septagon.

They might turn into a serious threat to the cosmos if they did that. Which was exactly why Kathra was pushing today. Why Wyll was burning cash reserves keeping several Ovanii warships in combat commission.

Why the Mbaysey weren't just walking away this time.

"Crence, is your frenzy ready to deal with it, if Rostami comes here as part of a fleet and we do decide to attack them?" Kathra asked.

Daniel appreciated the way the Trademaster's hammer flexed both directions before he spoke. Better than immediately blustering an answer.

"If they bring a single Septagon, plus whatever number of Patrols they think sufficient?" Crence asked. "Absolutely. We've got Scout-2 and Scout-6 teams just sitting in the darkness watching and listening. I'm still not sure we can take on two Septagons."

"We know how they'll fly," Ndidi said, drawing all eyes around to her, Kathra and Erin included.

Jaws might have fallen open.

Ndidi looked like an ancient crone come for everyone's souls when she smiled. She even took her time studying the other faces, enjoying her moment of supremacy.

"The only thing that can hurt *MorningStar* sufficient to make me stop is the Axial Megacannon," she observed with about as much emotion as one might express when boning out a chicken. "That leaves a blind spot, where we have twice dropped out and attacked. So either they sail side by side, all set to rotate inwards so I can't sneak between them, or they sit in orbit facing each other so they have coverage."

"You've figured out how to defeat that?" Kathra asked, perhaps a shade breathless.

But like him, she was not a naupati, trained in the maneuver of big ships and dangerous guns. Only Ife, seated across from him, and Ndidi, next to Ife, had that expertise.

Ife smiled now, late to the realization, but arriving before anyone else.

There was a reason Ndidi Spoke for *MorningStar*, after all.

"Defeat?" Ndidi smiled. "Probably not. Savage? Absolutely."

"Tell me," Kathra commanded.

"They think in two dimensions, Kathra," Ndidi smiled. "The third only comes in to play when they want to bombard someone and tip the ship carefully over on its nose to open fire on a planet. What happens if *MorningStar* comes out below them in orbit, rising like one of Crence's megalodon nightmares? Would you give the order to open fire on a target, with a Sept planet likely to be struck with an Axial Megacannon shot if you missed?"

Daniel was not alone, shuddering. Was there a commander ruthless enough to chance it?

Yes. Amirin Pasdar would do such a thing. Daniel only had to reflect on memories stolen from Hadi to know that.

But that might be the only naupati out there who would.

"Pasdar," Daniel croaked.

"Yes," Ndidi nodded. "Who else?"

He could not dispute that logic, and he knew them all

better than anyone else at the table, having been a Sept citizen in good standing for a goodly period.

"Any other naupati or aspbad will hesitate," Ndidi said. "Might even refuse the order, unwilling to chance it, especially if you are fighting over an important planet. Might be worth trying."

Daniel licked his lips and considered this idea.

Twice he had fought Septagons in the Star Turtle, winning one and fleeing, while being mortally wounded by the second. Commanded by Naupati Amirin Pasdar.

But twice Ndidi and *MorningStar* had attacked Septagons, wounding one and killing the other.

Merde, was it possible to win this war?

What would happen to the Sept if even two Septagons weren't enough to protect you? Would the Empire suddenly decide to sue for peace with the Merchants Bank and possibly even the Free Worlds?

Anything to keep Ndidi Zikora from attacking their worlds?

Wyll's willingness to spend credit like water suddenly made far more sense. If the Mbaysey could force the Sept into peace, then trade was likely to happen. Anndaing goods flowing into Sept households, who might become rather cross if the Emperor decided to declare war later and cut trade.

He was a chef, used to planning meals and menus. The women, and men, around him were obviously thinking in generational terms.

Kathra let the emotions settle, looking at everyone one face at a time.

"Daniel, you will track Rostami," she ordered. "I will return to *GhostStar* with Crence and Dane, ready to lead the frenzy back to Aeovan if they come, or to trail them to a place where they might even think they are safe. Ndidi will continue to Speak for the Mbaysey."

Daniel nodded. The others did the same.

Ndidi would *Speak* for the Mbaysey, of that he had no doubts.

What would she say?

56

DEEP SPACE. Hadi felt like a hunted beast, suddenly safe up a tree or deep in a bramble, where the hounds could bark, but not get to him.

For now.

Daniel had changed. Hadi wasn't sure what or how. Consulting his Ishtan memories while safe in the depths of valence drive space, those ancient ghosts were even more aghast than he was.

Urid-Varg had never done anything like some of the chef's recent actions. He had always been a beacon in the darkness they could stalk, always carefully hiding themselves and the things they did to undermine his various empires.

Only when Daniel had taken up the power had he been weak enough for them to strike, and even that had turned out badly.

Today, it was left to a pair of humans, all that remained of that ancient battleground, and Hadi was no longer sure he was Daniel's equal.

What had happened at Vorgash? How had the man been able to focus so much energy? The turtle had existed expressly to do such a thing, but the turtle was dead. The Ishtan had watched from a porthole on Septagon *Vorgash* as its corpse fell into a star and melted forever.

Now Daniel could mask himself somehow. Only in moving across the empire would Hadi be able to detect enough parallax to suggest where Daniel was waiting for him.

For their final battle.

One of them would successfully end the other, and be free to leave his imprint on a defenseless galaxy.

Daniel Lémieux had already thrown his lot in with the aliens. Their potential victory over the Sept Empire would see humanity eventually submerged into some strange, alien sea where the thing that made them unique and powerful was extinguished. Where humans served creatures, rather than the natural order of things that the Sept had assigned. They didn't have to be sex slaves like Rhages, but they must serve.

A chime alerted him. Hadi noted the time and began to make his way forward, bodyguards in tow.

They were not on a Septagon. None existed that could be spared to merely transport Amirin and his aide to Uwalu, where Septagon *Singara* had limped in order to be repaired. Before *Vorgash* claimed primacy in the immense drydock capable of forging such vessels.

Or reforging them.

Singara's crew had been reduced to a skeleton, and then augmented with repair engineers. Perhaps only thirty thousand men labored on the beast right now, as it had no Patrols aboard, nor responsibilities except to prepare the ship for the graving yard and repair what could be done while it flew nearby.

Except that it would not.

Hadi had made sure that the Shah of Earth did not know the truth, but the man always seemed to suspect. That decisions were occasionally foisted on lesser men, but Umek Sardari was not one of them.

Even Hadi respected the man too much for that, once things had been set in motion.

But orders from the Shah had them in flight to Uwalu in secrecy. And the Shah had contained an expectation, there at the end, that Amirin Pasdar would *somehow* be able to convince the necessary people to hand over *Singara* to him, even in such poor shape, for the challenger to the throne to fly on to Rhages.

Umek Sardari had not known the truth at a conscious level, but the man *suspected*. And Hadi found it a measure of the man that he had gone ahead and done these many things, rather than possibly unmasking Hadi Rostami as an alien imposter to be killed as an outlaw.

How far had the Empire fallen that even men such as the Shah of Earth were willing to hide their eyes from some truths?

Perhaps enough that Amirin Pasdar could tear the rotting carcass down and replace it with something better.

Hadi dared not think about destroying all of humanity's strength, at the moment when aliens might take their independence away from them.

Should he kill himself and Amirin, like some bizarre, romantic tragedy the ancients loved to immortalize? They were not lovers, merely partners. Hadi was a knife that Amirin would use to assassinate an emperor and his fools.

And then hope that they could sustain the Empire long enough.

He had no good answers as the guards allowed him onto the ship's bridge.

Fast military transports didn't even have a Command Node. Merely a large room for several men. At least they hadn't taken one of those courier vessels that always reminded Hadi of a bordello in the way they were overly-decorated for senior officers who could not bear to be away from their pleasures even for a flight between two other whorehouses.

This room was at least bare metal and utilitarian. Far less insulting to the military men they transported.

Hadi found Amirin already present and making small talk with the aspbad who commanded.

Hadi reached out a mental hand and reinforced all the mental control he had been forced to unleash on the man and his navigator. He needed them, needed to be able to point a hand and have the two men tell him what lie along that line, so that they could possibly locate Daniel.

But they would immediately scream in terror and kill him if he allowed them to even contemplate why he needed such a thing. Or what it meant.

Possibly, the ship would be lost in jump somewhere after that, flying directly into a star as a way of hiding the evidence and eliminating even the potential for witnesses.

Hadi knew sorrow, but there was no other way to handle things at this late in the game.

At least the crew he would need to kill would be small.

He seated himself without addressing the other three men. Easier to simply shield their minds if he did not interact with them. Maybe it would be enough.

The clock counted down the time to emergence.

Hadi meditated on the sorts of evil he had become, nearly the very thing that the Ishtan had feared from Urid-Varg, when Daniel had never taken those steps.

Only Hadi Rostami.

At least the last four Ishtan would be waiting patiently for him in hell when he got there.

Starlight.

Hadi opened his mind, keeping the tiniest thread on the others as Amirin fell silent.

All of the cosmos sang to him, but he was looking for a particular note.

Fear suggested Aeovan, so he looked in that direction first. At least as closely as he could estimate.

But he was rewarded with success.

Daniel's mind stood out there like a light in a dark room.

Still, he had survived this long on patient attention to detail. He read off the right ascension and declination to the navigator. Waited.

"Aeovan, more or less," the man replied after a few moments to calculate and triangulate.

This ship was following a predictable flight path from Earth to Uwalu. They would never be more than half a light-year from their destination on landing.

Daniel was waiting for him at Aeovan.

Even Hadi could see the neon lights proclaiming a trap.

He closed his eyes and let go a sigh.

You have failed, my nemesis. I will be to Uwalu before you can understand. Rhages before you can stop me.

Hadi rose and made his way from the chamber, nodding to Amirin as he departed and released most of the hold on the other two minds. They would perhaps remember seeing him present. Perhaps not.

But at least he had escaped the doom of visiting Aeovan.

A bigger doom awaited.

57

Kathra gave up trying to read the book in front of her, unable to concentrate.

It was her war around them, but Kathra was reduced to relying on others to fight it for her.

She should have gone home after awakening Daniel, a princess finding the sleeping man in the tower, to respond to a kiss. That should have been sufficient, except she knew better, now that she had been to the front to see the status. She should not be here, risking the future of the Mbaysey when she had promised all those old women she would outlive them, except that by being here, she might be able to end the war now, rather than win it in years or have to fly into the darkness to escape.

It was coming close to whatever end it would reach, and she needed to be able to guide it at the end.

Something must have shown, or some sound, because Erin looked up from her reader and grunted quizzically.

The two of them were in the crew lounge on *GhostStar*, killing time with books as a way to not climb the walls in boredom.

"We could take one of the Scout-2s and make a run for it," Erin suggested in a voice only half kidding.

"Don't think I haven't considered it," Kathra fired back. "But I keep feeling that something will go horribly wrong if I'm not here. Some failure at the last, possible instant that I could have averted, were I but within arm's reach."

"Should we be on *MorningStar*?" Erin asked, putting the reader down now to stare at her, much more serious than she had been.

"That's Ndidi's realm," Kathra decided. "And the place that a Septagon will focus most of their rage and firepower. We can lose all of them, Daniel included, and still escape and rebuild the tribe, but Adaku is not ready."

"Hell of a dilemma," Erin noted with a half-smile.

"Everything is building to some terminal crescendo," Kathra said. "But I need to be off to one side watching, rather than center stage. Daniel and Rostami will fight their final battle, but there's not much I can do against a naupati commanding a Septagon. That's Ndidi's job."

"Then why are we here?" Erin asked.

"If I knew that, I'd probably be rich," Kathra smiled.

Erin started to say something but the intercom chirped.

"Kathra?" Dane asked the chamber.

"Here," she said.

"We've just got a message from *MorningStar*," Dane continued. "Rostami is indeed moving, but appears to be headed to Uwalu, although that had a very high degree of uncertainty on that scan. But absolutely not coming to Aeovan, at least not directly."

"Agreed," Kathra said. "I think we probably need to gather everyone that is in-system and prepare to move as a force."

"Just woke Crence up and he said almost the same thing," Dane laughed. "Got any ideas why Uwalu?"

"No, but I will let you know," Kathra replied.

The line cut with a beep and she settled back into her chair.

Erin seemed pensive, so Kathra left the book and stared at her best friend.

"Uwalu has a shipyard, right?" Erin said.

Kathra nodded.

"One of the biggest ones, if I remember," Erin continued. "*Singara* was there first, but *Vorgash* had to limp there when Ndidi was done with them."

"That's what Crence's scout spies reported," Kathra confirmed. "Does it matter? They've got enough firepower in that system to keep us from attacking directly, regardless of what they do."

"So does Earth," Erin said. "There has to be a reason to go to Uwalu. They aren't launching any new Septagons right now, not if they have to rebuild *Vorgash* and then *Singara*. The system has two more protecting it like they've been doing. But it's got to be a Septagon. Pasdar is a combat commander, reputedly one of the best alive."

Kathra cocked her head and considered what she would do there.

"He has Rostami," Kathra began. "That means controlling people. But we also suspect the man has higher ambitions than just fighting."

"That would be Rhages, not Uwalu," Erin said. "All the important people are there, including the ones you'd want Rostami mind-controlling. Hell, if Urid-Varg hadn't run into us first, Daniel always feared that the *salaud* would have eventually conquered the Sept Empire like he did the K'bari or the z'lud. Just control the right people to get yourself close enough to the Emperor that you can take him over. Or kill the man and replace him with whatever heir is next in line and…oh. Oh, shit."

"What?" Kathra opened her eyes from where they had half closed as she listened, focusing intently on Erin's voice.

"Rostami just has to get close enough to someone to make them do things the way he wants," Erin said, a little breathless. "Urid-Varg would have used the gem to mount some poor sap of a prince and lived out that fool's entire life as emperor, counting on being able to hop from body to body when he needed. Eventually, people forget the past if you work hard enough at it."

"Okay?" Kathra asked.

"So he doesn't have the mind gem," Erin continued. "That means that Rostami cannot be emperor in body. Do we know if Pasdar is still human? Has Rostami been controlling the man since *SeptStar* got back to civilization? Maybe this is a play to get Pasdar on the throne? He's certainly got the reputation that people would follow."

Kathra rose abruptly rather than answering and keyed the intercom herself.

"Dane here."

"Get me Daniel and Ndidi on the line," Kathra said, gesturing to Erin to rise and join her. "I'll be right there and we need to think about something."

She didn't wait for an answer, but opened the hatch and started forward. It wasn't that many steps to the bridge, even on a Scout-6, but every second might matter right now.

What if those two were about to take over the Sept Empire?

58

Daniel listened to Erin and Kathra walk slowly through their explanation, listening with the parts of him that had been Urid-Varg, as well as the memories he had stolen from Hadi Rostami at Ogrorspoxu when the Ishtan had died so loudly.

Something triggered, so he went inside and found himself in that salon where he liked to take visitors. Arsène surprised him there, already waiting.

Daniel rose, but Arsène stopped him by holding out a book. A memory, taken from Rostami, from the Ishtan.

"This is what you seek," the K'bari scholar said simply.

Daniel opened the book and fell in.

He emerged a moment later and stared at the K'bari scholar with new respect.

Arsène shrugged.

"You might have been dead," the man explained. "We needed to interact with your friends when they came, so I took to cataloging everything you knew in better order."

"Better?"

"You would have eventually noticed that your memory

had grown nearly eidetic," Arsène smiled. "Humans have an amazingly poor system of organizing memories, so Pheryoutl and I had to improve it so we could find things."

Daniel nodded and emerged from his fugue.

On the screen in Ndidi's office, Kathra's voice was still echoing.

Still, she and Ndidi knew he'd been gone. The others might suspect.

"I have a memory," Daniel explained. Everyone on this circuit knew the truth. "Hadi was speaking with the Ishtan, right before they offered him power comparable to theirs. They had a conversation about Amirin Pasdar becoming Emperor of the Sept with Rostami's help."

"And they gave the man the power anyway?" Erin snarled.

Daniel shrugged.

"I suspect that they were tired of immortality," he replied. "And expected the Sept to succeed in killing me, either at Ogrorspoxu or afterwards. But for Ife, they would have done just that."

"So they gave him power comparable to you?" Kathra asked.

"Potential," Daniel corrected. "Not actual. I can do things Urid-Varg could not. Or never tried. But yes, Hadi can control minds like the Ishtan could. Or anyone bearing an Ishtan mind gem, like me."

"What did they foresee happening?" Crence spoke up now.

"Amirin Pasdar was already maneuvering to get himself made Emperor of the Sept," Daniel said. "If he did not try, the Ishtan believed that the Empire would last perhaps another three or four hundred years before it fell apart, as all human empires to date have done."

"And if he did try?" Kathra pressed. "With Rostami supporting him?"

"That he would succeed," Daniel shuddered as he remembered the words of the alien beings. "That nothing could stand before them, if I was gone. At the same time, they would destroy everything that the Sept Empire stood for, and have to build something else in its place. The Ishtan did not tell Hadi this in so many words, but they expected the two humans to fail. I saw that in their own memories."

"They set them up for destruction?" Ndidi's eyes got bright. "Destroy the Sept from the inside, by giving a human the power to do such things as you two can?"

"I cannot express the words," Daniel said. "I'm not even sure I could merge myself with you to show you. But after eleven millennia of attempts by Urid-Varg, the Ishtan seemed to have come to believe that star empires were themselves evil, regardless of their stated goals."

"Would you describe it as handing Adaku a loaded pistol right now?" Kathra asked.

"*Oui*," Daniel said. "They expected to die, I think, and took steps to make sure that Hadi might live long enough to bring the rest of the Empire after us, if they did. No more empires for Urid-Varg or Daniel Lémieux to capture. They gave him enough of themselves to be successful. But I do not see any inkling on their parts that their deaths would give Hadi that much power. It was supposed to have faded by now, so they might have imprinted themselves on his mind directly."

"Meaning?" Crence asked.

"Meaning that he is Ishtan in human form," Daniel said. "That he has all their abilities, but perhaps not their power."

"Not enough power?" Kathra asked.

"Not to fight me directly, no," Daniel said. "But they have Septagons, and we have only *MorningStar*."

59

CRENCE TAPPED his open fin down on the table top enough to get everyone's attention without being a complete ass about it.

All eyes centered on him now, present and across the gap on a screen.

"Wyll warned me," he began, pressing his lips together almost to the point they hurt as he considered his words. "It had been an absolute last stand kind of thing, but he was maybe planning farther out than any of us."

"What did he see, Crence?" Kathra asked in a quiet voice.

Like a big cat stalking prey in the grass. He tried not to shudder too loudly.

"We beat the Ovanii with the Armada," Crence answered. "Summoned up every captain in the entire Anndaing Merchants Guild and threw them at those *salauds* like a swarm of rats going after a bargee. Took the verks down eventually, but the cost was hideous. Still surprised we took any alive, but even those bargees understand death, and apparently still have cultural stories about shark frenzies."

He took a deep breath.

"Wyll told me to pay attention to see if there would come a point where we needed to summon the entire Armada again and throw it at the Sept," Crence concluded.

At least everyone else's mouth dropped open, and not just Dane's. Crence was glad that one transcended species. His hammer was as far down as it would go without tearing anything.

"No," Kathra said.

Boxing his eyes might not have been as surprising.

"No?" he goggled at the human woman.

Worse, she actually smiled at him, but it was that same smile a bargee sees as the cat landed on its back and started tearing chunks off.

At least he'd never understood women, so not fathoming this human version wasn't that much of a stretch for him.

"No," she repeated. "How long would it take to gather the Armada and get to Rhages or Earth?"

Crence did the math in his hammer. He had a pretty good idea where each world was located on a map, but had never been that deep into human space. Even now, they were only sort of close to the human homeworld.

"About two years," he said after a moment. "Sail time both direction. Call and Answer. Whatever battles we'd need to fight to set up and defend forward bases big enough to feed that many frenzies. Major undertaking."

"Daniel, what could you do with two years lead time?" she asked the chef.

"Own an entire Empire so thoroughly that you'd meet a wall of Septagons, like the battle of Masairctug."

His smile was even worse than hers, if that was possible.

"Masairctug," Kathra nodded. "Seventy-five Septagons sailing in formation. Most of the human fleet at the time. You have twenty-three Battlemasters, Crence. They'd lose."

"So what do you propose?" he snarled at the woman in spite of himself.

Her new smile topped Daniel's. Crence had wondered if anyone could look even more dangerous than Ndidi when that one was on a roll.

He should have known where the younger woman learned it.

Hell, just the cold rage in Kathra's eyes right now might make Sept men fall over dead at forty paces. Then she turned to Erin.

Crence had a scholarly understanding of the barcode tattoo on the side of the woman's face. She cut her hair into a thing called a mohawk to draw attention to it.

And he had met the venerable Ezinne that everyone called Grandma. Ancient by human standards and still one of the most dangerous humans Crence had met.

Worse, Erin just nodded, like those two had Daniel's powers to communicate telepathically.

How bad had things just gotten?

Crence Miray felt like a pup swimming with hungry megalodons.

At least Dane had gone pale, hammers back in unconscious fright.

Probably unconscious.

Maybe he could see the future.

Kathra turned back to him and Crence suddenly understood human theologies containing war goddesses.

Plural.

At least three of them, because a glance showed that Ndidi had ascended to that place as well when he wasn't looking.

"Yagazie," Kathra said simply. As if that contained everything that needed to be said.

"Can we pretend I'm just a dumb, Anndaing trademaster,

please?" Crence asked.

"Her mother," Erin said, helpfully.

"I'm aware of who Yagazie was, thank you," his tartness leaked out in spite of his fear.

"It started with an assassination, Crence," Kathra said. "The Sept sent someone out who killed my mother, in spite of everything her comitatus could do to prevent it. I was a teenage girl suddenly thrust into command of the Mbaysey. All because of them. Everything I have done—we have done—since then originates at that point."

"Two points," Erin corrected her. "Ezinne."

Oh, gorbak.

Crence suddenly wished that the gift of prophesy had descended on him. Maybe the touch of some *salaud* deity with a black sense of humor. Anything to make him understand.

Worse, Daniel nodded now.

Crence felt like the only person here without a private communication channel going, but Dane looked close to passing out, so maybe it was a human thing.

Hadn't Daniel said that he had fully merged with Kathra, Erin, and Ndidi? The others had been inside his mind, like Crence, but those three women had become him.

And, quite possibly, each other.

Ndidi looked like she was chewing fittings with her bare teeth. But she kept her peace.

"Who?" Crence finally asked.

"We would like to bring down the entire Sept Empire, Crence," Kathra smiled the sort of thing that painters would commit when they wanted immortality. "Amirin Pasdar and Hadi Rostami are already going to do that for us."

"And then?"

"And then Erin and Daniel will deal with them."

60

———

Hadi eventually got over his surprise. He had spent years expecting Amirin to finally step up and whisper to people that they needed a new emperor, a competent one. One like him.

All the maneuvering in the distant past had been sufficient to convince them that the naupati was as good a commander as they were ever going to meet. After the first trip to Tavle Jocia, building *SeptStar*, the man had spent the years since playing the aristocrat and making nice with people.

It had paid off.

They had arrived at Uwalu with maneuver orders from the Shah of Earth placing Amirin Pasdar in command of a greatly reduced Septagon *Singara*.

And people had accepted that.

Hadi had only needed to adjust a few minds to keep them from reporting anything to spies and secret police, then transports started arriving to fill the vast cargo holds with food and supplies. Thirty thousand men consumed far less food than three hundred thousand, but still required many loads.

He stood at the very tip of the Command Node on *Singara*, enjoying the view of the stars and nearby stations orbiting with them. The graving yard was due aft right now, which he also found rather fitting, since *Vorgash*, the first great love in his life, was slowly being put back together inside that complex, years from being whole.

Hadi still would have just scrapped the vessel and started over, but he understood that the Empire might possibly never admit the level of defeat that *MorningStar* had inflicted on a Septagon in single combat.

The aspbad that had been overseeing repairs on *Singara* had been assigned to ground duties to get him out of the way, but Hadi still remembered many of the men on the deck below him from the mission to Tavle Jocia. They would remember him.

More importantly, all of them remembered the mighty Amirin Pasdar, most of them with some level of awe in their minds. Hadi reached out to listen and noted that the naupati was approaching, exactly on time as always.

He turned his mind now to the twenty men below and reinforced things. Those twenty would be the key to a revolution that would see all of them as heroes of the empire, or executed as rebels.

Not even Hadi's power could erase the trail of minds twisted and lives shattered if they failed. Too much would be out in the open if they failed.

It would be as well if they succeeded, but he would have years at that point, hopefully, in which to slowly adjust minds and memories to something less damning.

The hatch opened and Naupati Pasdar entered.

They both had considered reverting to their military uniforms to go along with the ranks of command of this vessel, but in the end had decided to remain in the simple desert robes of the Court on Earth.

Theirs was not a military mission. Septagon *Singara* was merely a chariot bearing them to their destiny. They would be civilians here.

Hadi turned and smiled grimly at Amirin before walking to take his place next to the man at the rear of the chamber. They both sat, his aspbad's throne smaller and less ornate than the naupati's.

"Are we prepared?" Amirin asked in a voice loud enough for the twenty men around them to hear clearly.

"Septagon *Singara* is ready for flight, Naupati," Hadi answered.

He was not surprised when Amirin rose a moment later and began to walk. The length of a Great Causeway, running down the center of the Command Node and elevating the two commanding officers above everyone else, was just long enough for the man and such pacing had become Amirin's norm.

"Navigator, take us into jump," Amirin ordered as he got to the front of the room.

They waited for several minutes while the ship made final calculations, but Hadi had already prepared everyone and everything ahead of time, so *Singara* gave a good accounting of herself.

Hadi nodded as the stars outside faded.

"Warriors, it is time that you learned a great secret," Amirin announced after the ship had made the jump onto valence drives.

They were away from Uwalu now, and no message could be sent that might incriminate them at this late a date. *Singara* would arrive at Rhages before anyone figured out what Pasdar or the ship were up to.

Amirin Pasdar continued to pace, voice raised enough to rattle the portholes but still clear.

"For many years, we have fought the Free Worlds," he called, building slowly. "Taking them one by one because they could not resist us. But they have alien allies now, terrible monsters from the galactic interior set to push us back from our destiny."

Hadi watched the way that voice and those words worked their way into the men's minds like worms burrowing.

"In spite of that, we reached out a mailed hand and closed it around Tavle Jocia like a fist," Amirin said triumphantly. "Took it like the jewel that it was. You men did that."

Smiles on the faces at that. These men had been there. Had been part of that glory. Many of them had forgotten it in the face of the embarrassing failures that had come later.

"And then the Emperor recalled me from duty. Returned me to Rhages to attend him and those fools," Amirin's voice got darker now. Hadi helped keep the men cold, playing on their anger at subsequent events. "He ignored you and left the fleet hanging when the Mbaysey and their alien allies came. You have been betrayed."

That was a hard word for the men to swallow. All of them saw themselves as proud warriors defending the empire and helping make it bigger and better.

But each of them harbored some suspicion that the naupati spoke the truth.

"*Singara* barely escaped the attack, because the Emperor chose one of his *flunkies* to command," Amirin growled now. "They arrested the Shah, the new naupati, and even the aspbad in a whorehouse filled with aliens."

Singara had been gone, but the rumors had followed the mighty vessel home.

"Do you know what I saw at Rhages, when I was forced to wait on that fool?" Amirin continued. "More alien women for the men of the court to fornicate with. At least we think they were women. I did not participate, so I could not tell you what disgusting perversions went on in those chambers. I was too busy watching our emperor drink himself into a stupor every day."

Hadi knew a good line when he heard one, so he bored into those minds now, hammering home the thought of aliens, perversions, and even the copious alcohol that was supposedly *haram*.

Forbidden.

He felt a harder rage take hold in these men. It had always been there. The flight from Tavle Jocia had been the first time any of these men had ever tasted defeat, so it was easy for Hadi to implant the idea that they had been deceived.

They had not failed. Others had turned on them. Set them up to die.

But for luck and timing, they would be dead because of the Emperor and his follies.

His incompetence, wrapped up in perverted debaucheries at Rhages, hidden well away from the upstanding men of the fleet that protected him from the very aliens he fornicated with.

Hadi leaned back and marveled at the taste of pure wrath emanating from the men around him. It might be strong enough for Amirin to feel it, or at least smell it in the air.

These twenty men commanded the one thousand who normally commanded the entire three hundred thousand. That there were only thirty thousand minds within range of Pasdar's voice would not change the things they would say.

And these twenty men would back up those words. Would support the naupati who did not blame them for losing Tavle Jocia, unlike the others at Uwalu who had taunted them, however quietly.

Singara had been betrayed.

That rage would carry them to Rhages.

And then they would ask hard questions of a drunkard, in front of the entire empire.

Hadi looked deep inside to see if he even had any pity left for the man, but it had been burned out by the sight of alien slaves being dragged off to a handy couch for whatever rapes those men had come up with today.

Dana Bahram Tabatabaei, Keyaksar and Padishah of the Sept Empire, had this doom coming.

61

Erin completed her preflight checklist and set the clipboard back into its holder. She was buckled in. Daniel was seated beside her, waiting patiently, but she never rushed this.

Eventually she was done. Erin looked over and he nodded.

MorningStar had given chase, such as it was, once they guessed where Hadi Rostami had headed. From Earth to Uwalu. Spies had reported the sudden loading of Septagon *Singara* with excessive supplies, when the vessel had been quietly orbiting close to a repair yard since *Vorgash* returned from the dead.

Singara's flight had been observed by Scout-2s lurking in the darkness, so Anndaing pilots had been able to establish the probable baseline flight. Everything pointed to Rhages, the Sept capital world, so Ndidi had begun to chase after them.

"They really won't see us coming?" Erin asked Daniel again, for what seemed like the twentieth time.

"He'll see me," Daniel corrected her. "But Ndidi and

Nwanyiudo are flying a specific path to Rhages, so it will look like I'm still more or less in the vicinity of Aeovan when he tries to find me."

"I thought he could tell the distance, too," she said.

"He could, before I died," Daniel grimaced. "I have learned things about the power that not even Urid-Varg explored, mostly because he didn't need to. Some of my ghosts are in awe, but at least they no longer fear me."

"So he'll look back and see you, thinking you haven't figured him out?" Erin asked. "Is he that stupid?"

"No," Daniel said. "He is among the most intelligent humans I have ever encountered, in terms of the organic computer and encyclopedia in his head. But the Ishtan did not understand us."

"And you really think we can just sail in there and nobody will notice?" she asked, toggling the last settings to unlock them from the flight deck.

"Oh, they'll notice," he shrugged. "I will do things to them so they don't care."

Erin shuddered, but understood.

After he had come back from the dead, all of them had gone to the bottom of his soul again, reassuring themselves that it was still Daniel in there and that he was still the man they remembered.

Not submissive, but one who had submitted. Who willingly allowed the three women to direct him, because he could not trust himself with the immense power he had. She grinned inside that he had even asked for others to make sure that he had not used his power to accumulate a harem. In the end, it was just his quiet competence that impressed those women.

Erin would never touch the man, even as Kathra had explored certain things, but Erin had gone back to the very first Mnapyre ghost and inspected them all, clear to the present.

Daniel was Daniel.

Erin opened the comm line.

"Spectre Two, ready for launch," she said simply, glancing around the interior of the last SkyCamel in the squadron.

It even felt like an ending, seeing the two seats for her and Daniel. The storage closet on one side, immediately across from the small head. Aft, the deck and walls had been dinged by decades of use and abuse, until the jumpseats were barely visible against the marks.

Then the two big storage bins for holding smaller things so they didn't fly around in zero gravity. The airlock hatch that she had used on so many TradeStations, hauling ingots, sheets, and gases for trade.

It was the last SkyCamel left on this side of the galaxy, with the rest all back home aboard *SeekerStar* awaiting her return.

All the others in this bay were the larger transports the Anndaing used, but *MorningStar* had kept a SkyCamel so that they could easily shuttle people and supplies back and forth to *SeekerStar*. It even had valence drives, but the two of them would be living in zero gravity for a while.

It was just a shame that she didn't have her actual Spectre to do this in, but it was back in storage on *SeekerStar*.

In the end, she had started this strange adventure with Daniel while flying a SkyCamel, so maybe it should end this way as well.

End?

Perhaps.

Comitatus.

Kathra certainly couldn't do this. Nor could Ndidi. A'Alhakoth had the skills, but she was a Sword these days, just as Nwanyiudo was a Pilot, and *MorningStar* needed them more.

No, this was Erin's mission.

"Spectre Two, you are cleared to disengage," Kathra's voice came over the line. "Good hunting."

So much wrapped up in those two words, an inside joke from when they were still innocent fifteen-year-olds going to take on the galaxy. When Yagazie was still alive and expected to lead the Mbaysey to many grand adventures for decades, leaving her and Kathra to be unruly.

Erin pushed the button and the deck magnets released. Thrusters lifted them clear of the deck and then surged forward through the open lock door and out into space.

MorningStar didn't dare get too close to Rhages. Too much risk of a Patrol stumbling across them at the time they needed maximum secrecy.

But space was huge, when you scaled things out properly. There were a lot of places to hide in a cube several light-years across. *MorningStar* rode in one of them, with *SwiftStar* as her wingsister.

The others were headed home to that forward base with all the Anndaing raiders, to lay in supplies and perhaps turn themselves into pirates if this worked out.

And maybe if it didn't.

Erin brought up a rear camera on her main screen and watched *MorningStar* slowly dwindle with distance.

"We will be back," Daniel said emphatically. "Will see them all again."

"How can you be sure?" Erin asked, more from curiosity than fear.

"Because I am not done," he said, sounding more like a top-rated chef who had decided to turn himself into an assassin. "There are meals to cook. Books to translate. Women to seduce."

"You will never be my type," she grinned at him.

Daniel responded by getting a haughty look on his face.

"You say that now, madam," he said in a mocking voice, head up and shaking like a character on a vid. "However, challenge accepted."

His demeanor quickly fell apart into giggles, ruining the effect, but she laughed with him. That might require years of patience on his part, and for her to get extremely drunk first.

So he would have to survive that long. And stay with them.

Erin could not envision a future for the Mbaysey that did not include the bantam chef from Genarde.

But they were about to invade Rhages, just the two of them against the entire Sept Empire.

To take on however many Septagons might be there, and the entire ruling caste of the Sept. And a man who had been turned into another Daniel by the Ishtan.

But they had never truly understood what it meant to be comitatus, those *salauds*.

They would be facing Daniel at the height of his powers.

And Erin Uduik, with a barcode tattoo on her face.

62

AMIRIN HAD NOT FELT this level of uncertainty since his first mission as a mere sardar, commanding a team of elite killers he had inherited from an older man killed in action.

The sharp end of the stick, as those soldiers liked to think of themselves. Literally, in Amirin's case.

A hand rose and traced the scar on his left forehead as he sat and contemplated *Singara*'s flight through valence space.

He didn't even remember the name of the man who had given it to him forty years ago, the blade just missing Amirin's eye when he ducked. All head wounds tended to bleed profusely, so Amirin could only imagine what he had looked like to his men as he had killed the rebel with his own knife and stood over the last corpse with blood running down his face and onto his uniform.

Certainly, his men had accepted him as one of them after that. Other men, once they knew the story, also lived a little in awe, as had the few women he had taken in his time.

Soon, he would be to Rhages, and have to trade on that reputation. And the symbolism of arriving overhead in the broken Septagon that he had first taken to Tavle Jocia when he conquered the system for his inept masters.

Amirin Pasdar, of the Pasdar. Sardar. Naupati.

Emperor.

Properly, he should have arrived at the head of a conquering fleet, a line of Septagons sailing in proud glory like the old days.

But he could not trust that Kathra Omezi and her alien allies would not take advantage of a Sept civil war. This had to be fast and surgical.

Dana Bahram Tabatabaei, Padishah of all men, needed to be removed from power before he finished the job of destroying the Sept. The rest of those perverted scum needed to be lined up against a wall and shot.

Once the truth of those men's daily lifestyle was known to enough people, he could blackmail the ones he wanted to keep alive for political reasons.

But Amirin was absolutely planning to execute a significant chunk of them as worthless examples of failure as humans.

Amirin checked the clock. Early yet, as ship time went. Hadi would not be asleep. He moved to the intercom and sent a ping to Hadi. He didn't think he needed reassurance, but some nights he was not willing to lie to himself.

No man walks into the arena where death is on the line without some reservations.

"Sir?" Hadi asked simply.

"Tonight is a night where it would be nice to sit and talk with an old friend," Amirin said.

He didn't bother couching it as a request. Both of them knew that Hadi would come immediately as though ordered.

"Tea?" Hadi asked.

"Yes," Amirin decided.

The line clicked off and Amirin sat back in the chair, contemplating his various options at destiny.

Singara could not resist even a single Septagon opponent for long, to say nothing of the defensive forces arrayed at Rhages.

But if it came to a fight, he had already lost.

A moment later there was a chirp at the door. Amirin opened it to the ancient face of his Tea Master, a man who had served his family since before Amirin was born, and who had been with him for more than thirty years now.

The man entered and bowed, a look of solemn dignity on his face. He moved to the bar area and immediately went to work.

Amirin checked that his guards were in place across the hall and left the door open. Hadi would be along shortly.

Amirin returned to his chair and watched the old man work. Hadi had once said that it was unnecessary to alter the man's mind in any way, as the Tea Master was utterly devoted to the Pasdar.

Frightening, in a way, but Amirin had always been a man to follow his own desires, seeking excellence in ways that might be impossible for another man to understand.

In that, he shared something with the Tea Master, as the man's wrinkled hands began to boil water in a pot older than Amirin's grandsire, with tea drawn from the various estates under the watchful eye of this man's daughter, whom he swore would outdo him one of these days.

An emperor would need a Tea Master. Perhaps he would bring her and her family to Rhages. Or let her train another generation or two into excellence.

How many other lives was he about to disrupt and uproot with his vanity?

Hadi arrived before Amirin could wander too far down a

maudlin path. The man took his spot in the other chair and they watched the man steep tea with the grace of a painter.

"I occasionally wonder if the Mbaysey did not have the correct approach," Hadi began out of thin air.

His eyes never left the old man.

"How so?" Amirin asked.

He had summoned the man from whatever he had been doing for some level of philosophical discourse, so he couldn't complain when that was what he got.

Hadi glanced at the door, as if confirming that he had closed it, before turning back to the ancient.

"They have carved out their own destiny," Hadi explained. "Reliant on no man, no outsider, for how they live their lives."

"And this would be an improvement?" Amirin wondered.

"Our fates are tied up with sad, deranged men at Rhages who have forgotten what it once meant to be Sept," Hadi said. "What would it be like if the Pasdar, or even just a Septagon's worth of men and women were to venture out, to colonize some place far out on the rims, beyond Sept Space but with the entire empire between us and the Anndaing?"

"Give up the Imperial dream?" Amirin asked, intrigued.

He couldn't envision actually doing that. The hooks were set too deep into his soul after a lifetime of seeking just that.

"The Ishtan calculated that the Sept had perhaps four more centuries before they fell," Hadi reminded him. "That all empires eventually fall apart. Such was the nature of humanity."

"I cannot," Amirin replied after a long silence.

"Nor would I expect you to," Hadi replied. "But should we send colonies out as insurance policies? Have other collections of humans out there that could grow mighty enough to resist some future alien invasion?"

"Do we even know what species we might find in that

direction?" Amirin countered.

He was not intrigued, per se, but he could see the value of doing it. The arrival of powerful aliens had not changed Amirin's drive to conquer, but it had changed the timing and the purpose.

Before, he had been convinced that nobody but him could truly save the Empire. Now he knew what he was trying to save it from.

"We do not," Hadi said. "I have consulted every source I could, and none indicate that any explorers we know have gone very far rimward from Human Space as we understand it today. There might already be small colonies of humans out there. There may even be another Anndaing that we have not yet encountered, just waiting to fall upon us from the other direction."

"And that, my friend, is a measure of our failure as an Empire," Amirin said.

He watched the Tea Master approach now, two steaming mugs on a tray that he placed on the coffee table between them before he withdrew to the corner to contemplate whatever Tea Masters did in the presence of treason.

"It will be a new thing, if we succeed," Hadi noted.

"I will rely on you to remind me that we need to build long-range scouts that we can send in every direction," Amirin said. "Urid-Varg went somewhere after he destroyed the K'bari, but the Ishtan were not sure where, as they never followed that closely. Humanity must find all those threats and push them back if we are to embrace our destiny and conquer the entire galaxy. The Anndaing must fall before us. As must all others."

"Easier said than done," Hadi nodded. "But I will commission a team of scholars to go through every record and assemble an *Encyclopedia Galactica* so we know. And we can build ships comparable to *SwiftStar* and the others to sail those great distances. But colonies will eventually rebel against us."

"That is the nature of humanity, Hadi," Amirin said as he lifted the mug in both hands and let the heat leech into his soul. "The Free Worlds were those who refused to accept the Sept as their overlords. In five hundred years, perhaps a new Sept will arise to replace what we will do today, but we must ensure that they are humans, and not some abomination who grants aliens equal rights."

"Plant the seeds of our own destruction?" Hadi grinned.

"Had any culture ever not done such a thing?" Amirin countered. "I have heard your lectures on the nature of empires, my friend. We have grown weak and debased because there was none that could challenge the Sept. Now, a challenger arises and we have grown so inward that we don't even know who else might be out there. Even the Upynth are the limits of our knowledge in that direction. What lies beyond?"

"Darkness sufficient to hide Urid-Varg for a thousand years," Hadi replied. "The K'bari were gone before we rose, else we might have met them. The Anndaing are ancient. The z'lud are no more."

"No more," Amirin echoed grimly. "Gone not just as a culture, but as a species. That is what I am trying to prevent. Kathra Omezi and hers are not the answer, although I could see them turning into the very type of warrior cult that might return in several centuries, recharged and ready to take over. That is what I need you to out-maneuver, and do so on a scale measured in centuries."

He noted Hadi's grim nod, but could not tear his eyes away from the smiling face of the Tea Master. Something about the man's mirth suggested that everything Amirin wanted to accomplish in his life was absolute folly.

Amirin could not dispute the man.

63

Darkness.

Daniel was not one to travel in deep space. Or hadn't been before he met Erin. Before the Mbaysey and not setting foot on the surface of a planet again until Ogrorspoxu.

But when he was down in his various kitchens, he didn't really notice the stars. Even his cabin had not had a window to peek out of.

The SkyCamel, however, left you no doubts whatsoever. Valence space out the wide front window. Zero gravity to sleep in, eat in, and learn how to go to the bathroom again in.

At least Erin was pleasant company. Joane, on that long flight to Ogrorspoxu, had been generally quiet and withdrawn into whatever books Daniel had been able to translate so she could practice her language skills.

He and Erin had spent several days in close company, but they had long since reached a point where one could grunt and point and have entire conversations.

Now, they were at the edges of Rhages.

Endgame.

Space was huge. Even within a star system, you measured things in light-minutes or even light-hours. The amount of kilometers a beam of light travels in sixty minutes was still a frighteningly-large number. More so in three dimensions.

The SkyCamel was just another asteroid, or perhaps a comet, this far out in the darkness of the Rhages solar system, one of millions like it.

They had shut down the engines and coasted for a day, just to appear silent and dark to anyone that might observe them. This would work so much easier if curiosity brought someone near, rather than fear.

They were buckled in, up front in the SkyCamel, while Daniel watched the cosmos around them, listening for minds and voices. Urid-Varg had done similar things, but that grandiose shit had probably never bothered sneaking up on anything in his life. Even attacking the Ishtan, he had simply killed everything that moved until he got to his target and killed the Eldest and every Ishtan within sight. He had dropped out of jump on top of WinterStar and the Tribal Squadron and grabbed all their minds at once.

Daniel was being devious.

The SkyCamel had passive sensors, but nothing had registered.

Erin was munching on a bar composed of dried fruit and nuts, wrapped with chocolate. Messy in zero gravity, but nutrient and energy dense, and that was what they really needed.

There.

A mind saw something on a screen and turned its attention this way. To Daniel, it was like a flashlight coming on in a dark room.

The beam turned towards him and he smiled.

"They have found us," he said aloud.

"About damned time," Erin murmured back, before

stuffing the rest of the bar into her mouth and chewing. "How long?"

He shrugged.

"Depends on them," he offered. "We appear important, but they may need to get permission to come over here, since we are not broadcasting a distress signal. The SkyCamel just appears to be a dead ship from the outside."

"Not helpful," she growled under her breath.

"Hours at least," he said. "Maybe a day or more. There will be time. You should nap, but I need to keep an eye on them."

She rolled her eyes at him, but didn't comment. Instead, he listened to her breath grow slower and deeper, meditation if not sleep.

Bon. There was almost nothing she could do at this stage of things, so conserving her strength helped them both.

In the middle distance, minds took notice of a small ship where none should be.

What would they do next?

64

RHAGES.

Hadi had once dreamed of being important enough to be assigned to the planet itself, and not just another bureaucrat trapped on the moon overhead, safely removed from the ruling caste behind domes.

Later, he had actually walked those hallowed grounds, at the time too busy trying to keep from throwing up in disgust, or destroying the minds around him, to appreciate how beautiful the planet supposedly was.

Now he had returned, in a broken Septagon filled with symbolic weight and righteous rage.

They were minutes from emerging from that final, fateful jump. Both he and Amirin were on the Great Causeway, pacing in opposite directions that crossed at the middle of their lines.

They say that nothing centers the mind like an impending execution. His Ishtan memories were helpfully displaying ancient z'lud designs for starships that the Sept could build to explore and colonize distant worlds.

The z'lud had been explorers in their early days, covering even more worlds than humans did right now.

Until Urid-Varg had come. After that, the empire had turned inward and grown blinkered, rather like the current Sept. How frightening that the enemies of Urid-Varg were going to use their powers on a place that would have welcomed the Conqueror and absorbed him.

How long would a human empire of Urid-Varg's have lasted?

The Ishtan had no calculation, as only the z'lud had been anything similar at the start, at least until the Ishtan helped undermine it. But that had taken thousands of years, as they had been barely working iron before they managed to steal a few memories from Urid-Varg and chase him into space.

Hadi paused in his pacing as he considered how long-lived the Ishtan had been. Could his human form choose to live forever with these powers? Or at least until he got bored? The Ishtan had grown tired of living, and handed him the quest to destroy the last remnants of the Conqueror.

What would he do after that? Build z'lud exploration vessels?

Amirin had paused in his own pacing and was watching now.

"Nerves," Hadi said, unwilling to speak anything remotely incriminating before the men below them.

Not all were as loyal as a Tea Master.

"Always," Amirin smiled back and started to walk. "We have handed ourselves to the fates for judgment. Now we must find out what they have decided."

Hadi nodded and turned to look over the shoulder of one of the navigators. The countdown clock was large enough to be seen this far overhead, and ticked off the seconds of his life with impersonal, electronic efficiency.

They were close enough.

"All hands move to battlestations for emergence," Hadi said in a conversational tone.

They all should have been there already, but now they would have the confirmation that combat might be imminent. No more potty breaks. Put the book away.

Destiny was at hand.

Amirin took up his usual place at the very front of the Great Causeway, as if leading these men personally into battle, while Hadi watched from his throne. But then, Amirin had started out there, leading men in physical combat, so perhaps it made sense that the man reverted to a similar personal image now, when he was reaching for ultimate power.

The minutes turned into seconds.

The seconds evaporated all too slow and all too fast.

Septagon *Singara* emerged back into the universe, the warm smile of Rhages's sun on the outer hull.

"Locate Septagons *Darius* and *Xerxes*," Amirin called in a clear voice.

This last jump had been intentionally farther out from the planet than it could have been. Enough that they were not an immediate threat to the two naupatis commanding.

At least, not a military threat.

"Targets identified," one of the men below called. "*Darius* and several patrols are moving to challenge us."

"Open a channel to the Command Node on *Darius*," Amirin ordered. "Tight beam and scrambled. Conference mode at this end."

Hadi found himself standing in front of his throne without realizing it, so he sat and reached out with his mind.

Septagon *Darius* was not that close. Even the Axial Megacannon would not be lethal to *Singara* at this range, but that was changing with every second. Patrols would move up and surround them, tiny guns pointed inward to scour the hull, with only a handful of cannons capable of returning the favor.

But if it came to that, they were all dead and the mission a failure.

"Channel open," a voice rang out.

The air took on a different timbre. Hadi could smell Septagon *Darius* in the distance. He concentrated on that spot, midway forward on the top deck, where another naupati would currently be standing, questioning the arrival of *Singara* without any warning.

"Septagon *Darius*, this is Amirin Pasdar, aboard Septagon *Singara*," his commander said in a calm, commanding voice. "I am arrived from Earth with special dispatches for you and the naupati of *Xerxes*. I request permission for myself and my aspbad to board and deliver them. There is important news that cannot be broadcast."

If there was anything as Hadi listened, perhaps he detected the faintest hint of surprise at those words. This was not how a rebel acted, and *Singara* arriving like this heralded only a few possible options.

But Amirin would also intrigue them over there. Things that cannot be said over the comm because they are too sensitive for even secured, military channels?

Whatever could it be?

"News from Earth?" a man's coarse voice replied.

He didn't sound like a courtier, with silky tones to match with easy living. Perhaps the two Septagons protecting the Imperial Court were combat commands, after all. Hadi had had no way to actually determine without asking questions in places where rumors would spawn.

Better to trust his powers, and his ability to outrun gossip from Earth.

"Indeed," Amirin said.

Nothing more. Leave it at that. Perhaps sinister news. Let us come aboard where we will be under you power so you can learn.

Hadi smiled.

"I look forward to your news, *Singara*," the man decided abruptly.

But then, what did the naupati of a Septagon have to fear? They were, after all, the most powerful vessels in space. Two of them were a force that nothing could threaten or dislodge, especially not one barely-repaired Septagon with no Patrols attached.

Right?

But the Ishtan had understood. Urid-Varg had spent his entire life knowing that terrible secret. If you own the minds of the men making decisions, then you are the one making the decisions.

Amirin smiled at him now, a mixture of grimness and elation that they had passed the first, dangerous hurdle.

They would only get worse from here.

65

Kathra stepped onto the bridge of *GhostStar* and noted the ways that the three men here all reacted.

Jine got utterly relaxed, which was a sign of nerves in the nightflier. Dane stopped moving completely. Might have even stopped breathing, but she'd have to actually touch him to be sure, and he'd probably go ahead and pass out if she did that.

Crence rotated one hammer and an eye just enough to confirm that it was her and then blinked.

She didn't look that dangerous today, did she?

But Kathra supposed that she was exuding *formidable* like a scent. Daniel had accused her of it more than once.

She skipped over the polite chatter and cut straight to the heart of things. Crence would appreciate it.

"I see one of two options," Kathra said simply. "Either you hand me off to one of the Gun-2 escorts, or *GhostStar* goes ahead and hauls me to *SeekerStar* and the squadron."

Crence blinked again. Jine's fin actually rolled over like he was asleep.

She wasn't the least bit fooled.

"Because?" Crence asked in a carefully neutral voice.

"Because I need to have a conversation with Wyll and Obaj now," Kathra said.

"And you didn't know this before?" he hazarded, still careful.

"I've had time to think." She even smiled as she spoke. "To process it all and come to some conclusions."

"Would you like to share them?" the trademaster asked.

"I don't believe that Pasdar and Rostami can stop Daniel," Kathra noted. "Whether or not those two manage to overthrow the Emperor is a moot point, but the Mbaysey relationship with the Merchants Bank will have to change as a result, whatever happens."

"And we don't want to wait to find out?" Dane spoke up. "They won't be more than a few weeks, according to Erin's math."

"*MorningStar*," Kathra said.

"Huh?" Crence finally turned enough to look at her with both eyes.

"We only leased it and provided a command crew," Kathra reminded him. "*SwiftStar* I own, but might need to sell it back to you shortly."

"Why?" Jine perked up enough to engage, rather than being that utterly cool sleeper shark he liked to pretend.

"The war changes," Kathra said. "Whatever the outcome. If Pasdar is emperor and Daniel dead, then the Mbaysey are not safe where they are and must flee. Any outcome where Hadi Rostami is no longer a threat, means the war as I have planned to engage in is over. Either way, Wyll needs to send out a new set of officers and crew for *MorningStar*, and maybe *SwiftStar*, depending. That or recall the ship to someplace like Acran for a refurbishment. The Mbaysey will be done."

"Oh," Crence said. "I was afraid you were going to say something like that. You'd just leave?"

"Mbaysey means not tied down to any planet, Crence," she scowled at him. It was still a relatively friendly look. "Not even sectors of planets like the Merchants Guild. Personally, I'd like to buy or steal a human machine capable of putting out programmable chips and boards for the Stars and then all I need to buy is bulk food. I can get that from any farmer I encounter."

"Or build a Bishop ring to fly and grow it yourself," Dane said carefully.

"Or that, yes," Kathra nodded to the shark. "You've had years to prepare for this. The moment has arrived."

"Technically, I'm supposed to be in charge of this frenzy," Crence began. He waved a hand as Kathra started to interrupt. "But I also have latitude to put someone else in charge and haul you to *SeekerStar*. I could take you direct to Ogrorspoxu, you know."

"This needs to be done from my deck, Crence," she replied. "My people have put themselves out there long enough. Once Daniel and Erin return, we're done with your war and the Merchants Bank has to fight it."

Crence nodded. He had been warned, but Kathra didn't suppose that he was really ready for it.

None of them would be.

Like all things, Kathra had developed an instinct of when to cut and run, staying ahead of trouble. She turned and moved towards the hatch now.

"What if they don't come back?" Dane asked.

"All the more reason to run, Dane," she glanced back. "No place in the galaxy would be safe for us."

66

Today, Amirin was traveling unlike any other naupati alive, more than likely. Most of those men reveled in the pomp of their office, and could not even go to the head without a team of bodyguards and at least two assistants present.

He was aboard a shuttle with one pilot, himself, and Hadi. That was it. Even the Tea Master was being left behind, but this was not a social call, and if Amirin got killed in an hour, at least the old man would be safely returned to the family palace to retire.

"Coming up on landing, sir," the pilot said just loud enough to be heard, without intruding.

Hadi already owned this one. Certain people who got close to Amirin had to be held on short leashes, at least for now. Once he was emperor, other systems and procedures would take precedence.

"What do you see?" Amirin asked his Ishtan hound, gesturing to the vast ship around them.

"Intrigue, in all the various connotations of the word," Hadi replied after a moment. "Assassinations. Assignations. Betrayals. Conspiracies."

"So about par for two Sept gentlemen meeting for tea?" Amirin laughed, feeling some of the tension bleed off.

"Maybe a little reserved, compared to the men of the Court below," Hadi also grinned. "Two well-bred strangers, perhaps."

It felt good to laugh. Amirin had been tense all day. All month. All year.

His entire life had been building to this moment, and instead of arriving at the head of a conquering fleet of Septagons, he was aboard one lame horse, walking right up to the Emperor's front door and knocking politely.

The light in the shuttle brightened as they entered the flight bay of *Darius* and settled to the deck with a solid thump. Through the deck plates and landing gear, he could feel the great doors begin to slide shut. In a few moments, air would be pumped into the chamber and presumably a red carpet rolled out.

Or a firing squad.

Assassins and revolutions.

Amirin rose. Hadi did as well, gripping the messenger case with orders from the Shah of Earth to listen to these men and hear their words.

Umek had somehow known the truth, without that knowledge ever making its way into his conscious mind.

Words Amirin spoke would potentially ignite a revolution, but it would be a righteous one, as far as Umek Sardari was concerned.

Amirin just had to bluff his way into the great hall and challenge that old man for dominance. Assuming the bastard was sober enough to understand.

The hatch finally opened and Amirin emerged into the brilliantly-lit flight bay. Two lines of troops had been drawn up in the short time, but all were at rest, providing a backdrop for the scene, rather than preparing to take him into custody.

Or shoot him.

Amirin put on a serious face and began to walk towards the naupati in the middle distance, standing as they did, and he had, at the center of a swarm of aides and gunmen.

Too important to do anything alone.

Had he been that bad?

Amirin knew it to be the truth. Before Tavle Jocia and the Ishtan, he had been just another peacock. Perhaps a more deadly one, but almost as gaudy and self-important.

It had taken aliens inside his mind to break him of that pomposity.

It was a shame that the Empire would require the same, but at least something better would come of it.

Amirin walked to the correct distance and gave the man more of a bow than was required between two naupatis. And it would be the last time he bowed to the man, as Naupati Aghaei would be required to bend the knee to him when Amirin sat on the throne.

Amirin watched the man's eyes change as Hadi took control of him and began making adjustments.

Adjustments. Such a delicate, clinically-clean term for raping another man's mind and changing him to be the way you wanted him to be. The persona you demanded he become, when there was no power in the universe that could stop you.

Urid-Varg, but it needed to be done, if the Sept Empire was to survive.

"You are most welcome, Amirin Pasdar," the man said in a voice loud enough that everyone close would hear and understand. "I have a chamber prepared and tea, so that we can relax and talk like gentlemen of the Court."

"Thank you, Naupati Aghaei," Amirin replied, almost as

loud, but they were playing for an audience now. "I look forward to what we can accomplish together."

The man nodded back and they departed, moving side by side as equals for now, as they headed deeper into the great Septagon *Darius* and Amirin's destiny.

67

Daniel smiled as Erin shifted around a little. Because she was taller, the woman was standing pressed up behind him, against his back with her arms around his stomach and her head on his shoulder.

But having her chest squished against his back was not doing anything to improve her humor.

"Soon," he said to her.

They were floating in deep space, contained inside a bubble of air that his lime green and white suit could generate and maintain for the two of them. It even made things warm and comfortable as they waited, but Erin was just feeling grumbly.

The SkyCamel was shielding them from any view of the vessel approaching. This far from the star, Patrol vessels operated alone, covering great distances as they explored.

Daniel and Erin had walked out of the SkyCamel and stepped into the cold depths of space with nothing but his power to protect them. Here, they waited.

Inside the approaching vessel, he could hear the command officer issue bored commands to his subordinates, while keeping up a running commentary to the Tender off in the distance.

Daniel insinuated himself in the man's mind and dialed up the *ennui* another notch.

"Just another abandoned derelict," he told any listeners out there. "Looks like it has been here a while. Probably left behind by some smugglers about the time I was born."

The two other men on the bridge with him were less sure, at least until Daniel reached into their minds and tweaked a few things. The Patrol vessel didn't have the ability to dock the SkyCamel, other than to attach on a lock, and nobody who could fly it once Erin removed a few key parts and stowed them out of sight.

"Anything showing?" the commander asked.

"Negative, sir," one of the men replied.

"Hail them again."

"No response on any channels."

"Guns locked for surprises?"

"Affirmative. Still no response."

About now, the commander had the authority to just destroy it as a hazard to navigation, but Daniel wanted an extra escape route if they needed one, so he leaned on the man.

"Come alongside and dock," the commander decided aloud. "I'd like to see what clues they left behind."

Both other men shrugged and gave orders for a boarding party to assemble.

A handful of other minds perked up and Daniel listened as those moved to the airlock with guns.

This was why he and Erin needed to be elsewhere. If those men boarded an empty ship and reported it thus, their superiors would not expect any further reports. Daniel would only need to deal with adjusting a few minds, and they could keep sneaking slowly inward.

Thieves in the night, but for what he and Erin were there to steal nobody would believe. That was fine.

The Patrol came alongside the SkyCamel and the airlocks connected.

Now was the risky part.

He pushed off from where they hid and slipped across the gap between ships, listening to the minds on the bridge and hoping they had nothing pointed this way that might notice the impossible sight of two humans swimming in space without suits.

Just another nightmare, right?

Nothing changed as he moved them over.

Now, they were just below the airlock itself. Daniel could feel the edges of the grav field inducer, but they were still outside the range.

And below. That was important, because humans didn't tend to look down.

He listened to the commander's mind.

"Anything aboard the vessel?"

"Negative, sir. Temperature just above freezing and the air system is off. Things are a little stale. No cargo except food packs."

"Bring the food packs with you for inspection. We might eat them later."

"Yes, sir."

And the men withdrew, taking all of the leftovers with them. Daniel touched Erin's mind and left a reminder to steal some if they needed to use the SkyCamel to escape later. He felt her nod.

The airlock disconnected with a ringing thump through the hull. Daniel made sure he had attached safety lines for both of them as the Patrol vessel began to back away.

He waited until the ship engaged engines and began a slow burn for withdrawal, listening always.

The boarders had gone back to whatever they did. The men on the bridge had reported nothing amiss and were returning to their rounds.

He nodded to Erin and they climbed up and into the airlock.

Without suits, it was just like when Urid-Varg came aboard *WinterStar* after seizing all the female minds within range, never accounting for a male on the ship. Daniel lacked that *salaud's* power, but not his intent. He reached out and slowly began claiming minds aboard the vessel.

Non-critical personnel decided that they needed a nap and sat down where they could and went to sleep for twelve hours. Critical engineers developed a strange, partial amnesia where certain things could not stick in their minds. Bridge crew also found a strange sort of blindness.

The gravity in the airlock was set weak, about what *SeekerStar* kept the innermost deck at, rather than the heavier stuff further out.

Erin led, pistol in one hand. Daniel followed.

An engineer came forward and opened the airlock from the inside, so that there were no strange alarms. Daniel couldn't do anything about security tapes, unless he just caused these men to destroy themselves and their ship, but he needed quiet right now, not surprises and emergencies.

The engineer stared at them glassy-eyed and went back to what he was doing with his generators aft. From the man's memory, Daniel found the storage closet he needed, and got them both Sept Patrol uniforms.

She was still a woman, but having her in navy blue would make it easier for him to fuzz everyone's memories for what was coming next.

The two of them went forward to the bridge. A ship like this only had a crew of around forty, crammed into a space that made his worst kitchens look spacious. Kathra would be banging her head almost everywhere she walked.

"Here," he gestured.

Erin nodded and keyed the door open.

He and Kathra had spent a lot of time on this part of the approach, calling in experts and sailors. Most had agreed that it would work.

Daniel climbed into the mind of the commander and watched as the door opened and two figures entered. He had already adjusted everyone, but left things purposefully vague until he was close enough to steal the memories he needed.

"Good afternoon, Inspector," the commander said to Erin, seeing her as a tall, Persian officer, male even, who was here from central headquarters to watch him and his crew operate. "What are your orders?"

The man wasn't sure why, except that maybe the folks back at base had seen his ship as exemplary and wanted to watch him in action for training. Maybe he'd get a commendation and a promotion if he impressed this officer.

Daniel found it weird, watching the scene that was so radically at odds with what his eyes saw.

Erin glanced at Daniel and he nodded.

"We think that the gear you picked up aboard the shuttle might be contraband and should be inspected back at base, rather than at the tender," Erin said, following the script.

"Very good, sir," the man nodded brightly. "I'll see to it immediately and let my team know."

"Notify us when we get close," Erin said, turning and withdrawing now.

The ship was too small to have spare cabins where they could be bunked, and trying to adjust so many minds and not leave behind clues was more effort than it was worth.

Instead, they moved to the crew lounge area and sat in a quiet corner.

Daniel woke the men who had gone to sleep under his mental touch, but left a command not to see the Inspector or his assistant as they worked. No, these men should go about their normal duties as though the two were invisible.

And they did.

"You're nuts, you know," Erin whispered to him as two men sat down not that far away and one told the other a particularly off-color story about a recent shore leave.

"You were aware of this before you decided to invade the Sept capital world with me," he grinned back at her.

"Doesn't mean I thought it would actually work," she huffed.

"Then why do it?"

"I wanted to see the look on that *salaud*'s face when you finish him off," she smiled. "Dying afterwards would be worth it, just for that."

Daniel nodded, his face pensive.

"I have something much better in mind," he replied.

68

———

Hadi carefully studied the minds around him, one by one. The naupati was fully twisted to the point that Hadi would need to come back at some point in the next six months and undo a few things, lest either the man's mind shatter or everything broke loose and perhaps the naupati *remembered*.

The man's aides were easier to adjust. All of them had taken the change of heart from their commander and adjusted their own winds accordingly. Hadi did not have to do much to those men, other than perhaps nail a few things in place.

Again, it would all break free in time, but he would have fixed them. Or he would be dead, and beyond caring.

It pained him to think how much easier Daniel could have done all this, but the chef never would have spent the effort twisting minds into new shapes.

Hadi was seated now in the large conference room surrounded by aides and guards all marked. He was on Amirin's right as his aspbad, with Aghaei's aspbad seated diagonal from him.

"So what news do you bring from Earth?" the man asked after tea had been enjoyed and gossip exchanged. Amazingly, only thirty minutes or so had evaporated.

Lucky for everyone the news they brought wasn't time-critical.

How had the Empire survived this long, when long-winded, bumbling fools ran things?

But Hadi understood. The Sept Empire had been poisoned by its own success. Nothing could challenge the status quo, so every little thing that had gone bad had been frozen and gotten worse.

It would continue to do so.

Amirin leaned forward like a conspirator, and then glanced around the room at the many men lining the walls.

"Perhaps it should not be shared with everyone," Amirin suggested. "At least, not yet."

It even sounded reasonable, coming from the man's mouth. You had to know him to understand how out of character the tone was.

But these men didn't know Amirin Pasdar, except as the mighty and perhaps even legendary commander of so many great successes.

And Hadi was sitting inside Aghaei's mind, pushing buttons and moving levers.

"Yes, I believe that you are right," the other naupati said. He snapped his fingers and then gestured to everyone not seated at the table. "Clear the room and secure the door."

A breach alarm wouldn't have gotten those men moving as fast, even as badly run as this ship appeared to be.

Quickly though, it was the four of them. Hadi had even made sure that none of the men were aware of listening devices they could tap. Such things were here, but the men controlling them were the aspbad's personal troops. And they would listen to reason shortly.

Hadi took the aspbad's mind as well. Aghaei was not that much to control. The aspbad was far more competent, but base born, so the man could never command a Septagon.

Wasn't that the exact problem with the Empire? Only the Seven Clans could lead, regardless of how exceptional a man might be.

Even Hadi Rostami would never rise above the naval rank of aspbad, or the civilian rank of *andarzbad*, Advisers to the Emperor, but not Companions.

Never Companions.

This aspbad made sure Septagon *Darius* ran well enough. Aghaei's vices ran towards Terran racing horses, rather than mistresses, so he spent time on stud farms, rather than brothels.

As things went, at least it was a reputable hobby.

Hadi Rostami had read histories and biographies. Amirin Pasdar had studied tactics, strategy, and close combat fighting techniques.

"We have come from the Shah of Earth," Amirin said simply, gesturing to Hadi to open that case and withdraw appropriate documents. "He sends you and the naupati on *Xerxes* his greetings."

Hadi reached out and handed Aghaei the envelope with the orders and notes detailing that Amirin Pasdar was to travel to Rhages and take command of all naval forces in-system.

He let the man read things, keeping a warm hand over all those emotional centers so the naupati would consume the information and process it rather than calling for his guards to execute the two of them.

After a moment, he had Aghaei hand the documents to the aspbad at his side, where Hadi had that man read the pages while Hadi watched.

It was a bizarre way to think, seeing yourself in several

different bodies at once like on security cameras, but he managed. It helped that the Ishtan had been a single intelligence spread across several furry beings, rather than having any individuality.

Hadi was not, but he could see how it would make things easier in a situation like this.

The aspbad read the documents and recognized treason when he saw it, but Hadi did not allow him to even think the words to himself.

It was a fierce if silent struggle. The man was much more stubborn than he looked, but then, a commoner had to be to make it this far, aspbad on a Septagon assigned to guard the Emperor himself.

Hadi felt his control over Aghaei slip as he forced the aspbad to change.

"This strikes me as…" Aghaei started to say, but helpfully Amirin cut him off.

The aspbad was not going down easily.

"It is necessary, for the good of the Empire," Amirin said in a forceful, commanding tone, leaning forward to stare at the man, bringing the full force of his personality to bear. "You need to understand that we are taking these actions to save us all from ruin."

Weirdly, the way Aghaei had been twisted, those words wormed their way right in and found agreement, even in that split second when Hadi lost his hold on the man while he crushed the last bits of resistance from the aspbad.

Both strangers looked glassy-eyed now. Hadi wasn't sure whether or not he had done permanent damage to either man's mind. Hopefully nothing that could not be remedied when he had time later.

They just had to save the Empire, then Hadi could atone for the trail of sins and mental rapes he had left behind him to get Amirin this far.

"The good of the Empire," Naupati Aghaei repeated with hardly any prompting on Hadi's part. "Please, I implore you to remain with us tonight as my guest, and then you can continue your mission to *Xerxes* tomorrow."

By the time he finished speaking, the man even sounded mostly normal. Hadi would work on both men more over dinner, and perhaps after most of the other officers had retired.

Hadi gathered up the papers from where the men had spilled them as they lost motor control. He was nervous himself, but they needed to be off alone so he could meditate and look deep inside himself.

As they got to the very climax of all their planning, was his power finally beginning to fade?

69

Erin disliked the uniform she had been forced to wear, but understood that it made things easier for Daniel to handle. These men were expecting blue, so they did not awkwardly react to her like they would if she was in tangerine. They were expecting a male, but Daniel had keyed most of them to see her as such when they looked.

If they even saw her at all.

The Patrol had bypassed their tender to head straight in to a base, with a comment that they had found unnamed contraband and needed to turn it in immediately. Such things were uncommon enough to comment, but not so rare as to be an emergency. As a result, they were headed inward on a burn that had already lasted a little over twelve hours and would see them to a Sept base.

She had napped earlier, uncomfortably aware of men around her who avoided her feet without realizing it as she waited.

Daniel could not rest, but had assured her that he was still used to going a few days with minimal sleep.

She didn't believe him, but there was nothing to argue about.

He reached out a hand and prodded her. She looked over and he smiled.

"Time to go pretend to be important," he said quietly, a sly grin peeking out.

Erin rose and made her way forward to where the airlock was. The commander had slept, showered, and met them there, eyes still unfocused as he stood on Daniel's other side, a metal-sided briefcase in his hands.

They waited as the ship made noises from docking.

Erin found her hand dropping to the butt of her pistol as the door beeped, so she went ahead and put her hand at her side. She could draw and shoot faster than any man here, but her nerves were wound up too tight, even for her. It would not look right for her to be threatening these men, even as much as she wanted to kill them all.

The Sept officer stepped forward as the door cleared and stood in the middle of the hallway, as though he was alone. She watched another Sept male standing directly across from him.

"You have something for me?" the newcomer asked hollowly, evidence of Daniel's touch in his voice..

"Contraband," the ship's officer said in a wooden voice. "I place the evidence in your hands."

"I accept the evidence," the local man said, just as woodenly, turning and immediately walking back into the base. "Follow me," he said over a shoulder.

Erin did, noting that Daniel was a little off-center as he did and catching him as he started to brush against a wall.

Over her own shoulder, the Patrol officer closed the airlock and presumably went back to the bridge, where he would have memories of having done all these things, and then head back out on patrol, hopefully none the wiser.

Or they were both dead meat.

The new man they were following led them deeper into the base, walking slowly and with great deliberation. She knew Daniel was controlling the man, and riding him much as Urid-Varg would have, only doing it with far less practice.

In the distance, she watched a man who had been coming towards them suddenly turn down a side hallway, when he had been approaching, so the zone of compulsion Daniel was emitting seemed to be working. She had foul memories of those furry shits on Tavle Jocia doing something on a much larger scale, to keep everyone away from their tower.

Here, it would send people down other corridors instead of possibly confronting two intruders in badly-fitting uniforms.

She wasn't sure where they were going. Daniel had had no clue how this scheme would work, other than they would be handed off by a progression of Sept officers who would presumably log the correct information in their systems to account for the strangers as they went. And whatever either of them had needed to do or say along the way.

The man opened a hatch and turned to them with a smile.

"This way," he said brightly. "I have made arrangements for you to deliver the contraband to the orbital base for processing. Good work, agents."

Erin nodded at the man and took the briefcase when he held it out, feeling like a stranger in her own skin. Through the hatch, she found herself on a small flight deck, with a courier-style fast shuttle tucked tightly in, like new shoes in a box, although she had never actually bought any that way. Still, most TradeStations had them if you shopped.

She went aboard the craft and closed the hatch once Daniel came aboard, finally daring to breathe.

It wasn't much bigger than her Spectre had been. Two seats forward with a small kitchenette and fresher. A single cabin that took up about half of the thirty-meter length, with storage and engines behind that. No valence drives, but it did come with grav field inducers good enough for maybe one third G if she wanted.

"I'll talk when they call," Daniel said, taking up his usual spot on her right.

Erin smiled and started a quick preflight. The courier was stored ready, with everything topped off and a top speed almost as good as her Spectre, if she wanted to push. It would get them to orbit in just about two days from here.

On the dash, a red light began blinking. Erin keyed the comm line.

"Courier Three, you are cleared to launch and your flight plan has been approved. You will be subject to terminal control beginning at turnover and Rhages will issue you guidance at that time. All clearances are being filed now and will be on record when you get there. Safe flight."

"Acknowledged," Daniel said in a terse but happy voice. "Launching now."

He nodded over at her and Erin pushed the button that spit them out of the side of the base like a seed. She brought the engines on line and let the ship fly itself with the instructions they had been given.

Two days, and she would be in orbit above the human emperor.

Just how crazy was it going to get then?

70

—————

AMIRIN STOOD on the Great Causeway of Septagon *Xerxes*, at the front of the chamber, overlooking the bow of the mighty warship. One shadowed horizon of Rhages preceded them, the terminator still below the horizon for another few minutes as the vessel orbited.

He tore his eyes away from the vista and turned back to the two naupatis and *Xerxes*'s aspbad, all standing a little glassy-eyed next to Hadi, back by the thrones.

He had moved so much faster than he had ever anticipated. In his earlier plans, the maneuvers had been quiet and subtle, shadowed from such men as these until the entire empire was calling for the current fool to be removed.

At that point, the Seven Clans would have already been meeting in secret salons and gaming dens, handicapping various candidates and horse-trading favors back and forth as they sought a consensus.

Amirin already knew that he would easily make any top twenty list put together by almost anyone, merely on his career to date as a brilliant naval commander who had done more than anyone in the current generation.

Tavle Jocia would have also played a part, as he had captured such a valuable planet away from the Free Worlds. It was only after a jealous emperor had recalled him for an incompetent favorite that the aliens broke Sept control.

All the more reason Amirin Pasdar should have been left in command,

He would have been able to prevent this.

Or so the stories were already being spread by friendly agents and men who believed that Umek Sardari, the very Shah of Earth itself, spoke the truth.

An earthquake was building in the outer worlds, far away from Rhages below them. How quickly it would get here was unknown, because Amirin had outrun it.

Hopefully, it would arrive just as he needed it to convince the bureaucrats on the moon overhead to support him instead of Padishah Tabatabaei.

Three Septagons in orbit, all of whom answered to him, rather than the man on the ground. Dozens of Patrols that would take their orders from the naupatis around the Septagons, rather than necessarily listening to the Argbadh, their Commander-in-Chief, who was also down on the ground, probably drunk out of his mind by now.

Or still.

Perhaps it was an ongoing condition. One never knew with those men. Amirin had not wanted to stay near them long enough to find out.

Amirin walked closer to Hadi, noting the way the other men seemed to be more stage puppets than anything.

"Gentlemen," he said grandly as he got there. "I do not think that the current Court serves the interests of the Sept. What say you?"

Naupati Aghaei spoke for the two as the more senior officer present. That was why they had taken *Darius* first, leaving Septagon *Xerxes* until today.

"Padishah Tabatabaei has failed us," Aghaei spoke loudly. "He has failed the Empire. He has failed the Seven Clans. He has failed humanity. We must remove him from power."

Amirin was amazed to hear those words from the man, but according to Hadi, Aghaei held enough to the old ways to be offended by the behaviors of those men below. Not much prodding had been necessary, once Hadi used his powers to loosen the man's political reticence.

The words were still treason. The kind that would get the man and his entire family executed by a vengeful Court. That the naupati next to him echoed the sentiment a moment later would not lessen the crime.

Merely expand the hangman's writ.

"Communications, open a coded channel to the Palace," Amirin spoke loudly enough that all of the twenty men on the mezzanine below would hear clearly.

The revolution had arrived, as surely as Amirin Pasdar lighting a fuse.

Amirin paced back to the front of the chamber to study the stars some more. Hadi would be hard pressed to keep the three men under control right now, and didn't need any additional stimulus possibly threatening his hold. That much he knew about the alien power residing in the man's skull.

He still had memories of the Ishtan thoughts and words emerging in his own mind, before Hadi had offered to fall on his sword instead.

Would he have ended up like that, had they not changed places?

Amirin shuddered at the possibility that he would be Ishtan in human guise right now. It was going to be interesting enough when he took power and needed to find the man a set of seven brides to represent the Seven Clans and help bind them to Amirin's throne.

None could bear Hadi a child. Amirin dared not chance

that the power was somehow encoded in Rostami's genes, to be passed down to a child that might reveal ugly truths about power.

And he needed Hadi. Too much of what they had been doing over the last six months had happened because the man could warp the minds Amirin needed convinced.

That, and the fear that the power might eventually fade.

Amirin needed to be secured on the throne before that happened, and the dice had been cast.

"The Palace is on channel six, Naupati," an anonymous voice rang out from the men below.

"Conference mode," Amirin said. "You men will support my throne. You need to be recognized for the power behind it that you represent."

That would straighten spines. Heads would come up proudly. Amirin had always had been able to rally his men to do the impossible. That was the task before them all.

"Who speaks?" a rough, angry voice emerged from the speakers like a wrathful djinn awakened when someone opened his bottle.

"Amirin Pasdar, of the Pasdar," he replied, letting tones of triumph color his words.

Those men needed to understand that they had already lost. It was not to be a battle, so much as a surrender.

"You were assigned to the Court on Earth, Pasdar," the man replied.

It was the height of rudeness among Sept aristocrats not to give one's name when meeting. But Amirin already expected poor manners from them. He would not let it derail him.

"The Shah of Earth has decided that Dana Bahram Tabatabaei, Padishah of the Sept, has lost the Mandate of Heaven," Amirin declared, listening to the many quiet gasps from the men around him, as well as the ones listening at the other end. "He must stand aside and let someone else take the power, before he destroys the Empire itself."

"I speak in the Emperor's Name," the man roared now. "I will have you destroyed instead, Pasdar."

Amirin smiled. Only one man spoke for the Emperor. It was useful to know that they had begun this conversation by putting Vizier Nasri out front, rather than some mid-level bureaucrat.

Already they feared Amirin Pasdar's words.

But then, he had arrived with a Septagon. And taken the other two without a shot or even a whimper.

Amirin Pasdar owned orbital space above Rhages, and possessed the only weapon in the galaxy capable of annihilating the Imperial Palace from here.

If it became necessary to unleash the Axial Megacannon.

At least none of the important people would be killed if he did, as most of the bureaucrats who actually ran the Empire resided on the moon under domes.

An anarchist would turn one of these Septagons skyward and blast those lunar cities into slag.

That would bring down the Empire faster than anything.

But he needed those men far more than the drunkards and rapists below him.

Amirin smiled at the other two naupatis and then Hadi.

"Vizier, I control all three Septagons in orbit," Amirin let his voice get conversational now. "Umek Sardari ordered me to take control of all military forces in this system, and I am doing so. From there, I will take control of Rhages itself. Then we will shine the light of justice on the behavior of your lord and master. And all the rest of you. Assuming the man is sober enough to walk to his own execution. Or any of you are when the rest of the Empire gets there."

More gasps. Utter shock. Even among commoners, such words were grounds for someone to be beaten. Sept gentlemen would demand a duel to clear their names and their honor.

Maybe one of those degenerates would actually challenge him to physical combat. Killing the Emperor's chosen champion would be the cleanest way to have that entire nest of vipers crushed, because it could only be one of the Anusiya, the Emperor's Companions who were such a poor shadow of Kathra Omezi's Comitatus, that would be allowed to challenge him.

And they were all badly overweight drunks who had not lifted a hand in anger in decades, except to perhaps strike one of their whores.

"Inform your Lord and Master that his time is over," Amirin continued. "I will give you an hour to consider your response and call you then."

He walked over to the communications officer and gestured. The man nodded and a beep signaled.

Amirin turned to Hadi with a smile that encompassed the other three men.

"Shall we have some tea while we wait?"

71

Daniel had slept. He always feared making significant changes to someone with his powers, because all he could do was something akin to pushing a bar out of its normal alignment. Eventually, he had learned from his ghosts, such things slipped back into their natural state.

Urid-Varg had contained so much power that it sometimes had taken years for that to happen. In that time, occasionally the mind grew accustomed to the new mode of thinking, and merely accepted it.

Thus had empires been born.

But eventually, enough people reverted, or perhaps the Ishtan had worked quietly enough, that the empires of mind had fallen apart, necessitating that the Conqueror move on. From the memories Daniel had relived, the creature had also grown bored rather regularly, and running an empire, even one where you were venerated as a god, took a lot of work.

Especially if you intended to live forever, like that being had originally done.

But for angry chefs.

He and Erin had alternated long naps in the bunk aft.

Food in the galley was sufficient sustenance that neither would starve. It was even a notch above station food, low as that bar might be considered.

They were both awake now. The burn had run automatically, so well designed and programmed this little ship was, and they were approaching turnover. That was the one downside, as far as Daniel could tell. The little runabout did not have anything like valence drives, so getting anywhere required time and direct navigation.

Things were so much easier when you could jump that distance in an eye blink and be where you wanted.

Erin grunted. Or grumbled. Daniel wasn't sure what it was, but she made a sound that caused him to perk up.

He glanced over, still securely buckled in, if she needed to do some crazy flying.

"*Singara* is in orbit," she said quietly.

"We expected that," he reminded her. "*MorningStar* was much faster through jump, but it took you and I some time to get this far, and they could go directly."

"Yes, but this means that Rostami can see you if he looks," Erin pointed out.

Merde. He had forgotten that, so utterly focused on sneaking his way into the system like a dormouse.

"Hopefully, he knows I am pursuing him, then," Daniel decided. "With any luck it will cause the man to make mistakes. We already know he is not a chef. I look forward to his soufflé collapsing."

Erin chuckled.

Still, maybe he should try to disguise himself even more than he had. Not even his ghosts had been able to find him for a time, so it could be done.

"I agree with you," Daniel continued sharply. "I will hide myself as much as I can, but that means that someone could sneak up on us."

"I only need you when we get to the station to dock," Erin said. "What story did you tell them back there?"

"That they needed to send a pair of agents to headquarters with special messages for the men in charge," Daniel said. "Again, I was vague, because that sort of evasiveness seems to be how they think, and to such men, it is natural. Frightening, but the Sept are not known for the universality of their laws. Mbaysey like us can testify."

"Amen," Erin said. "So they will meet us with a mid-level officer when we get to the station?"

"That is my expectation," Daniel nodded. "The man we left behind would have phrased it well enough to get us someone I could use when we got there. But again, you'll need to be more prominent, if I am to remain hidden from Hadi."

The smile on her face made him a tad uncomfortable, but this was Erin. He had just handed her a role to play, one that would make the Sept look like even greater fools.

"So," she smiled serenely. "The Sept believe that a Persian male of the right family is the height of social and legal standing, right?"

"*Oui*," Daniel replied, unsure where she was going.

"So what happens to the man we meet, if I'm dressed as a naval marzban?" she asked. "A black woman with a rank just one step below aspbad and amazingly senior in their ranks."

"That you were either an imposter, or the most dangerous human they had ever met," he said. "But the bluff will work well, because he will have that question front and center in his mind. It won't take me much to get him to center on that, as long as nothing comes up later."

"You are a *Rabic* male officer," she pointed out. "And we'll have you as a mere savaran, my assistant, if you will. We're both secret agents on some terrible mission. Perhaps I'm an assassin, and they don't need to know anything more than that, lest their entire careers be tainted by association."

"I think you will probably be enjoying this too much by the time we're done," he grinned at her. "But it will play to your usual swagger, and you will need to swagger at such men to back foot them. I can work from there, as long as we don't get too close to Hadi."

"Can he stop you?" she asked, turning her whole head his way now.

"*Non*, but it will be like a sound that awakens him from a light sleep," Daniel said. "I believe I am more powerful than Hadi Rostami, or I would have never suggested this craziness, but we will be surrounded by millions of Sept warriors, soldiers, and aristocrats. I am not Urid-Varg, able to wave a hand and turn them all into loyal servants. We would be trapped, and fighting for our lives, and they have Septagons."

"Should we take a Septagon?" Erin asked. "Use that Megacannon on whatever place Rostami is?"

"That will either be another Septagon, or the Palace on the surface," Daniel acknowledged. "I am not sure I can control enough men to have them open fire on their own Imperial palace. Not even the Sept are that low."

Erin laughed.

"What would it look like, though, if we could get them to start fighting each other?" she asked.

"Ugly and messy," he shrugged. "Maybe easier to sneak out later, but we'd have to be sure Hadi was neutralized."

"And he doesn't have a gem like yours?" she asked.

"He does not," Daniel answered.

She reached down and laid a hand on the pistol holstered on her thigh.

Daniel flashed back to that first day, when Kathra had *required* him to test Urid-Varg's gem. When he discovered some of its powers while eating lunch with the women of the comitatus.

When Erin Uduik had shot him square in the chest with her particle pistol from point blank range, after he had asked her to.

No, Hadi Rostami had no way to stop a particle bolt, just as he could not walk into space and fly between vessels. That required the mind gem of the most powerful Ishtan ever born.

"*Oui*," Daniel said. "You can shoot him, assuming he cannot stop you from pulling the trigger."

"That's what I have you for, Daniel," Erin smiled.

Daniel nodded. Somehow, he suspected that it would come to that.

72

HADI LOOKED around the compact room at the men he was sharing tea with. He had learned how to better realign the mental pathways of his victims over the last two days. Nothing like walking a tightrope in a high wind to develop your balance.

Both naupatis were now mentally committed to revolution in the form of Amirin Pasdar. This aspbad had not proven as formidable a foe as the one left behind on *Darius*, so Hadi had adjusted him once and he stayed put. Around them, twenty senior officers of the Septagon had also taken their cues from their commander.

It helped that Hadi was able to insert some of his own memories into those minds. They could remember walking the surface of Rhages. Or standing in the very Court of the Emperor, however far across the mighty chamber they were.

They could think back and see stewards walking around with trays of wine glasses or distilled spirits for whatever important men needed them. Or those same men grabbing the arm or tentacle of whatever alien creature happened to be handy before retiring to one of the side chambers for their perversions.

They hadn't always sought privacy first, either.

These men were stewing in Hadi's memories today. Marinating in his hatred.

Seething in revolution.

That was not what the Sept was supposed to be. Not how it was founded.

Not what humanity was supposed to represent to the rest of the sentient beings of the galaxy.

Perhaps all empires were flawed and should be done away with. Power corrupted. Absolute power corrupted on planetary scales.

Just look at Urid-Varg and all the damage he had done. The cultures destroyed.

The species extinct.

Hadi wanted desperately to end the Sept as a threat to the future, but he needed to make sure that Amirin Pasdar had the tools he needed to build something better in the aftermath.

Otherwise, the coming war would echo the K'bari in scope and nature.

Destruction.

Amirin put down his tea mug and rose. Hadi recovered from his daydreams and made sure the other three men in the room were still capable marionettes, however tangled their strings might be right now.

Eggs that might have to be broken to make an imperial omelet.

"It is time," Amirin said. "Come, let us hear what our friends below have to say."

"Indeed," Naupati Aghaei replied, joining them quicker than the other two. "We have the opportunity to make the galaxy a better place."

Hadi noted the sly look Amirin gave him, probably wondering how much of what the man said now were his own words, and what came from Rostami's mind.

It was about an even mix.

Hadi trailed the others out of the naupati's salon to keep an eye on them as they went over to the Command Node, entering onto the Great Causeway like gods standing above the mere mortals below them.

In a way, that perhaps described the purpose of the Sept Empire as it had been yesterday, before Amirin Pasdar threw down the gauntlet.

"Contact the ground," Amirin called as everyone stood before the two thrones. "I would have their answer."

The Vizier was with them in spirit quickly.

"The people of the Empire are loyal, Pasdar," Nasri said.

"The people of Rhages live in mortal terror of you and your master," Amirin snapped back at the man. "I have come to offer him and the rest of you the chance to retire gracefully to your palaces, before I have to take the Empire from you by force."

"Do you think that possible?" the man sneered.

"I already control three Septagons above your head, Vizier Nasri," Amirin's voice got cruel as he spoke. "It would not take much to convince them to make a demonstration of that control. I am an honorable man, and thus you will have exactly one chance to surrender to me. After that, we will be in open revolt and I will be forced to destroy you without any mercy whatsoever."

Hadi listened to the minds around him. Sept officers were generally selected for ruthlessness and willingness to obey the sorts of orders that might cause them to open fire on cities from orbit.

If the people down there knew it was coming, they were much less likely to provoke it, but even then, every decade or so someone got uppity and needed to be reminded. Sometimes, just blowing up nearby targets was sufficient, but once in every generation a city had to be destroyed.

More than one of the men around him had already calculated the coordinates of the main Imperial Palace down there.

"And yet, you are the coward, Pasdar," Nasri retorted. "A true emperor would deliver himself before the Court for judgment."

Hadi caught the subtle shift of words as the man spoke. He had said emperor, rather than rebel or pretender. And presenting himself at Court suggested that a sizable enough minority of the folks listening might have grown tired of the current drunkard.

Enough, perhaps, to vote for rebellion?

But therein was the worst part of the dilemma. Dare Amirin actually take the man up on his challenge?

If Hadi was with him, enough minds could be swayed, even for a short period, to break all the eggs needed. After all, if Dana Bahram Tabatabaei, Padishah of Man, was dead, then they would already be forced to decide who should replace him.

There was a whole suite of princes to pick from, all of whom were even worse knockoff copies of their father, selected merely for blood ties to a failing dynasty, without any personal qualifications beyond that. It would be easy enough to arrest all of them.

But how many of those men would want Amirin Pasdar as their Lord?

If you have a weak emperor and a strong general, as the ancient saying went, the strong man will turn inward and focus on aggregating power unto himself. A strong emperor with weak generals is surrounded by incompetence that limits his reach.

Amirin Pasdar would be strong, and force the weak out. But the other strong personalities would resist him. Perhaps even seek to supplant him in the same way he was about to supplant the throne's current occupant.

There was a risk of civil war that might last for a generation, much like the ancient empires had suffered time and again.

But the dice were cast. And Hadi Rostami had a thumb he could place upon those scales to tip them. Only Daniel could do anything to prevent it, and the chef could never get here in time to do anything about it. He was still waiting elsewhere for the failed trap to close.

Amirin turned to him now and walked close enough to have a private conversation.

"Can we trust these men to follow orders?" he asked in a simple, direct tone.

"I have broken them," Hadi replied.

"I am aware of that," Amirin grinned fiercely. "It was necessary to get us this far, and the right thing to do. Can we give them orders that they will follow if you are not here?"

"You can," Hadi decided. "If we took both naupatis with us, the aspbads on both vessels will listen to orders from you or I and nobody else. They would fire on the ground if you called for it."

"Deadman's switch, then." Amirin nodded. He moved to the aspbad of *Xerxes*, a nameless, almost faceless minion of his commander that had proven the easiest to control of all the men here. Hadi moved in Amirin's wake.

"I will go to the ground," Amirin said to the man. "You will command here in my name. I will check in with you every hour. The first time I fail to do so, you will wait ten minutes and destroy one of the satellite palaces. If another hour passes and you have not heard from me, or if they kill me down there, you are to destroy the Imperial Palace itself, with however many shots you deem necessary to eliminate all possibility of survivors. After that, you will place yourself under command of the first Septagon that comes to relieve you. Am I clear?"

"Yes, sir," the man said woodenly. "Satellite palace. Main palace. Devastation. Surrender."

Amirin took a deep breath. Hadi found himself echoing it.

Devastation. Half a dozen shots from the Axial Megacannon, all centered on the palace grounds, would annihilate everything. Every man. Every slave. It would be as though the greatest earthquake in history leveled it all, and then Allah himself came down with a blowtorch to eliminate the rest.

"Vizier Nasri, I accept your offer of safe passage to the ground," Amirin raised his voice now. "I will present myself to the Court and make my case. If anyone plans treachery, my allies remaining in orbit will destroy you all. Is that an acceptable offer?"

Hadi was expecting the long pause. The man could not have expected Amirin to call his bluff and come before them. One man, facing the entire Court and all the loyal troops the Emperor could call upon in a crisis?

It only took one lucky shot, and the rebellion would be over.

But Hadi had broken a number of minds getting here. Those men would likely come the rest of the way apart if he wasn't there to reinforce his control.

Three of those men had Septagons.

"We look forward to seeing you on the ground, Pasdar," Nasri replied. "You have always been among the bravest of men, as well as the luckiest. Do you have the courage to stand here and be judged by your peers?"

"Do you?" Amirin snapped back at the man. "This

becomes necessary because you have forgotten what it means to be Sept, Nasri. How many whores does the Court keep? How many barrels of alcohol are consumed there daily? When was the last time the Sept inspired anything but fear?"

Amirin moved to the communications officer and had the man cut the line before anyone on the ground could answer, so that no threats were issued that might have to be dealt with.

Tomorrow, those men could free the slaves and burn all the alcohol, and Hadi knew that Amirin would grant them a clean slate upon which to build.

Or die resisting the new order that would be born. They always had that option.

"Naupatis, I would have you join me," Amirin said brightly. "Aspbad, you have your orders."

The group began to move.

The last Ishtan wondered what tomorrow would bring.

73

Erin didn't know Sept military procedures. No bloody clue where to even begin, once she found the right bits and gewgaws to add to the uniform to turn her into a badass Sept agent.

She had swagger, though. Daniel was correct that it would carry them as far as it would, and then fail them.

Hopefully, they would be on *SeekerStar* making their getaway when that happened.

Daniel had found an identcard carrier for each of them along with the uniforms. He handed it to her.

"This is blank, but when you hand it to someone, that will make it easier for me to make him think he read it and approved everything," her chef smiled.

"Can't you just reach out and make him?" she asked.

"*Oui*, but this is far faster, because I don't have to fight him," he said. "Just add a suggestion that the pantomime you did was good enough. Less risk of him remembering the truth later.

"And the exact opposite of Urid-Varg," she noted.

"And the exact opposite of how that *salaud* did things," he agreed.

She kept her pistol, but put it into a Sept holster that held it well enough. If she had to quick-draw, it would probably be better to punch someone in the face and then grab the gun, anyway.

They made their way back to the bridge of the little ship and strapped themselves in. Turnover had gone well. Orbital control was tracking them in now, one of ten thousand signals moving around.

The orbital space around the three Septagons was clear. About what you saw in a bar where her and two other Spectre wingsisters were drinking and had intimidated everyone else into keeping their distance.

As she settled, a red light blinked, so she called up the message.

"Huh," Erin offered vaguely. "Trouble?"

Daniel read it as well.

"Am I translating this right?" he asked. "They have declared a complete no-fly zone over nearly half of orbital space for the next twelve hours?"

"That's correct," Erin said. "Usually, I would expect something big to be happening, but there's nothing on any of the other channels I'm monitoring."

"Will it prevent us from getting to the station?" he asked, concerned now.

"No, we're above and well off to one side," Erin said, calling up the map display and dialing it in, just to show him. And to be sure herself. Always double-check. "We're headed here. Not sure where we go from there."

"We'll burn that bridge when we get there," Daniel shrugged. "I'm tracking Hadi right now, but he is not even trying to find me, so whatever he is up to is keeping all his concentration down."

"We'll ask someone on station," Erin decided.

It was her mission. Daniel had to hide behind her, like the old days, but that was fine. They were both comitatus, and he was just another wingsister on her mission. If he could get her close enough, she could shoot Rostami and that would be that. The Mbaysey would be safe and they could flee.

Daniel nodded and lapsed into silence. She spent the time monitoring traffic, but not sending out anything other than navigational pulses.

No reason to call attention to herself, especially not if she was a high-powered Sept assassin returning home from some mission so critical that you don't even have the security clearance to know about her existence.

Erin smiled and let that swagger carry her down to the station.

They docked as far away from the central hub as possible, down at the lowest deck where the other vessels around them were carrying cargo, probably food for three Septagons close by and the many enormous stations. It would require a lot of flights to feed however many millions of people were in orbit at any given moment. Lots of traffic as well.

Good place to hide. Better place for a secret agent to be met.

Erin put on her best swagger. The kind that intimidated the entire bar, and not just every man in it. She walked to the airlock projecting *indomitable* like a pheromone. Daniel wolf-whistled at her as she went by and she just grinned.

The outer alarm rang, indicating that someone had opened the lock and was waiting for her.

Erin opened the door with Daniel off to one side behind her. The single man waiting was shorter than her by perhaps a centimeter, but it might as well have been a light-year from the way she smiled down on him.

Down.

"Papers?" he asked professionally after a long moment where his eyes seemed to unfocus.

Erin handed the man the two blank holders Daniel had found. She watched the man open them, study them carefully, and nod to himself before handing them back.

"Very good," he said. "Mission documents?"

Erin smiled grimly at the man and handed him the exact same two identcard holders he had just given her back. He went through them again as if they contained much more information this time.

His eyes didn't seem to be focusing on anything, so she presumed Daniel was talking inside his head right now, feeding him the information he needed to remember tomorrow.

"We have an Imperial Alert in progress," the man said, looking up at her again and handing her the empty carriers. "Permission to come aboard and brief you privately?"

"Yes," Daniel said, tugging on her tunic from behind with the hand the man could not see.

Erin stepped back and to one side as the stranger entered. She keyed the hatch closed and watched him come to attention.

"There is a rebellion to Imperial authority occurring at this very moment," the man said in a singsong tone that suggested he was reading a document in his head verbatim. "Amirin Pasdar, the famous naupati, has challenged the Emperor for control. He has already gained the allegiance of all three Septagons in Rhages orbit and has threatened orbital bombardment if he is not allowed to safely land and confront the Court in open session."

Erin sucked a hard breath through clenched teeth.

They'd been right, but nobody had imagined this scope of things. Could Rostami control enough minds to actually depose an emperor? Or blow the fool up with the megacannon if he got pissy?

Erin really wanted Daniel to change the mission right now. Shift them over to one of those Septagons and let her take potshots at the planetary surface. They might kill her later, but nobody would ever forget the comitatus after that.

But they were just here to kill Rostami. She really didn't want to face the Creator answering for juvenile delinquency on her part. Doubly so if they could maybe still sneak out again afterwards.

She was way too young and pretty to die doing anything *that* stupid.

Or something like that.

"You have new orders, Agent," the man spoke up again a moment later, as though having a conversation. "I understand that you have information critical to the Emperor and need to deliver it immediately. It will be necessary for you to take off at once and land on the surface at coordinates I will provide. Clearances will be added to the system to get you and your assistant to the Palace Courier service. They will take the information from there and deliver it. Do you have any questions?"

Daniel prodded her in the back with a finger.

"No questions, Agent," she said vaguely, wondering what the man was actually thinking.

"Good luck," he said, keying the hatch to open again. "The Empire is counting on you."

He nodded and walked out like he had just delivered the winning goal in a Forceball game. Erin reached a finger and closed the hatch silently, waiting for it before she turned to Daniel.

His grin was as wide as a Septagon.

"That man was the Head of Internal Security for the entire Station," he said with a mirthful tone. "What would you like to know about how those *salauds* watch people? I took way more of his memories than was probably pleasant, but I can force myself to forget them later, after we get home.”

“So he had the authority to order those things?” Erin asked, a little shocked that they had lucked into someone like that.

“They were concerned when they got the message about a special agent needing to come to Rhages,” Daniel shrugged. “Intrigued might be a better term. So they wanted to meet you privately and make sure who you were. Easy to do when I can assure the man. And now he has assigned this most dangerous woman another mission, this time to save the Empire, when Internal Security is concerned that things might come apart.”

“We’re Sept Internal Security?” Erin growled.

“Whatever it takes to get close,” Daniel growled back at her. “With Rostami gone, things might fall completely apart for Pasdar. Now, you need to fly us to the ground, hopefully ahead of the rebels. I need to turn my mind off for a while and hide.”

Erin nodded and kept the curses to herself. As covers went, that was about as good as it would get, but she would need a shower when she was done, and Daniel was the wrong person to scrub her back for her.

She headed forward and started her preflight, with one eye following the Septagons icons as the scanner tracked them on the other side of the planet.

It was a race to the Emperor now. What happened when they got there?

74

AMIRIN HAD LED ground assaults when he was a young man. Nearly lost his eye when the rebel surprised him with a blade. He had fought men armed with knives, pistols, and starships, but today left him with the greatest unease he had ever encountered.

One stray shot. One random ideologue who would rather die than admit he was mistaken. Anything might go wrong, because it was mostly out of Amirin's control.

Even he was willing to admit that he was a control freak, but it had gotten him this far. Perched on the verge of a throne, at a time when all of humanity needed him. Without this change, they would fall before the aliens, possibly in his lifetime. Become just another client species in someone else's realm.

Never.

Not while Amirin Pasdar still drew breath. Even if he had to use the alien powers of the Ishtan to do it.

Anything.

The shuttle departed from the main flight deck of Septagon *Xerxes*, three naupatis and an alien in human form flying down from orbit to confront the drunk fool who had led the Empire to the edge of ruin.

Hadi was so focused on searching out hostile minds around them that he could not speak. The other two men were so broken right now that they might as well be children's toys for all the depth of conversation they might offer.

Amirin was on his own.

As it should be.

He watched a screen showing the sun disappearing behind the horizon as the shuttle dove into the atmosphere, bleeding off heat as they orbited down like a corkscrew.

One gun commander taking matters into his own hands…

Amirin had no doubt that there were dozens of weapons trained on him right now, sniffing for weakness and intent on ending him as a threat.

But he had not been bluffing. Nor had Hadi.

Those Ishtan had seen the future with the jaundiced eye of immortality. Empires like grains of sand on a beach, pushed up for a time, and then blowing away without leaving any mark that they had ever existed.

How many thousands of human empires had there been? How many handfuls were barely remembered today? Only a few had survived and evolved.

Rome, transforming into Byzantium. The Liao in China giving way to the Song.

Amirin Pasdar was going to bet his soul on repeating that feat. The Sept Empire needed to die so that it could be reborn.

"Sir, message from *Xerxes*," the pilot came over the internal communicator.

"Put me on, pilot," Amirin said. He waited a moment.

"*Xerxes*, this is Amirin Pasdar. All is well with the first check-in."

"Acknowledged, Emperor," the aspbad replied.

Amirin didn't think that statement was entirely politic at this moment, but Hadi had taken the man and turned him into a loyal subject of a thing not yet even born.

It gave Amirin hope for their future.

Hadi continued to squint, as if in pain, so perhaps he was reaching out to find those rogue Imperial officers willing to die for a drunk, rather than believe in a future that could be better. Anything to get him to the throne room, where Hadi would be able to control the men Amirin needed.

And identify those that should be put down.

They landed like an imperial transport, troops lined up for him to inspect and a vehicle that took the party directly to the palace.

Amirin assumed someone was hedging his bets as they took off and flew over the base. If Amirin succeeded, the base commander would be able to point out that he had been among the first to welcome their new emperor. If Amirin failed, the man could fall back on the order for safe passage, claiming that he was merely showing due courtesy.

Oh, the tangled webs we weave.

The Imperial Palace, as he flew close, looked like an entire city from the air. A ring reminiscent of ancient Baghdad's design, with eight roads circling outward like ripples and eight boulevards forty-five degrees apart.

At the center, the palace itself, covering some forty square kilometers of gardens and artistically-pleasing buildings like a university. A million people served the Emperor directly from here, but they were all servants.

Amirin looked up out the window and saw the moon overhead, where all the bureaucrats lived cramped and crowded lives under the domes.

Other than emphasizing the place of the Seven Clans above everyone else, Amirin could not think of a single reason to put all the working men of the Empire's government so far away and in such bad circumstances. The Empire did not need an entire planet dedicated to the pleasures of one man and his close friends.

And yet, that was what it had become.

Which was why Amirin Pasdar was here to destroy it.

They landed in a quad dedicated to the most important men in the empire. Perish the thought that such men have to walk any distance to get to a shuttle. Amirin suspected that he had paced a greater distance in any year, just on the Great Causeway of any of the Septagons he had commanded, than most of the Emperor's Companions covered.

Fat, drunk, lazy, and satiated was a fine way to go through life, as long as you had a moon filled with hard-working men to see to the paperwork. Or a fleet of Septagons to keep the lower classes from objecting too loudly to the sorts of taxes necessary for men like this.

Guards were there to meet them. Amirin was not surprised. The men were armed, but the weapons were in holsters right now, rather than bared and threatening.

Vizier Nasri hedging his own bets as well, no doubt.

A man met their aircar as they got out. He gave Amirin a bow that was more than a naupati deserved, and less than an emperor, but trust these men to understand how finely to cut such things when all was in flux.

It was all perfectly in place, as there still existed another man with the rank of emperor. Amirin was merely a pretender to a throne right now.

That would change shortly. One way or the other.

"Lead," Amirin ordered the man like the newcomer was merely a servant.

As he was.

The troops parted and turned inward on some silent command, crisp and martial, creating a corridor for Amirin and his party to pass.

He had brought no weapon with him other than Hadi Rostami's secret Ishtan powers, which were not to be sneered at, so he represented no physical threat to the man he was meeting. This was merely a diplomatic overture that might yet devolve into open warfare.

At least he would be avenged a thousand times over on those fools if they did kill him.

He walked through the eleven-meter-tall double doors and entered the Court, surrounded today by every man who could be here.

Interestingly, none of the women had been admitted to the chamber, but ruling was not a woman's place, Kathra Omezi and her Comitatus be never sufficiently damned on the topic to the contrary.

Men's work, and men's alone.

Amirin followed the corridor of bodies that led him to the center of the great hall, ceilings thirty meters overhead pierced with enough skylights to bring a warm, golden glow to the polished stone room and showing the broken blood vessels and other signs of rampant dissipation on the faces around him.

The *Anusiya*. The Emperor's *Companions* who had aspirations equivalent to the Mbaysey Comitatus, however far short they fell in actuation.

Further away around the room were the *Andarzbad*, those men born as commoners and important second sons who could only be councilors to the Emperor. Essential voices on serious topics, but not men who shared the Emperor's friendship.

Bureaucrats in fancy robes, like Amirin Pasdar and Hadi Rostami.

Dana Bahram Tabatabaei had aged terribly in the short period since Amirin had seen the man. He wondered if the Emperor would have died of natural—or unnatural causes—in another year or so, precipitating a different kind of rebellious struggle among his sons and advisers to reshuffle everything.

Or for someone to cut a few throats when nobody was paying attention. Other successions had sparked short term wars in the past.

The Emperor was a tired, old man, almost the antithesis of Umek Sardari, back home and leading an exemplary life as Shah of Earth.

"We are disappointed in you, Pasdar," the man announced in a voice that was probably supposed to come off as grand and intimidating, but sounded reedy and weak today.

Probably, the man had consumed an entire bottle of whiskey to find the fortitude to actually climb up on his throne this evening, rather than hide in his chambers with his whores.

"And I have long been disappointed in your failures as emperor, Dana," Amirin fired back, using the man's first name like they were equals already. "It is time for you to go."

The crowd gasped. Then leaned further in.

This probably ranked as the greatest entertainment any of these men could have possibly imagined when they first arrived on Rhages.

"Go?" the man roared now, working up the sort of enthusiasm he probably had when they found a new species for him to fornicate with. "I am the Emperor of the Sept. Your lord and master."

"You are a drunkard, Dana!" Amirin snapped. "A fool. A fornicator. An embarrassment. I am here to save the Empire, before you piss it away completely in your drunken haze."

Amirin let his anger come to the surface. He understood that he was taunting a broken-down, old man, and someone in this room probably had orders to shoot him, but he had to rely on Hadi keeping him safe from such snipers.

He could take all of the other drunk fools down on the floor with him. Even without a blade.

The civilians around him roared now, drowning out whatever words the Emperor looked to have said. Amirin stood with arms crossed and scowled at the man as the noise engulfed them both.

In his mind, he held an image of Iruoma Emeka. *Spectre Eight* in the old Mbaysey comitatus, who was known for her scowl, according to Daniel Lémieux's memories that had been originally stolen by the Ishtan and gifted unto their emotional progeny.

Yes, Spectre Eight would have possibly approved his scowl, were she here.

He dared not take his eyes off the man on the throne to look at where Hadi was or what was happening. His aspbad needed to be a colorless, invisible remora attending Amirin Pasdar from the old days, so nobody suspected how much power the man had contained in his soul.

Or decided to assassinate Hadi right now instead.

Amirin had only his bluster and his rage to stare down an emperor. Hopefully, it would be enough.

He let the immense noise continue for several moments before he spoke.

"Enough!!" he roared in a voice expecting to be heard on the busy Command Node of a Septagon in mortal combat.

His tone broke through, even if the word did not. The Court tittered down to silence quickly.

"A new emperor is needed, and now," Amirin pronounced. "The Anndaing are coming with all their strange, alien allies. Already they have taken back Tavle Jocia after I conquered it in your name. Vorgash witnessed a Septagon come as close to destruction as possible because you have done nothing to chase the aliens off. Krusskyo and Aeovan have been attacked, as have others, and the Sept Empire you command has lain there, passively accepting that rape because men like you are too busy drinking and fornicating to lead. You must step aside."

Angrier roars now. It felt like about a third of the men in here, at least by volume, agreed with him. Another third were angry in general. The last third were the ones that might shoot him right now. The ones that would be the most displaced if Amirin Pasdar became emperor.

He would enjoy executing some of those. Hadi would be an excellent judge of whether a man had enough redeeming features to be *adjusted* to the new way of thinking.

Amirin just didn't expect there to be many.

"Quiet!" Amirin commanded.

They fell silent faster, so perhaps Hadi was able to do something to more men now and he didn't need to fear.

"I will offer you exile, Dana Bahram Tabatabaei," Amirin said. "And even a pleasant one. You will be free to live out your days in comfort and luxury. You will not even need to move, as I will cause the Imperial capital to be moved back to Earth and take all the bureaucrats with me. You will continue to rule as the Shah of Rhages and do whatever it is you need to sleep at night while I am busy trying to save us all from the aliens you have ignored until it was almost too late."

This time, the sudden silence was painfully deafening. Amirin thought he could hear heartbeats of the men around him, so quiet it had become in the space of an eye blink.

A squawk of strangled outrage caused Amirin to turn sideways and slip backwards, his hands up to ward off a blow, but no one was threatening him.

In seemingly slow motion, Naupati Aghaei growled,

stepped to his right, and grabbed a pistol from one of the guards that had been watching. Amazingly, the man did not resist.

Nobody resisted.

Nobody moved.

Aghaei turned and screamed a rage so pure that they could have used it to forge diamonds. He raised the pistol and Amirin had time to turn his head and watch an imperial mouth fall open in surprise as the man fired a single bolt.

And then Dana Bahram Tabatabaei was dead.

Before Amirin could react, or disable Aghaei to protect himself, the assassin put the barrel into his own mouth and splattered the contents of his head over a dozen men nearby. At least his and Hadi's robed were still clean.

The silence remained unbroken as Aghaei's corpse tumbled to the ground. Amirin wondered what Ishtan nightmare he had just fallen into.

"What have you done?" he demanded of Hadi, but his assistant, his closest friend in the galaxy and co-conspirator just stood there, shivering with shock.

"Hadi did nothing," a new voice spoke up. "I merely broke his control over the man and let the naupati do as he wished."

Amirin snapped around as he realized that the entire throne room had fallen so silent that he could hear blood dripping off the dais and onto the floor.

Two figures emerged from behind a distant pillar, seemingly unnoticed, but then again the entire Court had apparently been turned to alabaster.

"Who…?" he started to say, but Amirin recognized the man, even though they had never actually met in the flesh.

Daniel Quentin Lémieux. The chef.

Urid-Varg made flesh.

Standing next to him was Erinkansilemi Uduik. The

famous *Erin*, granddaughter of Ezinne, both women sharing the old barcode tattoos that some Vuzurgan, the First-Born nobles that rule the Empire, had once used to mark a person as their property.

Spectre Two. She was older than the memories that had been stolen at Tavle Jocia. Beautiful in ways that Amirin might have had to spend hours documenting.

Hours he did not have, as the woman had a pistol pointed at him right now.

He did not ask how they had gotten here. Both wore naval uniforms marking them as officers, and Daniel would be able to affect minds just as Hadi had. Perhaps better, as he possessed the last Ishtan mind gem known in existence, and the most powerful one ever seen.

Urid-Varg made flesh, just as Amirin had an Ishtan in human guise at his side.

"Hello again, Naupati Pasdar," Daniel said with a smile.

75

———

Daniel listened to the roar as the men around them howled with rage or glee at Pasdar taunting a pitiful excuse for an emperor.

The time had come.

He and Erin had managed to land, bluff the agents at the field, and get transport to the palace under their false guise, where other men got them this far.

He reached out and took hold of the minds around him. Or rather, cast a web that reinforced what Hadi was trying to do, bringing all of the men in the room under control and silent.

Hadi really was Ishtan. Daniel was enough Urid-Varg to remember them, and the Conqueror had downloaded the lives of all the men he had ridden prior to the gem so he would have access to their memories later.

It was strange, not seeing Hadi Rostami covered over with pink fur.

Daniel closed a fist and the room belonged to him and an Ishtan.

But he was not here to help those two conquer the Sept

Empire, so he reached out with something his mind saw as a sakimaru knife, perhaps like the one Ndidi carried in a pouch on her thigh, even when commanding a warship. Daniel slipped the knife in and cut a single strand.

Naupati Aghaei, commander of Septagon *Darius*, broke free of the control that Hadi had maintained, roaring with rage and agony in the silence of a thousand, frozen men.

The Sept man stole a pistol and finally destroyed the thing that his twisted mind saw as the greatest threat to humanity in history.

Little did he know that Urid-Varg was standing not all that far away. Not that he could have done anything about it.

"What have you done?" Amirin Pasdar screamed into the hollow silence.

"Hadi did nothing," Daniel replied as he nodded to Erin and they finally stepped from behind the pillar that had been hiding them. "I merely broke his control over the man and let the naupati do as he wished."

Amirin Pasdar. He had only ever seen the man in Hadi's memories, exchanged during that fracas above Ogrorspoxu when the last Ishtan died.

Or so everyone had thought.

The last one stood at Pasdar's side now, straining with all his might to keep control of the minds Daniel had handed him.

And probably not smart enough to simply let go. The guards would turn on him and Erin first, but they would also remember that something, someone had grabbed their minds. They would remember Rostami's touch.

Daniel smiled.

"Who...?" Pasdar began, but fell silent as recognition hit.

"Hello again, Naupati Pasdar," Daniel said with a smile.

"Again?" the man asked, more surprised than anything.

"The very first time you chased down the Mbaysey,"

Daniel said. "I was there, newly hired by Kathra and actually riding in the front seat of her Spectre as she confronted you. That was before Urid-Varg."

"So you've come to conquer the Empire finally, alien?" Pasdar snarled.

The man glanced over at Hadi, but Daniel was watching with his mind. The other man had enough strength to hold everything, but too much fear for himself to release his grip and let the fates decide.

As Daniel had expected.

It is a terrible thing to have such a clear understanding of your enemy.

"Not me," Daniel smiled at the warrior, happy that such a distance still separated them.

Amirin Pasdar looked like one of the few men Daniel knew who could have wrestled with one of Comitatus women and stood any chance. Shaved bald head with that legendary scar. Dark brown eyes scowling out from skin just a little lighter than Daniel's *Rabic* brown.

The mark of Persian nobility going back however many generations.

"Then why are you here?" Pasdar demanded.

"Because an alien is about to claim the throne of the Sept," Daniel replied. "Because you have brought Urid-Varg himself to this place. Hadi Rostami is not human and you know it."

Telling blow. Pasdar's head snapped around and he stared now at his wingsister, ignoring Erin's pistol completely.

But Erin would not shoot until she was ready. Or Daniel needed her to.

"I command here," Pasdar snarled as he turned back, Rostami's eyes unseeing as he carried the weight of the room, Atlas-like, on his shoulders. "I will be emperor, not him."

"Do you really think your mind is your own, Amirin

Pasdar?" Daniel smiled as he slipped the first knife into the man. "The last Ishtan were more powerful than Daniel Lémieux when they lived. Not as powerful as Urid-Varg, which is why they fought him from the shadows, but more than enough for one man."

Daniel paused and held out both arms, gesturing to the room.

"Look around you, Pasdar," he continued. "Hadi is holding every single one of these men silent right now, unable to move, to speak, even to shoot one of us. Do you really think your mind has been your own since he returned from Ogrorspoxu?"

Amirin Pasdar flinched.

Paled under that swarthy skin.

His eyes got big as he turned his vision inward and tried to study himself in a broken mirror.

Erin lifted the pistol and aimed, but Daniel glanced over and shook his head.

Not yet.

Soon, but not yet.

On the road to Damascus, a man must first come to understand himself.

Erin nodded and waited.

"I do not believe you," the man finally said after a long wait, his eyes returning to the surface and studying them now. "I can find no scars, no marks."

"There would not be any, Amirin," Daniel said. "The men we've encountered over the last week will go to their graves believing that Erin is one of the top secret agents in the empire, because there will be no welds left in their heads. No memories broken. That is how the power works, when it is done right. Hadi never bothered."

"Bothered?" Pasdar asked.

Daniel watched the man's mind as much as his stance, but the naupati was not about to challenge Erin's gun.

Not yet.

"I have followed a trail of broken minds," Daniel said. "Hadi never bothered sneaking up on the men. He just reached out and twisted their minds when they stood in his path. But that is the Sept way, isn't it? Brutality, rather than guile."

Daniel let his anger show.

Amirin Pasdar had not caused him to flee human space. At least not initially. Angel did that. Caused him to abandon a Golden Diamond and walk away with nothing but a duffel bag. Kathra merely hired him, just before this man, this Sept Naupati with his own Septagon, chased him and the rest of the Mbaysey from imperial space.

Later, the man had driven Kathra outward, her chef in tow. It had worked out, but they were all here now.

"What do you want?" Pasdar snapped.

"Erin wants to shoot you," Daniel replied conversationally. "She's convinced that your death will be sufficient, but I know better. You've brought an Ishtan to the very threshold of your Empire. Even if you die, he could find another creature to ride."

"Ride?" the man asked hollowly, fear finally taking root.

"Urid-Varg lived twelve thousand years as a conqueror, using brutality because nobody could stop him," Daniel said. "What have you seen me do with the power?"

"Septagon *Uwalu*," Pasdar challenged him angrily. "Septagon *Vorgash*."

"Nobody died on *Uwalu*, Amirin," Daniel reminded the man. "I caused them to flicker so I could escape. *Vorgash* had it coming, because you had already started a war with the Mbaysey and the Anndaing Merchants Bank. The only time I have used my power to make people do what I want was to come here, now, so I could confront you. Erin can testify to that. I have an entire tribe of women who regularly climb inside my head to make sure I have not turned to evil. What have you done?"

"I'm going to save the Empire," Pasdar growled, fists clenching and unclenching, even as his feet never moved.

Carefully didn't provoke Erin to end him.

Not yet.

"How?" Erin spoke up now. "I have been Daniel, so I know his memories of you and the Ishtan as well as he does. They did not say you could save the Empire. Only that you could destroy it, and then perhaps, *perhaps*, make something else to replace it. I remember them telling him, *me*, that."

"If I don't, then the aliens win," Pasdar said in a hard, taut voice. "Humanity will be swallowed up and become servants, like the Mbaysey and the Anndaing."

"Is that what you think we are?" Erin asked. "Servants of the Anndaing?"

She punctuated her reaction with a harsh laugh.

"You, of all people, should know better, Amirin Pasdar," she continued. "Do you see Kathra bowing to any man? Any person? We are sovereign. Even the Merchants Bank understands that."

"And *MorningStar*?" he snarled. "Or *SwiftStar*? Any of the other alien vessels in your fleet?"

"They sold us *SwiftStar*," Erin snapped. "And Kathra has talked about selling it back when we're done, because she doesn't want to be beholden to anyone, even to the Anndaing Merchants Guild. *MorningStar* is leased, and the Merchants Bank is paying us tribute to raid you, but the entire squadron only has about two hundred humans on board. The rest are Anndaing, Kaniea, Anic, Wisp, and others who have volunteered because the Anndaing don't want a war if they can avoid it."

"They traded with the K'bari for millennia," Daniel spoke up. "Before Urid-Varg took that empire as one of his own and turned it inwards, like you wish to do with humanity. The K'bari are gone now, mostly reduced to pre-industrial technology on the few worlds where they survived."

"Then who built *MorningStar*?" Pasdar demanded.

Daniel smiled.

"The Ovanii, originally," he said. "Thousands of years ago they were a race of traveling merchants and raiders. Before they encountered the Anndaing and started to attack those worlds. The Merchants Bank summoned the Anndaing Armada, Amirin. They destroyed the Ovanii fleet so thoroughly that the survivors chose exile on a single world. They turned inward as well, like you would do, convinced of their innate cultural superiority and unwilling to admit that trade with aliens might benefit everyone. Like you, they saw things in stark black and white terms. Like you will, they failed."

"You don't know that!" Pasdar's voice had an edge of hysteria now.

Fear that humanity was not the preeminent species in the galaxy. That the entire Sept mindset of *caste* was somehow wrong.

"The Ishtan knew it," Daniel and Erin said in harmony so perfect they both glanced at each other and laughed.

"I applaud your expectation that you might be able to build something better," Daniel continued. "But I've seen what it would look like. The Sept would simply return to what it was originally. The Seven Clans would still rule with an iron fist. All you would accomplice is to allow a few more men a better place at the table. Nothing you did would make anything better for the rest of us."

"The lesser do not deserve to rule," Pasdar snarled.

"And yet, they do, right now," Daniel snapped back at the man. "You will replace the dead man up there with another Sept aristocrat, rather than perhaps finding the best person to rule. Ninety-eight percent of humanity will continue to be held in chains. To have barcodes tattooed onto their faces, like my sister here."

"So you've come to stop me?" Pasdar stood up to his full, impressive height, nearly Kathra's.

"In the most juvenile, mean way I can," Daniel smiled back at him. "Erin, please don't let anyone kill me while I'm doing this."

And then he stepped inside himself.

76

Daniel opened his eyes and he was back in that salon where he always brought visitors.

It was empty today, but he wanted to have a moment to himself. He rose from the couch and made his way over to the bookshelf.

As always, it was stuffed overfull with tomes, each representing chapters of his life, or the lives of the men he had inherited. His mind had them all appear as books, whatever the color or texture, but that was just to make it easy to visualize. They were really just bits of bioelectricity imprinted on the innards of a mind gem by a xenocidal maniac.

But they also represented a goodly number of his friends.

Shortly, he would bring the Ishtan here, but Daniel wanted a final moment to himself.

He grabbed the book representing that perfect ratatouille, the night before Angel upended his entire existence. Remembered how everything had seemed to come together as he worked, until it achieved rare flawlessness coming out of the stove.

Even Ndidi had been impressed, remembering it with him, and she was one of the few humans he knew who had a valid opinion on things that happened in a kitchen.

Arsène and Pheryoutl had originally helped rewire his mind so that he could attack Septagon *Vorgash* without the Star Turtle. When he had almost died afterwards, they had reorganized his memories, like a team of librarians taking the entire building apart and putting every single book back where it should have been, rather than where it had ended up when someone stuffed it randomly onto a shelf.

Every memory was at hand when he needed it, stretching back twelve thousand years. That included everything Urid-Varg had ever known or learned about a species of sentient, psionic snakes known as the Ishtan.

He would need that knowledge.

Daniel returned the last book to the shelf and looked upward, as though he could see through the ceiling at the world outside his body.

He surfaced into his mind just long enough to look around.

The Imperial Court on Rhages.

The Padishah of Men, *Keyaksar* Dana Bahram Tabatabaei, lay dead on the dais next to his throne, thrown there by the force of the particle pistol that shattered his skull.

Eight hundred and seventy-three men surrounded them, frozen still by the terrible thing Daniel had done to Hadi, turning the man into Atlas holding up the entire world when Heracles tricked him into taking the weight again.

Hadi would fail eventually, but his strength was sufficient for now. His rage at these same men. The Ishtan flavors had swirled through his entire mind, until Hadi Rostami was just one of a group of beings in there.

Unlike Daniel, he was not always in control. Nor did he realize that.

This would hurt, but Daniel had the strength. The mindgem would provide a much stronger platform, so he could do two things at once, where Hadi could only do the one.

Daniel reached out and took control of all those minds away from Hadi, holding them motionless himself now, rather than having trapped the other man into doing it.

The weight was enormous. Impossible. Unquenchable.

But a Golden Diamond still weighed more, and Daniel had carried one of those far longer. He could do this.

Hadi's eyes snapped open when it no longer took everything he had to remain standing. His head started to turn, to understand what had happened while he had been distracted, but Daniel grabbed the man's mind and pulled.

They were in the Salon again. Two men, having tea. Sweet in Daniel's case. A hot, chewy green in Hadi's. Something Amirin's Tea Master would have made.

"Where are we?" Hadi asked.

"Inside my mind," Daniel replied, adjusting everything with a slight grimace as he held all eight hundred and seventy-three men in place, relying on Erin to not be overwhelmed by Amirin, or to just shoot the man out of hand.

Not yet.

"Your mind?" Hadi asked.

"The mindgem Urid-Varg took from the eldest of your kind," Daniel said. "He altered it to contain all the memories of all the men he had ever ridden, even the ones before the gem. When I met the man, the gem was sitting in a housing made of platinum that contained a tiny power source and a secondary computer network that somehow held all of Urid-Varg himself. His mind, his memories. Everything. Kathra

Omezi destroyed that part, and ended the Conqueror, but he had a backup that had still come within moments of capturing me and making me bring the man back from the dead."

"All of his memories?" Hadi asked in a voice split midway between wonder and horror.

"*Oui*," Daniel nodded. "I remember the Mnapyre, the rest of Urid-Varg's race that he destroyed rather than allowing any to survive who might be able to stop him later. That was why he destroyed the Ishtan, not realizing at the time that a few of you had managed to hide from him. Nor that they had stolen enough of his memories that they could develop technology and chase him for so many years, upending his various empires eventually. I remember the z'lud, the K'bari, the Roahrt, even the Byormi. All of them are gone now."

"Why am I here?" Hadi demanded, still sitting, but it wasn't like he could rise and attack Daniel, not in this place.

"Because you have become me, and I you, Hadi Rostami," Daniel said. "Urid-Varg was a maniac intent on conquering the galaxy and living forever. He didn't give a fig for who he had to hurt or destroy in the process, as long as he got what he wanted. The Ishtan who you absorbed would be appalled at what you have become. I know that because I also absorbed some of them when they died."

"Your evil will not stand," Hadi snarled, echoing the very Ishtan he had once become.

"I am a chef, Hadi," Daniel snarled back. "And a scholar. I have spent my time making new recipes and translating old books. What have you done with the power they gave you?"

"Urid-Varg must be destroyed," Hadi repeated louder, through gritted teeth. "He is a cancer on the entire galaxy."

"So you will conquer an entire human empire and set yourself up as the eternal ruler, just so that you can keep chasing after me and Kathra Omezi?" Daniel heaped scorn on his words.

"This form will not live forever," Hadi replied.

"The power was already supposed to have faded, Hadi," Daniel pointed out. "I remember telling you that when I was Ishtan. It has not, so you have become one of them. Immortal. What will you do when the body does not age? Does not die? How will you explain it to Amirin Pasdar, when he does grow old and you don't?"

Silence, but Daniel was expecting that. He'd given a lot of thought to the memories he had absorbed from the Ishtan, carefully recatalogued by Arsène while they slept and studied on the flight to Earth.

"Urid-Varg must be destroyed," Hadi repeated, much more weakly than before.

"And I have," Daniel said. "You have my memories of beating the *salaud* to death with a fire extinguisher. The Ishtan rather relished that part. The Conqueror is gone. But we have a problem."

"What?"

"You have become Urid-Varg in all but name, Hadi Rostami," Daniel accused him. "Look at the trail of broken minds you have left behind. I can see in your own memory the rationalizations. How you planned to go back and *fix* these men again after you broke them. Your ends entirely justified your means. You have become just another rapist with power."

Hadi stirred angrily, and then fell in on himself, much as Amirin had.

Even a broken mirror will still reflect enough self-image if you look closely.

Hadi returned to himself with a wild scream, like an animal with a foot caught in a trap. His breath grew ragged.

"Urid-Varg must be destroyed!" he screamed, rising now and throwing himself across the room.

Daniel rose as well and caught the man midway, hands clenching hands like two playground bullies trying to force the other down by main strength.

Daniel kept his silence, even as Hadi howled like a coyote or some such creature. The man had the strength of the raging insane and for a moment Daniel wondered if he had been too arrogant.

Too sure of himself and his strength.

Four Ishtan fueled the frenzy he was facing, in addition to a human convinced of his racial and cultural superiority.

Hadi drove him back a step, which surprised Daniel more than anything.

The man should not be that strong.

Maybe, just maybe, the gods had finally decided to end the war in the best way possible, by wiping out everyone on the battlefield and letting winter cover it all over with snow?

Hadi could kill him here, and he would die there. But he would make sure Rostami drowned with him.

When that happened, those eight hundred and seventy-three minds around them would be freed from Daniel's control. Erin would kill until she was overcome by the mass of a dozen men tackling her, but her first shot would kill Amirin Pasdar, so they would both win on the scale of disrupting the empire.

It would be an acceptable way to die, on balance. He had almost chosen it after Vorgash, when the pain had been so great that Daniel had thought that death would be the only way to escape it.

Before he had retreated to his kitchen to brood.

And cook.

With the last of the Ishtan gone, Kathra would finally allow him the option of death.

But Daniel found that he didn't want to die. For the first time in years he actually wanted to live. Perhaps he had finally recovered from everything that Angel had done to him. Except she had not. She had just been the trigger, that first mirror that showed him he was broken.

Daniel had healed.

There was a new fire in his belly, even as he considered surrendering to the man.

Letting Hadi kill him, kill them both.

Kill them all.

Non. *I will not have it.*

The weight of eight hundred and seventy-three men was an enormous load on his mind, even as he tried to fight Hadi Rostami's madness to equilibrium.

But the mindgem weighed far more. Demanded so much more. Daniel had carried that burden for years.

And then there was a Golden Diamond. The heaviest weight of all.

He snarled in Rostami's face.

"You will not win," he said simply, driving forward now.

All of the rage from that night when Angel broke his heart. All the fear and wonder of walking away into the darkness and trusting the fates to find him a place. Urid-Varg coming to take everything away from him again.

Daniel belonged in a kitchen, bringing people joy and solace with his food.

Kathra had promised him that he could be free, but if he was going to fail here, at this last battle, Daniel would not go alone.

But he still had a meal he intended to cook, and two Sept rapists stood in his way.

Daniel drove Rostami a step back now, silent in the face of the man's redoubled howls.

A second step.

A third.

Fourth.

Something in the man finally broke under the weight of Daniel's cold anger. Hadi Rostami fell silent, fell to his knees.

Daniel reached into the man's mind and took all of his memories as the light flickered out and Hadi Rostami died. A new bookshelf appeared on the wall next to the window and all of the Ishtan got filed. Eleven thousand years and more of accumulated knowledge and perhaps even wisdom. Arsène would enjoy sorting it all out later for whatever scholars needed to know.

"I'm sorry, my old nemesis," Daniel said to Hadi Rostami's corpse.

And then he surfaced into the Court.

77

Erin watched both men with a pistol in her hand and hot murder in her heart.

Daniel had said not to kill the tall man unless she had to. She let the Sept fool see that in her eyes, though.

No questions. Right, princess?

Pasdar seemed to understand her just fine. He was frozen in place, even as Rostami rocked and moaned quietly. Interestingly, Daniel also moved a little, when Erin was used to him being perfectly still when he went deep inside.

A pulse of power sprayed over her like the life support system kicking on, or maybe like stepping into a blood-warm shower. Everything changed in an eyeblink, but nothing at all was different from what it had been.

"You're just going to kill me?" Pasdar asked out of the blue.

"That's up to Daniel," she replied. "Without your Ishtan sidekick, I don't think you're dangerous enough to be a threat to the Mbaysey. All we have to do is leave. But Kathra might feel differently, so maybe I do have to kill you after all before we leave."

"I would ask what I have done to you, but the mark on your face is sufficient," he said, still carefully not drawing fire. Her safety was off. And any excuse would be *sufficient*. "We had hoped to change things."

"Good luck, then," Erin said. "Like Daniel, I remember you that first time. I was in the Spectre next to Kathra when you arrived and threatened to drag all of us back to a Sept prison. Or maybe a Sept world like Tazo."

"The Sept have gone wrong," Pasdar said. "It must be brought down so we can build something better in its place."

"And that's why I think Daniel won't mind if I did shoot you, Sept," Erin sneered. "I'd like to see a galaxy without your kind in it. I tried to convince Daniel to let me take over one of the Septagons in orbit, just so I could annihilate all of your sorry asses, but he wanted to talk to Rostami one last time."

She liked the way the man's face got a little paler at the thought of her controlling a Septagon. Or a Sept world being melted down into glowing rubble because she had her hand on a big enough trigger for once.

Rostami made a strangled noise and then collapsed. Pasdar started to move towards the man and froze when her pistol came up.

"May I see to my friend?" he asked through gritted teeth.

Erin took a long step to the side, backing away from the two men before she nodded.

"This would be a much better place if your kind had ever learned to ask, rather than just taking," Erin replied tartly. "Grandma Ezinne wouldn't have to be an example of all the bad things out there that need to be destroyed first."

She watched Pasdar step over to where Rostami was down, but she didn't think he'd be able to do any good.

Erin knew a death rattle when she heard one, and that

sure sounded like Hadi Rostami going directly into hell with the fee already waved by the boatman.

Daniel opened his eyes a moment later and shivered like a wet dog for a moment.

"It is done," he said quietly, looking down at the two men and then meeting her eyes. "Hadi Rostami, last of the Ishtan, is gone."

"What do we do with him?" Erin asked.

She didn't really care, if Rostami could no longer threaten the Mbaysey. Kathra could just give the order to move beyond the Anndaing. Go somewhere else and be gone, like a thief in the night.

Daniel closed his eyes for a moment and the air changed again. Erin didn't feel a breeze shift, but it had a similar effect, like something had brushed her mohawk ever so lightly.

"Amirin Pasdar, I had considered letting her just kill you," Daniel opened his eyes again, drawing the living man's face up.

Pasdar's body followed, until he was standing over the corpse of his sidekick. She could tell the man wanted to scowl, but he'd already lost his best bet, and Daniel still had her.

"Why don't you?" the man replied calmly. "As Erin said, that ends the threat to the Mbaysey once and for all. No one will have a reason to chase you with me gone."

"Because the empire would go on without you," Daniel smiled and Erin felt all warm and tingly inside. Whatever Daniel had planned, it couldn't be good. "I have all of Hadi's memories, his entire life, stored for when I need to know some answer in the future. And all of the Ishtan as well."

Erin shivered in spite of herself. Urid-Varg had stored entire lives that way. Daniel was no Conqueror, but she would need to look deep inside him when they got to a safe ship.

Make sure he hadn't finally stepped over that line in his head.

The one that he had danced so close to, so many time, because they had demanded that he do it.

The place called *Evil*.

He'd had enough provocation this time.

"I do not understand," Pasdar said.

She could tell the man wasn't faking his confusion. His balance was off and backwards. His hands were wrong if he was about to do anything. His breathing had gone shallow and hoarse.

A man who just had lost everything.

"I have your memories as well as his," Daniel replied. "About a third of the men in here support you. Another third loathe you. The last third will decide who should be the next emperor to replace the dead man up there. I considered wiping out the entire room but that wouldn't do any good. No, this situation calls for something *better*."

Erin had been enough in Daniel's mind to understand that he wasn't making an idle bluff to kill the thousand or so men in range. Command their hearts to stop. Or have them draw weapons and start carving on the nearest fool, who was carving on them.

"Better?" Pasdar echoed hollowly, fear finally creeping into his voice for the first time.

"You have all those men up on the moon, Amirin," Daniel said. "The true power of the empire. If I was feeling mean, I would have Erin turn a Septagon around and destroy them instead. But that still wouldn't do the most damage. Not for what I intend."

"What?" the man demanded, hands finally coming up to gesture, even as those feet never moved. "What can you do that you believe will utterly destroy me? Destroy the Sept?"

"Nothing," Daniel smiled as she watched. "Nothing at all."

"Nothing?"

"Indeed," Daniel agreed. "I will gift you to the empire, Amirin. Perhaps you will succeed in your quest. Perhaps you will fail. But I'm going to leave you with all those men, who have been awake this entire time, watching, hearing, but unable to speak or move. They know the truth, Amirin. They know that you brought an Ishtan alien into the Court just so you could kill the Emperor and take the throne yourself. One that had twisted you on his quest into a tool of the Ishtan. Go on, convince them that you are still fit to rule. Erin and I will be gone."

"You cannot escape me, Daniel!" he screamed. "I will have the ports sealed. Every ship leaving will be searched with robots you cannot control. I will kill you."

"No, you will not, Amirin," Daniel said with a harsh smile.

Erin flinched and woke from a daydream to find herself seated in a pilot's seat, with Daniel on her right as always. He was holding her hand and smiling.

He nodded at her and she understood.

Erin closed her eyes and she was back in the chamber with the dead men, just as all the others were able to move again. Hostile eyes looked through her, all focused on Pasdar.

"Time moves differently in the mind," Daniel said carefully. "And you have all been—all of you—in mine for the last day or so. While we spoke, I took Erin and flew away, holding a thread so that both of you believed we were still there. Oh, and I told the men with their fingers on the Axial Megacannon triggers to stand down, so they will not fire on you and spoil my revenge, Amirin Pasdar."

"What have you done?" she heard the man who would be emperor scream, but his voice was fading with distance, even as her hands danced over the keys of this lovely armed transport Daniel had stolen for her and triggered the valence drives.

"Left you to your fate, Amirin," Daniel replied.

And then valence space swallowed them.

78

Daniel smiled, at peace finally as he set out the last of the cupcakes, each with a tiny candle burning on them. Around him, a dozen girls and three boys blew them out with a birthday wish, as the entire comitatus and special guests watched and cheered.

They grew up so fast. And Daniel had been gone for so long. Little Adaku and Kwento were celebrating their fifth birthday together, and the other children had all gotten to have their own party today as well.

Daniel's way of making it up to them, when he had been only a legend before now, the only male to ever serve in Kathra's comitatus, off with the other women warriors saving the galaxy.

Ndidi stood next to him, surveying the glorious mess. She had made half the cupcakes today, her own welcome home moment as well. Like him, she had finally healed. Come back from that terrible place she had gone in order to be the Speaker of *MorningStar*. The woman standing next to him was human again, after many of them had wondered if she had *Ascended* to some other state.

But their wars were over. *MorningStar* had been returned to her mooring at some secret, Anndaing base. *SwiftStar* and the others remained in service, but new Speakers and officers crewed them now to replace the ones departing with the Mbaysey. Not all of new Mbaysey were human, either.

Daniel watched the many proud mothers supervising the mess their bright, little warriors were making, even as they enjoyed their own cupcakes.

It was good.

Ndidi reached a hand around his back and hugged him to her side. He returned it. She and Erin had spent the most time inside his mind on the flight home, so she understood what he had gone through.

What he had done.

The fuse that he had lit under a terrible bomb called *human civil war*.

But he had healed.

The news that Crence had brought when he arrived for the party was dire in a way that brought smiles to all the faces in the room. Neither Hadi Rostami's death nor even the truth about the creature had turned that many more men against Amirin Pasdar.

What had happened had been even worse.

The Court on Rhages had functionally disintegrated as every pretender to a newly-empty throne fled home to rally their own Clans and followers. War had broken out among the Seven Clans.

Civil war fought with Septagons.

Daniel returned Ndidi's hug and then made his way around to where three Anndaing males sat a little to one side, the object of utter fascination from little Daniella, terrible Iruoma's laughing two-year-old daughter. She loved the way Dane's hammers moved and eyes blinked at her, giggling and bubbly as she stood in his lap.

Iruoma was almost as bad watching over them. Who knew what motherhood would do to such a fierce warrior?

Crence looked up now and noted the serious look on Daniel's face, so he slipped away and left Jine and Dane with the little one. It was probably an even fight.

"Wyll's offer still stands," Crence murmured under the overarching noise of celebration. "The university at Therly would love to have you on staff, either cooking or translating. Or both."

"They are welcome to send graduate students with us," Daniel shrugged and smiled wanly up at the shark. "It is a mystery where Kathra is taking us after this, but couriers and merchants will always know how to find her."

Kathra had followed Daniel's path around the room. She was here now, little Adaku over across the room with a cupcake in hand under Erin's watchful eye.

"And you, Kathra?" Crence asked. "Where is the next concursion?"

"Inward," she said with a warm, dangerous smile. "And up-spin a considerable distance before we find what we're looking for."

"Which is?" Crence's hammer perked up.

Daniel already knew the answer, but only he and Ndidi had been privy before now. Him because he held the information Kathra needed. Ndidi because she would lead.

"The reason I sold you back *SwiftStar* was so that we could commission a new explorer vessel," Kathra reminded him. And evaded the question a little. "A larger vessel, big enough that we could expand the tribe beyond our present numbers, while not being reliant on Anndaing technology."

"I'm aware of that," Crence smiled. "I will remind you that I was the one that stole you the chip-printing foundry you needed at Tavle Jocia for that."

"And thank you, again, for understanding," Kathra said.

"The next step was something big enough to grow sufficient crops so we could sail great distances without having to constantly resupply."

"You still haven't told me where you are taking the ship," Crence pointed out. "Just that it would be so far away that no reasonable maps marked your destination."

"We're going to Pyrris, Crence," Kathra said.

Daniel smiled. The shark blanched and his hammer flexed as far backwards as it would without tearing anything.

"Pyrris?" he whispered in terrible awe.

Kathra reached out a hand and prodded him, so Daniel took up the narrative now.

"It begins there," he said. "Urid-Varg's long-hidden homeworld, and the original birthplace of the Mnapyre. They once had an enormous interstellar empire, some twenty thousand years ago, before they turned inward and began to develop their mental powers instead of their physics. Eventually, they were so few that they began to abandon world after world, colony after colony, and returned home to Pyrris, possibly to die. That was the place where Urid-Varg hunted down the last of his own kind before setting out to conquer the galaxy alone."

"What will you find there?" Crence asked, voice hollow and raspy as he realized that Daniel knew those coordinates.

Of course the Trademaster would lick his lips with greed. What Anndaing merchant wouldn't?

Daniel almost laughed.

"I don't know," Daniel said instead. "The place has been mostly empty for about fourteen thousand years, and abandoned for eleven. But it once held a culture at least as advanced as the Anndaing, about the time you were first discovering iron smelting."

Crence turned to Kathra, eyes fiery with excitement.

"Are you accepting other vessels with your squadron?" he

asked gleefully. "I happen to know a Cargo-6 in pretty good shape, with a highly reliable crew."

"You'll need archaeologists as well," Kathra noted with a warm laugh. "Make sure Wyll understands that most of what he'll find has been lost for twelve or more millennia. I don't expect any great technological breakthroughs intact, but you never know."

"You never know," Crence echoed. "How soon will you be leaving?"

Kathra turned and caught Ndidi's eye, nodding for the woman to join them.

"How soon will the ship be ready?" Kathra asked when she did.

Ndidi blinked and called up all the information from that bottomless, eidetic memory of hers.

"A bishop ring is a new thing even for the Anndaing," Ndidi explained. "Adding engines, Ram Cannon, and valence drives all the more so, but physics is physics, and Joane has everything under control, with Tanuss giddy at the possibilities. The ship should clear drydock in about six weeks, and then we need at least a month of shakedown cruises to confirm that everything is running right. After that, we're good to depart and chase the ClanStars all over the galaxy."

"There you go," Kathra said to Crence. "You've got three months to convince Wyll and thenrecruit or kidnap whatever scholars you can get to ride on *Koni Swift*, but I'm not allowing any other non-Mbaysey ships."

"I will, however, accept a dozen students," Daniel perked up. "However you want to divide them between linguists and chef apprentices. Bonus points if they can do both."

"I can convince them in that time," Crence noted. "Although knowing those bastards they might upgrade me to a Cargo-12 just so they can add more crew and space to store loot. Does the ship have a name yet?"

Daniel was surprised when both Kathra and Ndidi turned to him to speak. It was her tribe. He was just a polyglot cook. And Ndidi would be the Speaker for the single largest ship in the Tribal Squadron shortly.

But he supposed that maybe they were all here because of him.

"We considered many," Daniel said after a pause to find the right words. "In the end, this vessel will become something of the core of the Tribal Squadron in the way WinterStar once was, because it will be so much larger than the rest. It has about as much space as all the ClanStars put together. Most of that will be given over to agriculture, but there will also be schools, museums, and other things. We had joked a long time ago about building a CityStar, but that didn't seem like an appropriate name. This ship will sail in a straight line, more or less, while the rest of the squadron follows, stopping off from time to time to mine systems for gases, water, and minerals. Thus, it will lead, and we needed a name that reminded us of adventure, as well as the many homes we have left behind, even as we create a new thing called Mbaysey. I consulted all my ghosts, but they agreed that the original name Kathra had drawn from the depths of human history was the most appropriate."

"Indeed?" Crence nodded.

"Indeed," Daniel smiled. "We will call the ship NorthStar."

ABOUT THE AUTHOR

Blaze Ward writes science fiction in the Alexandria Station universe (Jessica Keller, The Science Officer, The Story Road, etc.) as well as several other science fiction universes, such as Star Dragon, the Dominion, and more. He also writes odd bits of high fantasy with swords and orcs. In addition, he is the Editor and Publisher of *Boundary Shock Quarterly Magazine*. You can find out more at his website www.blazeward.com, as well as Facebook, Goodreads, and other places.

Blaze's works are available as ebooks, paper, and audio, and can be found at a variety of online vendors. His newsletter comes out regularly, and you can also follow his blog on his website. He really enjoys interacting with fans, and looks forward to any and all questions—even ones about his books!

Reviews

It's true. Reviews help me sell more books. If you've enjoyed this story, please consider leaving a review of it on your favorite site.

Never miss a release!
If you'd like to be notified of new releases, sign up for my newsletter.

I will never spam you or use your email for nefarious purposes. You can also unsubscribe at any time.

http://www.blazeward.com/newsletter/

Connect with Blaze!

Web: www.blazeward.com
Boundary Shock Quarterly (BSQ):
https://www.boundaryshockquarterly.com/

ABOUT KNOTTED ROAD PRESS

Knotted Road Press fiction specializes in dynamic writing set in mysterious, exotic locations.

Knotted Road Press non-fiction publishes autobiographies, business books, cookbooks, and how-to books with unique voices.

Knotted Road Press creates DRM-free ebooks as well as high-quality print books for readers around the world.

With authors in a variety of genres including literary, poetry, mystery, fantasy, and science fiction, Knotted Road Press has something for everyone.

Knotted Road Press
www.KnottedRoadPress.com